The Misconceiver

SCEPTRE

The Misconceiver

LUCY FERRISS

SCEPTRE

Copyright © 1997 by Lucy Ferriss

First published in the US in 1997 by Simon & Schuster
First published in the UK in 1998 by Hodder and Stoughton
A division of Hodder Headline PLC
A Sceptre Book

The right of Lucy Ferriss to be identified as the Author of
the Work has been asserted by her in accordance with the
Copyright, Designs and Patents Act 1988.

10 9 8 7 6 5 4 3 2 1

A CIP catalogue record for this book is
available from the British Library

ISBN 0 340 70831 X

Printed and bound in Great Britain by
Mackays of Chatham PLC, Chatham, Kent

Hodder and Stoughton
A division of Hodder Headline PLC
338 Euston Road
London NW1 3BH

Acknowledgements

The author wishes to thank the Corporation of Yaddo and the Virginia Center for the Creative Arts for the generous gift of time to write. Thanks also to Mark P. Couzens, Patricia Gaynor, William J. Cobb, Rose Ann Miller, Kip Kotzen, Sarah Pinckney, and the research staff at Hamilton College Library; this book would not be possible without you. And thanks to Nick for the joke.

For my sister, Julie

CHAPTER 1

The first one I did was on my sister. Marie was five months along, but not even showing—she stood tall, slender but big-boned, and she couldn't have put on more than twelve pounds. I was fifteen years old; my menses had started just the year before. But Marie had been talking for almost a year about my joining the practice. "Family," she said. "That's all you can trust in the end, Phoebe. There's no point bringing in outsiders." And I'd watched, twice, while she did the procedure—one a much older woman just barely into her second month, the other a plump, terrified teenager well enough gone that the thing we pulled out of her was recognizably dead, as in previously alive. I was the one to dispose of the remains that time, while the girl wept and Marie patted her hand, saying, "It's over now, it's over, relax."

So I'd hardened myself to the sight when it came time to help Marie, but I was still nervous about the procedure—afraid I'd mess up pulling out the laminaria, or inject the anesthetic at the wrong time, or tear the uterus with the cannula and so infect my sister. She lay there, fully awake, while I inserted the speculum for the second time; the first had been the morning before, when I slid the laminaria in. I love the laminaria, though they're used only for second trimester; they're slender, pale green rods, made from actual seaweed and smelling up close of the salty rot of the bay, so much different from the metal and disinfectant I have to work with otherwise. You slide them carefully into the cervix, which looks like nothing more than a pink pucker at the top of the vagina, and then you wait for the seaweed to expand in the warm moisture of the body, much the way you used to watch "magic" coral grow from one of those dried kits you got at the science museum store. When they're ripe, you pull them out carefully, being sure none of the laminaria breaks and plugs up the cervix it's helped to dilate.

After I got the rods out I clamped on the tenaculum, a giant tweezer to hold the cervix steady, and injected the Xylocaine just a millimeter away. "How many fingers?" she asked, from way up on the table.

"Two," I said, double-checking.

"Great. You can put in the Pratts now. Second largest, then the largest."

"Did you feel that injection?" I asked, and I think she shook her head, but I wasn't looking. The metal rods felt cold in my hands, but she was numb now and couldn't feel temperature. When I finished, her cervix looked like a dark canal. I got the vacuum tube in—this was when our machine still worked—and as it started its low thrum, Marie reached down for a quick grab of my hand, just the way I'd seen other women grab at hers. Then she let me go; I needed both hands to keep the tube steady and direct the suction around the mass I could feel in there, too big now to make it through the cannula. Pretty soon we were in business, though, the tube lapping up blood and fluid and bits of placental tissue. You kind of slip out of time when you're vacuuming a uterus—it becomes mundane but exacting, like ironing a shirt, and you don't know afterward if it's taken you thirty seconds or an hour. Anyhow, eventually nothing remained to suck. "How are you doing?" I asked Marie, stopping to touch her arm after I'd pulled the tube out and hooked it back over the machine. The bowl behind me was a bloody mess.

"Okay," she said. "Forceps now. Use the tenaculum to steady the cervix." I noticed she said "the cervix" and not "my cervix," as if this whole event were happening to someone else's body—or not even that, but to a uterus that didn't belong to anyone's body and was just there to be performed on. I noticed but didn't remark on this; it was just Marie's way of talking, professional all the way. I held the tenaculum in my right hand and with my left pushed the forceps inside.

Right away they hit the mass still floating in there, and I dropped the tenaculum and took the forceps in both hands and opened them until I was pretty sure I was gripping something big.

"Still okay?" I asked, since I didn't have a hand free for her to hold.

"Cramps," she said, her voice tight. "Just pull it out, Phoebe. Slow."

"I got it," I said, and I squeezed the handles and twisted the forceps around a little as they passed through the cervix. It'll usually come in pieces, Marie had told me when I watched her working on the teenager; but what I pulled out of Marie slid quickly, once I'd got through the cervix, and came out whole. I had the head in the forceps, and I cradled it with my other hand maybe a half-second and then transferred it, warm, to the bloodied bowl. It looked like a rubbery, unfinished doll, mostly skull, with its lower parts curled inward like a crawfish's tail.

"Boy or girl?" Marie's voice came as she heard the clack of the forceps, closing on air.

"Girl," I said, not realizing till then that I'd noticed.

"All right," she said, "now scrape me out. Use the Teflon-coated one, there, you see it?"

"Yeah," I said. I did a slow job of curettage, mostly because I was afraid of puncturing Marie's uterus, but also because I didn't have experience with angles and positioning. My sister was very patient. "Clean as a whistle," I finally announced, trying to sound professional.

"You're sure."

"Positive."

"You checked down by the lower right, where there's that little fibroid?"

"All scrubbed," I said.

"Okay," she said, and her voice sounded faint and far away, "why don't you fit me with a pad, before I sit up?"

I unscrewed the speculum and pulled it out, and Marie's vagina collapsed like a balloon. "Not very much blood," I said, wiping her with a couple of Wet Ones before I strapped the pad on.

"That's the ergotrate," she said. "Soon as it wears off I'll bleed like a stuck pig."

Slowly, she sat up. Her pretty face, with its broad planes and wide-set eyes, had gone white and waxy as cheese; her lips were the color of car paint, unnatural maroon. "Here," I said, "let me help you into the wheelchair." It was an old one, Salvation Army, but most people were grateful for it.

"My sweet little sis," she said. "You couldn't even support my weight."

Which irked me a little, after what I'd just carried off for her, but she was probably right. When she'd let herself down from the table and gotten her bearings, she did what we never let any of the patients do. One hand on the table, just in case she got dizzy, she walked around to the foot, where the extractor sat in comforting robotic silence, and she looked into the bowl.

"I don't know what I expected to see," she told me, later. "Maybe I thought she'd look different from the others, or at least different to me, you know. But she looked the same. She was just one of the whole ones."

I didn't point out to Marie the biggest difference of all: right away, without thinking, she had said not *it*, but *she*.

CHAPTER 2

We've called ourselves misconceivers, Marie explained to me once, ever since that case in Grand Rapids where a lab assistant screwed up an in vitro pregnancy and a Protestant woman began carrying a Tay-Sachs baby. Dirty pipette, apparently. A similar thing had happened in Holland a few years before, only they hadn't discovered it till the baby was born, and there had been scads of lawsuits, public outrage, et cetera—so for a while they passed a mandatory amnio law here to back up clinic failures, and Grand Rapids was the first mistake they caught. It wasn't a question of anti-Semitism, the appeals court ruled, nor of paternal custody. It was a question of human scientific error, allowing for no moral judgment or assessment of natural biological process. The cells in the mother's uterus, the court essentially maintained, were like Frankenstein's monster—a misconceived thing, to be corrected only by being destroyed.

Needless to say, for a time that case was the rallying cry for the dwindling voices wanting to return to premillennial liberties—EUFIAM, they called themselves, for Every Unwanted Fetus Is A Misconception—but all that resulted was a handful of legal abortions followed by the banning of IVF procedures, and then the voices went silent. After the amnio law was repealed, amnio itself came under attack; no use knowing what it's too late to prevent, people said. Only the name, *misconceivers,* stuck—both as a badge of pride, remembering the last battle, and as a stigma for those of us who've supposedly got the whole miracle of conception ass-backward. Miss Conceiver, some of the ignorant clients call me.

We don't take such great care with language as they used to. Before, when the procedure was legal, I understand that the people who performed it did everything they could to make the women undergoing it feel fine about everything. They said *contraction* when they meant pain; they talked about "uterine tissue" and about "the contents"; they used *postoperative depression* to mean grief. Now, people like me get right to the heart of the matter. "You want me to kill this baby for you?" I've asked, and without flinching most of them—the same kind who, two decades back, would have stuttered over even the word *abortion*— say "Yes, please." Sometimes I make them repeat it back to me, "I want you to kill my baby." Then we know what the terms are; the same terms we operate on outside my basement, in the world.

That one in Europe, I asked Marie once, the one who got born. What happened to him?

The family got a huge settlement from the lab, she said, so I guess he became a very rich mistake.

I picture a fat baby, sitting on his Dutch throne with eyes wide open and arms waving helplessly. Destroy me! he babbles, while people gawk and throw money at his feet.

Of course, when I'm asked what I do for a living, I don't answer, "I destroy babies." For one thing, it wouldn't make me a living, though of course it could. I could get probably two thousand dollars a throw if I wanted, and compared to what I make at my day job— which is what I answer the question with—I could be rolling in money. But first of all, I don't see how a person can enjoy that much money without getting caught. In fact, that's what you hear about all the time, some idiot misconceiver who took one more trip to Italy than made sense, given his eighty-thousand-dollar salary as a hospital orderly, and who got nabbed at the airport. Second, I picture the look I usually receive from my patients, complicity and gratitude combined into a pale attempt at a smile. Do I want to watch those smiles curdle? With all of Lloyd's efforts to screen prospective patients, surely there would be one, sometime, in whom anger at such a high fee overcame relief enough so that she'd turn me in.

Lloyd's my agent; he's also my cousin—part of Marie's idea of keeping things in the family. Like everyone else in my family, it seems, he's considerably older—thirty-nine now, and I've just turned twenty-six. He's potbellied and balding, already in the thick of middle age. He was Marie's agent before he was mine, and he may handle clients for someone else as well; I wouldn't dream of asking. He gets very little for the work, especially considering the prices I insist on charging; ten percent of three hundred dollars is hardly worth an audiocall. "You are giving away a priceless service!" he ranted at me the last time we talked about it, which was just a week ago.

"I am helping women who would use coat hangers otherwise."

"You're helping them save their credit for more serious things, you mean, like another day's worth of X."

"Come off it, Lloyd," I say—though it's true I don't mind doing X-heads, there's something sweet and mystified about them. "You make up the patient profiles. How many blissed-out cases have you sent me in the last month? One, maybe two. They're just poor women."

"For whom you should not feel responsible."

"Who says I do? Just I don't think twenty minutes of my time is worth a thousand bucks, that's all."

"Twenty minutes of your time and the risk of your life."

"Not while I'm a cheap local resource, Lloyd, and not while I've got you to run interference."

"Look what happened to your sister!"

"And do you think it would have been any comfort to Marie to know she had fifty thousand dollars or whatever socked away somewhere?"

"Maybe it would have," said Lloyd, edging his lower lip out just a fraction. I dropped the argument; it was getting clichéd, with me playing the saint and Lloyd the practical businessman. The truth is that I'm more comfortable with a cottage industry than a glamorous racket. If I were being honest with Lloyd, which I'd like to be someday, then I would tell him the three hundred I charge—five for second trimester—is mostly symbolic, a gesture made for his sake as much as anything. I've even taken cash from some of these women, and what do you do with cash anymore? Money is not the issue. Why perform misconceptions, then? he'd want to know. Does it give you satisfaction to kill babies?

This is the tough question. It's satisfying, sure, to witness the relief on so many women's faces once the procedure's over; you're glad to be doing your tiny part to make their lives and their children's lives a fraction better. But, Marie would add—Marie, who was always honest—the deeper pleasure lies in the event, in zapping an incubus. It grows in a woman's body, she'd say. Grows there even if uninvited, grows at an astonishing rate, feeding on her, claiming to be the true owner of her body that once served her so well. You are these women's secret weapon, she used to tell me, the power that this dumb, growing thing cannot see or hear, and you do what you do.

And yet I am not a monster, of that much I'm certain. I believe I am like almost all other women—and I mean those with children and those without, those who thrill to the miracle and those on whom it is foisted. If Marie was right, they all know about the incubus. If I'm different, it's only in my knowing how to perform the procedure and having the equipment to do it. I see it sometimes on their faces, as we're saying our final good-byes: part of them wishes they were me.

I've got only one procedure this week, and a good thing too—with the kind of hours I'm putting in at Viratect there's no time to moonlight. Viratect's my day job, where I'm huddled up with my boss, Lydia Anderson, while the summer shadows lengthen. We troubleshoot viruses on big computer networks, and right now business is booming. Every day a new theory hits as to who's behind all the bugging—an organized conspiracy of retros, foreign terrorists—but the strains are different and arbitrary enough to figure on multiple contaminants, most of them accidental. "Yeah, *most,*" says my coworker Tim Williams, who's a Pentecostalist—he hates retros, among others—and would look for conspiracy in a bad batch of brownies. Work being frantic, I've had to put Lloyd off a bunch of times in the last six months. He reschedules the women, assures them one week won't make any difference; he uses the time to screen them. These negotiations aren't really worth his while, but I don't challenge him on what's in this for him.

Right now Lydia's punching in numbers on her laptop while we wait for the rest of the team and the sun sets over the Adirondack foothills. I've got a mild headache, and keep rubbing my temples, wishing it away. "What're you checking?" I ask, looking over her shoulder.

"History," she says. "Look here, this problem's cropped up before."

"I thought we pulled the database for Angel City," I say.

"For DMV problems, we did. This is a credit company. See here?" She scrolls down the screen. "Half the J's arbitrarily converted to K's, and then a few of them inverted the number next to that letter. Which isn't totally different from what we've got."

"So where was the bug?" I ask. She's scrolling too quickly—Lydia's a fast person, that's how she made supervisor eight years ago, at thirty-one—and I can't read the text.

"In the control panel," she says, pointing. "Had to dismantle and rebuild, and the company recoded two hundred thousand cards. Shit."

The DMV we're dealing with, out in California—Angel City, to be exact, that scorched earth that used to be called Los Angeles—has a bug threatening to scramble driver's-license numbers. None of the locals out there can track it. Next week we'll be on-site, so we can bring the network down; till then, we're a top-secret bunch. That's what Lydia tells me. If word leaks out that the Angel City DMV can't trace numbers, then the business of coding fake ID cards will skyrocket, along with thefts of cards, legal challenges to tickets, general mayhem.

"Well, it's all timing, isn't it?" I say. "I mean, so long as no one knows there's a problem till it's fixed, it can't cost that much to recode drivers. Just post to everyone at once and have them slide their cards through their systems."

"People can be away from their screens, Phoebe."

"So beeper them. There's not a car in the country without a beeper."

"Listen to you girls," says Tim, waltzing through the glass door to the conference room. "Counting unhatched eggs. Problem's not fixed."

"Lydia's found where this happened before," I tell him.

"Not *this*. Something *like* this."

"Still," I insist, "it gives us a pattern to match against."

"How cute," says Tim. "We can coordinate the bathroom, too."

Tim's a sardonic wiseass. His face, with its handsome clipped nose and knuckly cheekbones, its babyish pouch of skin under the strong jaw, has always seemed oddly familiar to me; Lydia tells me I'm recognizing a type. Back home he's got a pretty dark-haired wife and twin sons, a third on the way. He's not making enough to pay his mortgage and the installments on his car, and at his age—forty-one— he resents having to report to Lydia. What she really needs, I've overheard him saying to Jonathan, another member of the team, is to get knocked up. Big time. Bring her down a few pegs.

I don't let him in on the secret I share with Lydia, which is that neither of us could conceive a child at the moment. For me it's because my periods quit three years ago, around the time Marie died. The doctor checked my weight and various levels in my blood, then brought me into the clinic overnight to run a little mirror inside and peek— that was the word he used, eyebrows lifting—at my ovaries and tubes. No obstruction, he said, and urged me to relax.

That was the same year they took the IUD off the market. While I was relaxing, Lydia was getting her tubes tied. She wanted to do it, she told me, while she could still think clearly about it. "First abortion," she said, "then what they call interrupted implantation—they make you feel like a criminal before they make the thing a crime, right? This way, if they ever say you can't do anything, not anything at all, I can just reason that it was a youthful mistake and, you know. You say, oh well, and get on with life. You're not to blame, you're not *controversial*."

The women who come to me often ask about getting their tubes tied. They want to know if I do it—and I tell them no, it requires a doctor, and anyhow it's legal. Yeah, they say, but the waiting line's incredible, unless you're black. These are the white women speaking. The black ones don't ask—they know they can get it done on demand, just as they can get Norplant on demand. But they won't. It makes them angry just to talk about it.

"Have you run the numbers through?" Lydia's asking Tim.

"Right here," he says, unfolding his software case and flicking on the screen.

"No hard copy?"

He shrugs. "No paper," he says, but he doesn't make eye contact. This is a power move: he's got the screen.

But we gather dutifully around while he touchscreens and clicks keys. While he's laying out the numbers, Jonathan and Gerald come in. At close to forty-five, Gerald's the oldest on the team. Jonathan's just my age, but some kind of software genius; when I asked him once what he does for fun on Saturday nights, he answered, "Write programs." Which I knew was at least partly a joke, because from a week after he joined the company, he and Gerald have been hanging together. The only one who doesn't know this is Tim. Pentecostalists and Mormons, Marie told me once, were the only groups that lobbied *against* funding the AIDS vaccine. As I lean over Tim, the gold cross around his neck seems to glint in my eye. Jonathan wears a cross, too, but I tell myself it's different.

"So we're looking at the last three digits," says Gerald when Tim's got the chart up on screen.

"Right," says Tim, "and in random cases they'll be missing rather than scrambled, and then those patterns show up again whole—look here—some six or seven hundred entries away."

"Any patterns having to do with time?" asks Jonathan. He's hooked a long leg over the back of the chair next to Tim. "Cards that were run in the morning versus those run after lunch? Cards from before the big M versus those since?"

Tim shakes his head; I take pleasure in the quiver of his embryonic double chin. "Only the ones run in the last two weeks," he says, "because they're getting downloaded onto freestanding systems where whatever this virus is can't touch them. Memory capacity'll only hold out for another week or so, though."

"Phoebe, you'll be checking desktops, right?" says Lydia. She's settled back into a chair, her little message to Tim: I refuse to hover around you.

I tell her I will. "But people must think we're the FBI or something—they do not want to set up appointments."

"*I* haven't had a problem," says Tim.

Lydia pulls her laptop over and makes an entry. "There'll still be the security problem out there," she says. "You mustn't explain what you're up to."

"I know, I know," I repeat. While the rest of them puzzle over Tim's charts and numbers, I step away, still rubbing my temples. This isn't my bailiwick; I just do desktops. I become useful when we go on-site. From the glass side of the building I can see the new expressway curving out from the Mohawk River like a bow. Congress just voted to keep all Native names: Mohawk stays. So does landlocked Utica, which according to last night's Webspan isn't Native anyway but named for some seaport where Aeneas landed. Brooklyn will revert to Brokenland, so the people there can know what they're treading. Santa Monica changes to St. Monica, Crève Coeur to Brokenheart. Everything anglicized except heroes, the classics, and now tribes.

St. Monica's where we'll be next week, and I realize with a start, still watching the cars hum over the expressway, that I'll have to cancel next week's procedure. "Shit," I say aloud.

"You—ah—thought of a *snag*, Phoebe?" Tim asks.

"No, no, something at home, sorry."

I don't want to do the procedure at all, to tell the truth. Lloyd warned me I wasn't going to like this one, when he called to set it up. On the screen, his forehead knotted the way it does when he's got a hard sell. We'd already lined up this week's appointment. When I saw Lloyd's forehead grappling with next week, I shook my head at him. "How old?" I asked.

"Twelve."

"Christ, Lloyd." I sent the powerball rolling; Lloyd's image shuddered. "Is she sure?"

"I made her do a test, in the bathroom here. Pink as a rose."

"Shit." That was when my headache started, last weekend. The young ones are the worst. Not only are they more scared than I know what to do with, but they've also been indoctrinated early. This girl won't remember a time when the procedure was legal. She'll have to be brought to the red house blindfolded, in a closed car, for fear she'll freak out next day when the cramps hit and tell her parents everything. "Won't her doctor do something?" I said to Lloyd, squeezing my eyes shut. "Menstrual extraction or something, tell her the test was wrong and he's just regulating her?"

"Robertson's the doctor."

"Oh well, forget it, then."

"Look, she came to me with the money already—"

"I don't *care* about the money."

"—and she got the number from an older girl who'd been to Marie four years ago, and I checked the older girl's file, and she was very cool, no problem. And I ran the usual checks on this one's card number, nothing irregular—"

"Who's the father?"

"You know I don't ask that, Phoebe." He was talking fast, I remember now, in his scratchy baritone. Eyes closed, I can still hear the squeak of his office chair—Lloyd's little tic, when he wants to get off the system, holding the edge of his desk with his free hand and rocking the chair back and forth.

"Who?" I persisted.

"Her father."

"All right, then. There's no way she'll tell."

"There's always a way," Lloyd said. But he insisted she was a mature one, she knew what she was after. By next week, he thought, she'd be ripe. Now I'll have to postpone, and already he's on me about all the travel that Viratect's demanding. We've got to talk about it, he says, like a parent hinting at curfew.

Rubbing the back of my neck, where the headache's traveled, I step back to the conference table and bend toward Lydia's ear. "Any chance I could join you guys on Wednesday, next week?" I ask.

"What, you've got a hot Tuesday night?"

"No, it's the nurse, for my dad."

"Let her lag behind," says Tim, who has a knack for overhearing conversation. "The chance that this is a desktop issue—"

"No, I want the whole team there," says Lydia. Tim looks up from his screen, and they exchange a glare. "No one stays back," Lydia insists. "Phoebe's got to check out those two sites near the beach right away."

"Why? They haven't got the earliest recorded virus."

"But look how quickly it spread just there."

"Yeah," says Jonathan, "and the frequency of missing numbers, it's twice as much at those places."

Tim shakes his head, but it's clear I'm not staying behind. "We'll work it out about your dad's nurse," Lydia says, looking up at me as she zips up her laptop. "Let's go for a drink later."

"Okay," I say, though I'm thinking I should call Lloyd.

"Jesus," Gerald says, pushing back from the table with the others, "but I want to squash this bugger. You ever feel that way, Beeb?"

"Like what?"

"Like, who gives a whatever about the client. This is between us and a virus."

"You ask me," says Lydia, "it's like a hangnail. You know how sometimes they say don't yank it? Well, I always yank."

"You can leave the area inflamed, that way," says Tim, not looking up.

"Yeah, well, we may leave this *network* inflamed, if killing off this virus means what I think it means."

"Not the same thing."

"Not?" I say.

Tim snaps his briefcase shut. "A hangnail," he says, looking from Lydia to me, "is a natural thing. It'll take care of itself if you don't tamper. A virus—well, that's a foreign intruder."

"Sometimes," says Jonathan. He's got his hand on my elbow, steering me toward the door. He doesn't like to admit it, but he's a little frightened of Tim, of what harm Tim could do him. "Sometimes not."

CHAPTER 3

That night Lydia gets toasted on strawberry margaritas. We don't do this often—I don't, anyway—but when we do the scene is almost always the same. There are men, at first just hovering around but finally moving in, drawn to Lydia's big oval eyes like bugs to light. They break into our talk, and if we've had a drink or two we'll dance with them. Sometimes, when we're down on Genesee Street, we go to more than one place. We watch our entrances and exits, though, and in the end we're walking away by ourselves, practically falling down laughing at how doltish they all were, throwing us their best lines, trying to disguise the thing we knew they were after from the second we set foot in the place. Then we admit the good looks of one or two, the way you might roll your eyes over a dress you've passed up because it's too expensive—"But it *was* cute," you say, and that's how we treat these horny homeboys.

Left to her own devices, would Lydia ever go home with one of them? I study her raised arm as she orders her second margarita. Tonight she's got on makeup, which she never wears during the day, and she's changed into a black spandex unitard with one of those ridiculous apron tie-ons that I think look stupid on anyone but her. Women like her are scarce in this industry, just as girls were scarce in the advanced programming classes in grade school. Software was a boy thing, all that testosterone crowded around the screen, clicking keys and handling joysticks. My position's not so unusual; I get paid half what Jonathan makes, so people figure I'm just doing this until I find a man to marry. Lydia's crossed the barrier, made herself into the sort that never does marry because she never needs to. Yes, I figure, she would go with the right boy. Then why does she bring me along?

The margarita comes; she stirs it thoughtfully while I check my watch. I'm working on Bombay slingers, some house concoction with whiskey and pineapple juice. Tomorrow's a home day, but I've got a tennis match before work, and then the procedure for Rita Sanchez scheduled late in the day, while I've still got the nurse for my dad. Lydia's been telling me a story about her adolescence, when she lived in California and wanted to be a zookeeper. She'd been to San Diego with her parents, she says, and got inspired by the zoo. "The holding zone, you know."

"Holding for what?"

"For when we destroy everybody's habitat. The zoo'll be this sort of landlocked Noah's Ark, just enough species laid by to get the balance going again. I don't really like animals." She takes a slurp of her margarita.

"Hard to be a zookeeper, then."

"No no no no. Easy. I'm not the one who mops the cages, I'm the one who goes on the safaris, orders up baobob trees for the minihabitats, that kind of thing!"

"Oh, right. Sorry. Go on," I say, trying to wipe away her aggrieved expression. She is herself the last of a dying species, and she knows it.

"So anyway, I met this guy. He was, oh, twenty-five maybe, out of school, and he rode a natural-gas Yamaguchi, and I thought he was gorgeous. I mean drop-dead good-looking. And then on our third date, before we've even had sex, he takes me on this terrorist mission. To you'll never guess where."

"The zoo?"

"Bingo. Seems the rinky-dink outfit in my town's got hold of a mother bobcat who's been separated too early from her kittens. I guess they bond a lot, or something. Anyhow, my movie-star date thinks this is a bad no-no, and he's got a bunch of friends who've already kidnapped the babies and have them way up in the hills—"

"Where was this?" I ask. I know very little about Lydia, really— only that she knew Marie at one point, that she's zooming up the company ladder, and that, as I've said, she's destined to be a social misfit.

"San Bernardino. My date yammers at me how it's not so much these particular bobcats that are the problem, but the whole way we've manipulated nature. 'You ever seen a prison built and then dismantled?' he asked me. 'No! They just build more and more prisons. These are prisons for God's creatures,' he said, 'and if we don't haul them down now we'll imprison the whole ecosystem.'"

"Well," I say, "that's kind of what's happened."

"But listen about the bobcat. So he's got a key to the bobcat cage, right? I have no idea how he got it, don't ask. And he and this other guy go in there with a tranquilizer pellet gun and a big duffel bag while I'm supposed to wait outside for the night guard. As if I could waylay some big oaf of a guard! I was *sixteen*, for God's sake. I had on one of those long fleece vests we used to wear, studded with bits of glass that reflected the lights outside the bobcat den—I was a twinkling announcement that illegal things were going on. The place stank of cat piss. Finally they put the bobcat to sleep, stuffed her into the duffel, and lugged her out, and then we had to make it over the alarmed fence with this big clumsy weight—I remember, I ripped my shirt on that fence—and stuff the duffel into the other guy's trunk and take off."

"So you made it," I say. There are some guys now, lingering near our booth, not listening to a word Lydia's saying but only waiting for us to stop paying attention to one another so they can move in.

"Not exactly." She takes a big hit of her margarita and waves to the waitress, her arm swinging out practically in front of one of the guys' noses. She'll flirt when she's ready, not before. I've never seen her quite this drunk; more often, she'll quit after the second round and excuse herself to the ladies', where she does a very delicate line of cocaine. "We made it up the mountain," she continues, "where there's a bunch waiting with the cubs. They've been camping out, bottle-feeding them. I asked if the government wouldn't just track them all down again, and one of my date's friends said sure they would, but the group would be waiting. I'd already decided this was my last date with this guy, I didn't want to get into one of those EarthFirst confrontations."

"This was *when?*"

"Oh-three. You remember, they kept chaining themselves places, and people shot at them—"

"I was just out of diapers, Lyd."

"Oh." She flashes her wide, thin-lipped smile, a little goofy. "I forget. You baby. Anyhow, by the time we got to the site—we got a little lost along the way—the mother was awake in the trunk. Simon, that was my date, he opened the hatch, and you could see the duffel moving around. So he unzipped it and shone a flashlight, and when I leaned in I could see her yellow eyes and those tufted ears flat against her head. I'd never seen anything so full of hate, Phoebe. And I figured Simon saw the hate, too, but he just pulled the opening wide and made little clicking noises with his tongue. 'C'mon out, Mom,' was what he said. Then she came out, all right. She sprang out with every muscle in her hind legs, and she ripped his jugular open with her claws."

I gasp so loud the homeboys draw back. "But did you—" I start. "Did he—?"

"It took about a minute for him to die," she says. "One of the guys was a med student, I guess, and he tried to do a tracheotomy and tie on a tourniquet at the same time, but he didn't have any instruments, and while he was yelling at us to check the glove compartment, check the first-aid kit, get on the car phone, the blood just gushed out of Simon's neck, and by the time they got through to a crisis line, the med student had stopped screaming and just said, real calm, 'Don't give them the coordinates. Hang up.' I mean, you could tell this boy was dead. He'd just given this little groan, like a kid's toy'll give when its chip wears out, and he'd slumped down in the med student's lap. I was kneeling there, holding his ankles—I don't know why. I ought to have been doing something more, but Simon wasn't even my boyfriend, he was just a sort of problematic *encounter.*"

"What happened to the bobcat?" I ask.

"She'd sprung out of the car right when she raked him, and I guess the two guys who'd been nursing her kittens stood clear when she headed that way. By the time we were done scrambling around being useless, and my date had expired, the mother and the kittens had all disappeared."

"But didn't those guys have guns? You said they were expecting the authorities to come after them."

"Oh sure. They were armed to the hilt, from what I saw in their little cave. But they weren't going to kill the bobcat. Natural act on her part, and all that."

"Wow," I say. "Pretty cold-blooded."

She shrugs; with one finger she rubs off the extra salt from her margarita glass and licks it. Her eyes flick across my face. If she weren't drunk, I'd say she was testing me. "I guess," she goes on, her voice a little raspy, "they saw it as a war, and the bobcat wasn't the enemy. Friendly fire, sort of. Anyhow, I kind of lost it, after I saw the guy was absolutely dead, and the blood pooling all over the ground. I'd never seen death, or blood, or anything. So they took me in the other car back to town, and they gave me a lot of weed to smoke until I was calm enough to go home. You ever smoke weed? Before your time."

"What happened to his body?"

"I'm not sure." She hesitates; her fresh drink has come, but she just sips lightly at it, checking the taste. "One of them called the next day, to make sure I wasn't going to report anything. He said they'd made arrangements; said that above all they didn't want whoever came looking to link the bobcat's freedom with a man's death, it would ruin everything they worked for. Said Simon wouldn't want it that way."

"But it must have hit the news! Didn't you check on the Web, wasn't there a big uproar?"

"About the *bobcat*, sure. Simon had come out from Missouri and didn't have any steady work, and I think he lived with one of these other guys, so there wasn't anyone to report him missing for a while. I did see something on television a year or so later, a family in St. Louis reporting their son gone, but there was nothing to link him with the animal-rights people or even with California. That was before everyone was on-line. You could disappear and still be alive somewhere."

She pauses for a long minute. "What a weird set of priorities," I say, "about life and death."

"Well, you know, they're fanatics. Stick to their principles. In a way they remind me of the people on the other side of the spectrum. Like the Coalition. You know they're trying to put back that old law about natal hierarchy?"

"Natal who?"

"*You* know. The last frontier. Where you can't save the life of the mother if it means killing the baby."

"What's that," I ask, my drink beginning to hammer in my head, "got to do with the bobcat?"

"Bobcats kill boys, birth kills mothers. Natural process. Not that people die from pregnancy anymore or anything, but just the idea."

"Jesus," I say. "My sister would have a shit fit over that."

"You know," says Lydia, leaning in toward me—the barflies won't wait much longer to move in—"I was in on what Marie was doing."

"You were?"

"Jesus, yeah." Lydia looks over at the wall; old photos of the mill towns hang from the paneling. "She was a hero to me, Phoebe," she says. "And she told me, too"—turning back to me, her arm on the table, playing with the salt shaker—"how you're still doing that work."

It comes as a relief that Lydia knows, without my having told her, but still I speak carefully, out of habit. "You try to be reasonable," I say. "I don't know, maybe there was a time when the Coalition had its point. Just like your bobcat people had their point. But you shouldn't wreck people's lives for a bobcat, you know, or a fetus."

It's a nervous giggle we share. From the corner of my eye I see an apple-cheeked guy with a mustache head for our booth. "I went back to that zoo just once," Lydia says, "and when I filled out my college application I wrote 'computer science' in the box marked *major.* I wonder sometimes," she says, going for a big frozen-strawberry swig, "what that Simon guy would have been like. In bed."

I don't get a chance to answer her. The locals have run out of patience, and the apple-cheeked one slides in on Lydia's side of the booth with the very original line, "How are you lonely lovely ladies tonight?" Three bars and a couple of surreptitious lines later, Lydia presses against me and says the apple-cheeked one is pretty cute, and I agree but add that the tall one with the blond ponytail, who's joined us at the second bar, is even sweeter. And with that judgment we

move decisively out of the bar and hail a cab. Whisked through the
dark streets of Utica, we don't talk much. I'm thinking of the pony-
tailed one, who was rubbing up against me on the dance floor and taking kisses every now and then, natural as breathing. I figure Lydia's
thinking along the same lines. But then we know how it might have
turned out, a line of them outside some windowless room where one
of them's pinning us down while the next takes his turn, and no one's
got any protection—we're not talking sperm-egg hookup, obviously,
for Lyd and me, but there's a bunch of new STDs—and when it's all
over, there's nowhere to turn. Ever since Doe *v.* Chicago, rape's had
no meaning except as a way to garner child support. In cases of more
than one suspect, the verdict is moot. So we lean back, sweaty and
itching with desire, in the dark interior of the cab, and let the city rush
by us.

"It's your serve I can never get around," my niece Christel says next
morning, back at the red house after tennis. "That spin."

"Marie taught me," I say. In the kitchen, I'm mixing lemonade,
heat hammering at my hangover though it's not nine o'clock yet. I've
logged on already, careful to preserve my home-station perk.

"Wish she was around to teach me." Christel's a sophomore in the
local college, and a social fit if I ever saw one—though she's only in
college, as my sister-in-law explained when they came visiting Utica,
to please the ghost of my dead brother, Frank, who believed in business training, even for women. Christel doesn't believe in business
training; she believes in home and Jesus. She's a member of Young
Disciples, as is her boyfriend, and they go on a big singing tour every
year, all the way down to New York City. Each of the Young Disciples
has taken a virginity oath, she explained to me once, only it's all right
for the boys if they weren't when they joined. She's agog that I work
in software; she's got proof that bytes and nodes aren't natural for a
woman's mind, perhaps even harmful. But Frank died of TB-2 when
she was just seven and I was just fourteen, and her mother's sort of
barely there, so I have a soft spot for Christel. And while I always
beat her at tennis, it's a way to enjoy each other without pretending.

Keeping the red house, once Marie's, as my home office serves two purposes—it disguises the clinic downstairs, and it gives me a space away from my father. Already I've booted up the data on those two suspicious places in St. Monica; the machine hums while we sip lemonade. "This is about the only thing I can stand to drink, this week," Christel says. "I have got the worst bloating."

"Keep clear of caffeine," I say.

"I do. And it's not usually this bad. I'm usually right on time. This PMS has been going on for two weeks!"

I laugh. "Well, you don't get much sympathy from me. I've been premenstrual for three *years*."

Christel puts her lemonade down, shocked, and I explain about the missed periods, the little mirror that peeked at my ovaries. "It doesn't really bother me," I say. "In a lot of ways, my life is easier."

"But what about *babies?*"

"Oh, Christel." I shake my head. "I'll be fine. It'll come when I'm ready."

"You wouldn't catch *me* waiting," Christel says. She's moving around, picking things up and setting them down in the sitting room. I have a lot of old things of Marie's—*tchotchkes,* she called them; Christel says *knickknacks.* "You going to see my mom, in California?" she asks.

"Not the same part of the state, is it?"

"Well, not far."

"It's a business trip, Christel. We've only got thirty-six hours on the ground."

"Oh."

I look up from my workstation; something's up with this girl, and it's not just PMS. "Exams around the corner?" I try.

"Two weeks. No point panicking yet."

"How's the social scene?"

"Well, Geoffrey, you know." I try to place Geoffrey—Christel's always got some clean-cut white-enameled boyfriend, but they tend to come and go—and I must look momentarily perplexed, because she adds, "He sings in the YDs with me."

"Oh, right, right. You doing a concert?"

"Tour, after finals."

"Terrific." Christel starts on the tchotchkes again—a carved wooden elephant, a sleek pewter crane on the sideboard. They came from exotic places, though Marie never traveled—a lot of gifts from patients, she explained when I asked. I'm glad Christel doesn't have a local Young Disciples concert; I won't have to offer to attend.

"It's too bad," she says, putting the crane back, "you won't be seeing my mom. You talked to her lately?" Christel's voice always sounds the same—cheery, conversational. She's pug-nosed, small-eared, her tennis whites crisp and her hair caught in a barrette; she is at her prettiest now, at nineteen, a fact she hasn't had room to regret.

"We're not real close, you know, Chris."

"I know, but you might get another version from her."

"Version of what?" It's one of Christel's few annoying habits, that she speaks in a way that makes you think you've missed something from the last time you talked to her.

"Well, you know. She's getting married."

"Hey, no—I didn't know!" I picture another version of Frank, my brother who died—slender and shadowy, his arm protectively placed over Christel's mother's shoulder. "D'you like him?"

"I hate him." There is the slightest edge to Christel's voice, scarcely a difference I could pinpoint from the tone in which she might have said, I've met him. She's never expressed dislike for anyone before.

"Have they set a date?"

"No. Well, yes. But I don't think they'll stick to it." Christel's twirling her small gold cross; I'm afraid she'll snap the necklace.

"What's wrong with him, Christel?"

"Oh, nothing. Just he's slimy and, you know, tight with money, and he's Jewish, and—well, I just don't see it working. And, I mean, I don't *think* they're having sex, but the way he acts, and his religion and all, he *would,* if—" She stops, stares at me.

"I'm sorry." I bite down on my laughter. "But Christel, you can't not like him just because he's *Jewish.*"

"I didn't say that!"

"Okay, okay." I can't quite stifle a grin, though. "If I do see her," I promise, "I'll try to find out what's up with this guy. You should tell her how you feel, though."

"She doesn't much listen to me."

"Well, that's true, she doesn't."

"She doesn't have any respect for my values."

"Mothers never do," I try to say wisely.

"I mean, my values are more normal than hers. Or yours!"

"Hey." I keep the grin on now. It's my thin layer of protection over a yawning abyss. "You don't know much about my values, Chris."

She sighs. "I'm sorry, Phoebe. I'm just all pent up. I need to talk to Father Paul." Finishing her lemonade, Christel licks at the undissolved powder below the rim of the glass.

"Oh yeah?" I say, hardly veiling my suspicion. "What's *he* going to do for you?"

"He'll tell me how I can help my mom. How to pray for her."

"There's no one right way to pray for your mother."

"He brings me out of myself—all right?" Christel's voice rises to soprano, the closest she ever gets to acting annoyed. She knows I don't like Father Paul, but she doesn't know why. She doesn't know I watched him, from the wings, after one of the Young Disciples concerts while I waited to congratulate Christel. A tall, flabby-looking man, he kissed each female singer on the forehead as she walked off stage, holding her cheeks in both his hands and planting his lips on her forehead. At least, that was what he did to all the young women who processed out ahead of Christel. With Christel, he used only one hand, while the other strayed around her waist, squeezing her lower back just where her ass began. The one right after Christel he treated the same way, except that his hand, releasing her, came around to the front and touched her, frankly, between the legs. I could see the girl's intake of breath, then her nervous smile as he released her. The third girl, the last chorus member to walk off the stage, he kissed benevolently on the forehead.

"All right," I say reluctantly to Christel.

· · ·

During the day I drown in DMV configurations. Two sites with double the breakdown, though the virus reads the same as everywhere else. Lydia was right, though; there's a glitch in their handlers, which accounts for the failure of some numbers to boot when called up but doesn't explain the scrambling. Jonathan's at the office right now, trying to rebuild the virus, to see whether it's the program or the handler that's affected first. When we go out this week, I'll be in charge of containing whatever he builds, applying it to the stand-alone systems to test without affecting the network. Meantime, I'm running a program he gave me last year, trying to make sense of the new numbers. "There's just a possibility," Jonathan said to me as we left the office yesterday, "that it's a code. I don't mean a coded virus. I mean a code in the new numbers themselves."

"Why?" I asked.

"Prank, maybe," he said, and we agreed we wouldn't tell Lydia unless I stumbled on something more solid. Lydia's feet are planted on the ground like tenacious weeds; she can't stand conspiracy theories.

It's almost a relief when Rita arrives early for her appointment and I can log off. Down in the basement clinic, she pops the Valium I hand her without complaint. Last year, when I did her, she panicked and almost ran from the red house into the street; if it weren't for Lloyd's sales pitch, I'd have turned her down this time. "Medications in the last twenty-four hours?" I ask while I'm checking her. Her abdomen's firming up right at the center; Rita's got a big abdominal stretch, from carrying seven kids to term, and you can tell right away. My fingers feel good, moving over something besides keys.

"Just the Zoloft."

"Drugs?" She hesitates; I'm palpating her uterus now; it's tipped rearward just a little, I remember. "Grass, right?" I say. I can smell it, even though Lydia's right, no one I grew up with does that stuff anymore. "It's okay."

"It do help me relax, Doctor."

"But nothing else, no alcohol."

"No." Her voice is very small, a young woman's voice though she's well past thirty. I hate it when she calls me Doctor, but Marie told me never to object—it makes them feel easier, she said, to give you that authority. Sometimes they call me nurse, which I prefer, but curiously I also feel guiltier, that they would think I was trained at nursing, nurturing. Clients don't realize it's practically impossible to find a member of the medical profession who'll perform a misconception. They could get the equipment easier, and maybe there's some emergency they could handle better, but in terms of police work they are sitting ducks.

"You going to get your tubes tied after this one, Rita?" I say in what I hope is a conversational tone. I pat the bottom of the table, and she scoots her buttocks, slides her bare coppery feet into the stirrups. Down here in Marie's basement, you don't know what time of day it is; there's only the faint scent of mold, from the damp corners, and the fluorescent tube overhead.

"No, Doctor, I don't think so."

"You could, you know. With your background."

"Huh! Keep the dark population down."

"I'm thinking of *you*, Rita."

"Sure, Doctor." Sliding further down the table, she pats my arm as if I'm to be comforted. "But my husband wouldn't like it."

"Does he have to know?"

"I done promised him"—she draws a quick breath as I slide the speculum in—"one more."

"Christ, Rita."

She crosses herself as I take the name of her God in vain. "I'm just not ready yet, that's all. When my Alphonse is in school, maybe I can handle another."

"All right now," I say, getting the lamp positioned, "I'm going to start dilating you. You remember this part, don't you?"

"I certainly do."

The Pratt rods make a shiny stainless-steel line. I start with the half-centimeter, since Rita's early and still pretty tight. We don't talk until I'm at two centimeters; I can hear her clucking her tongue, rhythmically, a way to distract herself. Rita's a big woman, with most of her weight carried in her thighs; I feel myself framed by smooth-barked tree trunks as I work. While I'm sliding the last couple of rods in and out, I explain about the aspirator being broken. "So I'm going to do an old-fashioned D&C, instead," I say. "It'll be slower, but there's not any more risk, really. Just tell me if you feel any sharp pain, besides cramping."

"I never liked that machine's sound anyhow," she says from the other end of the table. "Too much like something eating at you." She makes a slurping sound with her mouth. "Makes me think of my cat, how she chew up her placenta."

"Well, I'm trying to find someone who'll fix it," I say, "but it's a question of parts, I think, and they're restricted to government issue now, so they're hard to come by."

"You a good woman, to do this for people. My mom told me your sister used to do this sort of thing, too."

"Yup." I've got the three-centimeter rod in now; we're almost ready.

"That how you got in the business?"

"Yup."

"What happened to her?"

"How'd your mom know about Marie?" I ask, pulling the rod out.

"Oh, she went to her once. When I was twenty-two and had my first two already. She wasn't about to carry hers to term, no sir."

"Well, that brings us to the main question, Rita," I say. I've got the curette ready, but I put it down and take both of her hands in mine, the way I usually do. "Tell me now, and be sure," I say, moving around the table so I can look her in the eye. "Do you want me to kill your baby?"

Rita gives a soft laugh, slowed by the Valium. "Oh, I sure do," she says. "I want it more than candy."

"Okay, then," I say, and move back down to the end of the table. She's forgotten about Marie. For the next minute, two minutes, she's conscious of nothing but the movements the metal scoop is making in her, of nothing but this careful, deliberate ending of things. "Breathe," I tell her when I realize she's not. "Let your breath down," I say.

"Ahh," she says. "Ahh-yee." And I can feel her biting down on the beginnings of her grief, and I clench too—but after a few minutes I'm done; I give her hand a squeeze, I make my own breath come easy, I start to clean up. Please, Rita, is what I say to myself—but there's no use begging her, she can't hear me now, I've gone through it enough to know.

It's not as bad as the time before. Then, she hissed at me and tried to sit up, tried to run her head into the wall as soon as she was recovered enough to get off the table. This time she lies still, and there's only sound coming from her, a loud steady wail by the time I've got the instruments away. "Hush," I keep saying, like a mother to her baby. "*Hush.*"

If we mourn less for the more aged, it is because they leave less of their lives unlived. I put the pink contents of her uterus away, and come back to hold Rita's shoulders as she starts to sit up, as she keens in the gargantuan grief of a whole life lost. "*Ai-ya-wha-a-o-h-h!*" she cries, looking wildly to see what I've done with the baby, and then her dark torso shakes, her chin tucked down, tears and mucus spreading from her large eyes and broad nose.

"Hush," I say.

But she doesn't. The sound she makes descends from the screech of a hawk: "*Ai-ya-wha-e-e-e! Ai-ya-w-a-a-a-h! Ai-yah, ai-yah, ai-ya-wha-a-o-h-h!*" Her arms shake me off. She's way past me, in a world where planets collide and whole civilizations are blasted into space. "*Ai-ya-wha-a-o-h-h!*"

Only when I've fitted the pad, brought her orange juice and a box of tissues, does she go silent, tears washing her thick face like rain on a rock. "Rita, Rita," I say, but she won't answer me.

The afternoon nurse's name is Betty. She plays cards with my father; when alone, she reads detective hypertexts. "This is a good one," she says when I've dropped my coat back at my father's apartment. "Ten times through the program, double modes, and I'm still scared when that gardener shows up with the shears." After she's shown me the graphics—she counts on my interest in computers—I credit her on her Lap file. When she's gone, I click on the system: one call from my ex-boyfriend Rudi, but it's too late to call him back, just as it's too late to call Lloyd and postpone that twelve-year-old. I check on my dad, who snores evenly in his stew of dreams. He's easiest in the evening, when he generally sleeps or downloads old videos. Tonight I have the apartment to myself, and I stay up drinking sherry and playing a high-stakes Go game on the Web, a way of erasing the day.

Shortly after I fall asleep, I have a dream about Lydia Anderson's teenaged date Simon. I dream he's been dismembered by his fellows and fed to the mother bobcat; her kittens lick the bones. Suddenly I find myself gnawing one, too, only it's a very tiny bone, a fetal limb in fact, and it breaks in my teeth. I wake, shivering in the air-conditioning. God damn, I whisper aloud, God damn. I tiptoe to the living room, where my father's awake now, his round head nodding at the wall screen, some old romance. I heat water for tea, but leave it, only touching my teeth to the china rim of the cup. Finally I take a warm shower, touching myself first with the soap, then with my hand, easing myself to climax and calm.

CHAPTER 4

Marie was beautiful, and if videos are to be trusted, she looked like our mother, the only one of us who was medically trained, who died when a grenade hurtled through the window of the clinic where she worked. I was eleven at that time, and mostly remember her as being at work while my schoolmates' moms were coming along on the field trips or picking us up from the swimming pool. We must be poor, I used to think; only poor mothers had to work.

I take after my father—freckled and soft-shouldered, my hair untamable and my face remarkable only for green eyes, also my father's legacy. Marie's eyes were dark reddish brown, same as her hair, and she moved with that kind of fine, supple posture that makes you think of a magic string rather than a ramrod. It was Marie who acquired the equipment and instruments during the weeks and months before the amendment passed. She helped set up the Web site, too, which worked just long enough to get an organization going before the government managed to crash it as part of the CyberCensor Act. All this while, she was studying art, driving up to Syracuse four days a week for painting classes with Omar Jeffries—a neorealist, she told me, who was just coming into the spotlight then. I knew nothing about art, still don't. It was only after she'd been arrested that she told me she'd been sleeping with Jeffries off and on over the last couple of years.

"Look, I don't want him to know where I am just yet," she said when I rushed down to see her. She was at the precinct then; just booked.

"Why not? You can tell him you're innocent of the charges," I said. I wasn't sure how free we were to talk, in the space where they let us meet. It was no more than a cubicle, Plexiglas-partitioned from the hallway, with a folding table and worn plastic chairs, all of it left over from the last century. People passing glanced in at us with a frown.

"He wanted me," she said evenly, holding me in her brown gaze, her hair freshly combed but limp, bangs hanging over her thick eyebrows, "to make a baby with him."

Which was how I came to guess it had been Omar Jeffries's daughter we'd done in, my first time there in the basement room. I'd never asked; I wouldn't do that to Marie. Jeffries was married, that much I'd known, and had four or five kids of his own—but it was becoming stylish, in an underground way, to impregnate your mistress, in spite of the hefty child-support fees they could slap you with. Before, when there was a pill—I was too young to experience this—a man had no way of proving to outsiders that he was potent or even that he was having sex with you; or that he was the only one doing so. Now the proof, as they say, is in the DNA pudding. I do remember the first wave of books on paternity, on how it was going to rebuild the masculine ideal: the warrior as father, the father as society's new backbone. There were even pater cults, advocating marriage and fatherhood for boys of sixteen, a rite of passage "that we *can* afford." Those have died out recently, but they were big when Marie was arrested, and it wasn't impossible that Jeffries was into that line of thinking, at least as a badge of style.

"Do you think he—?" I asked Marie, sitting in the ratty visiting room. I wasn't sure how to finish, if we were being listened to. I didn't know how many people knew about Marie, where to begin suspecting a mole.

"No way could he accuse me of this," she answered, her voice still steady, her words carefully chosen. But when I squeezed her arm at the end of our time I felt how thin she was, and her voice quavered a little when she asked me to keep Dad in the dark. It was hard to watch her go back, attended by a stout guard, through the sliding door. That was the one thing I couldn't believe, that there was no bail for miscons. The idea being, as Lloyd patiently explained, that we could quietly terminate a couple hundred more lives while waiting for our trial date. There were some forms of heinousness for which society was willing to put a strain on its prison system, and mass murder was one of them.

She was so smart, Marie, and so careful! Just two months before, she'd built the one-room clinic underground, with the entrance through the trapdoor behind the furnace—and it couldn't have been one of the builders who turned her in, because the detectives never found the clinic or the equipment. Nor, Lloyd was sure, was it one of the patients, because he'd learned through the grapevine that the state had no material witnesses, only hearsay and what they called "evidence." Lloyd didn't think they had a case. He wasn't the lawyer, of course, that would have been way too risky, but he knew more than the earnest, terrified young attorney Marie had hired. Lloyd felt certain Marie would get off; the main issue was getting the case to trial. Prison'll drive her nuts, was what he said.

Driving out of town, I'm thinking about Lloyd—because I keep meaning to call him about the twelve-year-old—but I don't want to call him from the car, where I can't focus on his face, so I record a memo to myself on the dashboard system. I'm doing a Saturday chore for Mau-Mau, checking over a new shipment of instruments. Mau-Mau started out as Misconceivers' Association Underground, but the press got hold of the acronym and changed it to Mothers Against their Uterus. Now it's both. *Africa,* one of Marie's friends told me when I joined—*that's where the name Mau-Mau started, some tribe that wanted the white man out, they had horrible rites but clear goals.*

There's a detour from the new arterial, and I have to pass through the link from Utica to Rome. The sun's baked the asphalt, softening the new layer on Route 5 to a dark, tarry sheen. The roads are a mess, fallout from a hastily prepared five-year plan. Like fiberglass sardines, the traffic packs between the brick and concrete buildings of the old city, with everyone's car videos flickering from the dash as they switch to the traffic monitor, seeking advice. As I nestle into the snarl, sinfully longing for air-conditioning, my beeper flashes twice—Lloyd, then Lydia—but I know better than to take the calls.

No one expected Utica to come back this quickly, mostly because no one expected the torrential weather in the South to drive so many people northward so fast. But also they didn't take account of people like Peter Graves, the guy who owns the corporation that owns Viratect, who bought up a whole industrial park at auction thirty years ago, built his conglomerate, and waited for the boom. This is why half-assedly employed people like me get flown out to California to solve major network problems: no one wants to live in America's gardens anymore. They're getting washed out, burned up, broken by the earth they stand on. So they turn to us; they turn to Utica.

The Mau-Mau receiving barn is at the edge of Rome, or what used to be the edge; sprawl has taken over, like everywhere, and soon this old house—sign at the front, BAKER'S PROVISIONS—and its neighbors will be knocked down and replaced by shimmering towers. For the last few years, though, one of the men has rented the barn from the old lady who lives in the house and rents or sells arcane products like whale-shaped molds and preformed hard-sugar cake curlicues to the city's loyal Italian bakers. He needed an art studio, the man said—which wasn't entirely a scam, he was a friend of Marie's, a sculptor as well as a miscon. As I understand it, he doesn't do much by way of procedures anymore, but spends his time tracking down the tools of our trade and negotiating prices. Though I could be wrong, I don't think he makes much money off the deals, expensive though the supplies are; sources are scarce in the Western Hemisphere is all, and Customs very efficient. I'm on the list for extractor replacement parts, for instance, but he tells me I have another year, at least, to wait.

I don't know this man's name; I've only seen him a handful of times; he won't be here today. Each of us coming will let herself in with the hidden key, which we'll replace under the rock behind the raspberry bush. We could computer-code the door, but that would be a dead giveaway if anyone ever came snooping around this part of town. We're not buying anything today; it's just the inspection committee, checking seals and purity of serums, risking getting blown up when we slice open the boxes.

I park in a cloud of dust; the wind's kicked up, bringing in a thunderstorm. The barn sits on a rise from which I can see the low hills, the sky thickening toward the west. From somewhere far off comes the crash and clatter of a bulldozer. I shade my eyes to place it, but see only the shallow valley slowly filling with gray interstices of roads and buildings, like a graph on a monochrome Lap screen, the battery fading. Inside, the other two have arrived and are ticking off boxes on a sheet. "Raining yet?" asks one of them, and I shake my head. I don't know their names either, and they don't know mine, though we've been on the committee almost a year together; in July the skinny one rotates off, replaced by a new unnamed member.

"Look what I got," says the one making check marks on the sheet. I call her Pockface to myself; she's got lustrous hair, but both her round cheeks are acne-scarred, and she wears that pancake makeup that makes it worse. She holds out a slim device that looks like a remote video control. "Anything with a trigger, it's supposed to detect," she says. "This little screen, here"—she leans over and flips the top up—"gives a reading of trigger sensitivity."

"But does it tell you about the bomb?" I ask, turning the device over. "How big or whatever?"

"Nope."

"You tried it yet?"

"Yeah," says the skinny one. "No readings. Look, here." Taking the gizmo from me, she demonstrates: *00.00,* the screen reads. "Every box is the same. Of course, there could be some other kind, something with a remote switch, say, and we couldn't catch it."

"At least this is something," I say.

We draw lots for who goes first. Two boxes each, opened one at a time with the others standing far back. We've never had a problem locally, but I've heard stories from other parts of the country, places where the Coalition doesn't think the government's fast or brutal enough and where it has the resources to infiltrate just about anything. I draw the short straw, and take the razor to the two biggest boxes. It's always a sweaty-hands moment, pricking the clear sealing tape and gliding the razor down its slick surface, then peeling back the styrene flaps—but there's no explosion, of course, and inside lie shiny metal rods and plastic wheels, disassembled IV frames. "Wow—I suppose I should have one of those," I say.

"They're handy for fainters," says Pockface, coming forward for her turn. I hand her the razor and step back. The smaller boxes, I know, are filled with supply replenishments—ergotrate, Valium, laminaria, Demerol, Pitocin if we're lucky. We've got chemical compounds to spot-check, plus there are the individual seals to go over. There are only two windows in the barn, both high up, with a lazy overhead fan, and the humidity's building as the storm approaches; I run my hand around my damp neck.

"Long afternoon, huh?" says the skinny one.

"If it just weren't so hot," I say.

"You been busy?"

"Oh yeah."

She narrows her eyes, her arms crossed in front of her. "What d'you charge?"

I look at her, surprised. It's not a kosher question. We all know the general range, of course. And it's not as though money's an impolite subject; it's more serious than that. What we charge is what distinguishes us as individuals; it's not that far removed from asking someone's name. "Wel-l-l," I say. But before I can come up with a repartee, Pockface shrieks.

Instantly the skinny one and I flatten to the ground. My arms curl over my head on the cold concrete. One second passes; two; three; I don't hear Pockface running, and there's no explosion. Only my heart still beating, lub-dub, lub-dub.

Then comes the stomach-wrenching sound of Pockface vomiting in the sink, on the other side of the barn. I raise my head, get to my knees. The box sits open, its contents invisible. Pockface's back is to us, crouched over the soapstone basin. Slowly, crawling, I make my way toward the center of the barn. John the Baptist's head, I think incongruously, served on a platter. Then I draw close enough to get a whiff.

"Feces," I announce, standing. I can see it now, brown and gelatinous.

"Oh shit," says the skinny one.

"Exactly."

"Ha ha. No, I mean we can't open anything else now."

"Why not? We've got our Geiger counter or whatever it is. The worst is we'll get grossed out."

"No," says Pockface. She wipes her mouth and comes over. Her scarred cheeks are bright red. "Remember, the counter doesn't work for everything. And what this means is whoever shipped it knew what they were shipping and where to."

"Right," says the skinny one.

"You mean we've got to move this location," I say, feeling dense. "Find a new supplier, the whole bit."

"Well, that's a different committee, thank God," says Pockface.

"But there could be perfectly good medication here!" I say. "It seems a waste."

The skinny one leans down and picks the razor off the concrete floor. "You want to open the next box?" she asks.

We load the IV frames into the back of my car; Pockface and the skinny one each take half the unopened boxes. Some will go into the river, some into deep gullies where squiggly roads climb into the hills. We agree the dump is to be avoided. No one says anything as we haul the box of excrement behind the barn and toss it into the brush there, but I'm sure I'm not the only one to observe that it's undeniably human feces—fat, soft, coffee-colored cylinders mashed into one another, flecked with food particles. We don't say good-bye as we climb into our separate vehicles; we don't know one another, really; we just share the burden of the complicated process we have to set in motion—letting the supply guy know what happened, denying people their orders, changing the whole delicate structure of shipment. I tell myself as I start the car that I'll call Lloyd and double my rates, something's got to pay for this aggravation. Then, as I descend into Utica, I feel a sudden and undeniable urge that has nothing to do with money or hassle or even fear. I pull into a recharge station. *Call Lloyd,* my beeper rasps at me as I switch the car off. "Oh, shut up," I tell it, and step out to get the key to the ladies'. There, I pump the pink soap. I wash my hands, my neck, my face; I suck soap from my finger, scoop water, and rinse my mouth. I pull paper towels from the dispenser, wet them, squeeze a bit of soap on them, and do a quick swab between my legs, then take clean wet towels to approximate a rinse. Finally satisfied, I stuff the paper towels through the swinging top of the metal trash can and head outside, where with a crack the heavens finally open and fat drops of rain rush down, wetting my hair and skin in the time it takes to run to my car. Still, all the way through the storm back to town and my father's apartment, I smell the feces in my nostrils, taste it in my mouth, feel it clogging the pores of my skin.

It's hot on Monday, when I finally contact Lloyd on my way out of the Viratect office. The air-conditioning has that refrigerator smell that tastes, to me, like pineappled cottage cheese and fat tomato slices. Outside, heat shimmers up from the walkway; the goldfish pond in the little arbor they've built to alleviate the industrial-park tone of this complex looks stagnant, choked with algae. When you step outside, heat strikes you like a fist. My colleagues are all downstairs, waiting for the cab.

"I'll have to postpone the twelve-year-old," I say to the screen. "We're flying to California today."

"Damn. I'm not even sure I can contact her."

"Well, try. Or else she'll just have to find out when she shows up for the appointment." He sighs. He thinks I'm being mean. "I'll be back Friday," I say. "I'll take her on the weekend, it'll be okay."

"We've got to talk, Phoebe."

"I know, you want me to cut back the traveling. But when it's not my choice—"

"Not just the traveling. Look, I was going to call you this afternoon." He rubs his stumpy hand over his bald head and scratches at the back of his neck. He's looking down at his keypad, not at me. "I've got four clients who want something done tomorrow, only I told them you were booked, and then with you just accepting one a day, I was going to schedule you through most of next week."

"That's okay. There's just the twelve-year-old."

"It's okay *now*. But you could get called away again. Plus I know I'm going to get four more calls today from people who *also* want tomorrow, and they're not going to handle the idea of two weeks' wait very well. The fact is that the supply pool for this service is drying up while the demand pool is growing"—and your blood pressure's rising, Lloyd, I think as I study his heavy jaw, the way his mouth pulls into his cheek—"and right at that intersection *you* choose to charge basement prices and make yourself unavailable."

"I never said I was full-time," I tell him. I'm talking very slowly and deliberately, making track-ball swirls over Lloyd's image. He waits for me to say more, but I don't. I can't articulate to him how the only way I can bear to keep the business going is if I call all the shots. I know better than to tell him what happened in the barn on Saturday—he's not supposed to know about Mau-Mau anyway, under the general rule of thumb that the less knowledge we each possess, the less can be pried from us. And never having had anything to do with the hands-on part of this, there's no way he'd understand that if I took up the tempting proposition of full-time misconceiving, after a few weeks or even days of it I would simply vanish into the act, my hands become the hands of my dreams, pulling out human particles and emptying basins. It would be easy, so easy, to slip into that routine. Pockface, for instance, has done it, so that you look in her eyes and see pools as warm and stagnant as the goldfish pond outside. She touches life without choosing to touch life. I have to feel the hard, slippery, sharp edge of that choice every time. Words, Lloyd would say if I told him any of this. A lot of hooey.

"True, you never said it," his voice finally comes, his face leaning forward. "But I'm not sure I can accommodate you forever, Phoebe. All this special handling and no money in it—or not as many women helped as might be, if you want to look through that end of the telescope. This keeps up, may Marie rest in peace, I'm going to have to advise you to find yourself a new agent."

I'm stunned. Caught up in my own stubbornness, it hasn't occurred to me that Lloyd would ever lay down an ultimatum. "Wow," I say.

"I'm sorry, kiddo. But look, maybe it's a business you don't belong in. No one ever said you had to. Even Marie—"

"It's not because of Marie," I shoot back. The swirls covering and uncovering his face are turning to gyroscopes, tunnels on tunnels.

"Whatever. If this other job of yours was really turning you on, she'd say go for it. The poor are always with us—okay, so are the pregnant."

"I'm not quitting, Lloyd."

"Yeah, well, I need fifteen hours a week from you, guaranteed. And six hundred per procedure. That's still a *fraction* of the going rate. Maybe somebody else—"

"I don't want anybody else. Just let me think about it, Lloyd. I've got a lot of shit coming down right now. Just give me till after this California trip to think."

"And meantime I should reschedule the twelve-year-old."

"Meantime, yeah. Or place her with someone else."

It's the first time I've mentioned the idea that Lloyd represents other miscons, but he doesn't blink. "No one else has a slot free," he says. With a final caress of his bald crown, a final twist to his cheek, my cousin logs off. Before I can give it more thought, the intercom's calling me—cab's here, shut down and go.

CHAPTER 5

"Secrets," I tell Lydia. "I feel like secrets are the mortar that holds my life together. Everywhere you look, between every brick and stone. I hate it."

"I know what you mean, babe," she says, though of course she doesn't. "Having to carry on for Marie, that must be hard."

"I didn't mean that."

Lydia sets the speed to 80km; we're driving a rented Volt, they don't go much faster. "How many procedures d'you think get done every month?"

I draw a deep breath. She's not asking about me though, not necessarily. "You mean here, or in Utica?"

"Nationally."

"Christ, Lyd, who can say? Probably as many as ever. Maybe a million or so."

"God almighty," she says. She looks a little shocked, and for a second I wish Marie hadn't told her anything. "Those aren't secrets I'd want to have to keep."

"Nobody has to keep them," I say. "Not nationally."

"What are you, naive? There's a network out there, babe. And it's bigger than abortion, you can bet on that."

"I didn't think they called it that anymore."

"Oh yeah? What do they call it?"

My throat closes up. I point through the windshield. "Red light," I warn, but Lydia slides into a right-hand turn, onto the freeway entrance. "Close one," I say, but she just shrugs.

We stop talking for a while. The California freeway fits the car like baggy boxers—too many too-wide lanes, other vehicles scattered into the mirage. We'll pick up Jonathan at the beachside DMV where I worked alone all yesterday; if he's done we'll join Tim at the state office downtown, to put our bits and pieces together. Leaning back in the Volt's deep bucket seat, I shut my eyes and think about this job. What a fluke it was that I got it in the first place. There, at Marie's funeral, which almost no one but family attended—patients and other miscons, equally frightened, stayed away, a few brave ones voice-mailing regrets—Lydia came up and introduced herself as a high school friend of Marie's. She was wearing a dark blue business suit, her hair tinted copper, sunglasses hiding her eyes. "I think she and I are the only ones who haven't gotten married yet," she said, to which I pointed out that Marie never would now. I was in a foul mood that day, grief rising to my tongue like stomach acid. "You know how I remember you?" she went on, walking beside me back from the gravesite. "As a freckle-faced four-year-old. Marie'd have to baby-sit you, and we'd all take turns giving you tickle tantrums."

"I don't remember you," I said.

"It was just that last year of high school. I'd moved out here from California. I was sure I'd hate it. Marie was the first one to be nice to me."

"She had that way," I said absently. I didn't really want to be talking to one of Marie's chums from her former life, the life back in history where abortion was just another dirty word, where national legislation and constitutional amendments were just items on the phony list of things politicians campaigned for, nothing more. The Roe overturn had just been tested, if my chronology's right, the year that Lydia was talking about. But as we walked away from the loamy grave, with its piled flowers and silent neighbors, she was telling me how she'd headed off to college the same way Marie did, thinking there'd be men at school and then a career of some kind, and more men, with marriage a distant option to be blended with whatever stew of a life they would have come up with by then. "We thought people would just have to be more careful from now on," Lydia said. "We thought sexual *carelessness* was the problem."

"As opposed to sex itself?"

"No! As opposed to the *economy*. Who knew it'd buckle like that, in 'ten? And those pronatal packages that came down? God, who ever thought a single paycheck would be so freaking *chic?*"

I tuned her out, mostly. I'd heard it all from Marie—how corporations started laying off women when they married, how the political ads the next year presented a father feeding his family as opposed to a promiscuous young woman spending her paycheck. "I'll Take Care of You" was the song, that year.

"But you're still working," I said to Lydia.

"Until they turn up the heat a lot more. I'm single, after all. It's not a *legal* problem."

I knew what kind of problem it was, though—the staring eyes and clucks of tongues. Poor women didn't get that treatment, but Lydia didn't look poor. We were at her car by then. "Well," I said, "good of you to come."

"Do *you* have a job?" she asked, turning suddenly from the open car door.

"Well, no, not really," I said. "Freelance stuff, you know."

"What d'you know about viruses?"

"I'm not a doctor," I started to say automatically, as if I were talking to one of Marie's clients; then, "Oh! You mean *computer* viruses. Not a thing."

"I get lonely at the office," she said, "and I'm good at training people. I was going to ask Marie, before all this—this mixed-up mess happened to her."

She gave me her card, and a month later I called her. Lloyd was still holding back on getting new patients then—until we could spot the wire Marie had tripped, he argued, or the eyes she'd attracted, there wasn't any point in risking the same wire, the same eyes. The fact that the police had long since stopped harassing me would mean nothing until the shock waves that rippled through every cyberstream he touched had died away completely, and that would take close to a year. Until then, he was even in *favor* of my taking a job. Caring for my father wasn't enough to throw off the scent—it kept me at home, my schedule fluid, and since they'd never found the equipment they could conclude that it wasn't around Marie's little house after all, but secreted in the walls of my poor senile father's condominium.

From Lydia I learned that the most common viruses had acquired nicknames—Circe, the Vampire, Hecate. Incubi, succubi. I've learned that, like wombs, computer networks can blindly gestate fetal monsters that we have to zap before they become independent and go rollicking off, raising havoc in the Web.

Do I care about the job too much? I've never thought I cared at all; it provides money for Dad's nurse and a good cover, and with Lydia as my boss I take less than the usual amount of flak, but that's it. Marie would have given it up in less than a second had she been me and Lloyd asking.

Out in St. Monica, the DMV offices are cramped, the people who work here impatient. State offices like this still employ plenty of women—young women, Welfare-to-Work women, elderly women who trusted in Social Security. They glare at us—especially, I think, at Lydia and me—as if we're the problem and not their silicon chips and fiber-optic lines. We, who should have cleared this up weeks ago, are the ones not working right. "I got a crashing system out there!" one obese cashier is complaining, standing in front of Jonathan and the office manager. "Now, I got nothing to do with whatever your license problem is, I oughta be able to take the credit and log it in, paid!"

"Normally, you log it into a network by *number,*" Jonathan says, "and right now you've got a lot of numbers booted to your stand-alone hard drive, so if you're not careful about the floppies—"

"Just write it down, Jessica, all right?" the manager cuts in, seeing what Jonathan can't see, which is how her eyes are glazing over. "Just get paper and pencil from Adam and write the amounts and names and numbers and dates down."

"I am not *writing!*" Jessica practically screams. "I do not send my three kids to day care so I can come in here and chop wood and clean toilets and push paper!"

"It's not exactly the same—"

"It is the same thing! Go out to the wilderness, you want to do pencil and paper! Now you get me a good screen or I'll call WTW about these conditions!"

"You go ahead," says the district manager, stepping closer to the woman, and Jonathan seizes his chance to duck between them with a keypad.

"C'mon in here," he says to Lydia and me. We follow him into the narrow, fluorescent-lit room where I spent the whole day yesterday, now and then standing on a chair to peek out the high horizontal window at the blond beach that I could just spot between two rows of clapboard houses, the breakers foaming silently in. There's a wall screen, which Jonathan quickly fills with the numbers I isolated off the desktop. "Where's that HD?" he asks me. I hand him the disk I downloaded last night, which he dupes and returns while Lydia switches off the humming light. "Ladies and gentlemen," he announces when the thing loads, "I offer you the virus."

As the numbers mutate, I draw in my breath. "Where's the pattern?" Lydia asks. As Jonathan clicks keys, the numbers reflect on his long milky face; he glows with them. I like Jonathan, I think, a stitch of excitement in my chest. I don't want to quit this job and not spend time with Jonathan.

It takes two hours, the air growing staler by the minute, but in the end Jonathan's right—I bagged the virus yesterday, in my impatience and distraction not realizing what I'd caught. It's carefully constructed, a multiple aggregate code with time signals, no accident. Lydia squeezes my arm; Jonathan kisses me on the forehead, a blessing. "Now all we have to do," he says as we head, triumphant, out of the DMV building into the blast of hot air, "is turn the program inside out."

"Easykins," says Lydia. I say nothing; I feel smug as a blooming dahlia. As we pile into the Volt, though, I catch sight of the same group of retros I spotted yesterday, a couple dozen of them gathered in the alley that leads to the beach. Crouched down, they're trading cash money for used items, their clothes an assortment of bright ties and open vests, the women in pants like the men. At one point yesterday, one of them rose and came over to the Dumpster behind this building to add to his stash there. His head shaved except for a braid gathered in the back, he was short and round, like a tanned Buddha; looking up, seeing my face at the pinched window, he raised his wrists in their peculiar crossed salute.

"If it's not an accidental virus," I say, trying to ignore the retros as I slide into the hot seat of the car behind Jonathan, "then *people* are behind it. Right?"

"People like that, you mean," he says. He jerks a thumb toward the clump in the alley, a hundred yards away.

"Don't make me laugh," says Lydia, switching on the car.

"No, really," says Jonathan. "Some of those are brilliant."

"And they hate us," I say.

"But they don't know anything about networks," says Lydia. "They don't even have systems."

"Exactly," says Jonathan.

"My sister Marie never had a system," I hear myself saying, as we pull away from the DMV and the group in the alley. "I had to install one, when I moved my office to her house."

"Life without a system," says Jonathan. He's leaned back in the bucket seat and shut his long-lashed eyes. "What a golden time."

"Yeah." I chuckle sardonically, but I'm not tempted to contradict him; Marie's very name, in a situation like this, is my secret, and if I hadn't been so giddy with my little success I never would have let it out. "Real gold," I say, sincerely.

In fact, there was a golden time—just before they caught Marie. Not that life was easy; there was our father, for one thing, whose brain had already started shedding cells like a dog's coat in the spring. But Marie was strong and I was happy, basking in the sunshine of loving Rudi. I'd left school when they closed out liberal arts—I couldn't see my way clear to a major in home ec or business math. So I spent my time helping Marie. Only a few of her patients came through Lloyd— most were personal referrals, women who'd heard of her the way you hear of a foolproof faith healer or a saint. She'd sit with them in the cozy back den of her little house, and on the leather-topped coffee table she'd display the instruments. Making tea or answering the phone, I'd overhear them telling her—after they'd gotten through the technical details and were turned to each other on the flowered couch—how it had happened. A husband had yanked out the diaphragm, saying it hurt him. A lover had promised he was sterile from all the crack he'd done. A boss in the company had promised marriage (we laughed at that one later, cruel sisters that we were). I'm so stupid, so stupid, the women would say, and Marie would answer in her clear voice, Accidents happen. Vitamin C, some of them had tried; goldenseal, penny royal, valerian; baths so hot that one or two had second-degree burns on their bellies. Can't you get hold of a pill? several asked—a morning-after, or RU-486? Don't those things get smuggled in? I'd pay you the same for it, they'd say, as if Marie was holding out on them, as if she had a stash in the back but insisted on the medical procedure because who could charge five hundred dollars for a pill? They don't make 486 anymore, Marie would explain, and you'd be too late for a morning-after even if I could get hold of it. Believe me, she'd say, and of course they did.

Then, slowly, she'd get them to talk about family, friends, work if they had it. How amiably they chattered by this time! And I don't mean to imply Marie didn't care—she did care, enormously, too much—but by the end she had the caution lights she needed: a Catholic family, or a husband who wanted his wife staying home, or a custody battle that news of a misconception might doom, or a certainty that the woman would burn eternally for what she planned to do. Not that it changes my mind, an example of this last type might say, her voice hardening between sips of tea. If I can't get this thing out of me I will die.

Marie never told them no. Some she persuaded to give it another week, and mostly those didn't come back, though I cannot believe any of them betrayed her. They gave birth to their babies and loved them, and in a while—months, years—they almost forgot they had once planned to murder this person who filled so much of their life.

But I've said it was a golden moment. One weekend we paid a night nurse to watch after Dad, and Marie and Rudi and I rented a cottage on the coast of Maine. At first I was afraid Marie would feel left out. But she knew one or two people in the town nearby, and she either painted or went to visit them, and by the third evening she'd

brought a man home for supper, a muscular pepper-haired guy named
Clark who told long hilarious political jokes and stayed the night. In
the afternoons Rudi and I walked on the sand and splashed in the water, but Marie went out the day after a storm with a child's foam board
and rode the great waves in to the beach. "Yowee!" she cried when
she stood up, sand-coated, the ebb of the wave rushing back behind
her. "This is a thrill, Phoebe! You've got to try it!"

"Are you sure there aren't rocks out this way?"

"If there are I'm cresting over them. C'mon, Rudi, you give it a try!"

Challenged, he swam out after her and rode one in, cutting his
shoulder on a jagged pebble but stoic about it. After that we both sat
and watched her. She was thirty-five that summer, her body thickening around the hips. I noticed the long muscles of her thighs, her large
expressive hands, the still-dark hair that she tossed out of her broad
face. Her white teeth flashed, each time she soared in on a wave and
slid to rest a few feet from our toes.

Back home in Utica, when we'd cleaned up Marie's basement
room for the day and sung our father to sleep—he liked old show
tunes, "Try to Remember" from *The Fantasticks* and "Tomorrow"
from *Annie*—she'd stay at the apartment until late. Stretched out on
the rug together, we'd do leg lifts and rehash the day. "That woman
Ophile really felt it, this afternoon," she said once, in September, summer descending into fall.

"I don't know, I thought she was pretty even-keeled," I said. "Now
that other one—Sarah?—I kept telling her 'blackberry brandy,' because I know she's going to cramp like crazy. Her muscles were all
bunched up."

"I don't mean felt it as in pain," Marie said. She turned to her side and
pushed up on one elbow. Bent, her upper leg lifted and held, a meter off
the ground, then slowly lowered. "Haven't you noticed," she went on,
watching the leg as if it were acting on its own, a door opening and shutting, "how most patients have already stopped being pregnant by the
time we go to work on them? Mentally, I mean. They cry from the pain
or the stress, they're sort of letting go that way, but they don't have any
more sense that there's another life involved. They've decided *we're* doing this to *them*, not that *they're* doing this to their *babies*."

"Well, we are, too."

"Sure, but—" She pivoted her body, to lift the other leg. Now she was facing my ankles. "It seems to me that at a basic level all this involves an understanding of death," she said. "That's where this country's got it upside down, thinking it's about the preciousness of life. We kill all the time, we human beings—it's like we're killing machines, practically."

"Oh, come on."

"Name me an action we take that doesn't damage or destroy."

"Name me an action an *ant* takes that doesn't damage or destroy."

"They clean up debris. They irrigate the soil without salinating it." I shrugged; Marie could get fired up. "I'm not saying we don't belong on the planet," she insisted. "Just, we don't think about all this killing that goes with the package. But Ophile—I caught a glimpse of her face, right when the aspirator got going, and you know what? It registered death. Others come in here and go out, and return to being the person they were before they goofed. Ophile, she'll never be the same."

I let the silence fill the room. From down the hallway, you could hear Dad's snores—it was the drugs, deepening his sleep. "You change too, don't you?" I said. It came out a whisper. "Each time."

She nodded, lowering her leg. "There's less of me," she said, "and more of me. But, hey." The mood slid off her; she sat up, cross-legged. "So long as I've still got my house and my kid sister," she said, "I can take it."

We laughed a lot, staying up late. The first time I broke up with Rudi, Marie got such a fit of the giggles when I told her the scene (he'd hopped up and down on the sidewalk, he was so angry, and landed too hard, and then he'd pulled off his right shoe and shrieked, *See here? See this? You made me break my orthotic!*) that she had to rush to the bathroom to pee. Or she would describe sessions with Lloyd, whom I hardly knew then, so that we'd both end up thrusting out our chests and tucking in our chins and repeating what he'd said to her like that, *You know, Marie, what you're running is a business and a business has no place for wiffle-waffle.* We'd repeat that word, *wiffle-waffle,* until just saying it made us crack up.

. . .

Rudi and Lloyd, in fact, are the handles on the two messages blinking for me when I get back home from California, still flushed with victory. Rudi's is simple—not unlike the retros, he's uncomfortable with screen conversations, and he wants to take me to dinner. This prospect depresses me enough that I don't boot Lloyd's message, which has got to be about rescheduling appointments. My dad's in the den, playing cards with Betty, who—even though she always wins—has the valuable appearance of being devoted to my misty-eyed, slack-jawed father.

Dad's got Alzheimer's, of course, complicated by an eclectic series of infarctal strokes that hit at the strangest nodes of the brain. Before, when I was a superfluous girl child and he held a bench on the circuit court, he cared little for me, and so I learned quickly: to resent his elegant arguments, to spit out his polished sarcasm, to detest the doughy skin and spangle-sized freckles he'd passed on to me. When my mother died, he pulled Marie closer to him; when Frank died, I having failed to be the son that could replace my brother, he pushed me farther away. But now that he's decrepit of body and mind, he's sort of like a superintelligent shaggy dog, whose tail wags wildly when he sees me and who licks his plate apologetically, because Nature's forced him into certain habits.

"Hi, guys," I say, dropping my bag at the door.

"Well, look who's here," says Betty, but she doesn't look; doesn't take her eyes from the card game. Rummy, I see it is, played with real paper cards on a folding table. My father, though, raises his heavy head as though Betty's answer were instruction. "Did you go away?" he asks, and I can tell from the tremble in his lower lip that he's working on who I am.

"I had a business trip," I say, stepping into the light.

"I went out today," he says. I settle into the armchair while he takes his turn at cards; he picks a seven from the pile and sets down a king.

"You sure?" says Betty, and he nods. He's got his granny glasses on, making him look shrewd.

"I went," he says, to me though he doesn't look my way, "to the produce store."

I say nothing. We have no produce store in our neighborhood.

"Gin," says Betty, choosing the king and then laying out her cards. My father leans his chin into his claw, staring at them, then nods, and Betty picks up to shuffle again.

"I went," he goes on, "to get an onion. But the produce manager says to me, 'Sorry, we got no onions.' So I go on down the street." Betty clucks her tongue, but my father won't look up. He's got his red dressing gown on, the expensive one Marie gave him after his first stroke. "Then, you know how I forget things," he says. "So I get to the end of the block, and then I turn around and go back. I see the fellow stacking cantaloupes and I ask him, 'You got any onions?'"

"Cut," says Betty. She shoots me a look that says, Don't put up with this nonsense, but she doesn't know everything about my father.

"And he says," Dad goes on, sinking back a bit in the chair after he's shifted the cards, "'No, sir, we got no onions today.' Polite young fellow. I thank him this time and go my way, but at the end of the block I've forgot. Old man," he says, pointing to his chest and glancing quickly over at me. I nod.

"Last game," says Betty, "then bye to me and you to bed."

"The third time I go in, he's stacking turnips. Big purple things," my father says, using his hands—the left holding two kings and a seven—to indicate size. His voice fades in and out, echoes of the baritone that used to carry across a courtroom. "And I say, 'Excuse me, young fellow, you got any onions?' Now I can tell he's a little annoyed, but for the life of me I don't know why. And he says to me, 'Sir, what would ya get if ya took the blue outa blueberries?'" This is in my dad's best Yonkers accent, and I release a smile. "Well, now that's an easy question, even for a goat like me. I say, 'You'd get berries.' And he says, 'What if ya took the honey outa honeydew melons?'" My father turns full to me, now. His hair needs combing, a full head of white hair that won't stay put.

"Dew melons?" I try. I push off my shoes, aching from the long plane ride.

"Right," says my dad, "and next he asks, 'Now what if ya took the fuck outa onions?'" This time my dad looks at Betty first, who purses her lips and slaps down a jack. When he turns to me our eyes lock, closing Betty out.

"There is no fuck in onions," I say quietly.

"That's what he was trying to tell me! There ain't no fuckin' onions!"

His shoulders shake silently, his head wagging. I come up behind him barefoot, and crossing my arms over his chest, I kiss the top of his hair, which smells of cheap shampoo.

"You shouldn't encourage him," says Betty, and I grin at her.

It's funny, of course, that I ended up living with Dad, even before they took his favorite Marie away. She'd moved into her own house before I quit school, and even the late evenings that she came over, she almost never stayed. Well, I didn't have her early-morning art classes, so I could handle Dad's midnight madness better. Still it was weird, catching the look on his bewildered face every time she leaned over to kiss him goodnight. Only a few times did she say that her little house felt lonely. Then I got her a pillow and blanket, and she curled up on the couch. These were the times, I think, when she had a man moving out of her life. For whatever reason—too many secrets, maybe—they never lasted long. And when she stayed, she got up early and prepared Dad's tray, sometimes with a funny little charcoal drawing next to the plate, to cheer him up. "That Marie," he'd say, scrambled egg spilling from his mouth. "That goofball."

Tonight, after I've credited Betty—a huge sum, three extra nights, she's one happy nurse—he starts again, interrogating me about Marie. "When?" he asks, his legs bent and splayed under the bedcovers Betty's helped tuck him into, his wrinkled elbows hung over his knees as if his arms were loose hinges. It must be awful, I think, to rediscover people's deaths over and over again, to have grief assault you in all its raw terror with no hope that, once the moment has passed and your pain eased to numbness, it will never return in this exact form again.

"Three and a half years ago," I enunciate slowly, taking one of the loose hands in both of mine, my weight propped on the edge of the bed, "she was arrested."

"What for? What for? How come nobody called the D.A.? That's Cliff Nickelson, he's an old golfing partner of mine, he could have—"

"Mr. Nickelson retired, Dad. And they arrested her on charges of performing illegal abortions and trafficking in abortion contraband, which is a federal offense. I'm not sure he could have helped."

"Performing *what?*" His forehead furrows, his watery eyes squeeze in consternation.

I sigh; I'm jet-lagged, tired. I should have paid Betty for one more night. Once, when this happened, I gave up early and told him she'd been killed in a car crash. Tonight, though, the need for truth overrides pity; no more secrets. "Helping women," I say, "who didn't feel they could bring their babies to term."

"Never! My daughter never did such a thing! It's murder, pure and simple, and these women who think they can shirk the gift and burden of life God gave them—these women, *acgk,* these selfish, *grecch*—"

"Stop trying to talk, Dad," I say. "Here." And I hold a glass of water to his mouth, steadying the back of his head while he drinks. He spits into the glass, a yellow mess of water and mucus. I take it away. When I come back with a damp washcloth for his chin and hands he is weeping, his head hanging between his knees, the shell of his back trembling.

"When?" he asks again, more weakly this time, after I've got him wiped up. His freckles have begun to fade, with age, but at these times they stand out like a spray of rust across his face.

"She was in jail a year just waiting, and then the trial dragged on and on. They didn't have any evidence," I add, to comfort him.

"But you said. You said she died."

"Bad meat. In the prison. The E. coli bacteria, you remember about that?"

He nods sagely. "Thought they had it licked, by the time I was born," he says. "Then the antibiotics stopped working, it got tougher and they didn't."

"No, Dad. You're thinking of TB-2." This isn't the moment to remind him of Frank. If he's forgotten entirely, there's a whole raft of grief waiting to float him downstream. "E. coli just comes from meat," I go on. "Meat that's—that's come into contact with fecal matter. Which is why most people don't eat meat anymore, but they serve it in the prisons, and I guess there isn't much else. By way of protein, you know."

"She was poisoned," he says. The loose, thinning flesh seems to pull back against the bones of his face.

"Well, yeah. In a manner of speaking. I don't think intentionally."

"She suffered."

"Yes, she did. Terrible pains at first, and then a sort of meltdown of her brain."

"Like mine."

"More quickly," I say, smiling, "than yours."

"My baby Marie," he says. He's leaned back against the pillows, now; the tears flow wildly, covering his face. "My baby who never hurt anyone. She used to touch me here, and here," his scarred fingers on his cheeks and large nose. "Learned to count on my freckles. Told me once I had two hundred sixteen of them. I just sat. Patient. Let her. Count."

These last words come out as sobs, each a separate explosion. I tuck tissues, three into each half-clenched fist. When he's cried himself to sleep I ease his body down, relieve him of a couple of pillows, check his diaper. He does not look angelic, sleeping; dreams flit across his papery face like familiar ghosts.

Out in the foyer, Lloyd's handle is still blinking on the system. I'll check the message soon, in case Lloyd's still at his office, waiting. For just a second, though, I finger the disklet in my pocket, the one I caught the virus on. Far from my father, out there in St. Monica I did have my tiny moment of triumph. Tim actually *hugged* me, his chest like cardboard and his neck smelling of salt. Gerald, the big lumpy fag, twirled me around, and Jonathan and Lydia took me out for Bombay slingers at an interactive bar. Right now the pull of my family— Dad, Lloyd, doing misconceptions—is just a sharp yank, like a puppy grabbing at your ankle; I can break free if I want.

As I step through the French doors of the living room, out to the balcony, I breathe the humid summer air. This is a senior citizens' apartment building, in the old Polish part of town, where long ago there were lumber mills and sweatshops drawing in labor. Later, it became a dangerous sector—crumbling, abandoned buildings, drive-by shootings, drug busts. Now it's gotten fashionable, with old warehouses transformed into hives of boutiques and cafes; the elderly who live here choose it because it makes them feel young and they can walk everywhere. I didn't grow up here, but on the west end of the city, where nothing's changed since the twentieth century: the streets still wind into the low hills and lawns are kept close-cropped and hedged. But I like it here better. Not for the fashionable boutiques, but for the way the air smells, especially now: of hot brick and last night's wine, of pigeons and the rare window box crammed with petunias. Dad moved here a few years after Mom died, when he was sick already but could still make a so-called competent decision. He wanted to go back to roots, he said, to live where he'd been brought up as a boy, by his Polish grandparents. They let him into the building only on condition that another adult would be here full-time. I'd just broken with the boyfriend I had before Rudi, and I hated the school dorms. I wanted to be near Marie, who'd bought her red frame house just three blocks away; maybe, too, I thought of it as my last chance to take her place, to be the daughter my dad loved.

Five stories below, the streetcar stops and rings its tinny bell. That's the other thing people love about this sector—six years ago they closed off the streets to cars and started the streetcars up again. Men take them to the edge of downtown, to work; their wives take them as a shopping shortcut. New Oldtown, they call us, picking up on New Traditionalism, phrases that make us feel good—who doesn't want to be new and old at once?

The streetcar takes off, its bright red trim refracted in ground-floor windows all the way down the block. Stepping back inside—restless, the puppy still pulling at my ankle—I close the French windows. One more trip, Lydia thinks, and not until next month. Meanwhile there are local New York accounts to clean up. From Angel City, trying to call my sister-in-law, Roxanne, Christel's mom, in St. Barbara, I kept getting lively videotalk, like Christel's but with an older face, a throatier voice, and the hazy option that "we might be out of town, but we do check in, cross our hearts!" Between tipsy ventures onto celluloid at the inter-bar, Jonathan and Gerald had kept up a harangue about how slow the government is with the new inoculation program—until they'd both had too much and switched to telling funny stories about the bad old days. "When sex was lethal . . ." they'd start in. Finally— because I'd had three slingers and watched myself tumble from a sky- scraper on the video screen—I offered the opinion that sex still was lethal for some people.

"Like who?" Gerald said, his chin in his big hand. He's a paunchy man, handsome in the face.

"Like women," I said, the vodka urging me on. "They get pregnant when they don't want to, and they can kill themselves trying to mis- conceive."

"Oh, come on," said Jonathan, still grinning from the last story. "There are places they can go."

"Five years for a first offense," I point out.

He waved his hand. "There are always places," he said. "Look at XTC, you can always get X."

"They let the X dealers go," I said, "after a couple of weeks."

"Well, I for one," said Gerald, "am glad to know sex is still danger- ous for someone. Keeps the spice in it."

My eyes burned. They were just being funny, lighthearted; this was my night. They hadn't known about Marie. I'm tired, I told them a few minutes later, and took the subway back to the hotel.

The job or the basement hideaway, with its table and its instru- ments? I put the choice to myself as I move through my father's living room and approach the blinking system. The hideaway or the job. Which do I want? Is that why I'm so restless? Facing the dark screen, in my mind's eye I see the streetcar flashing by. You don't want either of them, a voice comes to me—you want a husband, a family. Not Rudi, but someone stable and kind. You want a home.

Yes, I say to the voice. And then I press RECEIVE.

CHAPTER 6

Driving east from the city, you follow the barge canal. There's been a drought this summer; the trees are pale, leaves smaller than usual, so it looks more like late spring than August. At first I'm not going anywhere in particular; these days, even today, I have to be back for the noon hour, between the morning nurse and Betty. Trucks pass me, whining down 90 toward Albany. I turn off at Herkimer for methanol and a Coke. In the window of the quickshop is an American flag next to the insignia of the New York Militia, and a poster from the campaign four years ago: AN EYE FOR AN EYE, A DEATH FOR A DEATH, with a drawing of a fetus on the one hand and a hanged woman on the other. The resolution almost passed the House, I remember, but failed in the Senate; Marie and a couple of her friends and I polished off a bottle of champagne. I thank the store owner, a heavyset man with a carcinomic-looking mole on the bridge of his nose, and start up Steuben Hill Road.

I'm not in a hurry—I even stop once, to hike a familiar trail in the small state park and take a look over the sprawling valley below. But the second time that I'm tempted to pull over, as three young deer cross the road, I only pause. I'm in sight of the first house my sister lived in, when she left our home in the western hills, before my father was diagnosed and she came back to the city. I'm not going to stop there; I don't want to turn down the long drive to the rambling old ranch house where Marie lived with her friends. I just move onto the shoulder, let the trucks pass for a minute or two.

They were all misconceivers—three or four of them shared the place at any given time—but the faces fluctuated. This was right after my mother died, and often I got to spend Saturday night at my sister's house, staying up late with whoever was living there and taking my invisible place on Sunday mornings, when a large patchy group gathered and filled the place with the smells of muffins and fresh-ground coffee and mounds of fruit salad. They traded gossip and gripes, news and fears. They touched each other a lot, not just arriving and leaving but passing in and out of the narrow kitchen, or sitting on the couch with legs flopped over someone's knees. I knew what was going on, though I'd never held a speculum or palpated a lower abdomen. I knew this was my destiny, the work I'd do as soon as Marie thought I was ready. And though I knew what had happened to my mother, and why, the ranch house—like the red house, later, when Marie went on her own—felt like a safe place. When Marie had gone through something traumatic, she talked it out with the group in the living room. Men and women, they leaned into one another over the coffee table, insisting and assuring.

But I don't have that luxury, and so I drive. I've driven miles over Rudi, miles over my mad stubborn father. I don't usually come this way. Today it's the twelve-year-old I'm trying to drive out of my system—the one I postponed, the one whose fate I learned of on voice mail and later, at Lloyd's office, where I insisted on showing up in person.

You shouldn't have come here, he kept saying. Yes, Lloyd, right you are, Lloyd.

How spacious his office is, how sunlit and cheery! As I paced before his desk, the air-conditioning floated its soothing *sshssh* from tactfully hidden ducts. Lining the walls were large, chaotic oil paintings and small cabinets with objets d'art that Lloyd has elected to keep for a while, probably waiting for their value to go up. This is how he makes the stable base of his money, dealing in what will be precious before it becomes so. The paintings, Lloyd once said, are by a Chinese artist who escaped from labor camp across the high mountains of Tibet and lost most of his fingers to the cold. Holding the brush in his palm and stubs, he paints what look like collages—bloodied, broken fragments. In five years, Lloyd's told me, these will be worth a million dollars each.

Marie drew miniatures, small detailed sections of the human body—a navel, a cracked toenail, the whorls of an ear—usually in charcoal. Lloyd doesn't have any of her work, at least not that I've ever seen.

But we didn't talk about the paintings this morning, because Lloyd was tilting his monitor toward me, with last night's headlines jumping off the screen. "I know," I said. "I booted it up as soon as I got your message. I've read the whole thing."

"Seen the video?" He pressed a button, and the anchorwoman Connie Day came on, standing in front of the girl's school.

"Yes. Please, Lloyd."

"All right." He flicked it off. "You know there was a note to her parents."

"That's what they said on the news. They didn't read it."

"Well, I pay a guy in the police department to read me things like that. You want to hear what it said?" I nodded; I had no choice but to nod. This was my assigned punishment, I could select no other. Lloyd cleared his throat and unlocked a new file. *"You thought you could stop me by locking me up,"* he read off the screen. *"But I can kill this monster whenever I want to. And now I want to. No one helps a person when they really need it. Tomorrow, they always say. Well, now it's tomorrow, and look."* He pressed a button and the screen went black. "She signed it and hanged herself," he said.

"I know."

"Fish or cut bait, Phoebe."

"The bait cut itself," I said. I was staring at the floor, at Lloyd's ancient Oriental rug, with its dull colors and mysterious geometry. "You want me to feel terrible. That's how I feel."

"They found my handle, in her system."

"Shit. There weren't any messages, were there?"

"No. But it's messy, Phoebe."

"The police called you?"

He waved a hand, dismissing that part of the equation. "I'd done some checking. Her mother collects old coins, almost two hundred years old some of them. I reported that the girl had called me, offering to sell her mother's collection, and that I suspected what she wanted the money for and told her she'd have to shop elsewhere. I showed them the record of our conversation." He booted up the screen again, the file neatly dated two weeks past, the notes dutifully spontaneous.

"God, Lloyd. This whole thing's so much trouble for you."

"Well, they won't stop with me. So this is what I'm doing, Phoebe. I'm cutting you off for a month, all right? No appointments, no calls. Then you contact me and tell me either you're in as far as Marie was, or you're out. Deal?"

"What about the ones who come to you in that time?"

"I'll have to tell them they have the wrong number, that they're mistaken. I'm being watched, aren't I?"

"Can't you send them to someone else?"

"There are not that many of you people. You should know."

I nodded, miserable. "Did you meet her?" I finally asked.

"Who, the girl? Once."

"And?"

"And what? She looked like a twelve-year-old who'd been knocked up by her dad. Her hair hung in her eyes, she had bad skin. When I told her you could help, she squeezed my hand so hard it hurt."

"Oh God."

"Don't oh God me. Just get lost for a while, Phoebe. Get out of town with your job, or go hiking with your boyfriend, or something."

"I don't have a boyfriend."

"Well, disappear."

He was gruff—I think now, looking back—he was as angry as I've seen him. But when I stood to go, he came around the wide desk and walked me to the door, his pudgy arm lifted high to wrap around my shoulder. "If you are thinking," he said, more quietly, "'Marie would never have fucked up like this,' then stop. We all fuck up now and then. And then one thing we can't do is change the world. People are dying for stupid reasons these days, yeah. But people have always died."

"If she just hadn't been twelve," I said.

"Go think," he said at the door, his electronic secretary discreetly turned to Sleep. "Go ponder."

. . .

So I do. I think, the familiar driveway receding behind me, of the time just after the aspirator broke, when Marie had been doing a D&C on a panicky seventeen-year-old, and the girl jerked and punctured her uterus. Marie had to drive the girl, screaming, to the one doctor forty miles away who would anesthetize her and anneal the torn tissue, and she paid him five times what the girl had paid her to have it done. *Not your fault,* her friend from the group kept repeating when Marie brought it up. *We've all done it, or we will.* But that doctor's gone now. We're all much more cautious—I'll give as many as four Valium if I spot a panicky patient—and no one ever gathers. Lydia thinks there's a national conspiracy, but I don't even know the others' names. The Mau-Mau phone number is an old message machine somewhere, not even a system that could be traced. There's no one to absolve me of this girl's hanging, no one to assure me I couldn't have known, or that I can't live my life around the possibility that I could have.

So I'm not going to the ranch house, where Marie's old friends have vanished—left the business, or been picked up and convicted, doing time. But I do know where I'm going. From the winding mountain highway I turn left onto an even narrower, potholed way. Second-growth fir and maple fringe the road; here and there an abandoned building leans out from the scraggly woods, a hole punched in its wooden side. Just past a rusted-open gate I turn onto a dirt driveway where an old retriever, the color of autumn brush, lies deaf in the sun. Roused by my loud honk, he hunches his hindquarters off the main driveway and stands, hoarsely baying, in the weeds.

"Yipes," says Jonathan, drying his hands as he bangs out the kitchen door. "What's brought you here, Phoebe? Something's wrong, isn't it? Oh, shut up, Norman."

The dog stops, shuffles back onto the dirt and sinks like a rug that's been aired. Jonathan holds my hand as if we were on a teenaged date and leads me into his house.

"Is Gerald here?" I ask.

"No, no, he's gone to his mother's for the weekend."

"Does she know he's living here?"

"You kidding? She gave us the bread oven for housewarming. We do have *some* friends, Beeb."

"Am I your friend?"

"I should hope."

"No matter what?"

"Phoebe. What a question!" We're in the main part of his house, a place I suddenly realize I love—cathedral ceilings transversed by broad pine beams that Jonathan hewed and planed himself when he first came up here; old, lead-paned windows fitted into tall narrow frames that look out over the clearing and the valley; a trapezoidal brick fireplace separating living from kitchen areas, with glass doors on this side and a bread oven on the other. Along one wall, hardbound books of the sort you used to find in libraries, dull leather spines without gleam. Jonathan's still holding my hand, turned toward me now, staring.

"The last time I was here it was so cold out," I say. "You had that thing stoked. Roaring like a castle furnace."

"What do you mean, are we friends no matter what?" He draws me into the living area, sits me down on a folded futon; while he waits for my answer he fetches me strong coffee in a glass mug. "Did you kill somebody?"

"Sort of."

"Not your father."

"No, no."

"Motive?"

"None. Accidental."

"Am I supposed to be taking this conversation seriously?" He's passed me a coaster and sits opposite me, slicing a green apple.

"Yes. No. Probably not. I didn't kill anybody." I'm sipping my black brew, starting to cry. Partly I'm mourning the twelve-year-old; partly I'm weeping because my life upsets me. Mostly I'm scared. What my mother did, what Marie did, what I do is like a bomb locked safe inside me; the slightest leak can trigger combustion. Jonathan offers me an apple slice, and I shake my head. From the side room, off this main area, comes a whirring sound, followed by a rapid series of beeps. "I'm sorry. You were working."

"No, no, just waiting for something to cycle through. I was doing dishes, actually."

I've been in the side room, Jonathan's workspace, as coldly functional as this room is aloft with beauty. It's his laboratory, his black-windowed entry into every room cyberspace can offer. But I don't even glance over at the source of the beeps and clicks right now. I say, "You haven't answered my question."

"Sorry." He smiles. "That's just like in those old movies, when the wife asks the husband, 'Are you in love with that girl?' and he answers like, 'How can you ask such a question?' and then you know of course he *is* in love with that girl because otherwise he would simply have said *No*."

"So?"

"Yes, we are friends no matter what. If you have cut up your father into little pieces and served him to the alley cats, we are friends. If you have cut up Tim and served him to the cats, we are especially friends. If you voted for that asshole sitting in the White House—" He breaks off, holds a curl of apple skin; he has to consider this one. "All right, even then we're friends, but you'd better have a damn fucking good reason."

"All right." Suddenly parched, I drain my mug and hold it out, and he jumps up to fetch water. "I'll have to start at the beginning," I say. And then it's too late to stop, though my voice rattles in my chest and I can almost hear the explosions. It's the twelve-year-old girl I want to confess—but I can't get to her except through the rest of it, and my need to be forgiven for the girl swamps the careful fences I've built. So I tell him what I haven't told anyone since Rudi—even though other men have lain in my arms, even though I've gotten completely smashed at two friends' weddings and lain in a heap of women confessing secret upon secret.

"It never really had to do with politics," I tell him when I've gotten past the early part. I've explained how networks were set up and how Marie trained me, first on her and later helping to hold patients' hands, take their blood pressure, get their heads straight afterward. The words come shockingly easy, now I've started. "It was this feeling I picked up on. Like there was nothing worse than to be at war with something inside of you. That if women couldn't be left alone to fight this fight, they'd pick another enemy—children, maybe, or themselves, or men—and fight those things instead." I stop, looking at him. An apple slice is halfway to his mouth.

"We're still friends," he says, and pops it in.

"I mean, all this talk about how men are the warriors. Little boys popping Arrowstorms off at squirrels and getting approval for it because it's their male instinct. You know what my sister used to whisper when she got the forceps on the fetal mass inside some terrified X-head? Just loud enough for me to hear. *Gotcha.*"

My fist closes on air. Then I tell him about the girl, how I postponed the appointment and she got caught out and hanged herself rather than carry the kid to term. There's a long silence in which I hear the system's friendly buzz again, the ding it gives on the hour.

"Okay," says Jonathan. "My turn."

"I'm ready."

"We're going out to California in a few weeks, for the last time, I hope."

"I bet it won't be."

"It has to. I think I've got a new detection program that'll clean out at least eighty percent without crashing the net. Gerald's working on rebuilders. But listen. If you ask Lydia for a leave now, she'll freak, but if you ask her when it looks like we'll lick this thing, she'll say yes without thinking about it. You've earned some brownie points, after all. What if you just stayed out there a while, got away from this?"

"In California, you mean? Why?"

"Phoebe." Jonathan wipes his face with his hand, as if he's got grime on it. "I didn't know you when she died. But I've heard you talk about her—I've seen the light in your eyes—and you know what? You don't *owe* her this. She wouldn't want you doing abortions if your heart wasn't in it."

"Misconceptions," I correct him quickly. "And yes, yes she would. You don't know. The last time I saw her"—I have to bite my lip, I remember Marie with her face sunken and gray, her body shapeless under the hospital gown—"she said this whole thing was bigger than just her. She saw me as a useful element by then. Oh, don't be horrified, she loved me, too. But nobody stood alone for her, nobody was separate."

"All right." Unexpectedly he rises and ducks into the computer studio, where he checks two of the screens and then sets something running again. "I still maintain," he says, striding back into the woodsy, old-fashioned space where I'm sitting, "that you don't owe her, or those women. People make choices, kiddo. They should be in D.C., beating down the barricades of Congress, not relying on you to fix a constitutional-amendment problem. Look, do you have a place you could stay, in California?"

I think for a second. "There's my sister-in-law."

"I didn't know you had a sister-in-law!"

I nod and take a long drink of water; it's from Jonathan's well, I can taste moss. Where's the horrified reaction? From the way Jonathan's behaving, you'd think I had merely a practical problem. "I was born the year she married my brother, there's a lot of distance," I say.

"And he's—"

"TB-2. A long time ago." Then I tell him about Christel—I even do a little imitation of her, to make him laugh—and how I'd promised to check on her mother, Roxanne, but not done it. He's stood up again and is pacing, fireplace to CD player and back over a thick square rug, blue pile. Already I'm feeling better. The twelve-year-old seems very far away, a sad little girl I never knew who could neither keep a secret nor learn to climb out a second-story window. "But I don't want to run away," I say to Jonathan.

"Can you think, around your sister-in-law?"

"I haven't seen her in a long time. I don't remember her being such a fanatic as Christel is. But I wouldn't want, you know, to tell her anything."

"Well, look, if it doesn't work out I've got some friends around San Diego. These guys are flaming queers—you can say anything around them." He goes over to a wall system and boots up his phone directory. "Hand me a disklet, I'll copy this," he says, and I pull one out of a cranny in my pocketbook.

"Now," he says when I've drained my glass, "lie on the rug here, and I'll give you a backrub."

I obey; and at the pressure of his large hands on my shoulder blades, I feel the breath stored up in me catch and then exhale, so that the vertebrae on my spine pop and a tingle flows over my shoulders and down to the tips of my fingers. "Oh, Jonathan," I say, grateful.

"Ssh."

With his thumbs he works from the base of my spine upward, and then fans out along my ribs until he is massaging under my spread arms to where my breasts begin, pressed into the carpet. When I've given way to the power of his hands, so chaste and bold at once, he begins to sing. To myself I think, Jonathan, I didn't know you sang, but my words don't find their way out. It's an old Indian song he seems to be singing, a kind of chant, with a lot of *da* and *chi* sounds, the rhythmic notes alternating between two different registers. I think it must be a healing chant, and I imagine myself learning it and singing it to the twelve-year-old just in time, or to Marie as she slips into coma. *Daveeda vahlachich vahlachich voh,* he seems to sing. Only after a long time do I realize he's stopped, and his hands have left my body.

"What time is it?" I manage to form the words.

"Quarter to noon."

"Shit." I push myself off the rug, all my muscles bunching at once. "My goddamn father! I'll be late!" Quickly I find my pocketbook, the tiny disklet with the San Diego numbers on it. "I can't stay in California, Jonathan. Not with my dad."

"Yes, you can. You figure it out and you can. And say, Phoebe?"

"Yeah?" I pause at the door, a headache starting in.

"I always knew. Guessed, I mean. That you were up to something on the fringes. And I won't breathe a word to anyone, not even Gerald. Though he probably guesses, too. After all, it's not an isolated issue, is it? Privacy, and all that."

I kiss him on the lips before I go. His lips are thin, cool, a taste of wetness in between. Outside, a wind's blown up, scouring the valley.

CHAPTER 7

Roxanne's house is completely white. She dresses in white, too—loose, flowing shirts over cotton pants that stop at the top of her tanned calves. She is the very model of the New Traditionalist, living at the top of a cliff overlooking the St. Barbara bay, with just enough quirkiness in her sleek decorations to ensure that they'll be talked about. Her daughter's all grown up now, and I figure she's never worked—this is family money I'm seeing in the house, plus a large life insurance policy from Frank, who died so young.

"Peaceful here," I say. I'm standing on the screened porch, over-looking a cove where sea lions bark on the rocks just offshore. Beside me Roxanne's sleek Russian wolfhound gazes imbecilically, wagging his elegant tail.

"I have always said," says Roxanne, coming up behind me with a minted iced tea, "that no matter what other accommodations you make in your life, it is essential to live in a beautiful place."

There's some truth to this—Utica, even now that it's booming, hardly counts as beautiful—and I don't wreck her point by observing that within the decade these cliffs will probably be uninhabitable, the sun scorching the lupine that runs down them. Already, I'm liking Roxanne better than I expected to. She's not beautiful—my memory of her, from the brief time she and my brother lived in Utica, is of a big-toothed woman, with the toed-out posture of a ballet dancer, who played the harp badly—but she carries herself well; she makes the most of her thick, frosted hair, her deep laugh, and a certain wizardry in the kitchen. Last night we had a salad of avocado, goat cheese, and pine nuts that still sits nicely on my tongue. We talked, too, about bigger things than I expected—the war that's been dragging Europe down for thirty years, AIDS inoculation in Africa, the postmortem on Social Security. "Marta keeps me up on the real world," she said when she'd finished explaining what Social Security might have done for my dad, for instance, if it hadn't gone bankrupt.

Marta's the housekeeper, young and square-built and chipper, but with a birdlike watchfulness that could make you nervous after a while. "You pay her in cash," I observed.

"Yes, my God." Roxanne rolled her eyes. "It's just the way Frank predicted," she said when she could tell I didn't get the problem. "This'll be the ax that cuts this country in two. Not all that messy stuff your sister was involved in. But *credit.* Credit and the system."

"She can't be all that poor, if she's working steady," I said. "There are public systems. She could at least get a card."

"But she *won't,* that's the thing." Roxanne sighed. Behind her, in the kitchen, Marta moved about, cleaning up. "She sees it as a *betrayal.* Frank said one day they'll be an armed camp, and I don't doubt it. Anyway," she said a bit wistfully, "Marta and I are friends, and she has her ways of getting the news."

Today we spent gardening—Roxanne passionate and diligent, me slow and absent-minded—and now we've showered and dressed in anticipation of Roxanne's fiancé. The back of my neck and my forearms are burned—fair skin at the edge of the ozone hole—but the view and the cheerful barking of sea lions are enough to make me forget why I had to come here. I'm wearing a white Grecian-drape thing Roxanne gave me when I arrived, with pink flowers over a bodice that makes me look busty. "Christel was right," Roxanne is saying, crossing the balcony to a chair.

"About what?"

"With a little softening at the edges, you'd be a terrific catch for some man."

"Christel said that?" I laugh, crossing one leg awkwardly over the other; I don't want to sit down.

"Not in so many words. But she likes you and is in a little awe of you, and I think she worries that you're lonely."

"Well, she needn't."

"I told her that if you'd stay ten days, we'd fetch you up someone."

"Christel's worried about you too, you know," I say, setting my iced tea down and picking up a miniature crèche, exquisitely woven from cornsilk and bright thread. I hadn't meant to go on the offensive so soon; I've been here less than twenty-four hours, leaving Lydia and the rest to wrap up details in Angel City.

"That's only because I've taken up with a Jew," Roxanne says. Her lips sort of kiss on the word *Jew*, as if she's tasting it.

"I tried to tell her I thought that was a little narrow-minded," I say.

"Oh, that won't work with my daughter. She treads the straight Christian narrow. Better than having a retro for a child, I guess."

"Oh, Christel's no retro," I say, though Roxanne doesn't laugh when I do. This afternoon she told me she's frightened of the retros, of the way they ditch their families to live in the cities like rats, melting their cards and feeding off the cash markets where Marta survives. If I told her about the network virus, she'd be ready to barricade her system. "Maybe you should introduce your daughter to your friend," I say.

"In time." Roxanne's large eyes waver a little. "You know what it is," she goes on, as if she has something to account for. "I have gotten out of the habit of being engaged."

"I didn't know it was something to make a habit *of*." I take a whiff of the salt air, run my index finger over the weave of the screen keeping gnats out. "I thought it was—you know, on the way."

"To marriage, you mean."

"I thought that was the idea."

"But engagement," says Roxanne, rising from her chair and setting her palms down on the wooden railing, looking out at the slow twilight, "is where you learn."

"Learn what? Sock darning?"

"No. To give up."

"Your freedom, you mean."

"No." Leaning on the railing, Roxanne stretches her legs back— left, then right, like an exercise. "The first time, you know, I did have a profession."

I set my iced tea safely on a side table and imitate my sister-in-law. It's a delicious stretch of the hamstrings, like testing a rubber band. Roxanne with a job—it's offensive, somehow. I ask her what kind, but she dodges. The point, she says, is the giving up. When you're engaged, she says, you love giving it up.

I stop stretching. I must give her a funny look, because she laughs, then switches her weight to the other foot. "Really," she says. "And before I bring Christel into the picture, I want to feel that way again."

"Maybe you don't have to give it up, Roxanne."

"Oh, you do. With all of them, you do. Don't let anyone tell you otherwise. Anyway," she says, picking up her own drink and heading back into the house, "there's nothing for me to give up now."

Before he arrives, we look at Roxanne's old album of pictures—Roxanne and Frank mostly, with friends and with their daughters and with the things that are now collected in this house. Looking at my brother is like flipping through snapshots of a stranger. I miss him only in the way you miss the things you never get to have. In these photos he looks like a mannequin, pasted in. His smile—more a grin, really, showing just the upper row of teeth, dimples in his lean cheeks—is exactly alike in all the pictures, and his hair is always cropped square across the top, with his neck uncomfortably tight in whatever shirt he's wearing. He's got Marie's eyes, though, and our mother's olive-toned skin. "It was awful, when he got the TB," Roxanne says, gently shutting the album. "I didn't take any photographs, I didn't want to remember him that way. He lost forty pounds, did you know that? Then he was suddenly better. They sent him home from the hospital. I'd bought him new pants, but he popped the snap, he'd put on weight. The girls sat in his lap at church. And then that night his fever shot up, and by morning he was gone." She pinches her lips together, then shuts the album firmly.

Just before dinner I call home; Betty answers, and I can hear her shopping program in the background. "He thinks you're off to college again," she says, smacking on gum. "Says he hopes you'll finish this time, since he has to pay for it. Oh, and your boyfriend called."

"I don't have a boyfriend."

"Said he was. That Rudi person."

"Oh, well," I say. "Ex."

"He said."

"Meds," I remind her.

"I am a nurse," she says.

Next I check mail: Jonathan and Lloyd, both of them upbeat, concerned that I'm having a good time and a chance to think. Both of them closing with encouragement to stay, undercut by the line, "We need you here." Where is here, I wonder; who are we? Viratect? Pregnant women? Lloyd is not a pregnant woman. There's nothing from Mau-Mau, though I managed to get Roxanne's handle to the message machine in case they found a new receiving barn. I'm curious to know about equipment and supplies—I'm almost out of laminaria, and if I don't get Valium in soon I'll have to switch to Demerol, which I don't like.

That is, if I'm going to stay in the business.

Arthur, the fiancé introduces himself. Arthur Levinsky, if I've caught it right. He's virile if not particularly handsome—midsized, quick in his movements, a squash player. I suspect he's a couple of years younger than Roxanne and doesn't know it. No, he volunteers, they haven't set a date.

We eat grilled tuna out on the patio, with the salt of the Pacific flavoring the air and the rhythmic crash of breakers filling the occasional silences. I like Arthur's speech, which is faintly European. He's a doctor, an orthopedist. "Long ago," Arthur says to my asking when they met.

"Not so long," says Roxanne.

"Well . . ." He tips his head, at her, as if this is something they've had to discuss.

"We met," explains Roxanne, reaching across the table for his hand, "when I broke my foot falling off a ladder in this place."

"She was hanging Japanese lanterns," adds Arthur, very slowly, as if it were a fact to regret and admire at once.

He asks about my work, and I give him the standard vague line about helping Angel City to implement detection programs. He asks about my father, whom—he says—Roxanne liked when he was sound of mind and body. To this Roxanne nods approvingly; he's got the history right. He asks what I plan to do during my visit, and I tell him walk on the beach, and a wave of relief comes over me as they both echo "Good plan!"—this will be a tonic after all, Jonathan was right.

When the audio rings, Roxanne goes to pick up; we can tell by her exclamation that it's Christel on the system. I feel even easier, sitting alone with Arthur. "You've never married before?" I ask.

"No." He leans back in his deck chair and holds up his glass of ruby-red wine, from an expensive bottle he brought with him. "Shall I tell you a story?" he asks, his faint accent gracing the question.

"Is it a story you'll have to interrupt when Roxanne comes back?"

"Yes. But you'll be here a week."

"Sure, then," I say. "First installment."

"I'm forty-one," he says. "When I was a scrawny kid at the university, I was in love with a—a slightly older woman. A dancer." He's turning the glass around, the Japanese lanterns that now hang from poles on the patio sending light through the wine. "After I graduated we went to Europe together—people traveled there in those days, before the war spread."

"Don't look at me like that—I've never crossed a border!"

"Well, we did, in those days. But the two of us had a falling out."

"Over what?" I ask gamely, when he pauses.

"Her career, in a way. She wanted to stay over there, to dance. *I'd* been admitted to med schools."

He looks at me, but I let this one go.

"So, oddly enough, she came back here, and I deferred admission for a year and tried London. When I landed in the States she was married. A baby girl was on the way. Which says to you—as it did to me—that I ought to have done my medical training on the other side of the country. Yes?"

"Yes indeed," I say. I glance toward the interior of the house; Roxanne is talking heatedly on the phone. It's hard for me to imagine Christel saying anything to upset her mother. Maybe it's someone else.

"For a very short time," Arthur is going on, leaning forward to re-fill my glass—he's balding, tanned where his forehead slopes past the hairline, and I have an impulse to touch the skin there but don't—"I lived with another accomplished woman, a surgical intern in Los Angeles. We called it that, then," he adds, and I don't know whether he means "lived with" or "Los Angeles." "Then she held her last performance—my dancer friend, I mean. She was leaving dance at last, for her family. And she invited me to come. Once I saw her move, on the stage, everything began again."

"Did she leave her husband?"

"No. She had her daughter by then. The laws were just starting to change, different sorts of judgments on custody were coming down in the courts, and she was certain she would lose the girl if she left. I broke off with the surgical intern—she sent me her wedding announcement a year later. When I got my degree, I set up practice here. I started making heaps of money, enough for a beautiful apartment that she could come to. I'd go watch her dance—little amateur shows that her husband didn't care to attend." He stops talking for a moment, and I begin to stack empty plates. I will tell Christel, I decide, that Arthur Levinsky is a hundred percent respectful of her mother's chastity. It's black night outside now; from the beach far below, sea-gulls set up a raucous chorus.

"What was her name?" I ask.

"I'll get to that. Her husband—have I said?—was a mutual friend," Arthur goes on. He leans forward, both arms on the table; from the corner of my eye I can see Roxanne's gone out and is getting coffee. "Neither of us wanted to hurt him. Still—"

He pauses, his attention drawn away by Roxanne. "These things have their own momentum," I say.

"Yes, well. One day I called her house at what I thought was the appointed time, and to my surprise he answered. On video." Arthur stops, cracks his knuckles.

"You can't stop there," I say.

"That's all there is to the story."

"No, it isn't. He said something to you. Something happened to your—to the dancer. You're here now. Roxanne tells me you two're engaged."

"Well, all right." Arthur releases his hands and turns up the palms, as if whatever's left is without consequence. "I stammered something awkward. Then he said—and he said it just this way—'Arthur,' he said, 'my wife and I have a lot of things to work out in our marriage and with our daughter. We are working on them very, very hard. And I would very much appreciate it if you would not call here anymore.'"

"Well!" says Roxanne, appearing with a tray bearing carafe and cups. "The two of you certainly look involved!"

"Arthur was telling me a story," I say, "but it's mostly done."

"On the system—?" Arthur asks smoothly, raising an eyebrow.

Roxanne's taken time to comb her hair, I notice, and a whiff of fresh perfume, jasmine, reaches me as she bends over with coffee. "Christel," she says, her voice like glass about to break, "is coming home."

"But the semester's just started," I say stupidly.

"Something is wrong," Arthur says far more intelligently. "Very wrong," he adds, as the coffee cup Roxanne is holding out to him shakes in its saucer.

"Christel," says Roxanne—and the glass of her voice doesn't break; remarkably, it rights itself and sits fragile on its shelf—"is going to have a baby."

Later, I walk on the beach. The moon is cut exactly in half; a handful of stars attend it, the rest wrapped in the fog creeping in from off-shore. Back in the East, Christel is packing her crisp clothes, keying for a taxi to the airport. Here, the sea lions are asleep, but the gulls party high on a jutting, abandoned cliff. In the faint, diffused light from the sky and the square yellow eyes of houses lining the upper reaches of land, I stoop to pick up shapes that look interesting—smoothly humped limpets, cracked abalone shells with their ridged holes, a living starfish that I toss into the deep water.

Arthur's interrupted story has got me itching with something that takes me a long time to identify as desire. A dancer, I think as I skip a flat rock over the black surface. I wonder if Rudi tells stories like that about me, about how he lost me, but I decide not. We did have dinner, the night before I left on this trip, and the one clear thing was that he didn't yet know he *had* lost me. And in fact, though it's been two years since we broke up, neither of us has gotten anything going with anyone else, so there remains the illusion that we might get back together. He spent most of the evening lamenting a fellowship he'd failed to get and using wounded pride to entice me to South America with him; no doubt that's why he's called my father's place, to give me a last chance.

My bare toes in the cool sand, I skip another stone. Rudi is a puzzle to me, a bafflement. He is way too smart to believe the crap he seems to believe. When you come to accept that he really does believe it—he's not just acting out some anti-intellectual rebellion or leftover teenage fantasy—he suddenly looks so dense that your own belief in what qualifies for smarts is shaken.

What Rudi believes in is extraterrestrials. His contract is to manage the UFO Room on the Web, a cyberspace for sightings and reports not only on disturbances in our atmosphere, but also on galactic events, supernovas, black holes, and alien abductions—anything having to do with our many neighbors in the stratosphere. Ninety percent of the Webbies he deals with, he tells me, are astronomers and atmospheric scientists, a fair number of them working for profit universities, so there's cost-benefit in there somewhere. It's a faith I just don't have, I tell him. Once, as he booted up the latest simulations of alien abductors reported by a couple of sane middle-class citizens in Montana, I observed that the aliens looked just like fetuses, with their huge heads and goggle eyes and limp limbs. "It's the revenge of the homunculus," he said in a sepulchral tone, staring at the screen. "You tear them piecemeal from the womb, and lo, they reappear to exact their revenge from the other dimension."

Now he's hanging around Utica, refusing to take No for an answer. *Peru,* he said to me over dessert, *Lima,* as if they were magic words. I told him I couldn't get away, and he pointed out—Rudi's followed my day job—that I had vacation time stored up. "It's not the job," I told him, "that I can't get away from."

"Get a nurse for the old man. He can afford it."

"Not that either."

"You don't have to do that—that other."

"We've been through this, Rudi."

"The ghost of Marie," Rudi said. "That is so fucked up."

It went downhill from there, our little dinner. Rudi tried reminding me how he's loved me for my softness and pliancy, how I don't have to "prove myself." He's very good at tossing the lasso, Rudi is. Even now, on the beach, my eyes fill as if I'm mourning that sweet creature he conjured up.

I like Rudi; I appreciate his energy, the way he wakes smiling in the morning and takes the trouble to charm whoever crosses his path, from waiters to homeless people hawking print newspapers. I like the way his body is formed, especially the muscles around his collarbone and the dip just below his neck, where the skin goes pale and you can see a few wispy chest hairs. But he hasn't got a hold on me. Maybe he never did, I only thought he did; we're trained to feel that way— aren't we?—as though the only emotions worth having are the ones that we give over. Maybe that's what Roxanne meant, about engagement. Maybe that's why I want to hear the end of Arthur Levinsky's story.

Settling on a rock, I look up and back at the white house ablaze at the far end of the cliff. I hope Arthur is staying, but something tells me not; one reason I took the walk was that the two of them were tense, Arthur persisting with questions about Christel that Roxanne refused to answer. Christel, I think, turning my thoughts to the present with a small ignoble grin of satisfaction. Well well well.

CHAPTER 8

Lydia's wrong, of course: there's no national network for misconceivers. Whenever one's been broached, either Web surveillance has
uncovered the plot, or the idea's been shunned from within Mau-Mau.
What we don't know can't hurt us, goes their thinking. If I know no
one to contact in California, then I have no one to report on in California—and I can be neither bullied nor bribed into betrayal. Mostly,
operating as autonomous cells suits me just fine; as Marie used to
note with a trace of reproach, I'm not a joiner.

But now I'd give a lot for a simple listserve. Not even names, just
supply sources. Speculum, Pratt rods, tenaculum, curette: that's all I
need. Christel is tough, she can take it without Valium, without ergotrate. Antiseptic I can get from a drugstore.

Why? Because she has asked for it. She's asked, and now I have to
deliver.

The instant I saw her I knew the magnet had swung around, pole to pole.
With all her beautiful hair shorn off, she stepped into the terminal
dressed in the twenty-first-century equivalent of sackcloth and ashes.
Her bare head and the frightened face above her jawline were surprisingly beautiful, though neither her mother nor I mentioned that fact.
Watching her approach through the airplane tunnel, Roxanne complained that Christel wouldn't tell her who the father was, as if his name
would provide a key to the locked cupboard that held her daughter.

That was how we began last night. Arthur Levinsky, needless to say, didn't come to the house for dinner, and Roxanne filled the silences among the three of us by ticking off immediate plans. "Tomorrow we'll get you to Dr. Harrison and do a whole workup. Then we can enroll you in some classes at the community college."

"I can't study, Mom."

"Darling girl. Idle hands are the Devil's playthings." Roxanne winked at me, acting the good sport. "You weren't studying *enough*, it looks to me."

"Please, Mom." Christel's round eyes blinked, a rabbit just before the pistol shot. Her lip quivered as her fork drifted over her angel-hair pasta, and I was reminded how some societies won't eat with forks because they have too much potential as weapons. If anything, Christel appeared gentler than when she was "pure"—like a fallen bird, broken-winged—but I got the uneasy feeling that rage could rush in any moment, an uninvited guest for whom the door had been left ajar.

"You needn't look as though you had nothing to do with it," Roxanne persisted, forcing her throaty laugh. "Though someone else did, as well, and he ought to—"

"Please please please."

"Chris, I am not the Inquisition. I am your mother."

"I know, Mom, I know. Please."

In the kitchen to fix dessert, Roxanne poured herself three fingers of bourbon and tossed in a rock of ice. "She's beat down," I whispered, clearing Christel's untouched plate.

"She is sullen," said Roxanne. Sipping at the drink, she drummed her fingers on the kitchen counter.

"That's a bit harsh."

"Have you noticed how sullen the retros are? That's the worst thing about them, those hundreds of thousands of stubborn jaws."

"You're just reacting to her hair."

"I am not."

I scraped Christel's plate. "Well, she's about the farthest thing from a retro," I said.

"That's where you're wrong." Roxanne glanced out at her daughter, sitting long-necked and demure in her high-backed chair, one hand stroking the wolfhound's bony head. "All the same dangers," she said, "lie in extremes. From the minute she went so religious, I've been scared of the other."

I didn't ask what the other was. Over dessert, a mousse from which Christel ate the small swirl of whipped cream, Roxanne kept calling her daughter *darling girl*. Smelling the sweet draft of Roxanne's perfume, trying to stay uninvolved, I vaguely remembered being sick with a fever when I was a child and Frank had brought his very pregnant wife home for the holidays. I'd fussed and cried; my parents had both given up on me and simply ordered me into bed, where I set up a louder wail. It must have been Roxanne who came in then, freshly made up with a drink in her hand and that same perfume. *Hush, darling girl,* she had said, kissing my forehead with her cool lips, *Hush and sleep, and you'll get well.* It had been like being put under a spell.

Finally, Roxanne pushed back her chair, rose, and came around the table to where she stood behind Christel. Crossing an arm over her daughter's chest, she kissed the downy cap that remained of her hair. "We *forgive* you, darling girl," she said. "We're going to *love* you and your baby. It'll just take some getting *used* to, darling girl."

Then she turned to me, winked, and quickly left the room. As if we had something planned, I think now. Admittedly, I knew what I was supposed to do: find out about the father. Like the lawyers for that woman in Michigan, the one who accidentally got a Tay-Sachs baby. For a moment I wondered if Roxanne were sniffing out an accident of that kind—race, or birth defect—in order to work up a middle-of-the-road reason, the New Traditionalist's rationale for looking toward a misconceiver.

But there'd been no accident. When was it that I realized exactly what had happened to Christel? When the door to the kitchen swished shut, or the lights dimmed and then brightened again? No—it was looking at the back of her shorn head, her shoulders hunched in the oversized T-shirt, her plate untouched before her. "Father fucking Paul," I heard myself say. Crossing herself, she nodded, just barely. Even with her pregnancy, she looked thin, frail, her round face unnatural on such a slender neck. I thought of the lonely twelve-year-old girl I had never seen, how the world itself must have seemed an accident to her. "Did you try telling anyone?" I said. How solid I appeared to Christel, with my hair pulled back and my arms bare and muscular. I willed myself to be solid, a freckled rock. She shook her head—a jerky motion, now that no hair moved with the gesture. Her ears looked smaller than ever. "People like him don't have any more right than anyone else," I said.

"I let him. I gave way."

"What are you, a fortress being bombarded?"

"He said he was testing me." Her voice, so bubbly on her system back in Utica, was down to a whisper. "Said he'd tested many, and all but me—" She broke off, but she didn't cry. As she wrung her hands, the tissue she held came damply to pieces. "I failed the test," she said.

"Oh, bullshit, Christel, you were seduced! Does he know your condition?" She shook her head. "Do you want this baby?" Again a shake, no. I scootched my chair closer and laid a hand on her arm. *None of your business,* I told myself. I was quitting; I'd come here to quit. "Listen, Christel," I said. Quickly I glanced around, but Roxanne's bedroom door was far down the hallway, and closed. Now was the time to give up; to say some soothing words and step away. "Don't talk," I said, "just listen."

I started cautiously; if there'd been a microphone planted in the ceiling, no one could cull hard evidence from it. To get my gist, Christel had to be on the same vector as I was, and that had never happened. But when I told her how I could help her if she asked, she glanced sharply at me and then down again. As far as I could glimpse under the saggy black T-shirt, her belly was still fairly flat. I calculated quickly—ten days ago, she'd complained of two weeks of PMS. Almost three weeks. A minor adjustment, I told her—that was what they used to call it: menstrual regulation. I told her about Thomas Aquinas and the idea of quickening; I gave her a capsule sketch of the Christian attitude up to the late nineteenth century, when everyone went nuts. Still, she didn't look up again, and I thought I'd lost her, until the thing slipped out of me that hadn't come from my training with Marie. "There was a girl," I said. "I was responsible for her— same kind of situation as you, sort of. She was only twelve years old." As the story went on Christel looked up—interested in this suicide idea, a sudden tension in her body as if she would run from the room and end the whole business over the cliff. "No, wait," I said. The tension didn't go away; she even pushed her chair back from the table, ready to run. "Do you know what I believe?" I asked. She shook her head, and suddenly an answer was expected of me, who had never much believed anything. At this very moment I was running from Utica and the dead girl precisely because they begged me to profess a belief. My mouth was dry as paper.

"I believe," I began, "God wanted that girl to live. To live, and He'd find another home for the soul of the unborn. Your body isn't a fortress, Christel. It's a temple, and if it's been defiled, let's clean it up. Build houses for souls when you're ready to build."

Well, Marie would have done a lot better, and her voice never squeaked on the word *God* the way mine does. She'd been valedictorian in high school; at five I'd listened to her practice her sentimental address: *Computers? Sure, we're computers—but if our brains are the hardware, our hearts are the software. And when we love each other? That's shareware, folks!* Sitting among a passel of her friends in our living room, I'd clapped wildly while they cheered and whistled.

But Marie's dead, I thought, so tough cookies, Christel. I kept talking, my throat tight, until the words stopped coming and I pulled myself up from the chair. "Need some sleep," I said. Inwardly I grimaced at Jonathan's picture of me, relaxing by the beach. If only I could marry Jonathan and live in the cathedral-ceilinged home in the hills, and grow grapes and tomatoes in the sunny backyard, and never think about incubi again.

But I have to think about them now, today, because last night—when I'd done surprising myself with an offer it had never occurred to me to make, when I'd tucked my chair under the table and stepped with relief onto the plush carpeting leading to the stairs—Christel finally spoke. "Please," was what she said. Only it wasn't the evasive begging *please* she'd dropped on her mother. Her voice was almost normal, not a whisper anymore. "Please, Phoebe," she said, and she held out her arms.

. . .

But there's no network, no supplies. I can't misconceive with my bare hands, and I'm afraid to go to Roxanne—who batted her eyes at me all through breakfast, and caught me after with "Got any news?" so that it was all I could do to lie and tell her No.

Where there is no network, I reason, where do you find the supplies? *At the hospital.* Who gets access to the hospital? *Nurses, doctors.* Are they willing to help? *Never.* Correction? *Almost never.*

I boot up Arthur Levinsky's number on Roxanne's system and choose audio; I don't want him studying my face. I get a real voice, a receptionist. After a couple of go-rounds of urgent, serious, no-he-can't-call-me-back negotiating, the receptionist puts me through to a nurse who puts me through to his audiomail. I give him my handle, and an hour later there appears on my Minilap, *I know what you want, and I am not trained.* So I E-mail him back, *I am,* and he writes *I don't know how I can help you.* I stare at that one on the screen for a while, all its possible meanings charging me at once. Of course he knows how he can help me, is my first response, what he's saying is he doesn't think he wants to. Or maybe he knows how, generally, and just doesn't know what my specific needs are. We haven't really got to know one another yet, after all. For all the evidence he has, I'm not really here vacationing—I've been brought in by a group of pregnant movie stars who don't know where to turn. Doctors live in a different world from us, Marie always said. She steered clear of them, as did most of her colleagues; the AMA sold us down the river was all she would tell me. Maybe what Arthur Levinsky is saying is, Pursue this line of questioning, and I'll turn you in. But I'm reckless. *Meet with me and I'll explain,* I write. And to my surprise he says he can just take time for coffee between his early patients, can I come downtown now.

"Roxanne," I whisper, standing at the door of her room.

"Come on in," she says in full voice. "I'm frosting my hair."

I step in. Her bedroom is exactly above mine, but twice the size. In the center is a skylight—white, now, with the fog around the house—and to my right a bougainvillea brushes against a huge picture window. "I'm going to run into town a sec," I say.

Roxanne is standing in front of her dresser mirror, in white pants, with an oversized pink towel thrown over her bare shoulders. A transparent rubber cap clings to her head, with spikes of bleached hair shooting out of it like spray from a fountain. When she turns toward me, her face has the startled look of a victim in a horror flick, who has been transformed overnight into her worst nightmare. "I can't believe she didn't tell you," she says.

"I'm still working on it. Maybe when I get back. I have to pick up tampons," I add—and then I'm fearful that she'll offer to loan me, but she's turned back to the mirror and is dabbing at the roots of the white spikes with a Q-tip.

"Take the Saturn," she says.

"Want me to pick you up anything?"

"A wig for Christel." I'm halfway out the door when she says that, but I turn back. Alarm must show in my face, reflected in the mirror, because she laughs in her throaty way and says, "Just joking. She'd probably wear it over her face."

Sun washes the bread-colored adobe of downtown St. Barbara as I drive through. Santa Barbara, I think, and remember that *barbara* means *stranger,* why not St. Stranger? Everywhere hang flowers, reds and violets, so different from Utica this time of year when the leaves are starting to dry their way into color. No brick anywhere. Live in a beautiful place, Roxanne says. Though there's a grim satisfaction knowing that cataclysm strikes at beauty first. Last year, I remember, there was a firestorm not far from here; Christel worried about her mother. Everywhere in the town electric cars purr innocently along. I think maybe I'm on another planet, where the old rules don't apply— but they do, I can see that from the look on Arthur Levinsky's face through the window at El Siesta Coffee Shop, near the hospital.

"Does Roxanne know you're here?" he asks as I slide into the booth across from him.

"No. Should she?"

He shrugs. "I worry," he says with what must pass for a smile, "about her good opinion."

"I wonder how well you know her," I say, too brazenly—his head jerks back, as if avoiding a blow. "What I mean is, I think she loves Christel. That's all it's about, for her."

"I know she's a brave woman." He sips his coffee a moment, then sets it down and takes my hand. His own is warm, though nervous. "I am a coward," he says, his accent closing on the *w* of *coward*.

"So am I. I was running away from this problem, isn't that funny?"

"Funny, yeah," he says, and the smile broadens a bit. I like his mouth better than anything I've seen in a while. It's not cynical, but it serves mostly to temper melancholy; the edges of his mouth curl down even as he smiles. "Are you sure you know what you're up to?" he asks.

"It's . . . you know. My profession," I tell him.

"Ah. You're not what I would—expect," he says. His eyes stray a little, over my body.

"What, are we all supposed to have hooked noses and ride broomsticks?"

"No. You're supposed to look like con artists."

"There are those." He sips his coffee, and I think of the story he never finished, about the dancer he loved. But this isn't the time to finish it; already his eyes have darted down, twice, to his watch. My stomach's leaping. This isn't Jonathan, isn't someone I've known long enough to trust. *Family,* Marie always said. But I've gone too far to stop. "Are you going to help?" I ask.

"How?"

"Equipment's all I need."

"But I wouldn't even know where to start finding the stuff." He whispers, but fiercely, with a quick glance now and then to the street. "You people have a mistaken notion about what any given doctor might be locking away from you. The hospital does D&Cs occasionally, but only the OBs take care of them. They rushed us through the procedure in med school, for obvious reasons."

"Are they really so obvious?" He looks puzzled, his eyes narrowing a bit. "I am asking," I say, perversely refusing to lower my voice, "if you're sympathetic, or if you vote with the Coalition on this. Because if it's the Coalition, I'm wasting both our time."

"I'm a doctor, not a politician."

"I'm a misconceiver, not a politician."

He sighs, puts his coffee cup down, checks his watch more dramatically. I put a hand on his wrist, detaining him. He has the strong hands of a surgeon.

"Can you get hold of some ergotrate?" I ask quietly.

"I think so, yeah."

"Pratt rods?"

He rubs his forehead. "I wouldn't know where to start looking. I'm good friends with one of the OBs, but I'm not sure he'd stick his neck out. Anyhow, he's out of town till next week."

"By next week Christel's going to start burning herself with cigarette butts."

"Is it so bad?"

"It's everything she's lived for down the tube." I tell him about Father Paul, what I saw at the concert and what Christel confirmed with that little nod of her head.

"Somebody ought to shoot a sonofabitch like that," says Arthur.

"Somebody," I counter, "ought to vote back the laws that would've let Christel defend herself against him."

He shakes his head. "Those were difficult laws," he says. "Got a lot of good men into trouble."

"You don't believe that."

He smiles weakly, the curl downward again. "I don't know," he admits with half a shrug. "I have no idea what I believe."

What he says he'll try is to beeper his OB friend, who's in Texas, and persuade him to code a release for four Pratt rods and a curette, which can get buried in the log if nothing else rouses suspicion. "Don't you need a vacuum machine?" Arthur asks.

"I don't exactly see you wheeling it out of the hospital. I'm used to working this way, don't worry."

"All right. All right." He finishes his coffee, wipes his mouth with a red napkin. Then he brushes a finger against my sleeve. "It's for you I'm doing this," he says.

"For Christel."

"I don't have the least bit of passion for Christel." He glances sharply at me, too quick to read his eyes. Then he's getting up from the table. "I'll try to have these by tomorrow morning. Now I'm due in surgery," he says. Standing, he puts his hand gently on my shoulder. "Stay and have breakfast," he says. "The *huevos rancheros* are excellent, and they'll put it on my account."

So I do. I'm unaccountably hungry as I watch him speak to the waitress and then exit, walking briskly across the sunny street and through the gates to the hospital. There goes a conventional man, I say to myself. But I can't account for my feelings. The eggs come, steaming and flecked with peppers, the tortillas wrapped in a warm cotton towel.

I vaguely remember this town—this sky like a china bowl over the baked red roofs, the squat palm trees planted along the street. We must have come here a few years before my mother died, maybe when Frank was doing graduate work, after he married Roxanne. I remember stepping off the plane into the dry warm air, and later running through the surf, splashing and leaping into my mother's arms. Marie, I think, didn't come with us—there were only my parents hovering around me on the sunny beach, letting me buy trinkets at a sidewalk craft sale. I remember crying when we had to board the plane again, to return to winter and the bickering that marked our household.

Just outside the restaurant window, a group of retros has set up, shaggy and menacing; one of them, a thin blonde, has hair cropped close, like Christel's. I watch while the waitress brings them a basket of last night's chips and three bottles of lime soda. A stream of businessmen swerves around the group on their way to work, their suits pale and lightweight to match eternal summer and its attendant catastrophes. For a moment a school bus draws up—bright blue, oddly, not the yellow I'm used to, but of course this is an electric one, its little battery spinning away under the abbreviated hood. The children look out the window and make faces at the retros.

I have an urge to call Lloyd and tell him what I'm up to. So now you're fishing, he'd say to me, and next week will you cut bait? My niece, I'd tell him, and his sigh would travel three thousand miles over fiber-optic. You and Marie with the family bit, he'd say. The Mafia sisters.

No, I won't call Lloyd. Punching my card into the system by our table, I key in a tip for the waitress—who knows, maybe Arthur *is* tight with a dollar—and walk down to the ocean before I drive back to Roxanne's. Waves are coming in on slowly rolling breakers, flat unfurling sheets of slate blue. The sun rises over the water here, just the way it did in Maine—because the land curls around, Roxanne explained to me, but I can't feel it in my body, this facing east toward the Pacific. The main pier, old and creaky, is lined with fishermen. When I ask one how anything can be left to fish up, he explains that the boats don't go out anymore. "Nothin but farm fish, and the lobster's been gone for ten years," he says. He muffs his words a little, because his front teeth are missing; on his chin, a gray stubble. "But we catch 'em here, close in. They come in to eat the garbage, see." He's got bass in his bucket, fat and metallic-looking, and I pull out my card to buy five.

Late that night I ask Christel if she wants to hunt shells with me. It's a full moon, the waves glittering as they roll in toward the sand, low tide. "Fine," she says, with a spoonful of forced cheerfulness. In the still night, the plank steps leading down past lupine and beach strawberries sound hollow against the white noise of the retreating water. It was an awkward supper, though Christel had an appetite, at last, for the bass. "They're poisoned," Roxanne kept insisting. "Nothing within fifty miles is safe."

"What about that tuna?" I said, guiltily broiling the fish.

"Japanese. They have regulations, they don't dump, they have international oversight."

"Wow." I wanted to stop cooking, but Christel was hanging over the counter, determined on the bass. "You're a fount of information, Roxanne," I said.

"All tactics," she said wistfully, watching me dish the risky stuff up, "no strategy."

Her newly frosted hair hung limp; bags pillowed her eyes. When I'd come back that morning she'd been plucking at the harp, its strings flat but the execution lively and precise, better than I remembered. As we set the table I wanted to ask if Arthur was coming over, but bit the question off at the root. No, I whispered when she pulled me aside in the kitchen, I still didn't know about the father. Behind me, in the dining room, Christel was going through the motions of cutting the fish meat; placing it in her mouth, she chewed automatically, as if she could neither taste what she was eating nor choose to stop. "Give it time," I told Roxanne, wanting to tell her more, and noticed how she'd been biting her fingernails, not a habit I'd had a chance to see. Now, while Christel and I step down to the cool sand, Roxanne's gone to the park to exercise the wolfhound and try to puzzle out her role.

As Christel wades after shells, pants rolled up, I explain what will happen to her, if this friend of mine—I don't name Arthur—manages to get what we need. I explain in detail. Then I put the usual question to her.

"You know what my nightmare is?" she says by way of answer. "That you won't kill it all the way. That you'll leave something in there. That I'll grow a baby made up all of hands, or eyes. That it'll look at me, or point at me, and say, 'There she goes, the *virgin*.'"

"It wouldn't have a mouth," I say.

"It has one already. I hear it in my mind. It won't shush up."

"We'll shush it up," I promise—though to tell the truth, with Christel I'm not so sure. We select the tiniest whole shells we can find, leaving behind the broken, the marred. Offshore, the sea lions bay, mating calls.

CHAPTER 9

Unbelievably, Arthur gets an extractor, and not only that. "I've checked you into the Royal Palms for two nights," he says on video. "That is, not you, but someone named Lee Jones. So either of us can answer to it."

"They didn't ask you for ID?"

"Wait until you see this place." He smiles with just a corner of his wide mouth. His *l*'s come from the back, as if he's about to swallow them. "I rolled the machine right through the back door onto the freight elevator. No one stopped me. I hope there aren't cockroaches."

"And the ergotrate? The Pratt rods? Speculum?"

"They're all up there. It's Room three-five-six. I also brought you some extra sheets and disinfectant." He sounds competent, efficient, strangely excited; below the screen his hands are moving, checking items off a list. "Did you need something to relax her?"

"Shit, the Valium. No, she'll be all right," I say, knowing that Christel *will* be all right, at least through the procedure. What's happened to her goes deeper than a simple freak-out at the sight of Pratt rods.

"I have to wash my hands of it, then. You understand, in my profession." His voice is warm, but eager to be done. "There've been resolutions passed, oaths taken. And a lot of sick people to care for, these days—"

"Stop it. I understand."

"All right." He smiles faintly, crow's feet by his eyes. "I'll leave the key in an envelope for you, at the front desk of the hospital. It'll have your name on it, since you do have to show ID."

"Thanks, Arthur. Arthur?"

"Hm?" He was about to log off; his face swings back to the screen.

"Are you going to come by Roxanne's? I know that Christel—well, it's possible she could change her views. Toward you, I mean."

There's a pause. Then he says, "Christel's prejudices aren't why I haven't been at Roxanne's house."

"What then?" I ask, and think, What business is it of mine? Or at least I should be asking Roxanne, who is right now in the kitchen furiously mixing sweet cheese and eggs for some kind of tart.

He clears his throat. "Look, I have to go, I have patients waiting. Why don't you get in touch with me. After."

"All right," I say, and we hang up. I sit looking at the monitor for a long while, then I go to find Christel and give her the news.

Walking on the beach that night, I think of the one doctor we all knew of, years ago, who did misconceptions. He went nuts, everyone said. He was a late-term guy, one of the few who'll perform an evacuation at seven months. That was one of the things Congress banned just before my mom died. She used to leave the lobbyists' photos around the house—cute little not-born babies getting their skulls crushed. That these were skulls with bloated brains in them, or attached to spines that carried no messages from brain to body, or that the blood which ran in babykins's veins was going to kill both him and his mommy was not mentioned in the photo captions. Sometimes, my mom said, the decision is only about what way your heart is going to break, not whether. Still, when this guy was caught—he'd kept performing them even after the ban—they showed him the pictures again and again, and he couldn't hang on to the reasons he'd done the procedures. He just cycled through the memories he'd never allowed himself to have, before: the fullness of the limbs as he pulled them out, the blood warmth of the shrunken chests that never drew breath, the open eyes. It was the eyes that got him in the end. Could he be sure the procedure was necessary to preserve the mother's life? Could he be sure the child would have died within minutes of birth? Could he say what the value of this so-called potential life might have been? No, and no, and no, he said in court. And then he began to shriek, and to stare at his hands.

He had performed ten thousand of them.

I never knew this man, though Marie had met him once or twice. She said he played classical piano, Chopin and Schumann especially. In my teens I sometimes lay awake wishing I had met him, wishing I could say whether he went mad because he had lost his reason or recovered his compassion; whether, before he was caught, his nerves had been of steel or stone. He was of Japanese descent. After several months in the Men's Detention Unit, during which time he spoke to no one except to shriek at the sight of their eyes, he managed to get hold of a very sharp knife and to disembowel himself.

"Lie back," I tell Christel. "There's sheets we can throw away underneath, don't worry. All the way back, that's right. Now just let your knees hang open. This is cold, okay?"

"I'm scared," Christel says. Both her hands are fingering the tiny cross around her neck.

"You want me to stop?"

"No."

"All right. Well, it's okay to be scared. It's normal. There, now I can see what I'm doing." Papered in peeling flower designs, the room we're in smells of cheap air freshener. I've got the shade off the one bedside lamp, so its light can shine between Christel's legs. I tell her there will be a pinch, for the Xylocaine, and she doesn't flinch. "Last chance to back out," I say, as casually as I can manage.

She raises up to look at me; her eyes are perfectly round. "Don't ask me that," she says.

"I have to. I'm not making the choice here."

"I made it once. Just don't ask me again! I *made* it."

"All right," I say. "Just so we're sure you're sure." Slowly I ease in the first rod. "Think you'll come back to school?" I ask. This is part of what Marie taught me—how to make idle but not irrelevant conversation. In silence, patients tense up. "You could probably enter classes late, so long as you caught up on the work."

"What are we going to tell my mother?"

I chuckle a little. "'We' aren't going to tell her anything. You've lost the baby, is all. These things happen all the time."

"It's awfully convenient, isn't it?"

"Maybe. Maybe she'll guess at the choice you made. But from what little I've seen of your mother"—I pull the rod out and prepare the next one—"she'll be mostly relieved."

"Are we almost through?"

"A few more minutes."

"No one will marry me now." She says this practically, as an observation.

"Don't be silly. Men don't check for virginity anymore. That's centuries old."

"The kind of man I want will. He'll have saved *him*self for *me,* won't he?"

"Only," I say, starting on the third rod, "because his favorite parish priest never cornered him after choir practice." This isn't a good line of conversation; after a moment, getting the aspirator ready, I try again. "We should do a follow-up, when we're both back in Utica. Get you back on the tennis courts."

"I can't imagine. Doing stuff like that again." Christel says this flatly; then, after a sharp intake of breath as I wiggle the vacuum tube in, "Did you meet the Jew?"

"Yeah. Yeah, I thought he was great. Smart, you know, and sort of charming."

"He's not right for her," Christel says. The back of my neck flushes warm. I ought to tell her not to judge—but I'm nodding at her words, passing my own judgment. The tube's in now. Reaching up, I touch one of the hands that's furiously petting the crucifix.

"You need to be all the way back," I say, "and relax. This'll feel strange. You can hold onto me."

But she doesn't. She holds onto her crucifix the whole time, and the tornado is over very quickly.

· · ·

"We have to pick up a couple of things," I say as we're driving back to the house on the cliff. I've cleaned up, but left the supplies and rolled-up sheets for Arthur; the key's in an envelope at the seedy front desk. The clerk barely looked up as we checked out; Arthur must have precharged the room, or even found a way to pay cash. "I told your mom I was taking you shopping." There's a row of fashion boutiques as we turn onto the beach road. "You want to come in? Or should I just get you something?"

She looks blankly at me. "Just get something," she says in a mono-tone. Then, suddenly, as I'm swinging open the car door, a transfor-mation comes over her. "No, wait!" she says. I turn in the bucket seat. If the Blue Fairy had come down, waved her magic wand, and turned Christel from a puppet into a real live girl, I couldn't be more sur-prised. There's a sparkle in her eyes—almost the same as the sparkle I used to see back in Utica, when she was about to sing a concert with the Young Disciples, but something at the edge of it shines a little dif-ferently. She's holding back a smile, as if she's about to laugh at a rude joke. "I want to come in!" she says.

There in the boutique—Mexican imports, mostly, with a few beach togs and swimsuits—as she tries on fresh flowery clothes, Christel's cropped hair looks sleek instead of sad, her thin upper body chic rather than unhealthy. "What do you think?" she keeps asking, and every time I say, "Looks nice," she tells the saleswoman she'll buy it. She moves faster and faster, pulling embroidered tops and lightweight skirts off the racks, ducking into the dressing room, coming out to twirl in front of the mirror until I pray that her pad's holding tight. Even the mood of the dark, brooding saleswoman goes from grudging anticipation to wary suspicion. "How you paying for all this?" she asks at one point, fingering the pile of clothes on the counter as if they're rotten fruit.

"Card," says Christel gaily, and swishes back into the dressing room. The smile won't leave her face. It's her father's smile, I realize at one point, the one plastered on in all those old photos, with the up-per teeth exposed. Finally I follow her through the swinging door.

"Let me feel your forehead," I say. It's cool, a little sweaty. "I'm not sure your mom can afford all these clothes," I say.

"You worrywart. She likes me to buy blouses."

"Not so many at once. It's not normal, Christel."

"Since when should I be normal?"

"Since we're on our way to your mother's house and by the wee hours of morning you're going to have had a miscarriage, that's since when."

"I'll be fine," she says. She looks bemusedly up at me—Christel's shorter than I am, I realize; I'd always thought of her as taller. She's got on a puckery green dress, and her eyes—green like mine, like her grandfather's—pick up its color. Beneath the hysteria, I can see she's serious. "You probably don't know," she says, her voice gone breathy, "how it feels."

"Not from your end of it, no."

"It must be like this, being in a war," she says, "when you think you're going to get hit by a shell, and then the soldier next to you gets hit instead. It takes you a minute to realize you're alive, but when you do, life is just the sweetest thing. *It* died; I didn't. That's what I just realized, in the car."

"Did you think I was going to kill you, Christel?"

"No, I thought *it* was. I thought it had."

I assume *it* means the fetus. Later, when we've picked four blouses and a sleeveless dress out of the original stack and are driving back to Roxanne's, I think maybe she means something else, or something more. I remember what Marie said: *Most patients return to being the same before they goofed. Ophile, she'll never be the same.* What Christel's changed into, I can't tell. Most likely she'll grow her hair back, go back to college, keep singing with the Young Disciples. Her friends will see the change as gradual, evolving over time as change often will. On the other hand, she's close enough to the edge right now—or maybe she's always been close—that Roxanne's right, she could slip right over. Christel reversed, Christel retro. Either way, as I watch her bound out of the car with just a little care taken for the pad secured between her legs, I'm already mourning her lost twin, her shadow-self, the one I vacuumed out of her along with the blood and the tissue, the amniotic fluid and the small, soft, cartilaginous bits.

· · ·

The second installment of Arthur Levinsky's story is considerably shorter than the first. He manages to tell it while I am letting my hand stray over his naked hips, before he gets aroused for the second time. "In my condo, by the beach in Ventura," he says, his voice floating over my head, on the pillow of his bed, "I had a sort of shrine, you might call it, to this woman. There was a shawl she liked to wear if we stepped outside on a cool night—a red shawl, trimmed in black. There were little objects, blown glass mostly, that we'd picked up at shops when we met downtown. There were performance programs from her earlier life, and some photographs, and a tie clasp she had bought me for my twenty-sixth birthday. I wrapped everything in the shawl, and in the middle of the night, during an ebb tide, I went out to the end of the pier and I threw the bundle into the ocean."

"And then?" I say to his chest when silence falls.

"I left St. Barbara for twelve years. I practiced in Oregon, I almost married. Then I came back here, when I thought it was safe."

I stop caressing him for a moment and raise myself on my elbows. "Why are you telling me this? Has it got something to do with—with Roxanne, or—?"

He catches my hand; laces the fingers and twists the opal ring, the ring left to me by Marie, around my third finger. It was this ring plus the one on my pinky, an onyx, that lured me here, after three days and two E-mail messages, to this gingerbready frame house on Garden Street. I'd left them, he explained in the first message, on the bedside table at the Royal Palms; he'd scooped them up. "I am breaking off with Roxanne," he says softly.

"But the story—"

"The story's like the Ancient Mariner's, perhaps."

"Who's that?"

"Oh, an old figure. From an English poem, but we learned about him in Russia. A sailor condemned to tell his tale over and over until he purges his guilt."

"Are you guilty?" He's let go my hand, which strays southward again. "Are you?" I persist.

Turning, he touches my left breast with the back of his fingers. "Did you know I went for a walk with Roxanne? Outside the hospital, yesterday?" I shake my head. "It was while you were waiting, for—for your niece to be discharged."

"I wondered where you'd gone." The process was interminable, I remember, boredom at the hospital finally outweighing my anxiety that I'd cleaned Christel up too well, that in the perfunctory D&C they'd figure misconception rather than miscarriage. Roxanne kept reminding me I could leave, and I kept worrying that Christel would come unhinged—as she almost had, early that morning, when Marta arrived at the house and took maybe half a look at her to know. *That girl aborted,* she said to me in an undertone while Roxanne and Christel were in the bathroom; and when I asked how she was so sure, she said she could tell the difference by the way they walked. I didn't ask if she knew more, if she could have helped. She watched from the porch as we tucked Christel into the Saturn to go to the hospital; I thought she began to lift her hand, to wave, but then she seemed to think better of it, and only nodded.

"Roxanne is interested in—in pleasing me. In making me comfortable," Arthur is saying, his answer just ahead of my question. "There was a time, I suppose, when that was what I wanted."

"Not now?"

"Not now."

I can still see what Arthur never saw, Roxanne coming back late to the house that night after the interminable hospital, an odd brightness in her eyes and her arms full of exotic groceries. I was sitting on the screened porch with Christel, who was still cramping; we'd resorted, finally, to blackberry brandy, and I'd nipped enough myself to be hearing the sea lions as if in an echo chamber. After a short time we were smelling asparagus and lemon, white wine and basmati rice. Later, after a candlelit supper, Roxanne insisted on Christel giving us a fashion show of the new blouses and the dress. *Look how sweet,* she said over and over; and once, *At least she'll keep the figure for it.* Long after I went to bed, I heard her stroking the harp, hollow tunes.

I shift my body as Arthur touches me between my legs. "Still skittish?" he asks. That's what I told him I was, when he drew me into his arms right at the door.

"No." Laying one hand on each cheek, I kiss him on the mouth, and our bodies press together in a salty postcoital embrace. He wanted to slip on a condom at first—doctors must have a source for them—but I told him I was a risk-free zone. What was the cause, he wanted to know. Just the way I am, I told him—not ready to get into Marie, or how I knew the cycle would come back, just not wanting him to examine me like a doctor. Skin against skin then, he said at last, and seemed pleased. Now his glasses are off, and like most myopic people whom you usually see behind glass, his eyes are more protuberant than I'd have expected, with laugh lines cross-hatching the soft skin below and to the sides. "One more thing," I say.

"Only one?" Moving, he props himself on the pillow and puts on his glasses.

"Why do people put on their glasses to think?"

"That's the one more thing?"

"No, but—" I glance around. "There's nothing in this room to help you answer any question of mine."

"No doubt." He laughs. I work my fingers, both rings in place, into his thick patch of chest hair. "I don't know, I guess you feel you're putting things into perspective if you can get the visual part taken care of. Or maybe it just makes us look smarter."

"One more thing," I say again.

"*You* got me off track."

"If I had anything to do with your breaking off—"

"You know," he interrupts, "I am not a revolutionary man. My mother brought me over from Russia and beat old-world values into me like salt into pierogi. My early affair—the one I told you about—and my aiding and abetting you: those have been the most daring acts of my life."

"You aren't answering the question."

"You haven't asked it."

"If I was somehow the cause," I say—carefully, my words like marks in stone—"am I also the effect?"

"You mean future." He smiles, gently; I can see the crinkles by his eyes, behind the glasses.

"I'm flying back to Utica tomorrow."

"Don't." He kisses me. His kisses are surprisingly quick, his tongue darting in and out like a fish; at the taste I want him like food, now and now and now.

"I have to," I manage.

"No, you don't."

"I want to." Reluctantly I pull his hand away from my mound of Venus and hold it.

"Why?"

"Ghosts," I say. "I have to reconcile myself with a couple of ghosts."

When he's hard again, I take him inside me. He touches and moistens me, and I indulge in the sheer pleasure of the act. This is love, I think, this is love. This physical thing we make together. His hands on the backs of my thighs, his cock reaches deeper than I've been touched before, pulls back, touches a deeper place, and I cry out and come against the hard bone of his pelvis, and he makes a wordless sound. Finally lying back, cooling off, I lick the hair on his chest; I press my cheek against his jaw.

Before I leave his gingerbready house, we bathe together. The bathroom's down a dark hall from his small, sparsely furnished bedroom, with its poster bed and gray-striped sheets, framed photographs, black cello case in the corner. The system's hidden down another hall. Elsewhere, wood furniture clutters the house; paper books stack next to the CDs. A nest, I think. The bath's new, sunk into the floor, mauve-colored and thermal-heated. He stands while I soap his testicles and thick, delicate penis, then he slides back into the water and makes a chair for me of his chest and knees. The water trickles through the overflow, the only sound in the room.

After we've dressed, he presses his face into the damp waves of my hair and inhales. "Don't go," he says again.

"I'll come by the hospital tomorrow. My plane's not till ten."

He holds me once more against him and I ache, marveling at the perfection of our fit, groin against groin, breasts against hard chest, mouths locked. "Arthur," I breathe.

"What?"

"Nothing. Just your name. I'm just saying it."

· · ·

California, Marie told me when I was sixteen and studying geography, was the last holdout, the last state to keep first trimester legal. *Oh, California,* she'd say, as if she was disappointed in a friend. She'd gone there to lobby, the year Congress passed the Human Life Amendment, but it was no use. *We trusted the fucking states,* Marie said too many times. *New York, Oregon, New Mexico, California. They all said they'd keep choice.* Everyone forgot how choice costs money. No state wanted vagrant pregnancies crossing its borders from all points of the compass, no state was begging to go up against the Coalition. Corporations moved out, tourists boycotted, and California caved.

The plane drifts across the shadow-molded scrub of the desert valley, then soars over the Sierra—the Pacific long gone, more desert ahead, then patchwork below the clouds. I don't know if I'll be back to California soon, or ever, I don't know about this man I have loved so briefly. I know only that Betty waits impatiently for me to take over the care of my father, and that on Monday I'll be giving my notice at Viratect.

I will have to think about money.

Marie used to say that money was the one thing they could simply take away. But she was talking about the trajectory of the law, not about personal finance. Funding and states' rights, she said. That was where the Coalition got its breaks. Not from moral judgment or religious faith. You could forget the argument about when life begins and turn it into a question of why should society pay for some trashy girl's negligence. You could allow her a choice without being obligated to pay for the consequences. That was the first thing they got past Congress—the taking away of the money. Then they turned to states' rights. Privacy, they pointed out, was nowhere in the Constitution. If a state wanted to invade it, they could. If they wanted to privilege something else, say, like the incubus.

Still, that move came after the defunding. Think, Marie said, if they passed a law that military research couldn't access a cent of government credit. Pretty soon those guys with the stripes would look pretty damn frivolous, hey?

There's one sitting across the aisle from me on the plane, a guy in

military green, stripes on the shoulders. He looks anything but frivolous. His tray screen booted, he's explaining artificial cockpit vision to
the older woman on his right. They used to have this sort of dropped
nose, he says, drawing an elegant hook onto the screen design, but
that added six hundred pounds. So we replaced the cockpit window
with this computer monitor.

His manicured hands reconfigure the screen. The woman's attracted to him, but he doesn't know it. He wears a wedding band,
wide gold. Poor Roxanne, I think, a wave of guilt washing through
my chest. Last night, after Christel had gone off to bed with a heating
pad—the flow slowing at last, after three days—Roxanne told me she
and Arthur had broken up. "He says it's marriage he doesn't want,"
she said, leaning over the open balcony off the kitchen. The wind was
strong, thinning her words like a comb. "Not me."

"And that's not—all right with you?" I tried.

"You mean, just to keep company with the man? No, it's not." She
tore off a sprig of scarlet bougainvillea, sniffed it. My heart began to
slow from its mad scramble. "I grew up," she said, "in a time when
the boundaries were blurred around everything. I always hankered after definite arrangements. For the few people I know who are happy,"
she said, "it's the arrangement that works. More than the person. Oh,
do I shock you? You're still so young, Phoebe. You're an idealist. Like
Chris," she said, and the shadow of worry came over her face.

I should have told her then, I think, shutting my eyes as they dim
the plane's cabin lights and the system screens start to glow—little
windows on the back of every seat, too small to crawl through. If
Arthur hadn't got mixed in with it, I'd have told Roxanne about the
procedure. She's right to worry, after all, with Christel still so flighty.
Only after the cramps hit home do patients understand what they've
done. Soon as I land, I'll get Roxanne on the system and tell her. I
don't have to mention Arthur. I'll just tell her about Father Paul, and
Christel's choice. It was the father's name Roxanne was always after,
anyway. If it was that Geoffrey boy, she said before we came in from
the balcony, and Christel had carried the baby to term, she'd have
arranged a marriage. There was money to help them out, she said.

Next to me, a flatheaded businessman's booted up an intermovie where he gets to manipulate a space-alien plot. I glance over now and then—it's really about birth, as these movies always are, voracious alien mothers tending their horrible pods—and I think nostalgically of Rudi, who believes in these outer-space creatures. For Rudi, money's always been something other people have and ought to give to him. The grant proposal pays for the telescope and the software and dinner, all at once. If he'd known, like Lloyd, what I could charge for a misconception, he'd have been after me to push the market rate and then shave off a big slice for him.

But, I think, I will never misconceive again. Sorry, Rudi. Sorry, Lloyd. It's not just the twelve-year-old. She's almost gone away, these last few days; only at night, waking once or twice, have I seemed to see her frail body suspended over the deep blue of the ocean below my window. And it's not Christel either, exactly. What, then? "Marie," I say softly, turning from the gruesome movie to the window, its shade cracked so I can look as we descend through the mattress of cloud cover into Utica. Almost three years now she's been dead, and I have used up the reservoir of competence she left me with. The suicide girl was a sign; Christel was a bonus. Quit while I'm ahead. Sorry, Marie.

Still, I'll have to find money. And I remember how Marie used to say it, chant it practically. *After they take away the money—*

They've already done that, I'd say.

—and after they've made sex itself dirty and shameful—

That, too.

—then they make the stakes too high for the other party, meaning us. The money not equal to the risk, the long-term benefit not equal to the short-term loss. Morality, she said—holding one finger up—*and finances*—holding the other right next to it, glued together.

Which is why Arthur could be fired, if he were found out; could lose his license. The thought catches in my throat, and I twist the rings on my right-hand fingers, the onyx and opal. His mouth on my breast, his broad hand lifting my buttocks. Do I dare do I dare do I dare.

This morning, having directed the cab into town, I couldn't find Arthur at the hospital; he's in surgery, one of the receptionists said, and I left my name and a message, *I'll call.* Now, as soon as the plane's landed and started to taxi, I connect my Minilap; but there's no message.

I'm tired, I tell myself. Which may account for why I don't see them until I'm at the baggage claim. I'm tired, and missing the obvious clues. Still, I'm not entirely surprised when my shoulder is tapped and I turn to see a badge flash at me out of a plainclothes jacket. Maybe every miscon prepares for this moment. I don't know. But my heart doesn't come into my throat. "Just let me get my bag," I say.

"We'll get that for you," says the officer who takes my arm, and he hands my claim check over to a young one standing off to the side. "Shall we go quietly now?" he says to me.

I nod, and with three men surrounding me, memories of yesterday afternoon filling my body with the bittersweet flavor of a last moment, I head out into the windy and autumnal New York night.

CHAPTER 10

"They'll have to put your father in a home," Jonathan explains to me. "You're allowed to have some say about where, but with your assets frozen and no salary coming in for the time being, the pickings are slim."

"Does he know?"

Jonathan shakes his head. "He thinks you're still in California."

I was allowed one phone call, and I'm not sorry I chose Jonathan, though I did feel bad having to track him to Gerald's so late at night. He came all the way down here, to the First Precinct, and he hugged me and said the most cheerful things he could think of. I didn't want to call Lloyd. I didn't want Lloyd's help. Family, Marie had always said, but family wore thin when it came to extreme favors. I could just see Lloyd's face, sweaty and exasperated, cursing his loyalty as if it were an affliction, like psoriasis or a trick knee that can't be ignored. And for all I knew, Lloyd was in the shadow himself. In any case, Jonathan promised to track down a lawyer first thing in the morning.

Now it's the next day, and no lawyer has said yes yet, though one agreed to find out what could be done about Dad. Talking to Jonathan, I start to cry. "I wish I could see him. It's the little things, you know, like the way you cut the tomato for his stuffed tuna salad. If it's not done right he'll go over the edge. He was just starting to trust me."

Jonathan nods. "You told me about it."

"And when he's not confused these days, there's *sweetness* in him. I don't want to think what a—a home will do. He tells jokes, you know?"

"I'll check up on him, if they'll let me. From time to time. If you want me to."

"He won't know you."

"He'll manage to think of someone I remind him of." Jonathan forces out a grin. He met my dad once, I remember. Dad kept mistaking him for his dead brother, Phil, who'd been mildly retarded and was electrocuted, according to legend, when he was trying to play a primitive video game in the bathtub. You're a handsome one, Phil, Dad said to Jonathan, but you'll meet a bad end.

"I want you to make up some excuse about where I am, for the people at work," I say. "I'm not ready for them to know."

"Maybe they already do. Maybe old Tim turned you in."

"Tim didn't know anything about it!"

"You sure? You told *me*."

"But I'm not an *idiot*."

"All right. Calm down, I'll think of something. You had four more days in California coming to you, remember. And then there's the weekend. Maybe we can get this all straightened out by then."

"Dream on, darling," I say. But he raises my hopes, perhaps because mostly Jonathan's accomplished whatever he's put his mind to. He's brought me fruit—which is confiscated for fear of razors—and two hypertexts, as well as a game he's invented and a chocolate bar. They've confiscated the game too, mostly because they can't understand it, but they let me keep the h-texts and the chocolate after it's been sniffed.

"I love you," Jonathan says as he wraps his arms around me before leaving. And I almost laugh because it's so strange to hear those words from a man who never makes love with women, whereas from those who do—Rudi, long ago, and now Arthur Levinsky so far away—they have been absent. *Sweet*, those men say instead, and *darling,* and *yes,* and *good.* "We'll take this," says Jonathan, "one day at a time. Okay?"

"Okay," I tell him, though I've been in this room before where he has not, though I know how far one day at a time can take you, and it's only the short distance between life and death.

• • •

Next day they drive me out of town, south down the old highway where the leaves are starting to change. I know where we're going— Women's Detention Unit, a cluster of stone buildings high on a hill overlooking one of the booming little towns that line the valley. Once, Marie told me when she was lodged here, this was a college for rich kids who loved the snow; before that, it was a state institution built to assimilate the Oneida Indians. Before that, this road that winds up from the town center to the high gate, the stubbly fields, the main entrance marked WDU: ADMIN., was a path for deer descending to drink at the Oriskany River that rushes along the base of the hill.

They can hold me here, the state's attorney tells me, for three months without trial, such time to be deducted from my final sentence. That's a new ruling, a stopgap; we were leaking out of the judicial process, it seems, because of the bottleneck in the courts, a situation at which the attorney shakes his head disgustedly. "If it were a question of sending you down to State," he says, "we could move this along faster. We might even push you to enter a plea."

"State's for violent criminals," I say weakly. He's booted up forms for me to sign; beside me on the bench in this receiving chamber is my small bag of clothing; you get to wear your own at WDU.

"That's right," he says. "Mass murderers—and the like." His face is stone, no point arguing morals with him.

"Anyway," I say coolly, signing the pad for the last form—I should have an attorney present, signing these, but as far as I can tell they're about diet and procedures and my right to an attorney—"State's bursting at the seams, isn't it? I read five women in a room or something."

"You won't find Softjail exactly *spacious*," he says. That's what they called it when Marie was in, too—Softjail, dormitory rooms overlooking a college quad, the remains of a library tucked away somewhere. "But you'll have plenty of time," he says, snapping the Minilap closed, "to get used to it."

Almost as soon as I've deposited my few things in the one tiny cupboard in the room, the door opens (they never knock, I remember Marie telling me) and a tall, simper-faced woman stands there in gray uniform, her gun tucked inconspicuously under her jacket. "We've got your shift," she says, her voice fuzzy; cleft palate maybe. "Five to midnight. And there's a lawyer to see you. Court-appointed. Let's get moving now."

Miss MacDonald is the lawyer's name; it's clear from the way she introduces herself and the way she sits, small and stiff, in the chair opposite me, a small table between, that I shouldn't call her anything else. My heart sinks when I see her. "I had a friend," I say, "getting someone to—to represent me."

"He called our office." She glances quickly at me, head to toe, summing me up in less than a second. "The private firms," she says kindly, "are up to their ears." Meaning, *They won't take another one of you people.* Her face is powdery, the result of trying to look both more distinguished and younger than she is. I put her at sixty-three. Without having to ask, I can guess her story—laid off from the big corporate firm that hired her maybe thirty-five years ago, when it was still fashionable to hire brilliant young women. Unmarried, of course, and more desperate for income than she wanted to admit after the layoff, she took a public defender slot maybe eight years back. She hasn't won more than a handful of cases; she doesn't expect to win this one. Her body is shrinking, despite heroic attempts at good posture; she doesn't admit to the health problems she's started to have, either to a doctor or to herself.

"Oh well," I say, caving easily, "all right." Realizing that I could still stop this, could call Lloyd and ask him to tap someone—but I don't mind Miss MacDonald. She's got her desktop open on the table and is tapping the eraser end of a pencil against the side of the keyboard.

"I don't know what you've been told," she says.

"Nothing," I say. "They haven't told me anything."

"The charges are serious," she says, and I think, uncharitably, Well, duh. "They should be looking at this as a first-time offense," she says, "but there is the complication of your sister."

"Do they—" I begin, but don't know how to phrase the question. Long ago, when it was Marie in here, Lloyd explained attorney-client privilege to me, but it all sounded shaky; I'm not ready to confess to her with a question like *Do they know what I've done?* "What evidence do they have?" I ask instead.

"Paraphernalia mostly," she says. She clips her words precisely. "There was apparently a hidden room, beneath the house your sister owned—"

"Why should they think I knew about such a room?" Oh, I'm getting clever, playing games. There's sweat under my arms—how'd they find the clinic?

"It shows signs, I guess, of recent use." She's not looking at me but at her screen. It's maddening not to see what she's seeing; I want to stand behind her, to point and shout. "When your sister died, the house title transferred to you, is that correct?"

"Yes, but I've never lived there. I live with my father; he needs round-the-clock care. Are you the one dealing with my father's situation?"

"No," she says flatly.

"Do you know who is?"

"There's no name here." She pulls out a small paper pad and pencils a note on it. "Mostly that would have to do with the possibility of bail, which they're not going to give you. But you say you never inhabited your sister's house, correct?"

"Right."

"Why keep the title, then? That part of town is booming, why not sell the house?"

"Why, I—" The answer is obvious, but she's looking at me now, deliberately putting me on the defensive, as if we are enemies. She wants me to improvise, I realize. If it's good enough, we'll use it; if not, she'll try to avoid the question. "My father's been in poor health," I say. "When he passes on, I'd rather sell the condo and live in the house."

"That's very reasonable," she says, and makes another set of marks on the quaint white pad.

"Who"—I lick my lips, all possibilities scare me now—"turned me in?"

"They haven't told me that."

"But don't they have to? Don't we have a right to know where this accusation comes from?"

"Only if the evidence doesn't stand up to scrutiny," she says slowly, her voice molding words like clay. "On the other hand, if you suspect a source that, let us say, held a grudge against you for other reasons, that could prove useful in building your defense."

Arthur Levinsky, I think, and can feel again the sure warmth of his touch between my legs, the bemused lust with which he took my breast into his mouth. Christel, with her round eyes and forced gaiety. Rudi, pissed off because I wouldn't go to South America. Or Lloyd, so annoyed with me over that poor girl; who knows if there's a dark side I've never seen? Maybe he sold Marie down the river, too. Even Jonathan, who couldn't find me a lawyer. My head swims with the multiple avenues of betrayal. Miss MacDonald is saying something. "Hm?" I manage.

"I asked, do you suspect any such person?"

"I suspect," I say, feeling my moorings give way, my boat adrift on the sea, "everyone I know."

She makes another note, on the pad.

They still have hope, my cellmate Mary Jo tells me, of rehabilitating some of us. Mary Jo's a hooker and proud of it. She's not here for so-liciting—that crime alone would stuff the Women's Detention Unit—but for dealing IUDs, which prostitutes try to self-implant, sometimes tearing membranes. There's nothing hotter than birth control these days, politically speaking; any case could become high-profile, and so Mary Jo gets stacks of visitors. Since IUDs actually cause misconception, they got deep-sixed right after the Human Life Amendment passed. Other methods got legislated by state. Right away condoms and foam went to prescription, and then the Coalition launched its campaign against the Pill and the cap. Married people can still get something, most places, and dealing condoms makes for a hand-slap mostly. "But the device is the thing for most whores," says Mary Jo. "You don't have to keep it safe or take it regular, and it's no hassle for the johns. So long as you got girls on the game, you got the device."

Mary Jo gets only two months. When I arrived, she was with her lawyer. My shift's the best, said my other cellmate, Sheri St. Clair: still nighttime when you sleep, and a block of the day is yours. To do what with? I asked. Kill time, she said. Mary Jo, when she came back—a short, doughy woman, a study in contrast to Sheri's angular darkness—pointed out the place where we produce labor for the state: a recycling plant house in the former field house, adjacent to the former gym.

"We pack the stuff for recycle—aluminum, glass, plastics, you name it. Shifts around the clock," Mary Jo explained. "I have to grab a bite of chow now, and then I pull the eleven to six."

"Long stint," I said; but I knew about it, of course, from Marie, who worked mostly with glass. It was the last governor's great plan, Marie told me—rehab prisoners, recycle waste. The joke, naturally, switches the direct object—rehab waste, recycle prisoners.

Sheri's a lesbian mother jailed for contempt of court—her lover has the child, and she refuses to say where. While Mary Jo was on her shift she ate, went to exercise, played games on her Webtouch. Each of us has a portable; there were systems in the rooms, when it was a college—you can make out the wall connections, the specially constructed cubbies—but they were pulled out long ago. "What the state refuses to recognize," said Sheri just before she left for her shift at the end of the day, when I'd been thoroughly processed and Mary Jo had returned, "is that half of us at least are political prisoners."

"And the rest?" said Mary Jo, rubbing her feet.

"The rest got caught," I said.

Mary Jo arched an eyebrow. "So that eliminates you," she said, "from political status."

I shrugged. I was looking out our barred window at the long shadows, striping the quad, that came from the tall poplars ranging along the entrance. This was a pretty place, I was thinking, in its solemn, stone-heavy way. What must it have been like, to look out on this quad with the window unbarred, with four years of freedom facing you? Maybe you'd lean out and call down to a skinny boy who was playing Frisbee on the lawn. It would have been green then, watered and pruned in the apprehension that physical beauty encourages mental growth. "Campus," I said out loud. From the word for field. That was what this used to be called, in my lifetime even.

• • •

Now Mary Jo's sleeping, Sheri's on her shift, I'm back from a late dinner where I gave away my meat, making myself popular. Tomorrow I'll call Lloyd and tell him about Miss MacDonald. I have to trust Jonathan—that someone's looking after Dad, that whoever it is has been clever enough to camouflage the true situation. Dad won't miss me, at least, the way he missed Marie. "Girl was never responsible," he'll complain to the new nurse in his raspy voice. "Couldn't find herself a husband." I can't spare a thought for the question of whether I'm a political prisoner.

Marie, of course, had prepared—sitting up late with her comrades, talking Gandhi and Mandela and Susan McBride, the first misconceiver to serve time in our century. I used to sit near them, doodling on the computer. It was a tragic history, but Marie and the others had lived it while I hadn't. No matter how much information they handed me, no matter how many dates and movements and newsbites, I would never understand how tragic it all was. There was Utah, for instance, where the Coalition built its first case that so long as the majority of the state's citizens believed abortion to be murder, the legislature had a mandate. So you got Utah *v.* Doe, making Utah what the Coalition called a prolife state, and then one by one, the other states had fallen into line.

"We went to Salt Lake," said Marie one afternoon, wiping down the metal table in the underground clinic. "We marched in the streets with that actress, that Tamar Lewis, confessing her abortion at the head of the line, and we got pelted with dead baby rabbits."

"What were *they* supposed to mean?"

"Who knows? The Coalition's not logical except in its political process. They made us look gross, was the point."

Marie didn't think of herself as gross; in no way did she hate what she did. Whereas I was out in the world, trying to be a teenager, learning that straight hair and an engagement ring were coveted symbols and abortion a vile stain, a subhuman act. Women had started staying home more, abortion wasn't a topic for polite conversation—I understood the order Marie put things in, but it was all steady-state for me, it was in the past. I helped Marie because she asked me to and because each woman that came in seemed to need us so desperately, that was all.

I did know the text of the Amendment that would land us both in Softjail. It was one of those disarmingly short, simple statements—*No unborn person shall be deprived of life by any person*—and the rights it gave began at fertilization. What did Mom think about it? I asked Marie once. Not that I couldn't remember my mother; she died when I was eleven, ten years to the day after the Roe overturn. But I'd grown up, till then, knowing there was something wrong, something messy or disgusting, about the work she did, and so at the dawn of my adolescence I'd been too shy to ask, and then she was killed. By the time we were through mourning, the Amendment had passed.

"She thought—" Here I remember Marie pausing. We were sitting, where? In the basement room, I think, after an especially difficult procedure, a woman in her forties who had fibroids littering her womb. Marie didn't talk about our mother very often; they hadn't always gotten along—tensions in Marie's teens. "She thought," Marie started again, "we didn't have any backbone, any of us younger people. She said we'd send the world back to the Dark Ages if we didn't make it unfit to live in before we had the chance. She had all the stats, you know, on world population. When she got pregnant with you, she wanted to abort."

"Well, she was awfully old," I said.

"It wasn't that, it was the two-child idea. Big symbolic deal back in the old days—two parents, two kids, no harm done to the planet. Only I found out. Dad told me she had a girl baby in her, and I begged her and begged her, I got religion, I stayed up all night praying she wouldn't abort my sister, and then I hurt myself, banging my hands on the brick patio, begging her to have you." Marie shook her head; a wan smile spread over her face. "I think I was quite a display," she said. "Anyway, Mom gave in and had you and resented me for it from that second on."

I took this news, of being an aborted abortion so to speak, with a certain sense of awe. There had been those two beautiful women, one thirteen years older than I was and the other almost forty years older, with their hearts thrown into the tussling and me hunkered down, gestating in the dark, selfish space of the womb. "I don't hate her," is what I told Marie when she finished the story.

"Neither do I anymore," she said. And then we worked together to clean up the basement room, done for the day.

But Marie's dead, and I'm in the same building where she spent her last days, before the hospital and the useless tubes that went in and out of her. I boot up my Minilap, grateful that it wasn't taken from me, probably because digital access is seen as good for morale. I can't get on the net, of course, but I have Jonathan's two h-texts tucked in my back pocket. I click in a disklet, which to my surprise registers as VIRATECT. DO NOT REMOVE.

Oops, I think. Wrong disklet—this is the one I downloaded in St. Monica, the day we captured the virus. The admitting people should have taken it from me when they took my address disk and checked my hard drive. But it wasn't in my pocketbook with the rest—I remember now, my pocketbook was on the other chair—I just tucked it in my back pocket. The new shape is so thin, so compact, it's easy to miss when you're checking clothes—that's a big complaint, they get laundered all the time, but I never washed this skirt. So it's a fluke that I still possess this locked virus. I go into the directory and boot a file—numbers, codes, arcane instructions, it looks like a child's war game, not something to foul up a whole district's numbering pattern. But somewhere people are spending a lot of energy impregnating huge nets with the gremlin in these files and mutating them each time they're caught. Funny how it baffled me before. I couldn't figure why anyone would have such zeal for screwing things up. Now, suddenly, it seems the only right thing to do.

And this—I think, drinking down the numbers filling my screen—is what I have become. Myself a thing that ought to have been removed, my natural sympathy falling finally with the virus rather than with those who put the system to rights. I shut the Minilap down and cache the disklet, my secret tool, my ally.

CHAPTER 11

Under the arch at the far wall in the refectory hangs our token male image—an oil fresco of Prometheus Unbound, muscular and naked, but with his genitals airbrushed out. "Every so often," the woman behind me in line explained my first night, "one of us will crawl through the air duct into this place late at night and paint them back. They always get brushed out again though." Indeed, the space between Prometheus's legs looks like a limpid bluish cloud, it has been scraped and washed over so many times. His face, surging upward, has a worried look. Tough luck, buster. We all smile together at him, like girls at summer camp sharing a bad joke.

Twelve days, now. I've been processed, adopted, put to work. I who had wanted to quit my job now have a new job: to go to trial and get out of here. That's one of two jobs in this place. The other is serving time.

Prisoners on food shift dish us up fatty pork chops, mashed potatoes, peas the color of algae. I give my chop to the woman behind me in line. I've got forty minutes to eat; then it's my shift on the glass belt. The noise level scrapes at everyone's nerves—no one near me seems to be saying anything, yet women's voices from all sides rise and clatter off the arched ceiling. Then as I set my food down at a long table, I hear something shouted from a distance, cutting through the din. *"Phoebe!* It's little *Phoebe."* Turning, I see a short, plump, older woman making her way down the aisle with her tray, calling my name.

"Heather," I breathe.

"My God, child, it has been ages," she says. She's close now, and

I'm sure of it—there's the scar on her lip, the one I used to notice in the old days when the miscons came from miles around to eat muffins at the ranch house in the hills.

Unceremoniously, Heather moves the tray next to me and squeezes in on the bench. "You poor darling," she says, and kisses me on the cheek.

"No more than anyone," I say.

Heather was never so obese, as I recall—rather a short energetic bundle a quarter-century older than the rest of them, a mother figure who handed out copies of the latest convictions and appeals, lists of statistics, promising editorials. Marie used to say it made her tired just to watch Heather work. Now Heather tells me she's been working inside the prison for three and a half years—same energy, different place; she's adaptable.

"How many are in here?" I ask, leaning across the narrow table.

"Didn't they tell you when you were admitted? Almost seven thousand, and growing."

"But I mean misconceivers."

She shrugs. "Who knows? We're all sprinkled in with whores, dealers, you know."

"But isn't there—I mean, I thought in a place where everyone was charged—"

"You mean," she says, digging her fork into her peas, her eyes bugging out comically, "isn't there a group? Don't we trade off techniques? Share stories of the biggest fetuses we pulled, the experiments we performed on the tissue, the wombs we sterilized? Isn't there"—she glances around, mock paranoid—"a *conspiracy?*"

"All right, all right. I didn't mean to sound like the Coalition. But when Marie was in here, I thought she had—you know—friends, at least."

"Your sister," Heather says, chewing, "was so steady. A guiding light. It's true—two weeks after she got in, she had a reading group going. The old hard-copy library was still here then, and she insisted on borrowing privileges. But not just for misconceivers. She didn't distinguish."

"It's gone now," I say. "The library. I hear they're putting beds in."

"Not gone, just underground. A few texts I'm making them keep. But your sister, now," Heather says, her mouth working as she speaks, "*she*'s gone." She puts away a forkful of potatoes, then examines me. Her face is puffy, unhealthy, her neck a series of creases. I can't tell her age. She looks like a lot of the others in here, four thousand criminals crowded into a place where eighteen hundred students used to frolic. "Marie would hate to know you were serving," she says. "She felt bad, bringing you into the whole business in the first place."

I shrug and move my peas around the plate. The noise level's rising; I hear Heather, though she's right next to me, as if through a tunnel of sound. "She didn't bring me in," I say. "I could've quit whenever."

"But you didn't, did you? You are Marie's sister." Heather's hair, thin and bristly, stark white, shakes as she nods her head. "How long did you say, until your hearing?"

"Six weeks, they tell me."

"Well, they will pass." With a strange delicacy, Heather takes her small square of a napkin and dabs at her lips. "Have you the ghost of a chance?" she asks, looking not in my eyes but at my lips.

"No," I say. Lifting a half-dozen peas to my mouth, I try to chew, to swallow them.

I haven't got a chance, Miss MacDonald would tell me, because I'm too obstinate to take one. "Well, you tell me," I tried yesterday when we met to go over the protocol for the hearing. "If they have proof of a person's performing misconceptions—"

"Abortions," she corrects, holding up a pale finger.

"If they prove you guilty, what kind of extenuating circumstances *are* there?"

"They haven't proven you guilty yet."

"But if they know about the twelve-year-old girl—"

"I didn't say they knew about her, and in any case there's nothing there to prosecute."

"But there I'm guilty," I say, though she waves a hand at me, flicking away what's personal. The more Miss MacDonald seems to want to exploit me, the freer I get in what I tell her.

"Just abortions," she repeated, "and when I referred to extenuating circumstances—"

"I don't qualify as insane."

"I wasn't planning to enter the plea."

"What are you planning then? I mean is the evidence they have just not enough, maybe?"

"It's enough," she said.

"Lloyd won't tell me—"

"He's clear for now," she said, pacing around the little room where we always meet, her sharp heels clicking on the linoleum. I often wonder how she lives, alone or with cats or with a young man, a gigolo who doesn't care whether she's in private practice or eating the mud of the public defender's payroll. "Mostly because the prosecution doesn't think they need him for this case, and to pursue a charge of aiding or abetting uses up valuable resources for what ends up being a light sentence. We're overworked, you know, those of us who toil for the city, and that's on both sides of any case like this."

"Well, *if*"—I still wasn't ready to confess, and Miss MacDonald hadn't pressed me yet, perhaps she didn't want to hear it—"they prove abortive murder, how on earth can you help me?"

"I am open," she said, "to suggestions."

She stopped pacing for a moment and leaned against a wall, like a man, her arms folded over her dark jacket. "Suggestions for extenuating circumstances," I said.

"That's right."

"My sister." She nodded, encouraging me. "You could argue," I went on, testing each word the way you test an old staircase in a dark house, to see what will hold your weight and at what part of the step, "that I was—coerced. Even brainwashed. Is that right, am I getting the gist?"

"It's I who am listening to you."

"You could argue"—I spread my hands over the table, my hands already nicked and scraped with the edges of the things we sort, in the recycling barn—"that Marie strong-armed me into performing abortions before I was old enough to have any moral compass of my own."

"Go on."

"And that given the history of my family, my mother—" I looked up, checking on her. Her small powdered face registered every word, tucking it into a prepared slot. "You could do a sort of perverted-family-values thing, I suppose. There's no evidence of any political activity on my part, unlike Marie. You could try to prove that I was a sort of cult victim."

"You have to tell me," she said, pushing herself off the wall, "about Marie."

"I can't."

"Not even to win your case?"

"No, please. I can't." My stomach pressed back against my kidneys; I looked at the blinking screen Miss MacDonald had booted up, my public file. "You can't possibly understand," I said thickly.

"She is dead, Phoebe. She doesn't care how you use her."

"I want this to go away."

"Well, it won't. Not unless you're willing to do what you need to in order to get out." She was at the table by then, leaning on her white knuckles. Her voice hadn't changed, but I saw her silver earrings, dangling from long white lobes, shake.

"Look," I said, rising from the table myself, ready to stalk around her the way tigers do around each other in a cage. "Nobody expects you to win this case, do they? I mean, the best the public defender has managed has been insanity. Even if you did win, it wouldn't exactly curry favor with any private law firm you wanted to work for. And if you lose you're not going to get fired. You don't owe me. Why not just walk it through?"

Miss MacDonald took a long time to answer. She sat down again; she scrolled the file; she shut the thing down and tucked it. "I am older," she said, opening the thermos she always brings and pouring herself black coffee, "than I look. To be precise, I am seventy-one years old. No one in my office knows this, though certainly they could check if they got suspicious. But I am not ready for a life of poverty yet, so I keep in shape and hope for the best. Fifty-five years ago, I was sixteen."

I add it up now, after I've joined pasty-faced Heather in the lineup and started down the long corridor to the recycling barn. Nineteen seventy-one. A time, Miss MacDonald told me yesterday, when things were pretty much like now except that there was so much paper everywhere and the ozone hole was someone else's nightmare. She'd gone, sixteen and pregnant, to a part of town where she wasn't allowed, to a colored man ("We called them colored," she said, as if it was code) named Johnnie Dee, who told her to come back the next day with the money.

Away from the din of the refectory, we women who march to our shift keep our mouths shut, our feet steady. Looking ahead of and behind me in line, I wonder if I am the only one who has never had an abortion. In some parts of the world, I remember Marie saying, it used to be the preferred way to keep the population down. It occurs to me that it has to be easier to have an abortion than to perform one. For Miss MacDonald, it was a question of pills, of letting Johnnie Dee put something sharp in her for a moment before drawing it out and giving her a handful of white pills to swallow. "This many," she said yesterday, holding forth her cupped palm and demonstrating a curve over it with her other hand, "and a glass of water, and he told me to swallow them all. Then he left the room. I had a wad of gum in my mouth, I remember, and I had to throw it out, so I lifted the lid of the wastebasket, and there, inside, was a little pink creature, about this long"—she measured a one-inch distance between thumb and index finger—"with all its little parts intact, and hardly a speck of blood on it."

She'd shut the lid and taken the first half-dozen pills, then she threw up her breakfast in his sink. "I remember," she said, something approaching a wry smile on her wrinkled, wine-stained lips, "he was very upset about that. 'Why'd you have to do it in the sink?' he said. 'They was a wastebasket right here.'"

And she told me she miscarried the next day, at church, and something came out of her that she knew shouldn't have, and after that she couldn't have children. She didn't say whether she wanted them, only that she felt lucky not to have died. "Now," she said, our time up, the hearing protocol still to go over, "you understand a little, perhaps."

"But I don't understand," I said to Miss MacDonald—who is at the public defender's office now, while I take my allotted smock and gloves, who at seventy-one passing for sixty-three is booting up old cases, looking for a crack in the system. "Not the way you want me to. If you get me off by painting my sister and my mother as monsters, then you will undo all the work you did, and you will have helped nobody but me. I don't understand that," I said, in my pride, "and it's not the way I want you to handle my case."

The work itself isn't bad. Like Marie, I'm sorting glass, which I'm warned to be careful of; though the tiniest particles have already been shaken through the vibrating screen, most of what comes along the belt is broken or chipped. I sort into amber, green, and clear, with a separate chute for the plastics that the air classifier missed. I have a special little knife, like a fisherman's knife, which I've had to sign for, to cut plastic neck rings. All pieces larger than my hand get sorted. The rest, shards of all colors, go from the end of the line to a pulverizer; they'll make sidewalks glitter, help gird foundations. Inside my gloves I can feel the irritation starting up on my hands, minuscule bits of glass that work their way through the weave.

"Don't complain," says my roommate Sheri during the coffee break. "Paper's worse." And she shows me her pink palms, little tears all along the insides of the fingers; sorting paper they can only wear the thinnest latex, there are so many grades to distinguish.

"I found a dead rat once," says Heather. "Smothered. It had tried to chew its way out."

"Hoo, don't tell me!" Sheri hunches her broad shoulders. "I get enough with spiders! You know how they nest in that crumply stuff? They bite!"

"At least if you find something in a wine bottle," says Heather, unruffled, "it usually can't get out."

I like Sheri a lot. I understand what she's doing here—understand better, though I wouldn't be smart to admit it, than I understand what Heather's doing here. Sheri doesn't care whether her case has any impact on legislation; she isn't moved by what her serving time might do for anyone else out there. She's here for her kid, period. Every couple of days she runs old videos of Benjamin on her Minilap—tiny pictures of a dark skinny five-year-old with her bone structure, playing catch and falling from the monkey bars, shouting "Looka me!" from the squeaky audio box. It's been a year now, and she says she'll stay in till they let her out. "It ain't so bad, when you know who you're doing it for," she says. "You ask me, I say you should tell that old goat lawyer go fuck herself, you're doing it for your sister."

Sheri's never gone for a man. "But you have Benjamin," I point out, and she says that's about something else, but I don't ask what or how. She's tall, and she works out so that when the recycling barn gets overheated and she strips to her tank top you can see her brown arm muscles, like a man's. Other women look up to her, even the retros—and retros in prison, I learned my first week, have gone past the point where, the way Marie put it, they can pretend to balance society. You can spot them not so much by the way they dress—if anything, they're more apt to wear the soft blue uniform, since they brought in no clothes—as by the jumpy look in their eyes and the way they move in a clump, like hyenas. But Sheri and I sit with a couple of them at the night breaks, around two A.M., and they chew over what they're in for—shoplifting, mostly, or vandalism; the system tampering I saw with Viratect looks way beyond their reach—and Sheri locks her ivory eyes on to them. "They're jus' angry as hell," she says as we move back to our places.

"No one ever explains why, though," I say.

"Think about it. You're born into a world that's closed out the thing that's at the heart of you, and you can't even go about finding a new place for that thing 'cause you never even seen it, they wiped all trace of it away from this world. Only place you find it is in what the other ones got missing, too."

"Only what the hell is *it?*" I say, watching three of them slide away together from the table.

Sheri shrugs. "Fuck if I know."

Last night—morning, rather, in the gray dawn that puts neither of us to sleep—Sheri asked if I'd ever been with a woman. Then she asked what I liked so damn much about men, and I said, "Feeling them inside me, I guess. The—the aliveness of them. How much they want."

"So you *don't* come."

"No, no, I do! Well, not always. But I like them for other reasons. Honest, I think I could come with a woman and it'd be about the same."

"Wanna try?"

"No," I said, because I didn't, and then I looked up sharply from my cot, afraid she'd be hurt.

"Jus' kidding," she said, and her teeth flashed. We went silent then, and I fell to thinking about Arthur, as I always do, about the moment he entered me, that moment that moment. I have to bite my lip to tamp down the feeling, and I whisper in my teeth, *betrayer.* Falseness in his high sloping forehead, cowardice in his hips, his wonderful belly. Or there's Rudi, with his favorite mode of sex, sixty-nine. Squeeze my face, he used to say, and I'd press my thighs inward, but his mouth was flaccid against my labia, and the only thing I felt was an acute ringing in my ears as *his* thighs pressed in on my temples, harder and harder until I thought I'd pass out, my head held in that warm, semen-scented vise. He'd come that way, and it was safe—but it wasn't sex at all, it was suffocation.

Marie could explain men to Sheri. Though I never could tell Marie about Rudi, and she wouldn't have approved of Arthur. And no wonder, I think as I leave Heather and Sheri to take up my shift on the glass belt, since the fucker turned me in. Watch for bugs! Heather calls to me as a fresh load rides up the belt from the tipping floor—and sure enough, in the third or fourth unbroken bottle there's a huge cockroach, born in the bottle maybe and now too big to squeeze out. I drop it down the green chute; it'll float out in the rinse.

The hours tick by like the black conveyor belt, jerking over its metal rollers. Through the high windows of the old field house comes the slivered light of a quarter-moon. From beams all around what must have been a pair of basketball courts—you can just make out the lines and semicircles on the hard rubber floor—hang the banners of the schools this one used to compete against: Bates, Colby, William Smith, St. Lawrence, all their colors faded, the white backgrounds yellowing. Connecticut, that's a state school, it's still in business. The others are what? Softjails, probably, trying to turn a profit; there's been talk of turning the administration of these places over to the private sector. From somewhere overhead, loudspeakers ring out orchestrated tunes meant to cheer us up. I'm tired, dreaming awake over ambers and greens and clears. People in this place seem either to sleep too much, like Mary Jo, who's got a day shift, or too little, like

Sheri and me. Awake, I dream of Christel, of hacking Christel's hair off with a blunt instrument like the little knife I use on the neck rings. Every now and then I slip and the scissors dig into her skull, releasing blood. Then Sheri's at my side, her coffee breath near my mouth. "You've got a visitor," she says.

"Huh? Who?" My mouth feels gluey, forming the words, just as if I'd been really asleep.

"It's still Wednesday," she says, "and the bitch lady sent me to tell you there's a guy at Bristol."

Arthur, I think, and despite everything I've been telling myself my heart swells, he's found out I'm in here, he's come to rescue me. And I'll tell him how unwise that is even to try, how they'll start checking up on him, they'll find out about the equipment he logged out of the hospital. . . . I hurry over to the waiting guard, whipping off my knife and my head scarf, wishing I'd thought to comb my hair before dinner or use Mary Jo's cheap perfume. I knew he'd find out, he had ways of finding out.

But it's not Arthur pacing around the square table at the center of the room. My cousin Lloyd looks up when I come in, gives a faint smile. I feel foolish in my smock, my frowsy hair. The one other time he's come to visit—getting the news through his own channels, the way he always does—we went around a few times over Miss MacDonald. *Family,* Lloyd said, just like Marie, and I pointed out just how much good family had done *her,* and I could feel him wanting to bring up the twelve-year-old, to punish me, but his jaw tightened against the flat pouches of his cheeks and he held back, and I cried and he patted my hand. Now he's back with a lost look, bags under his eyes like mine.

"Maybe I was wrong," I start. "Maybe I should've got you to recommend—"

He wipes the air clean with his hand; it's not that, not the lawyer. "I took your father in," he says.

"In? What do you mean, in? To your house?" I find the tattered couch where they let us sit together; but I don't sit down, just lean my knees against the upholstery.

"I thought it was the easiest solution, at least for the time being."
Stepping across the tattered rug, he holds both my hands. "But," he
says, "I guess it was distressing for him, more distressing than anyone
expected."

"I thought *Jonathan* was doing something," I say, not caring whether
Lloyd knows who Jonathan is. "He said Dad was going into a *home*."

"Yes, but I—I don't know, it was foolish." Lloyd shakes his balding
head, embarrassed at some strain of sentimentality. "But with Marie, and
now you—I wanted to get off my duff and do something, and I thought,
well, the old man's my family, too. My grandfather's nephew. Have a little loyalty, Lloyd, I said to myself." He's blustery, his forehead sweating;
he doesn't catch his own pun. "So I took him to my place. I got that
nurse, that Betty, to come the same hours she was coming for you, and
at first he was all right. A little lost in time, but eating, and quiet. Then
last night—I don't know where he thought he was headed, Phoebe. Betty'd told me to put up a gate, but I hadn't gotten around to it."

"He fell?"

"Down the front stairs. Hit his head on the newel post. They've got
him in intensive care."

"Christ, Lloyd."

"I fucked up, Phoebe. I'm sorry."

Then we sink together onto the couch, and Lloyd tells me my dad's
got a good-sized hematoma and a paralyzed left arm. The doctors are
worried about stroke, either a stroke beforehand or one caused by the
fall. They're doing tests. "I've got to get out of here," I say. "Isn't
there some way we can promise them I'll burn at the stake or whatever they want, but I've just got to go to my dad for a few days?"

"That's a job for your lawyer."

"Oh, fuck. Oh fuck fuck fuck."

"Ssh." He's crying now too, slow fat tears that don't mess up his
face. "She's actually a very good attorney," he says, patting my back.
"I did some checking. She might be able to pull something off."

"I don't even want her on my *case*."

"Time," comes the guard's voice from the door. It feels as if a
swarm of bees are inside my head, all the lack of sleep. "Stay with my
dad," I tell Lloyd as I back away.

"I'm going back there right now. He's conscious."

"Don't let him be alone. Tell him I'm coming to see him as soon as I can."

"I don't know if you should get his hopes up, Phoebe."

"Tell him. As soon as I can," I say, and then the guard approaches.

The rest of my shift I screw up—put greens in with browns, clear plastic with clear glass. Finally the supervisor—Jackson's her name, blond and thick-nosed—stops the conveyor belt. "You'll have to stay overtime," she says, sorting the mess to my right. "And you'll lose privileges if this happens regularly."

"It won't," I promise. Already I can feel the outer layer of skin toughening under the gloves with glass dust already embedded, brittle calluses. But I can't concentrate on the sorting. There's my father, hooked to an IV tube in intensive care, conscious but cut loose from place and time, wondering perhaps where Marie is or Frank, or angry again at my mother. You remember, I would ask him if I could—my hands focusing on brown and green, amber and clear—the summer we took that big vacation, all five of us, to celebrate Frank passing the bar exam?

You wanted to climb a mountain, he'd reply. Bet you didn't think your old man was up to it, hey?

I was only nine, Dad. You didn't seem old to me. You seemed strong.

He would laugh, remembering the moment exactly. Marie wouldn't go, he'd say, nor would Frank, and your mother was never one for exercise. But I said fine, didn't I? I went with you.

What was it called, that mountain?

The conveyor belt stops—a snag, down at the lower end. Shutting my eyes, I see the glen where we stopped to rest and drink watery lemonade from a thermos. I sat on a sun-warmed boulder while my father gathered fine yellow grasses and moss. Then he went foraging the other way, into the woods, and came back with a pointed stick that he said was hickory, and a fat piece of soft pine. Unlacing his shoe, he wrapped the lace around the hickory and dug the pointed end just a little way into the pine. "Grab a little of that grass, Beeb," he said to me as he began spinning the hickory with the shoelace, faster and faster, one direction then the next. When he nodded his head, I dropped in a bit of grass, and an ember appeared. "Moss, now," he said, a minute later.

And so I learned my father's one bit of woods lore. He could make fire.

"Statues don't get the work done," interrupts Jackson. She's standing in front of me with her arms crossed over her substantial chest, the conveyor belt moving again, glass trundling by. Then, in practically the same tone of voice—crisp, cynical, nicotined—"You all right, hon?"

Focusing on her, I feel the blood leave my head as if the plug's been pulled from a drain. I see my father, his face oatmeal-colored, trying to speak to these strangers—Lloyd, Jonathan—wondering where all his people have gone, why his language makes no sense to anyone. I see my mother's body, blasted at the center, so many years ago, a hole torn in her ribs. My knees buckle, and I go down. The piece of glass I've been holding in my left hand drops so that I land on it—a sharp pain to the hip, then black.

They get me up right away—Jackson, Sheri with her smoky voice, Heather. "She'll have to go to the infirmary," says Jackson with a touch of anger.

"No," I say. I can feel blood trickling down the outside of my leg. "It's my father," I say, looking around at them. "He's ill."

"You the one ill, looks to me like," says Sheri, holding onto my elbow.

"Take her by the nursing station," Jackson tells Heather. "Get them to bandage the hip. She can take the rest of the night off. You," she adds, "come back here, after."

"Yes, ma'am," says Heather, and tries to get me to lean on her, which I won't do. All around our sector, the other inmates have stopped working. They stand with cardboard and plastic and aluminum cans in their hands, as if waiting to offer them as sacrifices. Jackson claps her square hands twice, and they turn back to their stations, dismissing me as a welcome interruption now terminated.

Along the echoing corridors, Heather and I don't say anything, but once at the nursing station, waiting for the nurse to get off the phone, she takes a look at the coagulating mess on my cotton pants and asks what happened. I tell her about my dad, his fall. "Would they ever let me out?" I ask.

"If he worsens enough," she says. "You can always get leave for a funeral."

"I was trying to get there before then."

"You're the last of the family, right?" she says. I nod. "Then there's a chance, if your lawyer's smart."

Inside her cubicle the nurse is ignoring us. She's the same one who checked me in when I first arrived and gave me my month's supply of sanitary napkins, still untouched under my bedstand. The scar on Heather's lip moves as she talks, like a caterpillar clinging to the pink rim of her mouth. There's Heather's story in that caterpillar-scar, but I'm not ready to hear it yet. "My lawyer," I say, "is too smart."

"You'll just have to click your heels three times, then," says Heather. I look at her, puzzled. "You know, like Dorothy's magic."

"Dorothy?" I'm feeling very stupid, my head light again.

The Wizard of Oz. Oh, forget it, dear. Before your time."

The nurse clucks her tongue at the sight of me and tells me to take off my pants, which I do, though the blood has gotten stiff and pulls painfully on my skin. She's surprisingly young, black but china-doll pretty. She says nothing as she swabs at the gash in my hip; the stuff she uses seems to burn right through to the bone and I draw breath in sharply, but she doesn't stop. "You better be more careful next time," is all she says.

"I will," I promise, and she tapes gauze over the clean wound and helps me sit up.

"Here," she says, giving me a disposable sheet to wrap around my waist. Heather's waiting, holding the ripped pants, her eyes on the nurse as if she's got some power to change the nurse's life.

Again that night, I fail to sleep. My hip burns and, strangely, my lip. I try to transport myself back to that western mountain where once I hiked with my father and we loved each other, but it's no good. Sheri's restless too, turning from one side to the other on her bed, fighting her own demons. Under the sheet, I click my heels together three times, but I can't find any magic in it.

CHAPTER 12

My father lies in a bed of startling whiteness, as if the cloth for the sheets were made of ground bone. His breathing is regular, but his left arm jerks now and then in a strange half-gesture aimed at the side of the bed. He's not in a coma, just asleep—but ever since the second stroke, after they let him go back to Lloyd's house to recuperate from his fall, he sleeps more than he wakes. The nurse tells me it's the drugs and the fact that—this is her opinion—he has given up the battle.

The doctor is a severe, distracted man not much older than I am who doesn't like my presence here. The left carotid is ninety percent occluded, he told me earlier today, but under the circumstances he doesn't want to risk operating. If my father gets past this acute stage, once they can assess neural damage. . . . He went vague this morning, his eyes avoiding mine. Does my dad have any chance at all? I asked him. There's always a chance, he said, but not for what was there before.

"Could apply to my life," I told him, but his eyes didn't so much as crinkle at the joke.

Taking my seat by the bone-white bed, I study my father's face. It's been eight years now since the Alzheimer's was diagnosed. I try, but I cannot remember him as a sane man. His face, so frighteningly like mine with its freckles and broad cheeks and brief flare at the end of the nose, has come to seem a clown's face, his griefs and angers a performance. I take his right hand, the one that's not jerking, in mine, and I stare at his face and try to peel back the layers. What I get are glimpses, like the flashes on a computer screen when it's malfunctioning. My dad teaching Frank to golf, wrapping his long arms down over Frank's skinny ones, clasping his hands to guide the heavy club back and up, then down for an easy swing. *Now you try it,* and Frank would muff the drive, and my father's face would cloud over even as he followed the party line, *That's all right, practice makes perfect, let's try it together,* and Frank, determined to go whatever distance my father would go even if, afterward, you could see the bright blisters, like tiny pink seashells dotting the palms of his hands. My dad admiring Marie, beautiful in a summer party dress, *I get the first dance,* putting on an old ska CD and clutching her tight on her lower back, his hips thrusting a little in a middle-aged, clumsy way.

No glimpses of me with him, though I can see him, as if out of the corner of my eye, the way he looked to me when I was twelve, thirteen, fourteen, the years just after our mother died. He stands at the door of the kitchen and looks at me, perplexed—where have I come from, am I a housekeeper? This was before the Alzheimer's. Or at my high school play, standing apart while Marie did the sisterly hugs, waiting for parents and teachers to approach—which they did—with their rehearsed lines, *So good of you to come, Judge. The times sure are changing fast for you folks on the bench, eh, Judge?*

He's got good corners in him, Marie used to say.

That's because he likes you, I told her.

"Oh, I wish you would wake up!" I hear myself say aloud; and as if I've issued him a command, he does. He sees me; looks away at the window; looks back, suspicious that I'm there. "It's Phoebe," I try.

"Beeb," he manages, though it comes out *Behb;* his voice is slurred from what the stroke's done to the nerves in his face. This is only the second time he's been awake since I got here four hours ago. I've got the day, that's all. Even that took not only my father's second stroke but also Miss MacDonald's gathering all the evidence—physicians' reports, lab tests, documentation about sole living survivor, as well as a plea she dictated to me, pointing out my father's former esteem in the judiciary community and his devotion to family values. Miss Mac-Donald's in charge of me for the day—she's to make sure I return to Softjail tonight by eight—but she's got appointments till four-thirty, so I'm on my honor. Secretly, I've promised Sheri I'll try to manage a favor for her, but there hasn't been time so far.

"Behb," my father says again. He's shaking his head, back and forth but at an angle, like a cat with ear mites.

"Water, Dad?" I try, pouring from the pitcher on his nightstand. From the corridor there comes a series of high beeps, and several medical personnel hoof it on by, just like in the old movies. *Our Hospitals, Stuck in the Twentieth Century,* ran a series on *Dialog* last summer—Arthur Levinsky, I remember, got worked up about it that first night with Roxanne, who made concerned noises but buried her opinion. I shake my head—what was I thinking, falling for a doctor?

"Nuhver l-l-liked thet nehm," my father's saying.

"Really, Dad?" I tuck the blanket under his arms, careful of the IV dripping into his left hand. "What'd you want to name me?"

"George," he says, clear as a bell.

"You mean you wanted a boy?"

He nods like a bobbing cork. "Hulluva luht easier." Suddenly he looks up, startled. "Whurd Frunk go?"

"Who, Dad?" I ask, though I've understood him, dread starting deep in my belly.

"Muh boy, Frunk." He starts chuckling. "He lurvs thet joke."

"Okay," I say, hearing doctors' voices outside, trying to push *Arthur* out of my head. "Tell it to me."

"Muhgic slide," he manages to say, the eye on his good side beading at me to make sure I'm listening. Every now and then the cheek on that side twitches, too, as if a nerve's pinched. "Boy showts 'Guhld!' and he gets guhld at the buttum. Nuhther boy showts 'Silver!' He gets silver. So the thurd boy—the thurd boy—"

"Don't get worked up, Dad," I say. I bring my eyes back to his, the pupil of the good one dancing around. I touch the papery fingers. I want to be out of here—back in Softjail, anywhere. Around my neck I've got a silver rose that Sheri gave me this morning, Sheri who's counting on me. I swallow. "Go on."

"Thurd boy gets rehl ex-ex-excited. Showts, 'Whee! Whee!' And you know whuht he gets et the buttum?"

I squeeze the fingers. "Good one, Dad."

"Frunk luhved et."

"I bet he did. He'll be here soon, Dad," I lie.

I move to the window. Below—my dad's on the twentieth floor—the October sun ricochets off the city's flat planes. On the other side of the haze blurring the Mohawk Valley, the low hills have concentrated their green, like food coloring before it disperses in water, the beginning of fall. I try to remember when fall meant a last sweep of glory before a six-month winter bound in snow—but that seems like an old movie, someone else's world. Since my teens we've gotten very little snow; farther south, they don't get any, just torrential rains all winter, washing off topsoil and releasing another round of gloomy atmospheric conditions.

Seasons in the hospital, though, are always the same, the same air recirculated till the oxygen's all breathed out of it. I yawn and turn to my father. He's drifted off again. I check my watch, not yet one o'-clock. Carefully I glance around the curtain, but my father's roommate's asleep too—has been all day, a semicadaver hooked up to a feeding tube and breathing noisily. There's just a limited system by the bed—screen but no videophone, touchpad for the desktop—but I manage to key out to the number Sheri's given me. If a man answers, she said, or if anyone answers with anything besides, Hello, Sandersons, then hang up, all right? But if they say Hello, Sandersons, then you say, Can Benjamin play? and they'll know you're calling for me.

"Hello, Sandersons," a smooth alto voice picks up on the third ring.

"Can Benjamin play?" I ask.

"Sheri?" says the alto voice, releasing all its breath.

"Friend of hers," I say. "She wanted me to check on him, but I don't have a lot of time."

"Well, shit, I'm due at work for a couple hours. And you shouldn't come here anyway. I'll tell the new sitter to take them over to the park. You know Hamilton Park, the other side of the Northway?"

Them, I think but don't pause over it. "What time?"

"She should be able to get them there by—oh—two-fifteen. How's Sheri?"

"She's good," I lie, thinking of how she sits on her cot at Softjail, her long neck bending down like a wounded bird. "She runs videos of him."

"Well, he looks different, now. He has to, you know. We all do."

Only as I'm hanging up do I realize that I only know what the boy looks like from those old videos. I've got no idea of the baby-sitter, not to mention no car. But I key for a taxi and fish around the tiny dresser they've allotted my father. Sure enough, there's his wallet—and his card in the front pocket of it, but I won't take that unless I have to. And there sure enough, tucked in the little snap portion where most people keep tokens, a tight wad of soft green paper. Cash. I pull the bills out and spread them with my thumb. It's hard for me to believe these were ever worth something—still are, legally, though it seems such a weird idea, trading pieces of paper around. But my dad's always carried cash, has said he always will, at least until no one will take his greenbacks anymore. The little painted leaves around the famous man's picture in the center, the four different scrolls around the numbers in the corners, the eye above the pyramid, on the other side—it's all such playacting. But still, not traceable—and some say that's the idea, that's why greenbacks still hang around, not because people can't get credit but because they refuse to lead a documented life. With a shrug I stuff fifty dollars and a handful of coins into my back pocket and trot down the hospital corridor, ready to be stopped at any moment.

Outside the haze has begun to lift, high cirrus clouds muzzling the sun. I slip my sunglasses on, though I don't need them—it's disguise, I suppose, though a fairly silly attempt at it. As of now I am AWOL, betraying my friends Jonathan and Lloyd and my good lawyer Miss MacDonald. My heart beats as if I'm really running away—because that's what they'll think if they catch me, and everything Miss MacDonald's managed on my behalf will go into the file as a dangerous precedent.

But I'm not running away. I've promised something to Sheri, who sometimes touches my forehead in the mornings but doesn't push it, who's negotiated with the guards to get a message to Arthur Levinsky that can't be tracked—so that if he answers, I'll know, if not by the fact of his answer, then by the tone of falsehood and the links he chooses to use. I owe her a favor, and I've got two and a half hours. And however wildly my heart hammers, the risk—in the ordinary afternoon light, a Hyundai cab pulling up to the curb while visitors pass in and out of the sliding hospital doors, ignoring me—is surely slight.

"Hamilton Park," I tell the driver as I settle in the back. An eager Filipino, he drives fast out of the hospital neighborhood and slaloms his way through a snarl of traffic working its way from Genesee to the arterial. "Can you be back here in an hour?" I ask, handing him a twenty when he finally careens to a stop.

He looks at the bill oddly. People like me don't use cash; he'd booted up the machine already. "Change?" he says. As he looks through the bill at the windshield—checking the threads, I guess—I picture myself as Marta, as Rita, as those people outside the DMV in St. Monica.

"No," I say, sounding like a person on credit. "An hour from now. Right here."

"Righto, missus," he says. With a great yellow-toothed grin he pockets the twenty, and I turn onto the broad slope of the park.

A baby-sitter and a child. No, perhaps more than one child. I don't know what Sheri's lover looks like, but I'm sorry I won't be meeting her, safer though this setup may be—I feel sure I'd know her, just from the minute gestures of lonely guardedness she would make. The thin scrim of gray cloud that's come over the sun must have sent the crowd packing; at the bottom of the slope, only a handful of women and children cluster around the small sandbanked playground. I make my way down. An older, sacklike woman is brushing sand roughly off a little boy's shirt. From high up in a castlelike climbing structure a slightly older boy is shouting, "Liar, liar, pants on fire!" and ducking inside the pretend wooden tower for a few seconds before popping his head out to shout the same thing again. The woman turns the younger child in my direction, and I see immediately that it's Benjamin—or not Benjamin, Sheri's warned me, but Christopher in his new life. It amazes me that he hasn't been spotted, his identity's so clear—but then the D.A.'s office doesn't waste its time patrolling playgrounds on the lookout for little boys whose brown hair has been dyed black, with eyebrows deftly plucked and dyed to match.

"Five minutes on the grass!" the baby-sitter's saying. "Sitting still. And no juice!" She's got thin strawlike hair and the nose of a drinker. She glances up toward the climbing tower, but the older boy's disappeared. She sighs heavily and lands on one of the park benches that edge the playground. She picks up her Minilap, boots up a shopping channel. I crouch down next to Benjamin-Christopher.

"Hey," I say. He looks at me, then away. His eyes are red-rimmed, his nose thinner than Sheri's, running now. "Here's a tissue," I say, and hand it to him.

"Alex is a poophead," he says.

I look over at the climbing structure; the older boy's on the monkey bars now, his legs around a fat boy's waist, trying to wrestle the kid to the ground. "You're probably right," I say.

"I didn't say *anything*. Just nine times nine is eighty-one, and he started pushing me and stuff. He said it is not, it's ninety-nine. But I *know*. And the eight and the one add up to nine, and that's how you tell, and I told him, and he pushed me again."

"So what'd *you* do?"

"Threw sand in his face," says Christopher—I've decided I should think of him as Christopher—under his breath.

"Well, okay," I say. "How old is Alex?"

"Eight, and he's a poophead."

"How old are you?"

"Five and three-quarters."

"Is he your brother?"

"I wish I didn't have a brother."

"But he is, isn't he?"

"I guess." He looks up, his arms locked around his skinny knees. I can tell he's got something to add, but he chews his lip and holds it back.

Over on the bench, the sacklike baby-sitter's spotted me. "Ah!" she says with sudden, surprising alacrity. "You're here!"

"Did—ah—Christopher's mom tell you I was coming?"

"Yes, and I am so glad. I have got to get to the chiropractor." Rising from the bench, she gathers up her computer and a heap of knitting. Alex, the older boy, sensing a change in plan, comes running over from the monkey bars.

"I need a snack," he says, looking from the baby-sitter to me.

"Chips and powerbars and juice squeezers in the basket," says the baby-sitter. "This here's your mom's friend, uh—I've forgot your name," she says to me.

"Lee," I say.

"I don't know you," says Alex, narrowing his eyes.

"I just stopped by to say hi," I say. "I'm not taking over or anything."

"She said you was!" cries the baby-sitter, her arms hanging down straight, plastic bags attached. "She said you wouldn't have no trouble!"

"There's been a misunderstanding," I say. "I've only got an hour free. I know—I knew Christopher's mom a long, long time ago—and I'd heard she was in the area—and I'm just passing through myself—"

"Well, I got a chiropractic appointment," says the baby-sitter, bending her arms to lift the bags a little higher. Without waiting longer, she sets off down the asphalt path toward a little parking lot where a half-dozen cars gleam dully. "The boys know where they live!" she shouts, over her back.

"Wait!" I say. I take off after her. But I'm hesitant, and she's faster than she looks. She's taken off at a gallop, and reaches the car just before me. She tosses herself into the front seat like a bag of groceries. Just as I reach in to grab her arm, she slams the door shut; I have to jerk back not to get caught in it. Her eyes are small, beadily angry as she starts up the transmission and backs away. I bang on the hood, but she doesn't stop. When I turn back to the playground, the two other adults—mothers, I guess—are staring at me, but no one moves. Alex comes over and matter-of-factly takes my hand. "It's okay," he says. "We do know where we live. We don't really need a baby-sitter anyhow."

"Mom says it's the law!" shouts Christopher from the grass.

Alex shrugs. He's sucking on a juice squeezer. "She was new," he says.

"I should hope," I say. "We'll tell your mom to fire her."

"How d'you know my mom?" Alex fixes me with pale blue eyes. He doesn't look like Sheri or Christopher—he's got dark hair but straight, and light clear skin, a Spanish-Irish blend.

"From way back," I say. "Before either of you were born."

"Our moms aren't really the same," says Alex, finishing the squeezer and tossing it expertly into a latticed metal trash can. "I'm not supposed to tell you that."

"Then you shouldn't," I say.

"They just lived together. Then she"—he jerks his head, indicating Christopher, or rather Christopher's mom—"took off."

"If you don't know the whole story, you really shouldn't talk about it," I say.

"You want to see me do a flip in the air?" he says.

"Sure."

Alex steps to the grass and gathers his body into a knifelike posture. Bending his knees, he springs upward into a coil, twirls once, and lands first on his feet, then on his backside.

"Excellent," I say.

"Watch my somersault!" cries Christopher, running over.

"You're supposed to be sitting!" warns Alex.

"Don't be silly," I say. "She's gone."

After I've spent forty minutes with them, I try calling the number Sheri gave me from the antiquated cash phone by the parking lot, but I just get voice mail this time, impersonal at that: "No one is available to talk right now, but leave your name and number . . ."

"Well guys," I say, returning. The snack's gone; the air feels heavy, dustpacked. "I've got places to be. What do we do?"

"I wanna go home," says Christopher. He leans against me on the bench, and I feel the heavy weight of his body, his tired head. I gather him onto my lap.

"You're a good boy," I say to him. I have an urge to kiss him.

"Our house is that way," says Alex.

"How far?" He shrugs. "Too far to walk?"

"Course."

My heart sinks; I've been wasting time here thinking, they could be walked to their door, or a neighbor's. The cab could take them—but the house is probably locked, and neighbors suspicious. "Don't you have a car?" Alex asks, staring at me.

"No," I say, "and I don't feel right dropping you at home with no one there. You both better come with me, I guess."

"I wanna go home," Christopher repeats, his head nestled now between my breasts. "*Star Shooters* is gonna be on."

"We can watch it where we're going," I say. "Come on." I gather up the basket, empty now except for three plastic sand shovels and sunblock. It's not three o'clock yet; she said she'd be at work a couple of hours, surely she'll be back in time to come to the hospital.

"Where's that?" says Alex, lagging behind as I hoist Christopher on one hip and start over the grass the way I came.

"We have to catch a taxi," I say.

"Wow, I *love* taxis!" he says, catching up. "Can we get ice cream?" he asks, as if cabs and cones go together.

"We can get it somewhere," I say.

And so we appear over the rise together as the Hyundai sits waiting, and I give the driver another ten when he asks no questions but pulls us around to the main hospital entrance. I promise Alex there'll be ice cream in the cafeteria once we get settled. Christopher's fallen asleep, his moist mouth open, his eyes moving rapidly beneath their copper lids as his head rests in the crook of my elbow and I carry him up to my father's room.

When he wakes, my father's head moves first from side to side listlessly, as if he's shaking off an annoying but very slow fly. Then his eyes open and look fiercely at the ceiling, at the overhead screen playing silent cartoons, at the plate-sized clock on the wall, at me. We're all equally guilty. I've left a message on Sheri's partner's system, with this number. The two boys are sitting at the foot of the bed, their legs dangling over, their mouths rimmed with dried ice cream, their heads filled with the sounds I haven't let them turn up the dial to hear. My father punches at the bed with the flat of his left hand until I understand he wants to sit up.

"You slept a long while," I say.

"Turd," he says. The side of his mouth that doesn't work closes down on the word, worse than before his nap. The cheek that was twitching lies still, but like a sprung rubber band. The two boys, naturally, don't get it; not even glancing around, they laugh as if my father has supplied the joke they've been waiting for on the cartoon. I lift my father under the arms until he's propped against white pillows, and he glares at the boys while a thick stream of drool comes out of the side of his mouth he can't control. I smell the faint acridity of urine; his diaper will have to be changed. I've done it plenty of times, back at the apartment, but they won't let me here. "I'll call the nurse," I say.

"Burrs," he says, lifting his left hand a few inches from the sheet and pointing it at Alex and Christopher.

"Oh. Yes. Boys, right?" I say, sounding too eager—how had he pronounced the word an hour ago? "Alex, Christopher, say hello," I say.

"Hello," they chime, not taking their eyes from the screen; and then Alex adds, "Can we turn the sound on now?"

"Ah, ah fergot yuh hed burrs, Mareh," he said.

"I'm not Marie, Dad. I'm Phoebe. Can you feel my hand here, on your cheek?"

"Yur musser en ah alwehs wanted burrs."

"I *know* you wanted boys, Dad," I say, the resentment creeping in despite everything. "We talked about it last time you were awake, remember?"

Something catches in his throat that would, in other circumstances, have been a laugh. "Ah'll tull yuh a shicrit," he said, inclining his head in secret-sharing pose. I lean in. Christopher turns momentarily around, looking for an answer to the question about sound, but when he sees what's involved he shrugs, hops down from the high bed, and goes over to the chair where I've put the little bags of potato chips and pretzels we got at the cafeteria. "Yur Ph-Ph-Ph-" my father starts, the *Ph* like an explosion about to happen.

"Phoebe," I finish for him. "You used to call me Beeb."

"Behb," he repeats. "Yur uh skemp."

"I'm a scamp?" I try. He shuts his eyes, opens them, assents. *Call the doctor,* I order myself, but I don't. It's four twenty-five. I want Miss MacDonald here—however angry she gets at me—before anyone else sees these kids. My dad's face has gone to a gray color. With great strain, the saliva collecting in the back of his throat, he manages to ask me when I got my two sons. "Bertiful chuldren," he calls them. The gray skin is splotched with white.

"They are beautiful, aren't they? They're eight," I say, indicating Alex, "and almost six. Big boys." They've both turned to us now, the distraction from the cartoons too great to keep their concentration there. "C'mere, kids," I say, pulling Christopher close to the side of the bed and cueing Alex with my eyes. "Tell Poppa how you're doing."

"I can do a somersault!" cries Christopher.

"I don't know him," says Alex.

"Ssh," I say, turning to frown at him.

"Behb," I hear my father say again, only this time his voice comes breathy, cut off from his lungs.

"What's wrong with him?" asks Christopher.

Turning back from the recalcitrant Alex to my father, I find him struggling to lift his head from the pillow. The veins in his neck bulge. His eyes lock for an instant on me, then go up to the ceiling. His head whips violently to the left; I can see his tongue, clotting his mouth. I try to put my hand in, to clear his windpipe, and his teeth gnash down on my fingers. "Press that button!" I cry to Alex. I nod at the call button on the far side of the bed. The boy stands there by the potato chips, his jaw hanging open. "Goddamn you!" I yell. "Press the fucker!"

He doesn't move. I pull my hand from my father's mouth, shredding skin on the way, and lunge across his body. I hold the call button down as if it alone will save my father's life, until three nurses come flooding in, a tide that wraps around me and separates me from my father. His face is iron now, a clacking sound coming from his jerking mouth. I pull the two children whom he will die believing to be his grandsons away from the sight.

CHAPTER 13

"It was a major, *major* fuckup!" Sheri's shouting. She slams her hand against the wall for maybe the fifth time. I'm sitting cross-legged on my bed. Mary Jo's tweezing her mustache at the mirror. It's rare for all three of us to be in the room together—but I'm to be let out again for my dad's funeral, so I'm off my shift.

"Yes," I say tightly, also for maybe the fifth time, "it was, but it was not my fuckup."

"I never told you to keep him with you! I never told you to meet them in a park! I never even told you to *meet* him, for chrissakes, you could've just talked with *Dara*."

Dara is Sheri's lover, now accused of conspiracy though not arraigned. The boys are being held at Juvenile Hall, pending. "Look, I said I'd be squeezing it in," I said, "and Dara was out the door when I talked to her, and the park thing was her idea not mine and if she was hiring baby-sitters like that for your kid then she needs some serious help the county can give it to her." I stop for breath; there's a glass of stale water on the windowsill, and I drink some.

"What about Benjamin? Does Benjamin need the county's help? I'd say *you* need help! You need a fat—"

"Leave her alone, Sher," Mary Jo cuts in, finishing off her mustache with a wince. "Her dad's dead."

"So fucking what! He was old! We are talking about my *kid* here!" Sheri stops suddenly. She leans onto the cheap bed, facing me, her weight resting on her knuckles. "But you don't care, do you, Miss

Conceiver? You think I shoulda yanked him out before he was born, don't you? Well, you disgust me. You deserve everything you get in this place. I hope you rot here. I musta been out of my mind, letting you get near Benjamin."

She starts to cry. It's taken me a second to remember who Benjamin is: Christopher, I'd decided to call him. I'd discovered him still holding my hand, when the nurses had given up CPR and the doctor had finally come and registered the straight blue line on the cardiogram they'd set up to track my father's death, the death the boys and I had witnessed as it was being born. We were linked like cutout dolls, Christopher and I, our hands a mere crease in the paper. Before the doctor could even turn to give me the news—as if it were news, to us who'd seen it—I knelt down to Christopher. "Don't be scared, honey," I said. He shook his head solemnly. "Where's your brother?" I asked. With his free hand he pointed, behind the blue curtain hiding the toilet area. "C'mon," I said. We found Alex crouched in a corner, sucking his thumb, his skin like polished oak. The doctor parted the curtain before I had a chance to lift Alex from the floor.

"He's dead," the doctor said.

"I know." I squeezed Christopher's hand a little; it was moist and warm.

"These aren't your kids, are they?"

None of your business crossed my mind, but I'd never been good at that. "I'm watching them," I said as assertively as I could, "for a friend."

"He'th not my grandfather!" Alex said vehemently, around the thumb.

"It was a massive brain hemorrhage," the doctor said, getting business out of the way. "There was nothing we could do."

"I know."

"Perhaps you'd like to call someone. To—to make arrangements."

"Yes," I said, "I'll do that."

He stood there framed by the blue curtain, austere but unsure. On the other side I could hear the nurses, murmuring, unplugging various nodes. "Are you *allowed* to have these children here?" he finally asked. He took just a half-step toward me; Christopher pressed himself against my thigh.

"Please," I said. "Someone'll come for them. Just let us alone."

But of course he didn't, and the police got there long before Dara did. You couldn't of done better if you'd been *working* for them, was the first thing Sheri said to me, when I was brought back to WDU.

"At least she'll be let out now," says Mary Jo when Sheri's gone off for her shift. "Can't hold her in contempt of court now they've got the kid."

"She's right to hate me," I say. "I would hate me."

"Forgive yourself, babe. That's my advice."

"Will she lose him, for sure?"

"Shit, I don't know. Beats me why dykes like her want to have kids in the first place. You know what they go through to get one cooking, without having to let a penis inside themself? It's almost as back-alley as yanking one *out.*"

"He's a sweet boy," I say, "and real smart. She must be a good mom." Mary Jo flops on her bed, her large breasts loose in a man's T-shirt. "You have any kids?" I think to ask.

"Three," she says matter-of-factly. "But I gave 'em all up." She says this as if she's given up smoking, or a small business enterprise.

"Just like that?" I say.

"I nursed 'em first. They got my milk in them, six months each one. Even though it's hell on your tits."

"You never thought"—this seems strange for me to say, like self-promotion, but I go ahead anyway—"of a misconception?"

"*Yahggh,*" she says, giving a voluminous shudder. "Freak me out. I couldn't live with myself. Needles alone give me nightmares, shit." And she shudders again.

Picking me up for the funeral, Lloyd looks at me the way you'd look at an orphan who missed the adoption plan. "Not much left to our family," I concede.

"You think I don't know it?" he says. He looks harassed, the thin hair that he usually combs over his bald crown askew. "If your dad's brother Phil hadn't kicked, or my old man—"

"Or my mom, or Marie, or Frank."

"I'm sitting on all these locked files until we work out your little situation," he says, turning onto Commercial Drive. "If I had any influence with the D.A. I'd beg him to ignore the Constitution just this once just so we can get the will out of probate and put you to work making arrangements."

. "But you don't have influence."

"Fuck, no. Just do me one favor, if you ever do get out of that summer camp or wherever it is they incarcerate you ladies." He opens the car's ashtray and draws out a pack of antacids.

"Whatever you want."

"Get yourself a husband. Get yourself a kid. I do not want to go through all this again when *you* kick."

"I have Christel," I say. "Isn't a niece closer than a second cousin?"

"Jesus. Christel." He bites off the end of the package and slips an antacid tab into his mouth with his tongue.

"Where is she?"

"Back here, as far as I know. I mean, nothing happened to her, right? That's the official line. She just went a little nuts and cut her hair and went home, and then came back again. She's gone a little retro—"

"What do you mean?"

"I don't know, like she's not enrolled in her classes, her mom thinks she's living with a group, who keeps track? But the hair's growing out fine. Right, Phoebe? Isn't that the story, Phoebe?"

"Don't be sarcastic, Lloyd. Please. There are a few cracks in my armor these days." I can't help the one fat tear that rolls onto my cheek, but I refuse to wipe it away. It sits at the corner of my mouth, a drop of wet salt reminding me bitterly of Christel, of St. Barbara, of Arthur Levinsky, who's never responded to the message he was sent. So it was him, I tell myself, not Lloyd or anyone else. Lloyd doesn't say anything, but when we draw up to the funeral home he comes around and gets the door on my side.

By the semicircular stone porch a cluster of reporters is waiting—it's a story, my father's death coming just as his second daughter is indicted for abortive murder. "Don't look," says Lloyd, and I don't; when I step out he draws me into his arms. He's gotten stocky over the years, Lloyd has; there's no softness to him, but a bulky solidity, like one of those decorative pillows that's been stuffed to the point where it has no give. I press my face into his silk tie. He caresses my back, two rubs and a pat pat, two rubs and a pat pat. Behind us, I can hear the videocams humming.

It takes a while to pass through the gauntlet. "Yipes," I say inside. The hallway is cool, scented. "You didn't warn me about that, Lloyd."

"You make good screen, Phoebe, and America eats good screen for breakfast," he says. He's steering me toward a back room, and as we get closer the panic I ought to have felt just now in the face of a half-dozen thrusting microphones finally surfaces.

"Wait," I say. "I feel sick."

"Okay. Okay. Easy now." I've backed against the wall; Lloyd's got me by the elbow. I look from the shiny black tile floor to the worn acoustic tile of the ceiling; neither seems to help my balance. Dull-witted but kind, my father's former colleagues have gathered in the room at the end of the hall. They knew Frank and Marie; they used to call me "the little one." *How's the little one?* they'd say, and pinch my cheek. Well, the little one is not so good, thank you, Counselor. "What can I get you," Lloyd seems to be shouting from far off, though he's just a few inches from my face.

"Jonathan," I say. "If he's there."

He is, and Lloyd leaves us alone to go clear a path. I don't know what look I give Jonathan, but it must not be a promising one, because he lifts my left palm until it's vertical, presses his own—cal-lused, wood-splintered—against it and says in his wonderful voice, "You look like you just went three rounds."

"Did you hear what they asked me out there?"

"No, I was inside with the dark suits. But I can imagine."

Jonathan's suit isn't dark; it's denim-colored and out of fashion, probably the only suit he owns. It makes him look like someone's son forced to attend a dinner at the country club. "They asked me," I say to him, "if I thought news of my crime brought on my father's death. They asked me if *he* ever took part in the abortions. They asked—they kept asking how many. Give us a round figure, they said."

"They're idiots," he says.

"But they ask all the questions everyone else wants to ask. All those people in that room down there"—I nod toward the end of the hall—"have those questions in their heads. I can't face them, Jonathan."

"I'll face them," he says. "Your cousin will face them."

"But you can't, you're not his daughter, you're not the one who did all those terrible things."

"Do you remember," Jonathan asks, locking the fingers of our upraised hands together, "when you asked if I'd always be your friend?"

"Yeah."

"I'm still your friend. And as your friend, I want to know if you're here for your father's sake or your own." He says this gently, but it punches me anyway. I pull back, but he hangs onto the hand. "Because if it's for your own sake go ahead and wallow in it. But if it's for your dad"—he glances toward the end of the hall; his lips are soft, almost pursed—"then you'd better face those dark-suited folks and thank them for coming and if they ask you something ugly tell them to fuck themselves. At least if you think that's what your father in his right mind would have told them, which, from what you've given me to understand, it is."

"Wow," I say. I've freed my hand. Turning down the hallway, I tuck it around Jonathan's slim waist.

"What?"

"I've just never heard you give a speech like that before is all."

"No one's ever asked me to be their friend no matter what, before."

Our steps echo on the black tile; already the people in the room are turning, making a semicircle and then a passageway to where my father's casket lies ready to be transported; already their smiles of sympathy have been fitted to their faces, and I have composed mine the way you solve a child's jigsaw puzzle, with a few deft, sure placements.

My father never attended church, called it an expensive way to get your morning coffee. I have a vague memory of my mother bustling back from the eleven o'clock service, my father harumphing at her while she got the roast in late. Marie never went to church either, though I guess Frank started attending after he met Roxanne—*a real church, devoted to the spread of God's word,* is the phrase I remember, from what family argument or manifesto I can't recall. At the gravesite, the cemetery hill thankfully barred to reporters, my father's dark-suited friends stand stoically, listening to the strange words of the preacher Lloyd picked—*I am the Resurrection and the Life*—as if to make up for the deaf ears on which the words fall.

Hah hah, my dad would say. Deaf ears, that's a good one.

When the words have been dispensed with, when a handful of distant relations have embraced me and laid hothouse flowers on the coffin, I turn to the only one I need to see—my niece.

"Hiyya, Chris," I say. Christel's been hanging back, skirting my view but still not leaving, waiting like a butterfly at the edge of a meadow. Her hair's grown to a fringe around her head, giving her a sweetly boyish look; she's wearing heavy shoes and the sleeveless dress she bought in St. Barbara, no makeup or jewelry.

"Sorry about your dad, Phoebe," she says.

"Oh well," I say, "he wasn't living much of a life."

"Sorry about you, then."

I manage to laugh. "Well, neither am I, for that matter. Living much of a life, I mean."

"It wasn't . . . wasn't . . ." She fingers her cross.

"Because of you?"

"Yeah. Was it?"

"I dunno, Chris. I don't think so. Oh, thank you, thank you," I say to a powdery woman who steps in between us and squeezes my hand—where were all these people, while my father sat playing gin with Betty in his apartment? Betty came to the funeral but not the grave, said she didn't believe in seeding dead bodies like plants.

"I didn't know—where you were—till I got back East," Christel says.

"Does your mom know?"

Christel shook her head, as if shaking a bad idea out of it. "I'm not in touch with my mom," she says.

"But why? Did she—" *Arthur, Arthur,* the name hammers at me, but there's something in the way Christel looks at me, or doesn't look at me, at least not directly, that tells me she's not concerned with her mother and the Jew anymore; that in the last couple of months the world's taken on a different shape for her. "Lloyd tells me you're not in school," I say instead.

"Yeah, well, I'm going back. Soon's I can catch up, you know."

"But the Young Disciples? You're still singing with them, right?"

"Oh, come on, come on, Phoebe," Christel says in a voice tightening like a coil. It's as if she's impatient with me, as if there's a puzzle I ought to have solved by now. "I'm done with all that side of it, don't you see? Tennis and singing and games. Oh"—she glances up to the sky, as if pieces of it have been falling on her—"what a creature I was, huh?"

"A human creature, maybe."

Meeting my eyes square on, hers are bright blue as ever, but painted-looking; she doesn't blink. "I gotta be somewhere, Phoebe," she says in a new jagged voice. "I'm sorry for any trouble I cause you."

"But you can't cause—" I call after her as she hurries down the lawn. I don't finish my sentence. Not because Christel's out of earshot, though she is. But because there, down the slope of the hill just behind Lloyd's shoulder, jangling the keys to his rented car as if offering it to whoever might need a lift, tellingly tanned in this northern climate, stands Arthur Levinsky.

Back at Softjail, Sheri's gone. "Tomorrow her custody thing starts," says Mary Jo. "It's not criminal anymore, unless she kidnaps them again."

"Him, you mean. Alex isn't hers."

"Yeah, well, I guess Dara lost custody of Alex this time around. He's gone to her ex-husband, Benjamin's gone to Sheri's mom. You can be a gay parent all you want till someone else wants your kid. Man, is she pissed, Phoebe. If you ever get out of here, don't run into her on the street."

"Thanks," I tell her. "I'll remember that."

So now I have an enemy. Not somebody who hates what I do in general, but someone with a special vendetta. It makes me real, in a way; up to now, the people who hate or might hate me have all been people who hate misconceivers. I'll miss Sheri as if we had been real friends, quarreling and misunderstanding each other for years.

Missing my father, on the other hand, is like a phantom ache in a missing limb; I can't quite place it, and when I do, I discover the spot for the pain no longer exists. Instead, I follow the nerve track, and farther along I find the old pain of missing Marie, who was my father's darling—that was part of what made her the sister she was, just as his doting on her was the way he fathered. For me, to grieve for the one is to grieve for the other. My dead mother is buried somewhere back in the broad desolation of filial loss, dwarfed sometimes by this simple medical procedure, a mechanical adjustment practically, that for her was a cause and for us is a crime. I can't see her clearly, and so the pain of having lost her makes a rough equation with the pain of never having known her personally. Ah, but did she know me? She wanted to terminate me, to erase my future before I had a past. Could she have told me now, as I take my lukewarm shower after my eight-hour shift in the recycling room—paper this time, separating grade from grade—what it is that sets me apart, what I ought to mean to the world, what I want? Oh yes, I say as I hug myself in the bed, yes, she was my mother and she could have.

Phoebe, she would begin, *was the most beautiful name I'd ever heard.* I know she would say that, because she named me, after all. What she would say next, I do not know.

Perhaps, I think, addressing Jonathan, all grief for one's parents is grief for one's own sake. Perhaps all we can do is wallow in it. I sleep fitfully, wake with enormous hunger pangs, cannot swallow my food. I wait for news from the outside world—the world of trials, extenuations, witnesses, evidence, legislation and its overturning. I wait for Arthur Levinsky to visit me and run his finger along my collarbone, his lips along the crease above my eyebrows.

"I won't even be angry," I said to him that day by my father's grave, having tossed in the first clump of sod and watching as the somber, muscled diggers went to work. A few feet away was my mother's stone, next to her Frank's and Marie's—the whole family, I think, lined up like dominoes, no room left for me. "Just admit it to me, and it'll be over."

"I am telling you I didn't know until three days ago," he said. "Whatever server that woman used got the message mangled and missent a hundred times at least—it came on my screen with a couple dozen headers and the ends of lines missing."

"But before then—"

"I'd been calling you! Video, audio—I must've E-mailed you a hundred times. I couldn't very well ask Roxanne what had happened. I decided—well . . ."

"What?"

"That you were a beautiful young woman from the East Coast who in a moment of weakness gave herself to a middle-aged doctor prone to romantic longing." He looked away from me as he said this, toward the picket fence that ran around the graveyard. Down the hill, I could still make out the cluster of reporters waiting.

"It's a plausible story," I said—feeling myself weaken, desire for him surfacing, fought against, surfacing again—"but it goes nowhere toward explaining why a posse was waiting for me at the Utica airport."

"I cannot explain that," Arthur Levinsky said, his hand making a motion that, under other circumstances, would have been to grasp mine but just then looked as if he was investigating the breeze that had blown up, "except to swear it had nothing to do with me."

I laughed, a little yip. "Nothing? You get the Pratt rods, you bring in the extractor, you pay the room bill, you clean up the sheets, you—"

"Put my own liberty on the line!" he burst out, too loudly—the mourners, drifting off, some waiting to shake my hand despite what they knew of me, turned and widened their eyes at this strange expostulating man. The hand he'd been testing the breeze with was clenched now. I moved away, my face reddening, ashamed. I thanked people for coming and they said, as if in a responsive litany, We will miss him, and I said Yes. Christel had left shortly after I spotted Arthur. She came over to him, standing next to me, and reached her hand out to him in a way that suggested both that she'd expected him and that she would never see him again. "Bless you," she'd said, in an oddly sultry voice, and then she'd slipped away over the leaf-strewn lawn. Now there were only Lloyd, Lloyd's mother, and Jonathan waiting to get me back to my cell before five.

"Look, maybe I was wrong," I said, coming as close to Arthur as I dared. "But I don't know who else would've known, you know, who was aware what flight I was coming back on. And it makes sense that you might've finessed a bad scene for yourself. If you screwed up getting the instruments back or something, and some muckamuck nailed you and asked what's up. It was the obvious thing to do. I don't set such great store by my performance in bed"—here the shame left me, I was able to lift my chin and meet his eyes—"that it should earn anyone's undying loyalty."

"That," said Arthur Levinsky, "is surely one mistake you've made."

At which point Lloyd came up, tapping his watch. I got a bouquet of wild roses and forget-me-nots from the pile left behind by the hearse and laid them on the soft loamy ground where they'd tucked my dad. I told Arthur he could come see me next day during visiting hours, and I shook his hand in a forced imitation of the way I'd shaken the others. His index finger darted out, before he let go, and stroked the inside of my wrist.

"Who is that guy?" Lloyd asked, easing onto the expressway.

"Friend of Roxanne's. Christel's mom," I reminded him.

"What, she sent him? Or what?"

"I don't know. I've got a private life, Lloyd, okay?"

"Private life." He snorted. "Wake me up when you learn what a crock that is."

I looked out the closed, tinted window of Lloyd's car at the other traffic, at the burgeoning city. Right to privacy, I thought. The phrase hung in my head, but it took me a long time to remember where it had come from.

CHAPTER 14

He touches my eyelashes, my throat, the skin behind my ears. He holds the weight of my hair delicately in his hand, as if my coarse strands were spun of the thinnest gold. He places a fingertip on the mole at the base of my collarbone, above Sheri's silver rose. He lays the back of a fingernail against my lips, so I can press them against that smooth hardness. His eyes do the rest, lifting off my sweater, unknotting my tied belt, sliding under the unfurled waist of my jeans and easing them down, along with my panties, to my ankles. On the second or third visit, I manage to do the same for him—my eyes releasing buttons, freeing buckles and hooks with a *sproing,* lifting shirt from shoulders and buttocks out of pants.

Our eyes acquire miraculous properties. They taste, they touch, they hear and speak, they smell. As if she were witnessing real clothes peeling away from real bodies, the guard at the door stands stunned and mute while we stare. When our time is up each Wednesday, she clears her throat, and like a reverse-action film, our clothes rewrap our bodies, our eyes return to their sockets; we speak a few words as if to be sure that language has not stolen away from us altogether.

"I feel like Dimmesdale," he says the first time, walking me back toward the door he's forbidden to pass.

"Who?"

"The reverend. In *The Scarlet Letter,* you know. Hawthorne."

"Never read it," I say, and go in to be frisked. The next week he brings me the text on a basic disklet, no links or video, and when I get back to my cell from my shift that night I stay up and read the whole thing, stopping only when Mary Jo bangs the door open at eight and wants to talk about the crazy bitch on her shift who was sorting glass and went after the supervisor with a broken bottle. Stupid cunt, Mary Jo keeps saying, now she's got a free ticket to State, do not pass Go, do not collect two hundred dollars. I'm glad I'm outa here in a week. Ain't you slept?

Reading, I say, and when the days pass again to Wednesday my eyes rove over his body and lap him up again, and when we can speak I say, "You're nothing like him."

"Who?"

"Dimmesdale. You're nothing like him. He let her fry for the thing they did together. I was doing this long before you. Plus, Christel's not our daughter; she doesn't enter the legal picture."

"That's how I thought you'd know," he says, "that it wasn't me who reported you."

"No." I smile at the absurd nights I spent performing imagined mayhem on Arthur Levinsky. "That made it all the more likely, that you wouldn't mention the one activity that had involved you. But it wasn't you."

"Maybe it was," he says, but he's teasing. The guard clears her throat again; he runs his lips over that crease in my forehead. Our mouths never kiss. "Whoever put you in here," he says as we break away from one another, "I am going to get you out."

Which is what he always says, though he hasn't any power to do so and is taking far too much time away from his practice in St. Barbara as it is. For fourteen days, finally, he goes back, and I pace my cell during my few free hours, my skin itching. Mail arrives, downloaded to disk and censored: *I believe in you, I can't breathe right without you.* But it's all bytes and nodes, marks behind a screen, and for the first time I wish I lived in an age of paper, with all its surfaces and scrawls.

Wednesday at dinner they're whitewashing Prometheus's genitals again. Two workmen do the job—they don't trust us, Heather explains, we might draw 'em right back in invisible ink—and the hall's filled with hoots and whistles, *Start with his then do your own! You got one that size, big fella? Come visit me, I'll draw balls on you!*

It's been two weeks since my hearing; no trial date yet. Miss Mac-Donald's grown steadily sharper and gloomier, waiting for me to give way on the *argumentum ad Mariem,* as she calls it in her careful Latin. She doesn't want to call Rudi or Jonathan, certainly not Lloyd—they'd have to perjure themselves to proclaim my innocence. We can't locate Christel even if we want her, and if Roxanne knows why Arthur really left—which she must, by now—what little help she could have given is lost. What about the others from Viratect, Miss MacDonald asks, the ones who knew me as a steady worker? Lydia, sure, I say, but Tim's a loose cannon. She's even thinking of Betty, but I've told her Betty can't account for the red house; she never set foot in it.

Miss MacDonald's the only one allowed to visit me other than on Wednesdays. And even with her interruptions, the days have sunk to monotony—work the shift, try to sleep, eat, do my home assignment, work the shift. The home assignment is the state's attempt to make us more responsible women—we scrub the lavatories, wax the old linoleum, wash the linens; we "learn to take pride in a clean home," as the prison literature puts it. I'm on window detail this week, a fruitless task, because you can't get to the real dirt that lies on the outside, between the glass and the bars. Still I go through the motions each afternoon, the stink of ammonia spray, the comforting squeak of chamois cloth on glass. It allows me to move through the hallways, to hear the slight domestic sounds from the other cells—music, clicking keys, women's voices.

Today I've been working in a stupor. I haven't slept for three nights; even Arthur this morning noticed the circles around my eyes, the strain at my mouth. He wanted me to see a doctor and we argued for the first time. But the mood in the dining hall on the occasion of Prometheus's fresh castration is contagious, and I root for the white-washers and eat burnt toast with gusto. Next to me at the table is my new cellmate, a skinny shy creature who reminds me of Pockface and who's in for pulling out her mother's feeding tube. "That's awful," she keeps saying, hiding the sight of Prometheus's slowly disappearing wang from herself.

"Yeah," says Heather, winking at me, "shows you every really big dick is just an illusion. Hey, Beeb, is that for you?"

I listen above the racket, then spot the guard standing in the doorway at my end of the dining hall. "It's still Wednesday," I say.

"Knock him dead, babe."

"Don't be silly. Only lawyers visit this late."

But it's not Miss MacDonald. It's a tall woman with tawny hair newly permed so that there's a split second, while her back's to me, that I don't recognize her. Then she turns. "Lydia!" I say.

"Oh God, Phoebe, oh God," she says, and she rushes to hug me tightly. She smells of the world outside, perfumed soap and good coffee, and I've missed her. "I've been awful," she says. "I should've come *weeks* ago, and then there was your *father*—"

"Forget it," I say. I start to tell her about the scene in the dining hall—Lydia would appreciate it, women painting balls on a man and a man having to scrape them off—but she's walking around the dingy visiting room, appalled at herself and at me, not listening. "I meant to E-mail you," I try, "tell you how sorry I was to leave you in the lurch, you know, at Viratect, but I never—"

"Of course you didn't. God, what a place! I should've come first thing—"

"We all procrastinate, that's my point. Your plate's full."

"Yeah, but yours shouldn't be empty. Hideous," she says, palms up, to indicate the room.

"Yeah, I remember I thought so, when I came to see Marie. You get used to it, though. Used to be a school."

"Yeah, I know, Marie told me."

"I didn't think you were in touch with her," I said, "when she was—before she died."

"Oh yeah, I was," she says. She folds her arms, walks slowly around the room. "I must've visited her, I don't know, a couple of times. In this very room. We talked about high school, can you believe that? About boys we had crushes on. About you. And then she got sick." She wheels around, looks at me sharply. "You aren't eating the meat, are you?"

"No, and I'm losing weight."

"I'll bring you some good stuff. Fresh fruit, you know. And peanut butter. Whole-grain bread."

"Forget it. Every one of those can conceal a razor. They'll just be confiscated."

"Well, shit, Phoebe, I don't know what to do. I think that's why I haven't come. It's been preying on me, you know?"

"But you don't want to be controversial," I say.

"What?" There's something about her face, the way it's expressing enthusiasm or confusion. The lines are just a little bit exaggerated, or they appear a bit too quickly. It unnerves me.

"You don't," I repeat cautiously, "want to be controversial. Remember? That's what you told me. With your bobcat story."

"Oh! *Ssh.* I never told that story to anyone," she says. She looks in the corners of the room.

"I used to worry too," I tell her, "but it's not bugged. Really. Come on, sit down here. Tell me about the office. Tim driving you crazy?"

"Same as ever."

"You know, there was always something *familiar* about him, to me. It must be just the type."

"Type Pain-in-the-ass, you mean."

"Yeah."

Seated on the dull blue couch, Lydia loosens up a little. They did finish the job in Angel City, she says, though they had to bring in a freelancer to reprogram the desktops as a last go-round. "And that was just the tip of the iceberg. Hasn't Jonathan told you?"

"I only saw him for a few minutes, last week. He didn't talk about work."

"Well, this exact same virus is showing up in weird little pockets around the country. Doing the same shit, scrambling numbers in a megapattern. Each time we beat it, it seems to mutate a little. Like somebody's practicing—some hard-core group of retros or something, getting ready to scramble Social Security numbers."

Lydia's eyes are shining, almost like the parody Heather did of the Coalition. I tamp down a grin, feel fatigue settle over my shoulders like a shawl. "I thought you hated conspiracy theories," I say.

"Well, it's all happening so fast—we can't get a patent on the detection program Jonathan and Tim wrote, but nobody wants to steal it anyhow because we keep having to modify. And then there's *security* to worry about."

"Half of it's accidents, Lyd. Glitches. You used to say so, yourself. Gerald did that study."

"*Gerald,*" she says, just a trace of spite in her voice, "doesn't always know what he's looking at."

I manage not to laugh. This is Lydia, my best friend at Viratect. She only believes what lots of people believe, that whatever doesn't go according to plan must have been sabotaged. "Well, I'm glad I'm not caught in the middle."

"Shit, Phoebe. You don't know—!" Lydia stops herself, claps a manicured hand to her forehead.

"You never used to do your nails," I say, incongruously.

"I'm sorry." She takes the hand away and shakes her head. "I was going to say you don't know how lucky you are to be away from the mess at work. Can you believe I was going to say that? What an idiot I am."

"No, no, you're not." I lean forward, take her hand. She's getting nervous again, not like the Lydia I remember, who was in control even when the risks loomed large. "Maybe," I say, trying to talk her back to herself, "you could testify. You know. To how I was as an employee, steady and so on. That I didn't push political causes in the office."

"Oh, Phoebe, Phoebe. I would"—her eyes loom moist and dark as a doe's—"but I *can't.*"

"Why not?"

"You *told* me, don't you remember? You told me what you were doing. They'll ask me, Phoebe, and I'm a lousy liar."

"When did I tell you?" I say, sitting up.

"*You* know. Just before we left for California. It came up, about Marie, and you told me."

"Well then, I'm the one who's the idiot," I say. I try to cast my mind back. We went out for drinks, there was the bobcat story, the men in those bars on Genesee. How much did I tell her, when? The circuits are scrambled, I've got to start sleeping. Lydia's asking me what I'll do now. "I'll get off," I say, "or I'll serve my time."

"God, I wish Marie were here to help you."

"Yeah, well, in a way she is."

"How do you mean?

"Oh, you remember what she said."

Lydia smiles. She's relaxed now, the long dimple back in her cheek; she's just been working too hard, I think. "Marie said a lot of things," she says.

"No, I mean in high school. She gave the graduation speech, remember?" Lydia still looks puzzled, trying to reach back, so I give her the gist, the software and shareware. "If it weren't so corny," I say, waving my hand, dismissing the image, "I'd say she was my hard drive."

Lydia's eyes have filled with tears. "I remember now," she says. "And it's not corn, babe. Christ almighty, this is hard."

Hard, I think when she's gone. Yes, it is. But I don't feel like I'm up against something hard; I feel irked, like there's a bug crawling on me and I can't spot it to squash it. That had been Marie's speech, basically, I was sure of it. And Lydia would have been there, in the living room. I should have asked her about our couch, our mantel clock, our fireplace. Back in my little cell, I pace back and forth, window to door. "Quit it, can't you?" says Pockface Two, trying to sleep.

"Sorry," I say. I pull off my shoes, but keep pacing. There's something, something else. And yes, I'm sure of it. I *didn't* tell Lydia, she *knew.* She told me she knew. And just now she told me something else—about Marie, visiting Marie. "Shit!" I yell, just as Pockface Two's eyes have closed, and without opening them she grabs her pillow and flings it at me. I run out into the hall.

"You gotta pee? Pee," comes the guard's low voice from the end.

"It's not that," I call back.

"Then git back in your cell. Time out for visitors only."

"I've got to find out," I say, "if I'm getting any more visitors today."

"You git one, you git one. You don't, you don't."

"What time is it?"

"Git a watch."

"It's broken."

"Git back in your cell or I call the preceptor."

"Okay, okay," I say. When I'm back in the cell I do need to pee, but I pace instead. Lloyd's the one I want, but I can't send for him, I have to take what comes. Pockface Two's picked up her pillow and put it over her head. I can't stop moving.

CHAPTER 15

When she was at the clinic, my mother worked late afternoon and evening hours. If I kept myself awake, she'd be home in time to kiss me goodnight. The relationships in our house were formed already—capable Marie about to move out of the house, Frank already gone, my mom and dad like affectionate cats with a slight allergy to one another. When they got together, my parents and their two almost-grown children, they behaved like two couples, one older and the other younger, who share some odd, incommunicable interest. But when I heard my mother come home—car in the gravel drive, tone of the front door lock, the thunk of her overloaded pocketbook on the old-fashioned radiator—a little tremor would go through me from neck to ankles, and I would ready myself for my role. The still-young daughter, my mother's little girl. That's who I was as I stretched out in the bed, tipped my face toward the moonlight that stretched like an arm through the open window, and steadied my breathing as I heard her climb the stairs. Softly she called to my dad, "Yes, honey, it's me, I just want to check on Phoebe." *Check on* meant kiss.

She smelled of antiseptic—probably the soap she scrubbed her hands with at the clinic—and of the pizza or Chinese take-out she'd had for dinner. "Beeb?" she'd whisper softly when she stepped into my room. When she was sure I was asleep, she arranged the blankets over my shoulders and brushed her lips against my forehead. Sometimes she touched my chin with her thumb, blunt and callused; once or twice, I seem to remember, she settled on the side of my bed and hummed a song—"Where Are You Going, My Little One?" I think it was, with those verses about the child getting older each time the parent turns around, until "turn around, you're a young wife with babes of her own." I may have fallen asleep for real while she sang.

But in the mid-afternoon, while she dressed for work and I bent over my desktop loaded with Circus Math, I wasn't her little one, only an eavesdropper on her and her real, twentyish daughter, the daughter who shared her knowledge of the outside world and its machinations. One reason I didn't do so well at school was that my desktop was strategically located the other side of the wall from my parents' bedroom. Often, in the late afternoons, Marie would curl on my parents' bed, head propped on elbow, watching my mother get ready for the clinic. I was held in that space like a mosquito in amber, time arrested along with my breathing while I drank in whatever they said.

They never mentioned Lydia. That's what gets me started on this, the search for Lydia in the folders and files of memory—and she's not there, never there. But I was four, I remind myself; or I was seven, or ten, an age when older people look the same, taller and wearing deodorant. Yet these moments are the clearest of my life, these times when I was overhearing my mother and sister. I recall everything— the distraction of a mockingbird just outside the open window, the smell of carpet cleaner, my mother's voice a little raspy from a sore throat; she was always getting sore throats. They argued a lot about *we* and *you*. "I don't understand," I heard Marie saying, one rainy afternoon in my mother's bedroom, "why you people can't get more organized. *They*'re organized, right? That's why they keep winning."

"'We,' you mean," my mother said. I heard her open the closet door, the other side of my bookcase. "Why *we* can't get more organized."

"If women my age had some clout, you wouldn't be in this fix already."

"That's only because you can look back and see where it all came from," my mother said. I wasn't in the room, but now, as if I could see through walls, I remember how a dimple dented her right cheek as she instructed my sister. She was putting on her nurse's uniform, white slippery material with buttons up the front. Brushing her long hair, she explained what a surprise the Roe overturn had been, how no one completely realized what they'd lost when it came down, because they never really knew what it was they'd won back in seventy-three. "Shoot, girl"—here my mother gave a short little laugh, sweet in its tone but bitter at its edge, the only laugh I ever remember from her—"we thought it was about a medical procedure!"

I remember my computer screen wavering, wet spring breeze coming in at the windows. My sister telling Mom that she wished she'd been born a man. The laughter fleeing my mother's voice, little knocks and clicks on the dresser as she fished for a barrette to hold back her hair. "Don't say that," she repeated three or four times, "don't. That's something my mother would've said."

"Well, she knew."

"What does that mean?"

"She knew what it was like to be a girl."

"Woman, you mean." My mother cleared her throat.

"See? That's just it. I'm a *girl*, Mom. Noonie was a girl. We have the choices girls have. That woman thing—it lasted for your generation, then—*poof*."

I remember my hand, resting on the desktop's old-fashioned mouse like a dragonfly poised; my jaw open as I looked past the screen, listening. I remember them talking about Noonie, about my mother's mother. When she was ready for work, my mother would sweep into my room, peck me on the cheek, and glance quickly at my screen, now gone to fishes. Her hair by then was pinned back, her fine-boned face tense with the work ahead. She squeezed my shoulders with her strong, nimble hands, and then she was out the door.

They say no one felt anything, when the bomb hit, except for one woman who was in the midst of a procedure. That woman lost a leg in the blast and was in critical care for some time. A sidebar on the Web reported that she miscarried her baby—those were the words. The woman said the nurse attending her simply blew out of the room. Perhaps that nurse was my mother; I like, somehow, to think it was, to think of her flying out of the room like an angel. But there's no way to be certain, since everyone else was killed.

And then what changed, what changed? Did the real change take place in the law, or in my sister's heart? The procedure stayed legal in the state until two months before the Amendment passed, but none took place in Utica; my mother's had been the last clinic. Still, I don't think Marie learned her techniques from Mom. Rather, changing against the times, she moved out of the house, enrolled in art school; leaving me with our father, who doted on her, she began her training with Mau-Mau somewhere. When she thought I was old enough— thirteen, maybe—she started having me over to the ranch house in the hills, and one day in a state of high excitement she offered to let me watch a procedure. Yes, I said to everything she told me. And from then on I didn't have to overhear things, she gave it all to me straight.

There was a picture of Noonie on Marie's dresser—a stiff-looking picture taken in the nineties, of a thin, papery-skinned woman in a floral print shirt and green pants. Her smile looked tentative, as if she wanted the camera to like her. Carefully dyed strawberry blond hair curled back from her high forehead. It was Noonie who taught Marie how to work needlepoint; it was Noonie who taught her about husband material. Husband material was something Noonie was brought up to watch for. When the first man she loved—Jim, his name was, and he drove a truck—didn't seem to have it, she threw him over and settled for our grandfather instead. Only when she was very old, working needlepoint with gnarled fingers, did she point out to Marie that she'd made a mistake—this Jim, heartbroken, had gone out to Arizona and made a fortune in sunscreen windows, and when he died people took pains to tell her how he had still loved her, every day of his ambitious life. Noonie spent her last years, Marie told me, chewing on her mistake like a dog on old leather.

Heather, when she hears the story from me, disagrees. "She couldn't regret it that much," she says from the other cot. We're cellmates now, Mary Jo's time served. Heather's established herself emphatically with her collection of trolls, her assortment of talcum powders, her heavy paper books piled in the corner. "Not when she thought of your mother or her other kids. You can't regret your kids, it's just not possible."

It startles me, always, to remember that Heather has kids. On the wall above the cot she's got pictures tacked—her daughters at fifteen, twenty-one, getting married. She tells me the second time was a mistake. "That's when I was married to a farmer," she says, pointing at her younger daughter, who's standing on some beach looking at us over her shoulder. "Can you believe it—a guy who thought he could *farm?* By him*self?* Well, obviously, we couldn't afford a second child. And I'd had one misconception already, you know, the kind of thing you go through when you're eighteen and still stupid."

"You were never stupid," I say.

"Oh yes I was. I only married the farmer so I could remember whose bed I was getting out of in the morning. Anyhow, we couldn't afford a second, so I have Parker—that's the farmer—drive me on down to that little clinic where your mom worked. And they say they'll give me Valium, and I say, 'I don't want Valium. I have to work this afternoon, I can't take Valium.' And they say, well, I have to take it or they wouldn't do the procedure. So I walked out of that place and back to the truck in the parking lot where Parker's waiting with my daughter, playing hopscotch, thinking Mom's going to come out in an hour or so. And I said, 'Parker, it is just not in the cards.' And we drove on home."

"And had the baby? Just like that?"

"Just like that."

"You didn't check with my mom?"

"She said it was clinic policy."

"There were other clinics."

"Not many, by then. Anyhow, I didn't want to go through it with another clinic. I hate that Valium. I only gave it myself, later, when women insisted."

"So it was easier to have the *baby?*"

"I'm *telling* you," says Heather, "your kids are your kids. You don't have regrets. Look at Sheri."

Which is the last thing I want to do. Sheri's back in Softjail, in a cell on the other side of the quad but working my night shift in the recycle barn. This weekend they've moved me to The Box, on the compressing floor, where we load materials to be squeezed into usable cubes and shipped off to manufacturers. Everything but the glass goes out this way. Twenty thousand milk jugs, the supervisor told me my first day here, pressed into a cube no taller on one side than I am.

Earlier today—Heather knows this—I was onto aluminum, running the big yellow forklift to pull glittery, color-flecked squares from the mouth of The Box and stack them along the far wall. Marie used to talk about aluminum cubes like these, how long ago they'd have been placed in a sculpture show at the museum: found art. I was just beginning to wonder whether it was a virtue, her finding of beauty in everything. The forklift was ancient, belching gasoline—the aluminum's mostly from soft drinks, colored absurdly bright to attract us, like flowers for bees— and I was saying silently, to Marie, that you have to know it's ugly before you want to change it. The public weal, public welts.

Suddenly Sheri was beside me, hoisted into the passenger seat where there's no door. I'd seen her far off, by the metals. But now she was just on the other side of the hydraulic lever, lean-faced and long-necked, and she whispered, intimately, "I am going to flatten you inside one of those some day soon, my little Phoebe-bird." Her voice was sure as a knife, and instinctively I reached around my neck; but I wasn't doing glass, I didn't have my own little weapon. I punched levers to slide my prongs under the finished cube and put the truck in reverse. By the time I'd lifted my shiny prize—and swiveled my head, despite myself, to the right—she· was halfway back to her assigned station, as if she'd learned in her short absence from prison how to fly.

"She *will* flatten you, too," says Heather now. "I've seen her kind before, they don't mess around. You might as well have gotten between a tiger and her cubs."

Lying on my back, on my own narrow cot, I squeeze my eyes shut, remembering Lydia's old story about the bobcat. You don't blame the bobcat, she'd said, as if she understood these things. "What's Sheri in here for?" I ask, eyes closed. "She kidnap her kids again?"

"Who knows," Heather says, but she's no good at it; I can tell by the catch in her voice that she does. I open my eyes, prop myself up on an elbow, and stare her down. "Look," she says. "It was just one of those things."

"One of what things?"

"You know. An accident. A quirk of fate. Don't worry about it." But I'm waiting, not answering. Heather loosens the top button of her shirt; she's always warm, she's told me, she gives off heat. "They gave the boy to Sheri's mother," she says, talking to the wall, her head tilted back as if she's checking for spiders.

"I knew that."

"Well, I guess her mother wasn't the best care provider in the world. You know how Sheri bitched about her."

"Not really," I say, though I remember something vague. "She drank," I say. "The mother."

"Correction: drinks. And I guess her license got suspended ages ago, but the court goes and gives her this kid, and she lives three miles outside town, so she's gonna use the car. Christ, what did they think?" For the first time Heather seems just a little bit upset. She runs her hand through her cap of silver hair, then sits up, elbows on knees. She glances at her daughter's picture, the young one. "I guess the boy had an earache or something," she goes on. "The last thing anybody knows about was Sheri's mother audioed a late-night clinic to say she was bringing him in. When they found her, her blood alcohol was point two oh."

"She had an accident," I guess. "A car accident. And the kid died, didn't he?" I'm not looking at Heather, but I can feel her nod. My breath's coming short. "Oh, fucking hell."

"We used to bring up cases like this," Heather says, "when we lobbied for airbags. But we didn't get the airbags, and we couldn't bring the kids back."

I've started pacing the room. It's odd how I can't bring an image of Benjamin-Christopher to mind. I've pictured him a lot, since that day my dad died. Now it's as if the news has erased him—the more I try, the more I get a generic brown-skinned boy, all ears and outgrown T-shirt. I'm working to focus. "What's it got to do with Sheri being in here?" I say. "If her little boy died, what charges can they bring?"

"Assault and battery, for starters." I stop pacing and look at her. She looks very old, sitting on the bed; she's in ill health, but she won't say what it is. "My sources don't tell me," she goes on, "what kind of shape the mother was in, but I gather she didn't exactly walk off the accident scene without a scratch. All I know is, Sheri showed up in the room where they were keeping her, at the hospital, and started after her with a pair of scissors. Cut her up a little, I don't know how much. It's real messy, Phoebe. It never gets cleaned up, this kind of thing."

What Heather's saying is true—if only Sheri could have kept her kid to start with, none of this would have played out, and the boy would be at the playground instead of the graveyard. I point out, straw-clutching, that she could have posted bail.

"She didn't choose to post bail."

"Because she's after me now."

"I didn't say that. Not exactly."

"But she is!"

"*Now* she is, yeah. But if you think she hatched some kind of plan the second her son died—if you think she said to herself, I'm gonna get my mother and that bitch abortionist, too—then you're thinking plain wrong. Grief is married to rage, is all, and both of them are at a fever pitch when it comes to your kid. The most rational person in the world'll go off her nut."

"Well, sure," I say, "but—"

"But nothing. Dearie, I have to put it to you, there's a lot you've learned in your short life, but you don't know squat about how a mother feels."

My face flushes, then burns. All the dreams I've been having, of bits of tissue floating in red blood, seem to push from inside my chest. What I know about being a mother is death, that's all. And if I make myself look at them square, at the losses that piled up, one curettage after another, if I peel off the grateful face each patient presented to me afterward and look straight on at the churning grief inside, I know exactly the rage that Heather's talking about. No matter that they asked me to do it: I did it.

And what else I know about mothers, my mother, is that this thing, this death, is what they do. And now I've done it to Sheri's kid, with his soft hair and his eyes like chocolate drops. I ought to be executed, is what I think. But it's not what I say. I say I've explained what happened as well as I can. I say I feel lousy about Sheri's kid, about all that happened, but you have to admit—I point this out, my back against the old plaster wall now, my fingernails touching the paint—that none of it's my fault. "She should be after that freaking baby-sitter," I say, getting more and more control over my voice, "not me."

"Look, dearie," Heather says, her sympathy all with me, "just avoid her. You should spend the rest of your life apologizing, and get your head lopped off for it? Not by my rules. You've got worries enough, poor lamb." She rises and comes over to where I'm standing. Like a mother, she lifts my chin with her hand and holds it there, cradled in her palm.

CHAPTER 16

Sheri watches, watches from the other side of The Box, and I think what a noble act it would be, to go kneel in front of her and offer her my head to chop off. Which I don't. I stay away; I toss in my bed during daylight; I stew over Lydia and what she told me—*I visited her a couple of times. In this very room.* Finally, on Wednesday, Lloyd comes, the one I've been waiting for, bringing a touchpad for me to sign. It's time for me to say good-bye to the apartment, to my father's clothing and personal articles; disks and papers go to storage. Itchy and nervous, I've rushed out to see him, and I won't sign the pad at first but put it to one side. There are files stored, still, in the basement of the red house, Lloyd is saying. We can't sell it until after my trial anyway—the clinic in the basement being evidence—and he didn't want to wade through Marie's old things. Leaning across the table, I ask if he remembers the list we got hold of, the list from this very prison, after Marie died.

"What list?" Lloyd sits up in the plastic chair, straightens his tie.

"People who visited her. Before we knew what she died of. You thought, I don't know, poisoning."

"Jesus, Phoebe, that's three years already. Buried in some file. Not in the red house, though—those are all Marie's old things, from before."

"Well, look in your office, okay? I know you, Lloyd, you keep everything."

He snorted. "Yah, all right, I'll look. And if I find it, I'll have it zapped to the office here—"

"No, no, have it brought. I want a piece of paper."

"I got a busy afternoon, Phoebe."

"I won't ask much of you ever again."

"I'll believe that when I see it."

"Well, then." This is an unfair ploy, but I want what I want, and I'll use any cards I might have in my deck to get it. "If you're too busy, I'll send my friend Jonathan to go through old files. He's always been willing to help."

Lloyd's head jerks up; I've hit home. "That faggot is not family," he says, "and in my personal opinion you lean on him too much."

"I take my help where it's offered."

"Marie wouldn't like you taking this problem so much outside the family. Especially to a guy who might have his own legal problems."

"You mean because he's gay."

"They're not a popular breed."

"So, fine. You get me the list and I won't breathe a word to Jonathan."

"I am not a miracle worker. I can't bring the data back, if the file's been initialized."

"I mean if, Lloyd. You know I mean if."

Three days later I wake to pain—to painful light and a sense of being bound. *Sheri,* I hear myself mumble as I come around. With my eyes still shut I say the words in my head, Sheri has tried to kill me.

I open my eyes: infirmary. Everything's white, or else that blue that looks cold, the color of blue veins. People are moving around, some-where in the room, but I can't turn my head—it's my jaw that's wrapped, constricting movement. Sheri hit me. I remember this. Hit me and I fell. Sliding my eyes around, I make out an IV drip coming into my hand, a blue curtain pulled around the right side of my bed, a Microbook at the foot. Carefully I shut my eyes—if they come to check, they'll think I'm still out, and not ask questions before I'm ready. I start with my toes, which are bare under the white sheet, and concentrate on each part of my body as I move upward. Legs feel awkward but fine, likewise torso, though my bladder's full. The left shoulder's heavy and hot as lava; when I make a fist with my left hand it's like tightening screws in the bicep. My jaw's not broken, not in a brace, but uncomfortably swaddled and numb, and though I count my teeth with my tongue—all intact—I feel as if I can't open my mouth, as if a great weight's pressing on it. My head might as well not be there—that must be whatever narcotic they've given me, numbing the worst spots. I lift my good arm, and it touches thick bandage, wrapping from the jaw around the back of my head. Above my forehead I've got hair, but I'm sure they've shaved the back.

"You decided to join the conscious world, I see," comes a voice, and I snap my eyes open. "Don't try to talk. Let's check your vitals." It's the doctor, the one they get in here for Pap smears, the one Arthur wanted me to see for fatigue. His eyes, as they say, twinkle; he's got a long face and that sort of avuncular irony which makes you feel like his competence is a favor he's doing you. The nurse comes in, takes various readings, and punches in on the Microbook. "You had one very nasty run-in," the doctor says in his baritone when she's done and he can pull up a chair. "That's a cracked skull you've got, young lady."

I nod. He's reaching over, doing things to the bandages. Marie, I remember, dove into shallow water once and cracked her skull on a rock. It was the summer before her last year in high school. The scary thing for me—I was five—was that they wouldn't do anything for it, but promised it would heal by itself if she'd rest. The week or two after the accident, while she moved around the house in her yellow bathrobe, I used to watch for leakage, as if her skull were a vase that had cracked and the water inside it were sure to seep out.

Now the doctor's booted up and is showing me pictures. "Here are your X-rays," he says. "You can see the hairline fracture, right here"— he rotates the knob, and I get the top view, in 3D—"running from the lambdoid to the squamous suture. We could do some laser stuff—but the crack will heal itself in a month or so, if you don't push it. I've been worried more about internal hemorrhaging. That looked like a concussion, and you weren't exactly quick to come out of it, hey?" He stops and gives a little *heh heh*. "Now I'm looking mostly at the jaw, to tell you the truth. Whatever hit you was full of rust, that's sure. Gave you a tetanus shot, but we'll have to watch it. You're going to feel woozy for a few days, I guarantee. Now I'll just get Jennifer here to fix you up with a catheter, I bet that'll feel good, hey?"

Heh heh. I nod, scarcely moving my head. It was on the way back from my shift—I'm getting the picture now. In the corridor, that stretch where there's no guard, nothing but fluorescent tubes that run down the center of the ceiling, humming and snapping. The woman I sorted with had just turned off onto her wing—she's a slow, nervous woman with a collection of tics, biting the cuticle of her thumb, sniffling, smoothing her thin hair, squeezing her eyes shut and opening them—and ahead of me the XTC addict from the end of the hall was shuffling along, humming a tuneless song. I was thinking—yes, about Lydia. I hadn't been able to stop thinking about Lydia. I was trying to bring certain moments back to life—a story Lydia told by the water cooler, or the way she tilted her head and laughed, at that bar on Genesee—I was listening in my head for the point where the moment went off-key. I wasn't thinking about Sheri. Then something cracked over my head, and I was down on the wood floor, and there was a warm dampness in my hair, and the image of Lydia was wiped from my mind as if someone had taken a damp sponge to it.

And then what? I'm in this blue room, everyone speaks in whispers, I can't move my head. Then—yes—I was on the floor, and something sliced the light from the ceiling; it came down on me, fast. It was thin, hooked at the end, like a clumsy sort of sword. I rolled, and it clanked against the floor. And there was Sheri, standing over me. I couldn't get words out, by then; couldn't lift my head, either. The weapon landed sharply on my shoulder and cut the sleeve. *Look,* I started to say. I pushed up on my elbow. All I had to do was get up and run to the end of the hall, down the next corridor, there would've been a guard. Why didn't I do that?

The doctor gives another little chuckle, then follows my eyes above and behind him, where the assistant warden is standing. Her name's McGonigle; I remember her from when Marie was in here, she was the one who had to talk to the press about the E. coli outbreak, and from the way she talked then, you'd have thought Marie herself had chosen to eat poisoned meat. She looks much like the doctor—wire-rim glasses, gray hair, long face, an early wattle beginning on her neck—but she hasn't got the twinkle. "I'd like to ask Phoebe a few questions," she says, her voice as deep as his and more mellifluous.

"I'm not sure she's up to it," he says.

"I'm okay," I say, the first words I've uttered; they come out pinched—*okkey*, not unlike my father's after the stroke.

The doctor looks mildly irritated. He wants a job in the private sector. When he's vanished beyond the blue curtain, McGonigle settles herself into the one hardback chair. "Well," she says, trying for a he's-gone-now-we-can-talk tone. I suppose I don't respond the way she wants, because her thin smile evaporates as quickly as it came. "The only good thing," she says, "about having you people in here is that you're almost always smart cookies. You know what's best for everyone, you know how to cooperate."

I don't nod, not yet. She's got my record, she already knows I wouldn't name any names from Mau-Mau, I wouldn't even name patients. I keep my eyes steady.

"From the wound to your head," she says matter-of-factly, "we know you were struck from behind. But there's your jaw, too. Surely you got a look at whoever attacked you?"

My swaddled jaw tingles: *they don't know*. So they haven't got Sheri straitjacketed or down in solitary. She must have heard footsteps and dashed off. There are plenty of corridors branching off that main one, and others branching off those; if she could catch her breath quickly enough, she could just be returning to her cell like the other women. So there's a mystery, like a locked chest, that I can hold on to. "Did you find the weapon?" I ask McGonigle. My tight jaw makes the words come out in a monotone, like system talk.

"It was a curtain rod," she says—solicitously, for McGonigle. Christ, I think, a curtain rod, of course, the old metal kind; I thought they'd removed them all from the windows. And when Sheri swung that rod back and whipped it at me again I wasn't quick enough. Aimed at my throat, it caught me across the jaw, and the sharp edge—the edge that's supposed to be tucked under but they never are, there's always that warp—sliced me deep. That was when I kicked, and caught Sheri's ankle. When she stumbled I pulled to my feet. There was blood spilling from my jaw, spotting my shirt.

"The only blood on the rod," McGonigle's saying, reading my mind, "was yours. So we're not holding you on charges or anything."

I almost chuckle at that, the idea of me attacking Sheri. But then McGonigle's seen all those photos of almost-babies dodging the abortionist's lance—she thinks I practice violence for a living. "Someone just came after me," I say.

"But why, Phoebe?"

I shrug. What happened next, after the blood? What?

"Look," she says, scooching the chair just a little closer—she's got a mole on the side of her blunt-tipped nose, with a black hair starting out from it—"we know you people have your share of enemies, in our community here."

"Community," I echo, again like a computer.

"But you can't say there isn't blame to attach to both sides. We want to nip acts like this one in the bud. These things escalate. What we see in the men's detention unit—well, let's just say the difference between it and maximum security is one of degree, by now, not of kind. If you even knew what group was behind the attack—it doesn't have to be a particular individual. You could *help* us, Phoebe."

Help, that was what I'd called for. *Help, help,* the hall echoing with Sheri's and my labored breath and the clank of the rod, and I must have been hit hard in the head, I couldn't say any other words. I got my feet moving down toward the light at the end of the corridor, and as I glanced back I got a square look at Sheri. She was much thinner, gaunt even, the bones of her face stretching the skin like canvas over a frame. She was wearing just an undershirt, and in the faint light the hair under her arms glowed with sweat, tight and springy as the hair on her head. Her eyes looked puffy, as if she'd been crying or was about to start.

I try to focus on McGonigle. How can I tell her that Sheri's loved only one thing in the world and that was her son? That she tried to kill me, not from hate and not because I hadn't had a chance to explain but out of too much love, love that hasn't got anywhere to go now?

"It was personal," I say, and right away I regret it. However amazing it is that no one saw Sheri and that, even now, they can't look in the records and figure it out, the tiniest hint would send them her way. I don't ask myself why it's my job to protect Sheri; it just is.

"What?" says McGonigle. I am spared.

"It was dark," I say.

"But you weren't attacked for nothing. Think!"

"Look," I say, fighting the swaddling to make my words clear, this time, "I don't care to get cracked in the head. If I had any idea, I'd tell you. I need protection, don't I?"

"Exactly, Phoebe, exactly." McGonigle's nodding quickly, like a bird hunting bugs on the ground. "But we can't offer you that protection unless we know *who* it's *against*."

"I'll work on it," I promise, and I try to make my eyes melt, to work on whatever grain of sympathy McGonigle might have for a beaten woman. "Really," I say.

But she can smell defiance a mile off; defiance is what she lives with, it defines her days. The mole dips as she purses her mouth. "We'll wait to hear from you as you recover," she says. "But it's only fair to warn you, you're not completely clear of suspicion yourself."

I shut my eyes, though McGonigle's not leaving. *Sheri*—I said her name, finally, in the corridor. I heard it coming distinct from my lips, and it stopped me almost dead. I was still backing away from her but not running anymore. She was coiled up on the floor, where I'd tripped her, and it seems to me she sprang, like a dark cat. The metal caught my head again, and this time I gave a great shout—like a baby's cry when the doctor whacks it, except that I wasn't going from dark to light but the opposite; the hallway was speckled with black, and then all black, and my legs wouldn't hold me up, so I threw out my arms as I went down.

Standing up, McGonigle's saying something about an envelope. Jennifer, the nurse, has it at the desk. I can see it when I'm ready. My head's starting to hurt—the analgesic, wearing off. But I manage to pull a hand out from the covers to wave at her as she parts the blue curtain. Temper temper, I chide her silently. Her hard shoes click away, out of the room.

Envelope—Jennifer, too, is saying something about an envelope. I don't know how much later this is; I've slept. The IV's gone from my arm, though, and the room's staying still. I can locate the pain—clutching the back of my head, also my neck and shoulder, some minor stuff along arms and legs, that weight on my jaw. Envelope, such an old-fashioned word.

"Sure," I say. "Let's have a look at it." I turn her direction, and it's not Jennifer but a different nurse, dressed in white, like my mother, who nods and then vanishes. I tell myself I can move now, but I don't. I'm thinking of Sheri—who's free, or as free as you can get in this place—and of her delirious rage. It's her rage alone that cleanses me, the way fire cleans a needle. I'm not afraid anymore, I think, as the nurse comes back in with a small white rectangle. I break the odd flap, the paper wrapping; it's already been opened and checked, hastily retaped.

Inside are three sheets of white bond, the kind you almost never see. At first I don't know what I'm looking at, then I read Marie's name at the top of the page, followed by a list. Oh yes, the *list*. Lloyd's name and mine, with dates and times, followed by the lawyer Lloyd got, Omar Jeffries twice—the schmuck—and a bunch of names I don't recognize. Tim Williams, once—that stops me, what in God's name?—but it's a common enough name, or maybe someone from Mau Mau managed a fake ID, though it's hard to see how. "Tim," I say aloud, and shake my head, but no point in stewing over a common name. I wish I'd asked for the disk; I could run a search. Instead I scroll my index finger down. First I look for *Lydia,* then for *Anderson.* Then I start at the top and check *Andersen.* There's nothing, not even close, and my head is hurting.

Quickly I fold up the paper. Means nothing, I tell myself. The records could be wrong; she could have slipped by. Could have gone by a different name. She and Marie talked about me, she said. I shut my eyes and then open them on the white ceiling, and it seems to me I remember nothing clearly, and then that I remember nothing, period. Heather's told me that the paper books she takes care of down in the basement were once considered terrible threats; when printing was invented, it was feared that if people came to rely on paper records, they would lose their ability to remember things clearly. Then came bytes and nodes and hypertext, and now I don't trust these three sheets of white bond. I don't believe they recall the truth any better than I do. Why should Lydia go by a different name? *You'll have to ask her*—that's what Marie would say. And I will, Marie. As soon as I see her again, I will. I crumple the paper in my left hand, turning the flat sheet into a round ball.

CHAPTER 17

But I can't ask Lydia anytime soon, because she's gone. This is what Jonathan tells me, as if he's announcing a disaster: Lydia's left Viratect. Gave no notice, just walked into the CEO's office and handed him a polite note and cleared out her desk. Tim's been put temporarily in charge of the team, and he's rampaging over the rest of them; yesterday he tried to fire Gerald. "I've left maybe two dozen messages on her voice mail," Jonathan says, his hands on his temples, "and now her mailbox is full, and I drove by her place and didn't even see her car. I mean, it's not just the team, or Gerald's job. I'm worried about *her.*"

"No, you're not," I tell him.

I'm out of the infirmary, but confined to my cell and my home assignment. I get periodic headaches, which the avuncular doctor tells me is normal; they've run a scan of my head and the crack is mending. Last week Arthur got back from St. Barbara and went raging to McGonigle. *You can't tell me you're not investigating this violence! We'll press liability! You can't tell me you won't bring in a specialist! She is entitled to protection! She has her civil rights!*

At least, that's the gist of what he said. I wasn't there. I was only there for his visit when they finally let me out, and I treated him the same way I treated McGonigle and finally I sent him away. I'm fairly sure I told him he understood nothing about what had happened; I may have told him I didn't love him anymore. I hope those weren't my words, but words have been spilling out of me, steam from a pot, bearing little relation to what's cooking. That was a week ago, and he hasn't visited today, and my greatest hope and greatest dread is that he's gone back to California. Oh, I hate you, I say late at night when Arthur's face drifts into the cell I share now with Heather, though I say it the same way I might say I love you, a way of throwing a lasso about his irreplaceable body.

Still there is Jonathan, who has started treating me the way one does a person who's been sick too long, like an animal that needs retraining. "What do you *mean*?" he asks now, in the visiting room. "I care about Lydia. Jeez."

"But you're not worried about her. You know she's all right. You're just curious about her behavior, it's not making sense to you."

"Well, fair enough. But she's steady, you know? Rash action, it doesn't fit. And the project's been going well, and—"

"She might've turned me in," I interrupt. It's the first time I've voiced it, even to myself.

He frowns—a look so rare on his face that he seems to be clowning. "What do you mean, turned you in?"

"Told the police I was practicing misconceptions. Told them where to look for the clinic room."

"How would she do that? Why?"

"Who knows? Maybe she turned Marie in, too."

"Phoebe, Jesus! I thought you and Lydia were *friends*." Implying, not how could she do this to me, but how could I do this to her—libel her this way.

"I thought she and my *sister* were friends," I fire back.

"What's your sister got to do—"

"They were *best friends*." I jab a finger at the table for each word. Then I tell him how Lydia came up to me at Marie's funeral, how she talked me into trying the job at Viratect. "She'd just started working there six months before," I say. "And she claims she came to visit Marie in here, but she didn't. Is that the way you treat your best friend? And then you go after her sister."

"Are you saying this is personal?"

"Of course it's personal! Just like what's happened to me in here." I gesture vaguely at the bandage still taped to my head. "Maybe she got jealous of Marie, or she felt like Marie left her behind, who knows? Women fighting women, always personal."

"So you know who did that to you. Your head, I mean."

"Yeah, and I'm not telling," I say. The parallel hits me—if Marie knew it was Lydia, she never told. Jonathan's tipping his head to one side, skeptical. "Look," I say, "you believe me or you don't believe me?"

"Believe you got in a catfight? There's the evidence."

"No, I mean about Lydia."

"You haven't got any evidence for that."

"Yes, I do," I say, and I tell him about the paper list in my cell, still crumpled into a ball, stuck in my one drawer with my clothes. I tell him how I went down the list with my finger.

"It's not much to condemn a person with," he says.

"Shows she lied."

"Could be a computer error. Okay—I know, I know, I always say there's no such thing. Maybe she just wanted to make you feel better. You think she ought to have visited your sister, and if she didn't, she's let you down. And she meant to, but then your sister died. So she stretches things."

"That's lying."

"But it's a helluva long way from that kind of lie to turning someone in!"

"What if you thought she'd turned you and Gerald in? Would you give her so much rope, then?"

"She wouldn't," Jonathan says, gentle as a lover, "turn us in, Phoebe."

And even though I don't like the way he pats my bruised hand, touches the sling over my arm, it's a relief, oddly, to give up on my flimsy evidence. *May all your enemies be strangers to you*—Marie used to quote that one, called it the Paranoid's Blessing.

And so I give up on my suspicions of Lydia, and I live among women, and I live in fear. Over and over, I see what Sheri will do. A shard of glass stolen from the line—she'll climb up next to me in the truck cab again, and swift as a cat's claw, she'll rake it deep across my throat so I strangle on my own blood and can't cry for help. Or no, she'll get hold of some rat poison, they use it in the kitchen, and she'll sidetrack the dinner cart and douse my vegetables, which taste bitter anyway. Or a wire cord, they're not hard to come by, flexible enough to whip around my throat and yank tight. My hand goes to my throat, my mouth, to the bandage on my head. Getting up from my cot at dawn to walk down to the food hall, my head feels light, and I'm not sure at first whether my feet are touching solid ground. And then I find it hard to eat, hard to swallow the bites of food no matter how mashed or puréed. I'm so certain that Sheri will find a way to kill me that it's like having a swift and fatal illness: I try to grasp each minute that flits by, but each one feels hollow, like death. I dwell on regrets. If only I'd come to understand my father before the Alzheimer's took him, I'd . . . I don't know. If only I could see Rudi again. If only I'd finished college. If only I'd asked Marie all the questions I used to store up. If only Lydia, if only Arthur. *If only Rudi,* strangely enough, is the most common.

If only I could see Rudi once more, I'd confess there was a time— three months? six?—when I really loved him. Loved him differently from the way I love Arthur, if I do love Arthur—loved him in a more abstract way, the way you love music or a moment of time. When I met him I'd left college and was vacationing with Marie and some of her friends on Cape Cod. There was to be a starwatch one night in Provincetown, a night with no moon and a meteor shower. I'd grown antsy in the small house Marie had rented on the bay—I'd walked the flats until my legs ached, and swum the length of the long cove, sprinkled with similar houses, where we stayed. I was in mourning, hard as this is now to believe, for a boy I'd known in college—Gary was his name—a business major who'd decided I didn't fit his bill. That night, I borrowed Marie's car and drove the thirty miles north to Provincetown, which seemed a circus of gaily dressed people and street music, and then beyond to a long spit of sand that curled out into the ocean. The group sponsoring the starwatch had a telescope set up on the jetty; you slid your card through its meter, five bucks for three minutes. I stood in line behind a square-shouldered man, glad for the anonymity of the dark beach and the placid oddballs populating it. I can remember the instant when the man's gaze moved from the studded sky above to my face. Rudi Hauser, he introduced himself. He looked birdlike, as I've said, but also like a young Keanu Reeves, from movies made just before I was born. "You're here alone, aren't you?" he asked me, and I nodded.

"I accessed it on the local net," I said.

"I thought so. Usually the same people come to these things. What are you looking for?"

"I don't know," I said, wondering if I'd understood the question. "Falling stars."

He laughed at that, and without hesitation hugged me. "Stay the night," he whispered in my ear before he plugged his card into the telescope—and in the humid, salt-licked air of the promontory, with iconoclastic star watchers clustered around us in little groups, drinking and exchanging data, staying the night seemed like the only good idea I'd heard in months. Later we lay on his small bed in a rooming house north of town, with our clothes on until the dawn hours, while he told me of his research, his travels, his ambition to go up in the shuttle from Prague and take his own notes on interstellar movement. It was like hearing the light strains of chamber music all night, or like listening to the story of a prince who's set forth to find three apples of copper, silver, and gold.

But I can't mend any regrets over Rudi, or over anyone. I am stubborn, as Miss MacDonald keeps reminding me when we go over the State's offer to extend a suspended sentence if I'll cooperate with their investigation of prison violence. "They know you could bring a suit," Miss MacDonald says, tapping her polished fingernails on the desk in the small conference room they let us have, since the attack, whenever we need to meet. "For wrongful injury, maybe for malicious neglect. They don't need the publicity, not at a moment when privatization is all the legislature talks about. We could get you out *and* profit from it."

"I don't follow," I say, looking out the precious picture window of the conference room. It's midwinter now, night falling early. The stars should be more brilliant than in summer, but clouds shroud them. The burnt skin between my shoulder blades itches. Yesterday a friend of Sheri's—I figure her for a friend, at least—dropped a bowl of scalding soup down my back, and the soup is usually lukewarm at best. The day before that my cell door was marked with a cross in blood, which I washed off before a guard could see it.

"They want low-profile," Miss MacDonald is saying, "and they want economy. They're offering to bring you to trial, give you a year in here, then quietly let you go. Come now. I know you know who did it."

But I'm on the other side of a wall; she can't pull me over. The name of my enemy is more precious to me than my freedom. Miss Mac-Donald tells me I am self-destructive; she tells me I am self-centered; she leaves our sessions disgusted with me and my stubborn silence. And I return to my routine inside these damp walls, winter rain thundering in the black outside, full of weird pride and the word No stamped on my heart.

Until finally Heather pronounces the words. "We've gotta get you out of here, dearie." It's early in the morning, when she's back from her shift but not yet asleep, and I'm about to head off for my home assignment, rolling the dough for eighteen hundred biscuits. My last bandage is about to come off, and according to the scan my head's sound, but Heather's told me I moan in my sleep and grind my teeth.

"Sheri's got too many friends is the problem," I tell her. Pockface Two is still on her shift, smashing tin into huge cubes. I've got the Minilap booted up, trying and failing to key a letter to Jonathan.

"Have you seen her?"

"Sheri? Not since that night. But she's always just behind me. I jerk around and she disappears."

"What's your trial date?"

"Miss Mac says the Ides of March," I say, watching to see if Heather gets this reference. I don't. Miss MacDonald still scares me too much to ask what "Ides" means; I think of tides, saltwater washing March away.

"Trial!" Heather snorts, like a terrier with dust in its snout. "You won't be alive by trial date, if this keeps up. I've seen it before, Phoebe. Three years ago, there was a hooker in here who had it out for another hooker. The girl just deteriorated, and the people in the infirmary couldn't make sense of it. Finally she caught TB-2 and died, but everyone on the block knew she'd been poisoned till she was weak."

"Sheri's not using poison," I say matter-of-factly.

"Course not! That's too easy for her. She wants you to know each move. You haven't got past the first line of that letter in two days, have you?"

"There's nothing to say." I flip out the disklet, turn off the drive. Our letters flow through the netcache in the office, but it's not censorship that's blocking what I want to say to Jonathan. I've got my little stack of disklets on the corner of the tiny dresser; as I start to put this one back, the whole thing spills.

"You sure have enough of these," says Heather. "What's this one?"

She holds up the one that stands out because of the bright blue plastic, Viratect color. "Oh!" I say, taking it delicately from her square hand. "That's a germ. A big, bad germ." I turn it over. "In another life, I used to ferret these out."

"What would it do?"

"What, to a system? Scramble data. Alter codes. Block access to certain files, maybe. Set up crashes."

"Would it change numbers?"

"Well, that's exactly what it did do, in L.A. Fucked up drivers' licenses. Could've been mayhem, if everyone found out before we fixed it."

"Hm." She reaches out a stubby, callused forefinger and touches the disklet, as if checking for heat. "*Our* numbers?" she asks, giving the little round disk a last tap.

I look at her. Her eyes, heavy-lidded, sneak their glances. "I don't have access to the database here," I say.

"I do."

"How?" I say, and then I remember: the library. Heather's pet project, down in the basement. "Well, what good would that do, except cause havoc?" I say. "It's not going to change Sheri into not-Sheri."

"I am thinking only of you," she says deliberately. "Of your safety. Of how we get you out." She draws away and starts pacing the room, as if measuring a circle a million times wider than the disklet. She does look ill, I think—not thinner, but more weighed down by her flesh, sodden.

"Miss MacDonald has a way to get me out," I say. I explain about the WDU's offer, the suspended sentence.

"What's the matter with you," replies Heather, "is that you are too much like your sister."

"You'll be late for your shift," I say.

"Cripes. All right, dearie. But just don't get killed in the next eighteen hours, all right? I'm going to think of something."

She doesn't flinch at circumstances, Heather. She doesn't reflect, or sink into regret. I can picture her in the early days of abortion resistance, her hair already short but more tawny than gray, her breasts and hips ungirdled beneath brightly printed cottons, sitting in a circle of anxious women, focusing always on the next step—*We've got to raise money, We'll hold a demonstration outside City Hall, We'll get that senator out, next election, We'll mount a court case.* Lying back on my bed, my head throbbing, I watch her run a comb through her thatch of hair and leave for her shift. I don't want her to think—I want to do the thinking, to claim my life—but I'm wallowing, wallowing, and without someone to drag me along I suspect I'll sink. "Bye!" she says brightly, as she turns to go. I wiggle my fingers at her, listen to the click of the lock as she shuts the cell door.

CHAPTER 18

I don't get killed. In fact, my shift—five in the morning to two in the afternoon, minding the plastics chute to weed out Styrofoam and number sevens—is quieter than normal. One of the big women, a user named Helga, ran a high fever early in the day and has been taken off the shift; she'd been leading us in old labor songs, "Harlan County" and that sort of thing, and now there's just the piped-in electronic stuff that we're used to drowning out. My head's stopped hurting, and there's nothing left to the wound on my face but a nasty red scar running from chin to jawbone, which the doctor has guaranteed will turn white. I'm tiring easily; that's the only long-term effect, and I can't say for sure it's from the injuries, anymore. Maybe one grows old faster, in Softjail. Maybe I've grown lazy. All I know is, every ten minutes or so, standing at the chute with my long-handled picker, I find myself mumbling, "Jeez, I'm tired," which occasionally one of the other women will hear, prompting a "Me, too," that makes me feel like a slacker. At these moments I'm not very interested in whatever Heather's cooking up for me. I'd much rather be back in the infirmary, with its white sheets and its overheated, dry air.

"Hey, Chambers!" shouts the line chief. "You're letting egg cartons go by! Watch it!"

"Sorry!" I yell back, and try to blink my eyes wide; I rotate my shoulders to get the blood flowing.

But there's no incident on the line, and nothing walking back toward my cell. Only in the bathroom, nestled into the sink where I al-

ways wash up—freshly planted there, surely, since nine others use
this room, this sink—is a small pink fleshy object with a little tag
reading *Phoebe*. As soon as I see it I utter a little moan, the kind that
comes loud from deep in your gut but is almost soundless by the time
it passes your lips. I back against the cold metal of the toilet stall and
shut my eyes; but then I have to step forward again—as she knew I
would—to see it whole.

It's a four-inch fetus, just over three months old. It's clean, pink,
and stiff as a plastic pig. Its shut eyes look as if they're dreaming, anticipating; its buglike arms reach up, curling gently, ready to hold—
the tag's on the left arm, tied delicately around the wrist. There's no
smell. Between its rubbery bowed legs a tiny bud rests—a girl, I
think, and remember Marie's misconceived baby, the way she just had
to look at it and say which it was.

Even though I haven't eaten in five hours, I turn and vomit into
the toilet. I wipe my mouth with a rough paper towel from the dispenser. Then, with another towel, I reach under the fetus and cradle it
in my hand.

How many? I ask myself. Five hundred? Eight? Not a thousand,
surely. But I've pulled out enough embryonic people to fill all four
basins in this room to the brim, in their different sizes and weights,
like so many dead frogs. Only not frogs. Geniuses, to judge by the
size of this one's brain in relation to its body: a deep thinker, too ab-
sorbed to open her transparent eyelids, her mouth sealed and serious.
She could be anyone's—women come in here pregnant, or sleep with
one of the male guards, and Heather's told me there's always an old
hand here who will take care of the situation in return for a favor or
two. The slender black stub of a cord lashes her thin stomach, her
food supply cut off. I can make out the veins wrapping her skull, a
delicate pink rhizome.

I take the stiff pink fetus into the toilet stall where I vomited. There
are still some bits of half-digested bread in the water; I flush again and
wait. But then I can't do it—however dead the thing is, however natural a burial by water, I can't put it where we put our feces, I can't
send her through the dark cold pipes. Where else? Not the wastebasket; they empty once a week, it will smell and be found. Not back to

Sheri. I pull another towel from the dispenser and wrap the fetus up, then take it across the hall to my room. Heather's gone to group therapy, Pockface Two's on her shift. I leave a note on Heather's pillow: *Sheri gave me a fetus, ha ha. I can't bear to dispose of it. Will you handle? My drawer, left side.* Then I strip down, toss on a robe, return to the bathroom to shower—hot, stinging—and then, back in my cell, bright winter day sliding under the shade, fall into a deep sleep.

Barely an hour later, I jolt awake. Voices, out in the hall. Heather and another woman are laughing softly. I glance at the note on Heather's pillow, and suddenly it's wrong, all wrong. I stumble from my cot and take the note, crumple it. As I straighten up, I realize I was dreaming of Marie, of her carrying bowls of tissue and blood, of her neat efficient movements. I was dreaming of her large hands; I might even have been kissing those hands, in the dream, I can't say now. I open my drawer and draw out the paper-wrapped fetus. She's even stiffer than before, gristly almost. Her skin is stuck to the paper. I open the door to the bright light of the hallway and blink. Heather's standing there with a woman I've seen her with before, another misconceiver, and they both turn to me. "What's up?" says Heather.

"Something I've got to take care of," I say. "Myself," I say, superfluously. I've got the thing in my hands; I want to hold it out to them, like an offering. But I set my scarred jaw, and I don't. They let me pass, across the hallway, back to the bathroom with its snaky lines down to the river, to the ocean. And I do the deed. I take care of it myself.

But I tell Heather later, and I cry. Not normal tears either, but the kind of weeping you associate with maudlin drunks, or homeless people who've forgotten what they're shedding tears for, they just can't stop. That's when Heather lays her plan out to me, because, as she puts it, "Either this poor bitch is going to kill you, dearie, or she will drive you bonkers, and either way you're of no use to our people anymore." And I cry some more.

To join forces at the right hour, Heather instructs me, I have to fake a fainting spell on the line. I do it the next morning—"No point delaying," says Heather. I let my knees give, not while I'm working on the line but at the break, so the guard escorts me back to my cell and informs the night nurse, who won't budge on it unless I'm not up by morning. "She don't eat, that's the problem," I hear her say over the beeper. "Tell her she gotta eat if she's gonna stand up."

"Eat," says the night guard, offering no food, and she shuts the door loudly behind her.

Pockface Two's gone to breakfast, the only one of us who keeps almost normal hours. Heather sits up in her cot as soon as the door slams. "We've got five minutes," she says. "C'mon."

I follow her to the guard at the end of the hall, who writes us out a library pass without so much as looking up from the movie she's got booted on her screen. Heather's never taken me to the library before, but she's there most of the time, and they trust her. Briefly, as we clatter down the metal stairs and through the low corridor that runs underground to the next building, I wonder what trouble she will catch for this. It's not something I can ask; Heather would be insulted at the idea that some threshold of trouble would prevent her from doing what she thought was right.

"But we're not going to the library, are we?" I finally whisper, when we've passed underneath most of the next building and are headed back up another set of metal stairs, our steps ringing cold and loud.

"We're going through a corner of it," she says. "Through the side door, which gives onto the old illustrated volumes, and across to the catalog office, where there's a door that opens onto the main file room. It used to be fund-raising offices, when this was a college. They were all connected so the people who worked there could poke their noses into each other's business. They called it networking."

Now we're on the first floor, which is suddenly carpeted in a slate gray. However ill, Heather is walking fast, as she always does, like a little engine on full throttle. Somewhere behind us is the part of the library they've broken up into "areas," for therapy and retraining, high-ceilinged partitioned squares where they try to turn crack dealers into data-entry clerks. Sounds echo in those rooms; here there's a corporate hush. I can't believe that we'll be able to open any of these metal doors interrupting the wall, but Heather stops at the fifth one, puts a finger to her lips, and slowly turns the handle.

And then we step backward in time. I know this is just a side room, a place to store valuable junk, but still it occurs to me that I've never seen so many books in one place. I mean real books, with pages and covers. We had some at home, growing up—my mom liked to tuck her feet under her in the old wing chair and turn pages, she said she couldn't follow a story on the screen. And she liked mystery novels, too, which seemed all the stranger because they weren't in hypertext, so you couldn't follow any possibilities besides the ones laid out for you on the paper pages. But the rest of us in my family read files like everyone else, and by the time I was living with my dad in the apartment—how long ago it seems!—there were just three shelves filled with yellowing paperbacks and an ancient encyclopedia along the bottom row.

These books, though, stack up to the ceiling, and there's not a paperback to be seen—all maroon bindings and gilt letters on the spines, the metal shelves crammed end-to-end with black printed words on what must have been white paper once. Along the far wall, a glass case holds books the size of mainframes, opened as if to read, their pages puffing out from the center and settling in two striated waves down to their grainy covers. The room reeks of dust and a smell I remember from only once before in my life, that summer on Cape Cod with Marie, when one day we went on a tour of a maritime museum and the guard showed us briefly through the "map room"—stacks and scrolls of old hand-painted pictures of the earth, directions for voyagers. It had this same odor of dry paper, evaporated ink, musty leather.

I start to sneeze, and pinch my nose; Heather frowns at me. We're in a narrow alcove, unlit, at the back of the room; at the front, just visible through the overwhelming stacks, sits a prisoner under bright fluorescent light facing a laptop, scrolling through data; a paper volume sits open on her desk. Saving these books is Heather's pet project, and if we weren't fully staffed at the recycling plant, the administration would never allow it. We step across the narrow space—wood floor now—and Heather soundlessly turns the knob on an old wooden door.

The first room we stumble through is completely dark, but when Heather opens the door to the next, I can make out the comforting green glow and steady hum of a megadrive. Heather's mouth is at my ear. "I don't want the light," she says. "Can you feel your way?" I nod, though I'm not sure I can. Following the glow, I step around a desk, knock against a chair, and then sit in it; it swivels and rolls silently. I feel my way across the smooth surface to the oval keyboard and boot up. When it asks for password, I start with the most elementary—prison initials, nine-digit zip, and "login"; when that's rejected, I switch the order. It'll only give me five attempts or so before it shuts off access, but on the fourth try I hit it: WDUinit.utica. "Not real imaginative," I mutter under my breath. Heather shushes me; she's standing by the door, listening for footsteps. I rummage in the desk beside me, and she steps over. "What are you doing?" she whispers.

"Got to convert the disklet. Mainframe won't take a disk this small. Shit, I wish I had a flashlight." But just then my fingers find it, right where we used to store them at Viratect: a Chameleon, with slots for all five sizes, and next to it a stack of three-fives. "This'll just take a sec," I tell Heather. The surge protector's lit up, easy to find; I plug the thing in and get my poison onto a suitable disk, then go back to the mainframe. "Here goes," I say, though not to Heather. It scares me a little, what I'm doing. I have this peculiar instinct to warn the mainframe, to read it its rights. I've spent my short adult life, up to this prison time, relieving computer networks of these very viruses; I even had this neat parallel going, between what I accomplished at Viratect and what I accomplished in the clinic underneath Marie's house. Now I'm the incubus. I hesitate, the disk dangling from my fingers, the screen blinking its question at me. Then I flash on Lydia—on how she used to step into a procedure that was barely mucking along and punch out a string of commands that cut through to the heart of the system. Once or twice she lost the thread of what we were after; most times, though, she stripped the virus of all its disguises, so we could pluck it out without ancillary damage. Lydia wouldn't hesitate. I slide the disk into the slot.

"It's wonderful," I breathe. Heather tiptoes over. She watches as I order the viral program to unlock one directory after the other, as the programs obediently update and confirm application. Within subdirectories, I can make the infection automatic; the little pendulum that swings on the screen to suggest patience goes tick-tock a dozen or so times while one file after another blackens a bar in the application inset, and the message reads out, CONVERSION COMPLETE.

"How much longer?" Heather whispers impatiently after maybe five minutes.

"It's a big network," I say. "Give it a couple more minutes."

But it takes less time than that and never gives off a bleep or warning along the way. It's a rude form of the virus, surely; Jonathan or whoever may be called in will have it out of the system in a day or two. Still, Heather's right: it will give me time. "Done," I say, and exit the system, leaving the hard drive thrumming as it was when we came in, the green light holding steady.

"Hold on," whispers Heather. "Someone's back here."

We flatten ourselves against the wall—why, I don't know; instinct, maybe—while footsteps come back to the little alcove and try the door to the catalog office just outside this one. Too many clicks, maybe. I give silent thanks that we were able to work in the dark. The door closes. I hear the soft thunk of books being returned to their places, then a louder plop as one drops. "Shit!" exclaims the woman outside, and there's something of a scramble—maybe the binding broke when the book fell, and some pages have fallen out. Then the light blinks on in the alcove, filtering through both doors to us, and even after she's cleaned up and we hear her shuffling back to the front desk, it stays on.

"Keep low," Heather whispers. I peel myself off the wall and follow her. What will I do when I don't have her to follow? This sneaking, this business of sabotage and escape is new to me; I'm all thumbs at it. On the way through the alcove my toe stumbles on a book, more like a pamphlet, that the woman at the desk failed to scoop up. As if hiding evidence, I pick it up and tuck it into my deep shirt pocket.

Once we're safely back in the carpeted hall, we walk at the pace of a slow run to the exit stairs, down to the lower corridor, then through the dank hallway back toward the main building. I'm out of breath, not so much because we're moving so fast as because I can't bring air fully into my lungs. "Here," says Heather, and she takes a sudden left into a narrow corridor I've never noticed before. "Up this way," she says.

These aren't stairs, but a metal ladder, leading to a hatch in the ceiling. I glance left and right, sure we'll be found now. "I thought you were going to check in at the library," I say—stalling, I realize. "You know, so they wouldn't trace your whereabouts."

"Shit, I forgot. Do it after. Five minutes, and we'll have you on your way."

"You sure? I don't want them after you."

"They're too stupid, don't worry about it. You've got bigger fish."

She lifts the hatch, and I follow her up and through. We're in the food hall now, emasculated Prometheus staring dolefully at us from the far wall. Late-afternoon light filters through the arched windows. In the back, we can hear the clatter of pots—prisoners working the kitchen, preparing early dinner for Heather's crew. "So this is how people get in," I say, "to paint the genitals." I nod at the painting.

"Not in the past. Remember, that downstairs corridor's locked off at night. And there's no time between day shifts to execute a good painting." She grins at me, but we keep moving—like bugs, along the wall toward the lit kitchen. I spot the air shaft just before she stops and points it out to me: a latticed grille, ten feet off the floor at the kitchen entrance, one of those old-fashioned exhaust pipes with a tiny fan attached to the inside of the grille to blow smoke out if the kitchen got too greasy. "We used to climb in where it opens onto the guards' kitchen—you know, at the end of our hallway?"

"I thought they sealed that off!"

"That's why our friend's anatomy's been incomplete for five weeks. But listen now. The other end of this shaft comes out at the roof, the side by the woods. Take this." She reaches in the big square pocket of her flannel shirt and pulls out what at first looks like a huge crumpled plastic bag. "If you can drop down to one of the gables just below, there, you should be able to jump to the wall. There's bushes on the other side, and a mile to town once you find the road. Here." She hands me a wad of moldy paper.

"What's this?" I've unfolded the bag, which *is* a bag—or rather, a string of them, knotted one to the next, and double thick. Heather must have been retrieving them from the plastics belt for weeks, weaving them into a rope ladder. Now I'm looking at the green wad.

"Paper money. Cash. They'll still take it if you go to one of the smaller towns."

"But I've got my card. The numbers are scrambled—that network covers the whole state, I'm sure of it."

"You also said it was one of the easy bugs to get out. This"—she closes my hand over the wad—"is for when they've got it unscrambled."

There are voices in the kitchen: no time to thank her, to hug, to ask again why I'm playing at escape. Heather bends down and I hoist onto her shoulders, using the wall for balance as she straightens. It's easy to unlatch the air shaft with its little fan. Inside, the endless cylinder is dark and primitive as anatomy. I stick my head inside it, like the trainer in the lion's mouth, ready to pull out when the jaws close. Then Heather, smart lady, gives a little jounce with her shoulders, and I'm through the shaft—too narrow to turn around, to close the hatch behind me, but Heather reaches up with a broom handle or something; I hear the latch click shut, and I'm inside the tube, in blackness, pushing like a baby toward what I've heard rumored to be light.

CHAPTER 19

What astonishes me is how simple it is; what astonishes me is how little, past Heather's help, I need accomplices. Always, in the old hypertext games we used to play as teenagers, when the woman needed to escape danger there was a man at the ready. You had choices—she could signal for him, he could follow a set of clues, he could give his life for her—but whatever route you took, he helped save or salvage her. Well, there was Jonathan, it was his disk. But the script's still calling for a man, and love has been known to follow a script.

I walk, walk, walk. Through the back alleys of the town that's sprung up around Softjail, or just converted from what must have been a college town—low frame buildings, a church by the green—I wind onto the secondary road, six miles to Utica. My legs are aching by the time I'm in the familiar maze of gritty streets that connects upscale New Hartford to downtown, but it's nerves as much as the workout. I stop at a video arcade. Sure enough, there's an old system, tucked into a booth at the back. Punching in my number, I tell myself I'm not sending for help, only testing the virus. *Yes,* I mouth when it goes through—I'm still scrambled, my code still floating free among the fiber-optic lines. But that can't be all I wanted to find out, because I hang on still, until a voice comes on from the other end.

"Levinsky," he says, sounding tired, as if he's been playing a guessing game too long and *Levinsky* is the last choice he can think of. I can only get audio; the tiny screen's an underwater swirl of gray.

"I'm out," I say.

There's a long silence—or not so long, maybe, but just enough for panic to grab me, and I'm ready for disappointment in Arthur's voice, disappointment that he didn't manage to play the savior role, or even that he has to cope with me, now.

Then he speaks. Maybe there hasn't been a silence at all, just the lag of the lines. His voice gets under my skin, unsnags my muscles. "Tell me what to do," he says.

And it occurs to me that there's nothing for him to do, that despite love, despite the whole package, the worst plan of all would be for Arthur to do anything that would leave a trail. I detect a little sigh, escaping, flying over the fiber optic, and I can picture Arthur rubbing his forehead, as if it's a worry stone. A practical man, I think. Not a dreamer like Rudi. Marie, you would have liked him. No, you wouldn't have; you'd have laughed at his corny ways, at me and him together. I pull a clotted strand of lint from the sleeve of my khaki shirt; I picked them up, cobwebs and dustballs, on my way out through the air shaft, until when I emerged above the woods I looked like an oak hung with Spanish moss.

"Nothing," I say.

Funny, when I hang up, how loud the sound of the arcade is. From outside there comes a biting wind—something that's trying to be snow is being flung wetly up against the window, and pedestrians squeeze their collars up around their chins, imitating turtles. Somewhere out there, people in uniforms are searching for me: *Twenty-six-year-old female, height five-seven, weight one-twenty, shoulder-length brown hair, freckles, left-handed, no distinguishing marks.* Behind me, young men jam their cards into machines and go to battle; they slam their hips up against the control deck as they release agonies of death from the screens. Astonishing how these things have lasted. I slide my back down along the glass wall until I'm crouched, facing in. The corner next to me is piled with junk left behind—a hand-held game, a greasy hat, a ripped flannel shirt that's lint-strewn, like me. Half the machines are out of order. You can get any of these on the Web now, and I remember when Lydia said the arcades would just die out, like network TV. But there's something in the hot, rubbery air here, the shared sweat

of frustration, that keeps these guys coming back, to deplete their cards
in the slot for Mortal Kombat Ten or Desperado. Some of them stay
here for hours—they'll emerge at the end of the day like gamblers,
broke and dazed, not happy but with a burden lifted.

Besides me, there are no women here. They never come to these
places. I'm as good as invisible, hunkered next to the system; the only
reason for one of the joystick-plunging guys to notice me would be to
rape me, and they won't do that here.

But I can't stay. Out on the street, it's night. Taking the flannel shirt
with me, I step into the cold, my chin tucked into the plaid collar as I
pull it on, fastening the buttons that are left. Something falls out of my
shirt pocket, and I pick it up—the little pamphlet I grabbed on my
way out of the library. *Phaedo,* the cover reads, and I remember some
argument from college, democracy and freedom. In my pocket I finger the roll Heather's blessed me with. I'll start using it, I figure, when
I reach Canada.

Only I don't get that far. It's late at night, after all, and by the time I
hit Utica I'm tired. No, not tired, only cold and damp and vaguely
hungry. No buses will be leaving until morning. That's what I tell myself as I skirt my father's neighborhood, arms crossed over my chest
and feet moving relentlessly. Perhaps I make my way to Marie's red
house not so much for shelter as to say good-bye. I can't say. I only
know that I'm on the porch and then running the old pattern through
the door lock, and it still works, and I am inside.

Well, Lloyd, I think, as my eyes adjust to the darkness indoors, you
did your work. I stand free in my sister's house, and there is no sign
of my sister. The main room is empty except for a tattered oval rug
near the fireplace that I don't recognize. In the kitchen there's nothing
to eat, though the refrigerator's there, humming nicely, the inside light
like a voice of welcome. My footsteps clap on the hard floor; bending
stiffly down, I pull off my shoes and carry them by the fingers of my
right hand. Moonlight slides through the glass doors from the
screened porch, where Marie used to serve minted iced tea to her mis-

conceiver friends and probably to Omar Jeffries. Carefully I make my way to the door by the pantry, then shut it behind me as I descend the old wooden stairs to the basement. Here, I can switch on a light, its yellow glare squeezing my eyelids. Beyond the furnace, the door to what used to be the clinic gapes wide, and I can tell without stepping in that everything's gone. At the moment when I reach the last step, the cool of the concrete floor like a river beneath my feet, I'm socked with fatigue, and I sink down. Surely this wasn't the right place to come, but for tonight I can go no further.

There are a few things left, of course—I remember now, my eyes adjusting, scanning the big basement room, that Lloyd said he hadn't completely cleared the place out. Some boxes in the corner. I let my head rest between my knees, and the *Phaedo* falls out again; I tuck it into my back pocket. What things? I wonder. What bits of my sister, what flotsam and jetsam? Nothing to do with misconceiving, surely—they'd have removed all that. Clothes, perhaps? Or old cooking utensils—she was such a great cook, she could be excused for taking pride in it, and she replaced cookware as soon as it got scratched or dented. Blankets, maybe, that I can shape into a bed. Levering my hands against my knees in their khaki pants and rising up, I make my way over to the small stash in the corner. No blankets here, only a box of Marie's sketches—feet and shoulders—and the plastic toys she kept around for clients' kids, when they had to amuse themselves during the procedure. And behind the toy box, a smaller, plastic container—CD-ROMs and three-fives, half the slots filled. This surprises me—I'd think they would have been taken when she was arrested—until I see the labels: *Graphic Art, '06–'10; College Essays; Yearbook, 2005.* These were probably spot-checked and then left behind; Marie was too smart to keep lists on disk anyway.

Squatting, I hold Marie's high school yearbook flat on my palm, like food you'd feed to a horse. There's something here, something here. My mind's not working fast enough—I should make a pillow of the flannel shirt, a bed of Marie's sketches, and catch some sleep. But I keep holding the CD instead, until memory works its way from my palm up my arm and into a prickly place at the back of my neck. Unsnapping my Minilap from my waist, I boot up and slide in the CD.

It downloads slowly; my Minilap's failing, planned obsolescence. First I find Marie's photo, unsmiling though beautiful, her hair old-fashioned, some snippet of poetry as the caption; there's a link to five seconds of her playing basketball—very primitive video—and for sound, a tape of some girl group singing about freedom. She was always shy, I remember, about her own voice. Then I search Anderson. No matches, the screen tells me, and suggests Andreson, but that's just a boy with big ears. I scroll: Abbott, Alden, Anders, Archer.

"You never knew her," I say, as if to Lydia. "It's not just that you never visited her. You never *met* her." My heart's banging in my bruised chest. "Another name? Okay," I say, and I scroll from the beginning, linking all the colorful faces with their clear eyes and hesitant grins—Brindle, Buford, Caldwell, Chavez, Clemson—looking for the face unstruck by age, for the marks that don't change. Bone structure, eyes; I zoom to the set of the mouth. McWilliams, Mandell, Meese, Montgomery, Murphy, Murphy. It's been more than two decades, I remind myself, and I go through the alphabet backward—Wurstheimer, Wilson, Westover, West. Finally I boot up the Junior Class picture—maybe she was a year behind. Brightening the screen as far as it will go, I scrutinize all the faces lined up on the school steps, the names on the link. It was a sunny day and most are squinting, but even through the hazy edges of time and a bad photograph, none of the girls looks remotely like Lydia Anderson.

I shut down the CD and hug my Minilap to my chest. Tired as I am, my muscles are jumping to leave the house. Make my way to the bus station and wait for the first express heading toward Toronto. Get out of this trap—quick, before it catches me. But the moment passes, and the next, and by the third I know I can't leave now. Once again, I boot up the photo of Marie, and it's like one of those pictures of Jesus they sell in little chapels: her brown eyes follow me everywhere, no matter what angle I give to the screen. "For we are put on earth a little space," her caption reads—it's by a guy named Blake, I don't know him—"that we may learn to bear the beams of love."

· · ·

Two days later, I slip uptown to see Miss MacDonald. The wind is still, the weak sun shining, no one's discovered me, and I've got myself booked into a residence hotel for a month. I've loaded up on rice pilaf, canned fruit and vegetables, chili, a liter of Scotch, cooking and eating utensils; I've furnished myself a basic wardrobe; I've got a coffee can full of bus tokens. In the process of scrambling numbers, the virus managed to thaw my account—temporarily, anyway—but even so, my resources are limited. My father's savings and life insurance were never transferred to me, but to a trust account I don't have the PIN for. I've missed out on eight months' wages. When I charge a winter coat on sale at Ormond's, the clerk tells me there's a red warning on my file—less than a grand to go—and I thank her for the info.

The residence hotel was my only choice. I couldn't stay at the red house, which was surely one of the first places they checked. Any apartment rental agreement would have logged onto my account number for security. Long before the next payment came due, my number and my dossier would be matched up again. I could have put card money down on, say, a small trailer home, but there would have been installments; or even if by some miracle I'd been able to buy the thing in one transaction, there would have been utility bills, taxes, insurance—all drawn from my number, traceable. Everywhere I looked, I had to account for my number not just today but next week, next month, next year. The residence hotel—one I used to pass now and then, taking back streets from Marie's red house to Rudi's place—is giving me thirty days' reprieve. True, the roundheaded clerk took the number in case of long-distance calls, but once he'd downloaded a month's worth of residency, he didn't log it into any network where it could be traced. He was only too happy to have cash money up front, and I looked to him like a nice young lady a bit lost in the world.

Now, waiting outside Miss MacDonald's small office, I feel like a stranger to myself. I've cut my hair to match the fringe that's grown out over the scar on the back of my skull, and I've dyed it harsh blond, so that it resembles a brass helmet cupped over my head. The clothes I've bought with my scrambled card are far more drab and sensible than the ones I'm used to wearing—wool pants, turtleneck, boots, all in shades of gray. I look like a librarian caught unsuspecting by a kamikaze hairdresser. When Miss MacDonald motions me in and directs me to a smooth, sloping wood chair with paddlelike arms, she sits opposite behind her small desk and examines me, head to toe.

"I would know you," she says in her small, sharp voice, "but only from the eyes."

"I came to say," I start in, casting my eyes downward a little—Miss MacDonald's are hard to meet—"that I'm sorry about the trial. I wish I could have followed it through, I really do. I'm not indifferent to— to the situation of others."

She nods, quick bobbings of her powdered chin. She's dressed in bright red, a tailored pantsuit that sets off the white of her hair. For the first time I glance around her office, at the degrees on the back wall and the slender Indonesian carvings on the shelf above her law CD-ROMs. It's a tasteful office, even a daring one—on the wall to my right hangs a series of charcoal sketches of a woman's upper torso. As my eyes lock onto the art, I get a peculiar sense of dislocation, almost vertigo; when I turn back to Miss MacDonald, she's smiling. Abruptly I stand and step closer to the sketches—sure enough, there's *M. Chambers* scrawled hastily in the lower-right-hand corner. "You never told me you had her work," I say.

"You never asked. I met her at a little show at—where was it, now? Oh well, doesn't matter—one of those half-underground places where good and bad artists try to sell their things on behalf of good and bad causes. I try to buy from the good, when I've got the money."

"She was good," I say, my eye on the charcoals, still, regaining my equilibrium.

"She was," agrees Miss MacDonald, but she's looking at me, not at the art. "Not a saint, though."

"Why do you say that?" My question comes fast, a retort.

"I didn't know her." Miss MacDonald shakes her head, dismissing her own testimony. But I'm not going to let her off the stand. "People are susceptible," she says. "They begin by believing one thing, and then they are persuaded of another. Sometimes it's not fair, the means used to persuade them. But then you point out the unfairness, you try to persuade them back. And sometimes you succeed, and sometimes not. It's called living in a free society."

"You think that's what we've got?"

Miss MacDonald's mouth curls upward, the kind of smile she might let a jury see, in a courtroom, to suggest how absurd the evidence is without getting objected to. "There's your sister in you," she says, a remark that stings me in an odd place. I loved my sister, I want to say but can't. "Look," she goes on, "there were—still are—a lot of people who want to change this law. But not everyone who wants it changed believes that we should go back, that women should have casual access. The coalition targets the middle ground—and yes, some are willing to compromise; but they don't go out and betray individual people! They don't want the law to stay as it is!"

"What's this got to do with my sister's sainthood?"

"She more or less had a group that blacklisted people who waffled. This is documented." Miss MacDonald presses her palms against the warped wood of her desk, as if pressing on reams of paper. I think of Marie's friends, the spiced cider and iced tea, the laughter and odd silences around me in those days. "For Marie Chambers it was all or nothing, for or against. Where most of us want freedom, she wanted orthodoxy. And she lost us some friends. Influential friends. That's all I mean. It was her human failing, I think—not to allow for human failing."

I can't remember their names, not a single one. Only the way they greeted Marie, great wrapping hugs. I've started to cry. Miss MacDonald, her hand trembling, passes me a tissue. "And you think I'm like her," I say into my chest.

"No, I don't. That's why I had hopes for your legal case. For hers, there wouldn't have been a chance."

"Sorry I let you down." I blow my nose, wad the tissue. She shrugs, a gesture younger than her years.

"This thing's bigger than me, God knows," she says. "You're doing what you need. And no, I don't want to know how you managed the break. I am surprised to find you still in town. Do you know how fortunate you are?"

I shake my head, start to speak, but she holds up a thin hand. Then she tells me she's had three calls for me. One from Lloyd, one from Rudi Hauser, and one—just this morning—from the district attorney.

She told each of them the truth: that she hadn't heard from me. The D.A. wanted me to know, if I got in contact, that Sheri St. Clair raised a scene when she learned of the break, just last night. "She started after someone else with a curtain rod," said Miss MacDonald. "They recognized the style, you see." A slow, sad smile plays on her lips as she explains how Sheri's in maximum, up in Oneonta, with her bail held up now that she wants it. I can go back to Softjail without fear; or I can wait until that window closes and Sheri sues and they release her on bail. "To get the drop on *you,* you see," says Miss MacDonald, almost primly.

Lloyd and Rudi, it seems, left no messages. I stand up, shrug off my coat. It's suddenly warm in the little office. I step over to Marie's charcoal sketches, and brush dust off the tops of the black frames. "Sheri's the reason I left," I say finally. "But she isn't the reason I won't go back."

"The longer you're out—"

"I know," I say. I pick one frame off the wall—it's a charcoal of a woman's breasts, sloping away from one another, full toward the side. My breasts, I think. "My sister wasn't a saint," I say, "but she didn't deserve to die."

"She didn't even deserve prison! *That* was why I wanted to file your case."

"But people don't just get caught by accident. Especially not when they're careful. Look, it may all be water over the dam for you," I say. Putting the charcoal back, I turn to plant the backs of my knuckles on Miss MacDonald's desk and lean on my arms in her direction. "But I need to find someone, and I can't do it from the WDU. I'm giving myself a month, that's all I wanted to tell you. And if you choose not to handle my case when they do catch up with me, I'll understand perfectly."

She pauses a long while. Her right hand twirls an old-fashioned pen through the fingers, index to pinky to index, a tiny baton. Then she says, "Good," and sticks the pen back in its holder, as if it's given her the word. I'm disappointed, childishly—I'd hoped, of course, that she would promise to aid and abet, to step back in at the crucial moment like a petite white-haired knight. Where there isn't a hero, there's a fairy godmother. "We have another case, you know," she goes on, as if I've said nothing ominous, told her of no threatening plans. "A nurse who's been implanting IUDs. Since there's no fetus present at time of implantation, we'll argue, her crime can be no greater than that of dispensing a weapon to a potential murderer, which could be any of us. This reduces her sentence and throws the burden on the woman, of course, but we've got a whole line of argument up our sleeves for that."

"Great," I say. I stand straight, feeling a bit slapped by Miss MacDonald's cheerful coolness, her keeping to the path of legal action. But then I can see, from the nervous cast of her eyes, that I had better stop talking to her, telling her my plans. There are such things, her expression implies, as subpoenas. "I'd better be going," I say. "If I'm back at the old place, I'm sure you'll hear about it."

She stands to take my hand; her grasp is as firm as ever. "I have always believed in you," she says before I turn away. Which may be a reproach or a promise, it's impossible to say. I make my way out of her small, light-filled office, past the other legal offices on the corridor, back down to the anonymous street.

CHAPTER 20

It's like the deer seeking the hunter—fruitless and suicidal. Walking the streets of Utica with my brassy hair and my smoke-colored clothes, I hold my breath as police cars cruise by. Wherever I spot a possibility, I stop to ask about Lydia.

Workplaces first. Utica's got a dozen network service companies, five of them in the same park as Viratect. One by one I enter their doors, start to register on the touchscreen, and then tell the monitor I'm here for Lydia Anderson. *No such employee,* they each respond, blinking their little red warning lights.

Next, bars. Not the seedy spaces near my hotel, but the glass-walled Interbars we used to move through so freely, with their Virtual Rooms and Nightwebs. You can't buy a drink with cash at these places, so I don't linger long; I drift, as if looking for my date, until I reach the ladies' room, then I check it out and drift forward again. I get a little scared in these places—not of something happening to me, but of what's already happened to the way I look at things. Compared to the retros I see on the river landing, the young people in the bars—their fingers dancing over the little screens in each booth, their buggy glasses in the Virtual Room, their plastic cards sliding in and out of the slot on the drink tray—seem like some kind of cyberinvention to me; I can click them off with a touch of the right screen.

But I don't find Lydia in any of them.

The notion that Lydia could have taken another name occurs to me once or twice, but that's a ruse from the last century—you can't manage it now, not unless you plan to spend the rest of your life among the retros who gather by the river under the new expressway to trade their wares. We live, as the old video has it, documented lives. Mine is documented; so is Arthur's; so was my sister's; and so, unless she knows tricks the rest of us haven't caught on to yet, must Lydia Anderson's be.

I know the retros better than I did long ago in that other life, when I observed them by the beach in St. Monica or from the cafe where I first felt that queer stirring of the blood for Arthur. I pay with cash now—after a few days, the card became too dangerous—and so I shop at the pathetic little corner groceries that meet the needs of the cash class. Shifty-eyed owners size me up and figure I'll neither slip their merchandise off the shelves nor try to pay in pharmaceuticals. When my feet are aching from a day roaming the city for this woman who claimed to know my sister, who claimed to love my sister, I sidle down to the cobbled slope by the honey-brown river in the cold dusk and listen to the nightly music. The people there don't mind the way I look, though it doesn't fit with their shaved heads and heavy tunics. The other night, an older man—tall, with weatherbeaten face and hands but the frail mouth of a professor—offered me a cigarette that I figured fairly quickly for weed, the smell that same dark sweetness that I used to inhale around patients like Rita. He was talking with a crew that huddled on large rocks and stumps around a dying fire, steel-band music going not far off. Swallowing more than breathing, I enjoyed the taste of the weed, like malt edged with burnt almonds. As I leaned close to the group talking, I realized I was eavesdropping the way someone from Viratect would—listening for clues to the latest virus planting, keys to the conspiracy. But they were talking about children. "I am telling you motherfuckers," the tall one was saying to the rest, "it's a problem we oughta slam back in their faces. Just yesterday, in the river, froze to death, three days old."

"Take 'em to the orphanage," came a voice from farther off.

"Now there's an insane idea. Might as well shoot the poor creatures."

"I say shoot the bastards who leave 'em off," said a short, squat man about my age. "Baby killers."

"Listen to you, playing the Coalition's hand for them," said a woman's voice—I couldn't see her on the far side of the fire.

"For who? You see me leaving kids with swelled brains out in the rain to starve?"

"I see you blaming the girls who got no choice in *having* them."

"They can keep their panties on."

"That never made too much diff to you, Spade," came the tall man's voice again, and there was a general laugh. They went on about the abandoned kids—whom I'd seen, with groups of retros: encephalitic or palsied toddlers, kids with staring eyes or shrunken chests. What I'd heard was that they came from the drugs these people did, or the way they led their lives. The woman kept coming in, with her hard impatient voice.

"I am *telling* you," she said when they'd listed the ones who'd died, the ones who'd ruined the lives of people who adopted them, "we got to stop this jamming to each other and start jamming to media."

"Not till it's in print, I won't," said the tall man.

"Fuck print. You're not getting print back."

"Says who? There's that guy started a newspaper on the North Side—"

"And went under."

"Well, you cannot do battle on the Web," said the man my age.

"Their turf," agreed the tall man.

"Might as well get your card and sign on," said a man I couldn't see, his voice tight with smoke from the cigarette I'd passed back, or another, I couldn't tell.

"Oh, fuck the buncha youse," said the woman. "Inside, you boys're dying for your cards, and that's the truth. You hate 'em because you can't get 'em."

"And you're different, hey?"

"I see something wrong," she shot back. She was standing away from the fire, by then, her hands on her broad hips, her hair grown out almost as long as mine but spiking up from her head, her nose swollen with exposure. "I see something wrong with us 'tros playing nursery school for the freaks of this world. I see something wrong with the fucking system. I see something wrong with the fact with all your little homeless fuckdollies, I got no *women* to talk to around here." She turned to strut away as they snickered. "'Cept you," she added scornfully, passing me, and I felt what a spy I was.

And then, late, with the music faded to a low, stoned screech and the fires down to embers, I come back to my residence hotel with its odor of cheese and bad coffee and old, old vomit. A suitcase I found on the street yawns open on my room's one table, serving as a dresser for my fistful of clothes. I think about these things the retros say, and the divisions blur between them and the cash people, like Rita or Roxanne's Marta—and the rectangular slip of plastic that sits dead in my waistpac feels more and more like a sweepstakes ticket, a useless thing I've collected in the foolish faith that a group of people somewhere have a good thing planned for me.

Sometimes I think I am turning into a politician, and I laugh at myself on Marie's behalf. Can I clear the sand out of your ears? she used to ask me, when I slipped away from brunch to wash dishes. It's packed in there, from shoving your head so far in the sand.

Nothing wrong with sand, I think. Even now, on Lydia's trail like a heat-seeking missile, I want to know nothing—not how she latched on to Marie and then me, not what evidence she came up with, not whether she's acting alone. I only want to launch a bare fist at her face, twist her neck until she cries out. I want her to plead with me to stop, and ask her if she heard my sister's pleas.

And then what? Then what, Marie? I've started talking to my sister this way, as if she's watching me with the ghost of a smile on her face, waiting to see if I'll take the right path. Like all partners in imagined conversations, she never says anything. Then, Marie, I say, you will be satisfied. Because you know the answers to all those why-questions already, and I don't need to know them.

Two weeks pass; three. I'm low on cash. Every day it rains on the city, a steady disinterested downpour that tapers off in the evening to a cold mist. I shiver at night and drink the Scotch and pull my new gray wool jacket over my shoulders on top of the thin blanket the hotel provides. Upstairs, a couple fucks early every morning, a hard rhythm followed by the thump of his shoes as he slides them on and stands to dress. My head aches where the crack never healed right. I don't know what I'll do when I run out of greenbacks. Sometimes, standing in front of the slice of mirror someone tacked to the cracked wall of my room, I touch my body. I run a finger around my breasts and down across my navel. I name myself. I marvel at the facts—*this is the body of an escaped convict; this is the body of someone who spends only cash*—the way I remember marveling just after I first got my period, or lost my virginity, and I was amazed at how familiar I seemed to myself. I look at my hands—did they actually close on forceps, pull the thin, slippery not-person out from woman after woman? Surely not. *This is the body of a murderer.*

Then, making my way home from the cash market by the river, I find someone. Not Lydia. Rather a tall, round-shouldered girl stirring a pot of some sort of gruel over a makeshift fire. All I feel at first is that odd sense of being stared at, and when I look up she's got her spoon lifted in her hand, her eyes on me, smiling a little crooked.

"Well," Christel says, when it's clear I can't slide past or pretend not to know her, "looks like we're both hiding in the same hollow log, huh, Phoebe?"

"Good Christ."

"No, good Christel. You know, like the stuff you don't want to chip?"

"I thought you were going back to school."

"Changed my mind, I guess." She smiles, in that hazy space between shamefaced and proud. In six months she's put on twenty pounds, and it's an odd sort of weight—a grim fattiness around her chin and upper arms, distracting from the blue saucers of her eyes. She's wearing a vaguely melon-colored sweatshirt and khaki pants; her hair's grown out, and curls over her ears, which are both newly studded. "I couldn't concentrate anymore. The YDs—you remember them?"

"Your singing group."

"Yeah, well they kept coming around and talking about the right track, how to get me on the right track. There was this one boy, Jed"—Christel stopped to taste the soup, her face wrinkling at the sour heat of it—"he liked to sit on my floor with his legs crossed, and he had pointy ears and a thick neck, the girls in the YDs thought he was handsome, you could tell, and he talked about Jesus never was for mingling races—"

"Slow it down, Christel." Her voice has been coming faster and more breathy, as she stirs the soup with quick whips of her heavy arm.

"Right, well I just said to this Jed, I said, Man, don't you even have a cock? and they all went white and prayed for me. Oh, Phoebe, you would've loved it!"

Christel giggles. An older woman comes up, glares at me, and tastes the soup. Three or four others hover behind her. I want to move on. I've got my vegetables, and, apart from Lydia, I have no reason even to be in this city, much less in this other river-world that neither Christel nor I would ever approach in our real lives. "Does your mother know where you are?" I ask.

"I called." She grins, like a cartoon. "I talked to Marta, *she* knows I'm fine. But, hey, my mom's probably in town right now, snooping around for me. I tore up my card."

"You can always get a new card," I say. Christel doesn't answer this one, just leans down to smell the soup. I step closer, away from the ones hovering. "I'm afraid," I say, "I did this to you, Chris."

Christel looks at me. Her mouth hovers somewhere between the cautious smile of a child who doesn't want to be spanked and the arrogant lip curl of an old woman who's seen it all. I'm reminded, impossibly, of a twelve-year-old girl I never met. Most of the ones waiting behind her are men. "Come with me," I say, stretching out my free hand. "I haven't got much of a place, but—we'll get hold of your mom, she's not so bad. Or you can stay with me, we'll scrape some money together, I've still got my card. My—my business can wait. You don't look so great, Chris."

"She *is* great." A tall, stringy guy, his head unshaved but his thin dark hair plaited down the back, comes up to put a hand on Christel's shoulder. "She's busy," he adds, and then he turns to Christel and whispers something in her ear that makes her giggle and lift her shoulder, as if to brush him lightly away. The others take a step forward. They scare me. Christel won't look up; she stirs the soup, the hand on her shoulder like a mute button.

"I'm out of my element, Chris," I say, but she's deaf too, her newly grown hair hiding her face—I wouldn't have noticed her like this, would have passed her by. I'm standing on the knife of a ridge, my choices descending around me on all sides. "I've got to go," I say. Backing off, I move slowly; I'm waiting for someone to announce it: *You did this to her, forced her hand. She should have had the baby. This is your burden, carry it.* But no one announces anything.

People—retros—start bumping into me, though the cobblestones aren't crowded. The rank smell of the river drifts up. The stringy guy's whispering something else to Christel, and she shakes her head, shakes her head, as if she's flirting at one of the innocent dances she used to go to with her Christian friends. A guy on the far side of the fire gives me the signal, arms in front of his face and wrists crossed. I turn and walk rapidly away.

And so, Marie, I've failed. Have left Christel—who maybe should have borne her baby, who knows? women do such things and are happy—to the confused mass that comes at society like horses in an ether dream, from impossibly far away moving impossibly fast. Have lost Lydia and so got no vengeance for you. I'm down to thirty-eight dollars. Must I give up Canada, give up Arthur? You wouldn't make me, Marie—you made mistakes yourself, plenty of them.

It's five-thirty, two days after I've seen Christel. Tomorrow I'll leave—my cardboard suitcase in hand and my greenbacks in pocket, running away. Like a picnicker with a favorite hypertext, I'm resting my back against a tree on the grassy knoll opposite Viratect, a new angle from which to observe them all striding out of the building to their home stations. Here come Jonathan and Gerald, together but not touching of course, looking a little grim, parting ways at the curb. Three of the office assistants, checking their beepers even as they leave. Tim the Pentecostalist who always stops just outside the door, to unbutton or button his jacket, this time pulling his raincoat collar up at the back of his neck—damp weather, March. For a minute I think he's staring at me, and I see again that name, Tim Williams, on the list of Marie's visitors. Then he starts as if he's been daydreaming and heads off to his black Volt, and I meditate on coincidence.

So far I'm following routine, with Viratect the hopeless box I keep opening and finding empty. Last time, I tell myself. Pocketing today's disposable Newsweb, I haul to my feet and weave through the thin poplars to the parking lot. There's Tim still, leaning on the hood of his car, hooked up to audio and talking more energetically than I'm used to. He's a handsome man, in a coyote sort of way. The old uneasy feeling of recognition comes over me. Oh, help me here, Marie.

The first time I met him, making the introductory rounds at Viratect, I thought, I know that guy. And I did. I still do. I know his face.

Leaning on his car, he's got his jacket askew, a thumb resting in a belt loop. To see people, sometimes, you have to pull a trick of the eyes—lift them out of their surroundings, the walls and floors and parking lots that give them shape. What I know about Tim is a smell of coffee and cinnamon, the low background static of argument. His body would be half-hidden by a glass coffee table. I see Heather. I see a shelf of tchotchkes. I see . . .

Yes, I see him. See him the way he used to lean on the CD case in Marie's ranch house, and talk with the same energy, his Adam's apple jumping in his throat. I blink but still see him, long ago reaching for blue corn chips and laughing, that same disturbing high pitch to his laugh that used to get me on edge at Viratect. A beard, he had a beard then, and something else on his face, glasses maybe. Older than Marie.

I blink and blink, but the image keeps getting clearer instead of going away. Tim the Pentecostalist is—was—one of Marie's gang, the Sunday-morning-muffin group, her other family who disbanded only when they started going to jail.

Going to jail. Marie's list of visitors. *Tim Williams.* I have to remind myself to breathe. I have to watch, to see everything now.

Tim's eyes are fixed high up, across the industrial park, where I can make out a figure standing behind the glass wall. Squinting my eyes against the light fog, I can tell it's a woman—tall, full-figured. My heartbeat doubles. If Tim's not really a Pentecostalist, if he's a member of Mau-Mau, then whoever turned Marie in—whoever turned me in—is surely tightening the noose for him, too. And if that is Lydia, high up in the next building, waving down at him—

I almost call out. I take a step forward; my lips part. Then suddenly Tim shuts down audio, and the figure high up backs away from the glass, and he drives off. I've got no way to follow him. Tomorrow, I think. Tomorrow I can warn the man. And my heels click across the parking lot, running to the place where I saw—must have seen—Lydia.

The glass building isn't one I've checked; I don't know how I missed it. A narrow building with—I count floors—a laser-room designer's office on the twentieth. The virtual doorman's shut off, elevators key-coded. I cruise around the structure. Four entrances, each one leading to a different parking lot, and no car that I recognize as Lydia's in any of them. I crouch by one entrance for ten minutes, then move around to the next—but it's hopeless. One by one, the cars in the lots disappear, their owners leaving by the entrance I've just left or the one I haven't come to yet. As night starts to fall, two women pass me, but neither of them is Lydia and neither looks like the figure I saw standing behind glass, waving at Tim.

And then it's dark, and everyone's vanished. I walk back, down the curving drive and then the long streets, descending toward the city, the river.

Back in my room with its moldy carpeting and buried sighs, I don't know what I've seen, if anything. Tim's face seems to have no features anymore; I fill it in, like an Easy-Art program. Surely he wasn't around in those last years; the memory's diffuse, which is why—in addition to the beard—I hadn't recognized him before. And of course he would never come out to me. Fooled me, instead, with all that religious hype. But Lydia—Lydia at the window!

Lying on my thin mattress, I touch myself, uncorking wrath—*This is the body that could be making love right now, but for Lydia; this is the place where the skull's cracked; this is my young body, younger than Marie's; this is Marie's body, festering in the ground, this is . . . this is . . .*

No. No. This is not Marie's body. I sit up, switch on the yellow light. It's two A.M.; I've drifted but not slept. My breath comes shallow, rapid. Hugging my knees, I press my forehead to them; my head hurts. Tomorrow, I think. I'll just hang on until tomorrow, and then I'll find it was a dead lead, after all—Tim will look like a stranger to me, and the woman in the window will prove to be Sally Smith or Julie Jones, anyone but Lydia Anderson. And then—*then, Marie*—I will leave this town.

My watch blinks at me—two-fifteen, three-thirty, four. I've learned to dream while awake. Lying on my back, eyes to the mottled ceiling, I dream of the places I could have got to if I'd set my path out earlier—Mexican desert, Canadian forest, darkness and light. Arthur: *Tell me what to do.* The government can extradite you from Canada, but it takes a long time. I have been a fool. In the damp dawn, I rise unrested, place my back to the just-warm radiator, step in my cheap shoes into the bathroom I share with the three old men who live on this floor—leftovers, like the steam heat and the analog clock in the lobby, from the twentieth century. Here by the washbasin, the window's wide open—too much heat—and I hear the sounds of the city waking: the purr of electric motors, the clank of construction. I can even make out the smoke of trash-can fires down by the river where Christel may have spent the night. At this moment, back in Softjail, Heather is lining up for the morning shift on glass; the avuncular doctor is making his visit to the infirmary. Down in Binghamton, at State, Sheri is pacing her cell, a real cell, her lovely dark face ravaged by rage and grief; she's refused to work, surely, and punishments heap upon her.

I must move quickly, get up to Viratect to warn Tim, then stake out that other building. And then? I don't know; I'm not thinking clearly enough to know. I should have a weapon of some kind, something to make her come with me. A small knife, maybe, or a razor; I can afford a razor. The thought makes my hands sweat; wiping them on a thin towel, I step out of the bathroom into the communal hallway.

"Hey, Beeb."

The voice comes from the stairwell, to my back. "Lydia," I say, and the dark relief of surrender washes over me.

CHAPTER 21

"She just drew parts of bodies, I'm told," Lydia says when she's settled me back in my dingy room, the sheets awry on the bed. "Disconnected. Torn apart. Doesn't that tell you something?"

"She was interested in the little things," I say. "How they fit together."

"Not much difference between the hand of a fetus and the hand of an adult person," she says coolly. "Just one's bigger."

"But why turn in Marie, of all people? Where'd you get the idea it was your duty?"

"Who said *I* turned her in?"

I don't answer. I'm sitting on the bed, hands clutching the edge of the mattress; I'm looking not at Lydia but at what passes for a view from my room, the slice of sky past the air shaft and the ridge of a distant hill. If I let go of the mattress I will start to shake.

Lydia has a weapon. Nothing more than a stun gun, the kind you hardly need a license to carry, but still it shocked me—her pulling it out from her raincoat pocket in the hallway, motioning me in here. I'd forgotten: I'm the quarry. "If you think one person can put a misconceiver in Softjail, you haven't been paying attention," Lydia's saying. She's inspected my meager pantry, the empty bottle of Scotch and the peanut-butter jar. Now she's leaning on the back of my one chair. She looks exactly the same—the hair teasingly out of control, the doll-like nose. If I had the means, right this instant, I could kill her.

"What if you succeed?" I ask Lydia, biting on the words. "You're not going to stop women from terminating pregnancies. They'll take care of it themselves, if no one's left to help them. I mean, if prostitution's the oldest profession, infanticide's the oldest crime."

"And there are consequences for crimes. People have to take it seriously."

"They take it seriously, all right. You have no idea."

"I think I have some," she says quietly. I shift my gaze from the window. It occurs to me that I don't know this woman, don't know anything about her that's truth. Maybe her name isn't even Lydia. "You remember that bobcat story I told you?" she asks. I nod. "Well, I didn't quite tell it right."

"Your date didn't die?"

"Oh, he did. But he didn't bring me to that place. I brought *him*. And I *told* him not to stand so close, but he was stubborn—he wanted to see. I couldn't save him then—none of us could save him—so I said, you know, 'Don't call an ambulance.'"

"How noble of you." The words snake out; I can't get my jaw to open all the way.

"Later," Lydia persists, dumping some spring water into my coffee cup and tossing it back, "when I was going to have his baby, we thought it would be what he wanted. His name was Jeremy." She peers into the empty water jug. "Such a young boy's name, isn't it? And I was sure I was going to have a boy, so I called the baby that, to myself, from the start."

"Christ! You have a *kid?*"

"No. I'll never have kids."

"But you said—"

"I was young. Sixteen. My parents made me have an abortion."

"Misconception," I correct her. I can't help myself.

But Lydia doesn't notice. She did some coke before she came here, I think—I can tell by the haphazard way she's gesturing with the stun gun, pacing around my room. "I was going to run away, to my friends in the hills—God, Phoebe, what friends those were! Truest family I ever had—but in the end I lost my nerve. I don't know, maybe it was something my mother slipped into the food, nerve killer. Oh, she was very modern, my mother. This was responsibility, she said. Responsibility!" Her voice has gone airy, as if she's talking in her sleep. The stun gun swings to her side; I could pluck it off her in a second. It's surprisingly easy to picture her up in the hills, in mountain jeans and khakis, trying to save a wilderness that never really existed, privileging a mama bobcat over the boy who put his seed in her. How did I ever believe the first version? "I don't want that operation to be legal," she says, with a dramatic throatiness.

"Well, I don't think you've got much to worry about on that score," I say dryly.

"It was legal when I went through it. Tim—I mean, *they*—say it could be again, tomorrow."

But she's too late. As Lydia's neck flushes, I cancel the equation I made yesterday in the parking lot. A new one's already taken its place. "Does Tim know," I say acidly, "that you got your tubes tied, Lyd?"

Her head jerks. Bull's-eye.

He was, she insists, on Marie's side at first. "All that crap about choice—he bought it! Then he witnessed a couple of late abortions, and he knew what he was seeing, a baby being killed."

Of course they're being killed. I think this but don't say it. I concentrate on the distance between me and my half-filled suitcase, on the little table by the door. My muscles bunch. I order myself not to attack. There's no point to attacking Lydia anymore.

"Then he saw how your sister's group bullied people, how anyone objecting to a certain tactic got hushed up or kicked out."

"I don't think so, Lydia."

"He did *so*. He told me. And he found others who felt the same way, and one thing led to another."

"There were no others. Not in that group."

"She brought it on herself, Phoebe."

I disobey orders. I could be flying, I'm coming at Lydia so fast. Then her stun gun goes up and I stop, midair, waiting for her to fire. She points the thing at me. "Sit still," she says, "and let me tell you about Tim."

• • •

Three weeks ago, recognizing Marie's charcoals on Miss MacDonald's office wall, I knew which drawings were of my breasts because I could remember Marie sketching them. While I was still in school and Marie was studying art, I used to sit for her a couple of times a week. In summer, she'd light citron candles and we'd go out on the walled brick patio behind the red house, and I'd strip down and settle into her black wrought-iron furniture. Sometimes I'd bring my Webtouch out and log onto a chat group doing, say, "Postliterate Linguistics"—the last gasp of humanistic gassing, people were calling my sort of school, but it gave me something to do while Marie sketched. I usually drifted off the circuit to talk to her anyway, finally lounging back in the chair, the iron latticework cool against my buttocks, to watch the stars swim overhead.

We never spoke, those evenings, about the misconceptions. We did them on Monday and Wednesday nights—sometimes, as an exception, Thursday—and by the afternoon of the procedure I knew as much about the patient as Marie did. I'd get Dad settled—Infoweb programmed to local newsbreaks, soy milk and biscuits by the couch, remote programmed to my beeper—and I'd come to the red house for pizza or curry, and we'd talk about whether this one was a second- or third-timer, or how far along she was, or how old or how fearful. Then the woman arrived and I got her prepped—they were always startled, at first, by how young I was, but once they learned I wasn't doing the actual procedure they relaxed more knowing I didn't have age or wisdom over them—and the three of us entered the sacral space of the clinic room where the Pratt rods and the aspirator did their work. After a rough case, hysterics or vomiting, sometimes Marie and I sat up drinking vodka and debating how Lloyd might have warned us. But we never spoke of the actual procedure, of the distinct sound the curette made scraping out the last bits. We never described the forms that fell into the bowl. We might all have dreamed the same dream, it seemed so impossible afterward to translate what had happened in that room.

"The weird thing," Marie said once, on the patio, bringing a candle close so she could draw the lower curve of my thigh, "is that I think men's bodies are so much more beautiful than women's."

"Thanks a lot."

"Not yours particularly, silly. Just the lines of the body. Men's are much cleaner, more balanced. All the great old sculptors thought so. Michelangelo's David."

"He was gay."

"This isn't sexual! It's aesthetic. Think how centered a man's body is, in his scrotum. You can understand how his whole being focuses there. A woman—well, where's the center? Her breasts, her belly?" I didn't answer; I was still smiling over the word *scrotum,* the way Marie said it—flipping the *t,* precisely and without embarrassment, as if it were a medical term she needed to get comfortable with. "What's hidden between her legs," she went on, "that's too low down, too tucked away to count, really. Hold still, I want to get the shadow your other leg makes, there."

"Sorry I can't be your brother."

"I didn't mean it that way. God, can you imagine me sketching *Frank?*"

Marie did sketch men, though. The curled hair of a forearm, the Adam's apple; I never knew who the model had been. I figured a few were of Omar Jeffries, a few of our father. If she'd told me the rest were of a man named Timeon, it would have meant nothing.

He was a long-necked guy from one of the Plains states, who'd come East when the procedure was still legal in New York and who stayed on when there seemed to be an organization here, after the Amendment. He was fiercer than the others—more religious, is the way Lydia put it. Before the Cybercensor Act he'd initiated a Website provocatively called "Church of the Immaculate Misconception." He took all the heat he could draw. Men in the movement were pretty rare, in the first place; in the second, they were mostly mealy-mouthed statisticians, ready to spout about the freedom of the medical profession and the number of back-alley abortions that got done when you took away the right to misconceive. This Timeon was different. He used to argue, in his Web manifesto, that the lengths we went to to preserve fetal life suggested how arrogant we were, as a species. That for every fetal life saved, enough money to preserve a thousand acres of wetlands was lost. That with every thousand acres of lost wetlands we were five hundred years closer to extinction. He scared even the

ardent group of misconceivers around Utica and Albany. He scared—
I remember myself now—even Marie.

She'd never been scared before, not even by Omar Jeffries. She
flew to the man who called himself Timeon, at first, like a bug to
light. And when he dictated that they should keep their relationship
secret, that they mustn't endanger their professionalism, she nodded
and nodded.

Alone on the sidewalk a safe distance from the hotel, with the
streetcar clanging by, I piece it together—what Lydia said to me just
now and the postcards of the past. He didn't come every Sunday
morning. That's why he never made a strong enough impression on
me. Partly he didn't come because he was busy—traveling, smuggling
things in from Canada—and partly because he was more effective,
more powerful in his absence. He liked being an outlaw; he liked to
take the risks that the others didn't deem worthwhile. In the old fable,
he would have been the one to bell the cat.

I don't know how he got Marie pregnant. But I'll venture this.
Condoms were still available then because of AIDS. Marie relied on
them. His broke. Or maybe it didn't break, but was primed to break, a
pinhole at the tip, a wee tear along the side. Because struggling within
him were the Church of the Immaculate Misconception and the pater
cult. The vision he had of the world wrestled with the one he had of
himself. Men want to own something, after all. He assumed—who
wouldn't assume?—that Marie adored him.

And then she killed his daughter. Not Omar Jeffries's, but Timeon's.
Timothy's. Tim's.

How different the human species looks when it wears your face!
No doubt she told him, in the end—honesty was in her blood, the
badge of a stoic. Just as Christel went from Young Disciple to retro,
so Tim went from the higher calling of one church to that of another.
Only he took with him his outlaw nature, and when he first stepped
beyond the bounds of his new faith it was to snare Marie.

He even came to her in Softjail—a fanatic, like Rudi, having to see
the thing through. We were never visionaries, my sister and I, but both
drawn to the gleam in the eye, the quickness of movement, the
slightly desperate daring. And Lydia? Lydia's got her bobcat story.

She bows at the altar of Nature. Somewhere in her early dreams stands an unbathed, muscular man dressed in hides, his body scarred, his passion closer to animal rut than human romance. Ridiculous, surely, that the closest she's been able to get is this Pentecostalist from New Hartford, with his sweet wife and his newborn progeny at home—but how close do any of us get to what stirs our blood? He speaks with certitude—of the world and how people have messed with it; of the great scheme of things; of how he and she stand outside the whole blundering affair, the only ones truly free to act.

But now she, too, will disappoint him. Proving only how ordinary most motives are, how betrayal and murder possess the same roots as a snub at the office or a ganging-up at the playground. How we can all do the selfish thing, fall prey to it, walk away from it. What a tall order it is to act from any conviction at all.

She let me go in the end, obviously. After giving me the usual offers, the usual song-and-dance about joining the Coalition and being washed in the blood. What did I care, she pointed out, since I was through with performing abortions? Her face, the face of a nearly beautiful woman hitting middle age without husband or kids or even an acknowledged lover to show for her pains, kept tilting leftward, the eyelid heavier on that side, the carefully waved hair slipping over her temple. "You know what the recidivism of abortionists is?" she asked at one point, as the sun rose over the sill of my dirty window.

"I don't even know what recidivism is."

"Going back. Nearly a hundred percent of abortionists go back to killing babies when they get out. There are people—in the Coalition—who see just one way to solve that problem. Especially in the case of Marie Chambers's sister."

"What, you mean I should be *killed*?"

She shrugged. " But I told Tim, a wasted death is just a crime."

"A *wrongful* death is a crime, Lydia."

"But that's a matter of perspective, isn't it? Puts us back to the deaths you carry out. All of them wrongful, if you think about it."

"You don't believe that."

"Does it matter what I believe? I'm saving your life."

It was then that all plans of vengeance began to dissolve, a sand castle in the wind. I'd stayed too long among these buildings, chasing phantoms and wasting my freedom. "You had better stop me," I said, rising from the bed. I laid hold of my cardboard suitcase, the paltry cash and change of clothes inside, my Minilap and my copy of the *Phaedo*. "You told him you'd stop me. You'd deliver me, one way or another."

I turned my back on her. I ordered my body to stop shaking. I stepped from the room, through the hallway, down the clattering stairs. For an uncountable moment my rage was a whirlwind with no eye. Then, breathless, I reached the ordinary street.

Where I am now.

She didn't follow me. Not in those first high-voltage moments, stun gun at the ready, none but the old zombies of the residence hotel to witness. Not after, as my steps slowed and the queer dizziness of disappointment set in. I turned to spy on the entrance to the building. In hope, or fear? Or habit—I'd been casing entrances so long, my sights on Lydia.

She never came out.

The streetcar moves on. I rotate my shoulders, shake the panic out of them. Turning, I walk north. Two blocks farther, grackles quarrel in the eaves of the courthouse my father once worked in. Everything in me wants to go back to that hotel room. *I'm saving your life,* she said, and her pencil-thin lips pressed together, smug or else prepared to cry. Then she vanished.

Tim, I think. But the name rolls like a pebble into the gray, sluggish flow of the Mohawk River. He's someone else's battle; I've hung up my armor. I reach the levee, point of departure.

CHAPTER 22

Around me, people sell fruit and furniture and used clothes; occasionally I hear arguments. A smell of rotten fish comes up from the river. It's a beautiful day—funny how you notice such things when they matter least. Hurrying through South Utica toward this wasteland, you can tell we're a city on the move—sleek new subway stops, rows of battery-charging parking meters, the new walkway mall over the expressway. Unlike people, cities can die and come back to life.

With me I have my Minilap, my tattered *Phaedo,* my paltry wad of greenbacks. To reach Arthur's system or any system, to say *Meet me, find me, fetch me,* I must risk the sharp blue card that swims at the bottom of the case. The money's not enough to get anywhere without starving.

Congos echo from where the retros are playing, under the bridge— *pat a bum, pat a bad bum, pat a bad bad bum.* When I grow very warm, I trade my gray wool jacket for a loaf of bread, a hunk of cheese, five bananas, and a hat that I can wear or trade later. Only when I've eaten—late afternoon by now—do I really look around me. No Lydia, no Tim. Though it's funny how, having looked so long for the one and failed to recognize the other, I'm certain they're lurking behind a hulking Dumpster or an abandoned car. Or maybe it's the ghost of Marie I'm feeling at my back. I shut my eyes. Let me go, Marie.

Making the circuit of the cobblestones, I find a group talking heatedly around the iron pot that Christel was stirring three weeks before. Christel's turn, I think—to give me something to eat, a safe place to sleep, to send me on my way. "Rodriguez was not the guy to go to," an older woman with a shaved head is saying. "The man is a recovered X-head with a drinking problem."

"He's got steady hands," says a woman I can't see.

"Sold me a pound of bad hot dogs once. I had the shits all night," says a man.

"Wasting time—"

"—but I came looking for you last night, and your lady—"

"He's a good man."

"Y'know, Stu-boy's got a place—"

They're all talking at once, and I don't see Christel. I'm going on when the stringy guy who shooed me away before breaks off and comes near.

"Jesus H. fucking Christ," he says, planting himself in front of me, "it's got to be a miracle or some shit."

"I'm looking for my niece," I say. The bread and cheese feel solid in my stomach. I clutch the suitcase now holding the rest of the food and the hat, a magenta-colored mohair cloud.

"Your niece—" He stops, waves his arms as if pumping an imaginary accordion. He looks distractedly at the blue sky.

"Christel, yeah. Is she all right?"

"She's—she's—" He's handsome, or used to be, and much younger than I thought before—only his gauntness, and wrinkles from the sun, age him. "Down Railroad Street, over this way," he says, pointing and then starting that direction, meaning for me to follow. "All right, you maniacs, I'll check back!" he hollers over his shoulder as a couple of women call at him.

We cut across the lower arterial and past a fenced-off site where men are laying foundations. "It's been four, five days," he says as we get out of earshot, away from the congos beating under the bridge. "It might of been you she called for a few times. I tried to fetch someone, but she wouldn't have it. Anyhow they want card, at the hospitals."

"Not all of them," I say, but who am I to make claims? Arthur would know. "What's wrong with her?"

"You'll know," he fixes me now with his eyes, pale hazel like chips of mica, "when you lay eyes on her."

"She's not pregnant again, is she?" Counting the months, six since the procedure in St. Barbara, easily possible.

"Shit," he says.

"She is, isn't she? Well, look, I'm not helping her this time. It was a bad decision before. If she's so sure, she can find someone else—"

"*Shit,*" he says again, like a command to be silent: he's fed up with the lot of us.

I've never been on Railroad before. When I was growing up, the station was still here, but no one I knew ever took the train, and when the funding for the bullet train died the whole thing folded. Now it's the only part of the city still empty, the unrenovated ghost town. I'm led up three flights of stairs from a cobwebbed shop that reads UPHOL-STERERS on the window. The room the gaunt man brings me into is dark, especially after the bright day outside; I can just make out a figure on a reclining chair and another standing at a window. The air reeks; and at once—without yet making sure that the one in the chair is Christel, or the other one the woman I saw at the campfire by the river—I know what's happened.

"How long ago was she misconceived?" I ask. The woman at the window turns her head; she's smoking something.

"I don't know."

"Five days," comes a parched whisper from the reclining chair. At Christel's voice, I realize I'm not yet standing completely in the room, but have one foot on the doorstep, as if I can flee the place as quickly as I did my room with Lydia in it. I move the foot in, then step through the artificial twilight toward Christel.

Her forehead's hot, her eyes glassy. "Christel, honey," I say to the pale, heart-shaped face, "I think you've got a fever."

"No, no," she whispers. "It's just the baby, working me. Oh, get it out, Phoebe, please get it out."

"It's not that easy," I say. I put my hand on her long neck. The weight I saw on her before is gone now, slackened off. "If you'll help me," I say to the smoking woman, "we can get her lying down and slip her pants off. I'll have a look. But I think this is way out of my range."

Christel moves her arms feebly. Always pale, she's alabaster now, but hot and dry as just-burnt ashes. There's a pile of old drapes by one of the narrow windows; wordlessly the woman and I lay them out, then lower Christel to the floor. I ask the man where I can wash my hands, and he leads me to a closet with a basin—no soap, but hot water, enough to scald the skin. Coming back to find the woman helping Christel slip off her pants, an unforgivable annoyance flares in me. "How long'd it take you, Christel?" I say, soft yet astonished at my own cruelty. "Two months, max? That's about how long it would take for your period to come back."

"I never got my period," she says weakly.

"The first time was such hell for you," I say, crouching, "I'd have thought—" But I don't finish with what I'd have thought, because the smell from between her legs hits me like a fist. "Christ almighty, Christel," I say.

"I'm cold," she says.

"Cold, nothing. You're getting eaten away down in here." You can never be a nurse, Marie used to point out to me, you're too damn blunt.

"Just get it out, Phoebe. I don't care—what you have to take out with it." Christel's voice is small, but burdened in a way it wasn't, before, not even in that tiny hotel room in St. Barbara. On either side of my cautious hands, her unshaven thighs tremble.

"That's not the point. She's got a raging infection," I say to the woman, who's looking over my shoulder, trying to stay out of what little light filters into the place. A doctor would hide the news from the suffering patient, but I'm not in any shape to be polite. The smell is like week-old meat left unwrapped in a broken refrigerator. Bile rises in my throat. "I don't have the experience," I say, "and I don't have the medicines."

"Call Arthur," says Christel, from the floor. His name is like lighting a match.

"*I* should call Arthur?" I say. "*I* should? Me, who the police are looking for all over Utica and way out in Santa Barbara, too? Why the hell didn't *you* call Arthur, when it was clear that whoever did this messed you over?"

She shakes her head. "I . . . dunno. I kept thinking that I was just having a bad reaction. The people I was—with—gave me some tea to drink, they said it would stop the burning. It's just like my dream, Phoebe, and you can't help—"

"Oh, never mind. Stay quiet," I say, and while I can't rub away the harsh edge of my voice, I lower her thin legs and move to the side of the makeshift bed to stroke her matted hair back from her burning forehead. If she could drive a comb through the dense snarl, it would fall in streaky curls around her ears and pale neck.

"It wasn't me," comes the voice of the gaunt man, still by the door. I'd forgotten about him.

"Doesn't matter."

"Well, it wasn't."

I don't answer. "Where's the system?" I ask the woman.

"Don't have one."

"Phone, then. Does anyone live in this building? Do any of you people have codes?" I'm squeezing Christel's hand, trying to make up for my hard words. From somewhere below us comes the low thump of amplified music, flat and glassy, an old-fashioned CD player.

"We've, sort of, lost touch with all that," says the man.

"Paper, then." I bend and touch my lips to Christel's forehead, as if they can cool her down. "Something to write with."

"Now you're cookin'," he says, stepping back to the door. While he leans down and rifles through the pockets of a jacket that's been thrown there, I stroke Christel's temples and feel her pulse, which is fluttering.

"Do you know where your mom is?" I ask, and she shakes her head.

"Here we go," says the man. He offers me a limp pad of paper and the stub of a pencil, and I think briefly of the DMV employee, back in St. Monica, who refused to use paper; of how I saw the retros there, and was frightened by them. Keeping my right hand on Christel's wrist, I lay the pad on the floor and write, a clumsy effort.

"Just five blocks away," I tell the man. "Off Genesee, toward the new museum. Give the doorman—you know how to use an electronic doorman?" He nods. "All right, well give it this name, and go on up to the seventh floor. It's the big office just as you step off. Give my note to this person"—I point to the outside fold—"and tell him I don't care about the consequences for me. Do you follow? I don't care."

"Course you don't," he says with just a taste of condescension. He nods toward Christel. "She going to be all right?"

"Course she is," I condescend, and send him on his way.

Lloyd sends three paramedics and a private ambulance. While we wait, our ears pricking like dogs' at every siren, Christel goes in and out of delirium. "Hold me, Mommy, hold me hold me *save me*," she says at one point, arching her back and waving her feeble arms.

"Your mom's not here, Christel. She'll meet you at the clinic."

"Mommy! Mommy, get me *out*." She turns her round eyes on me, her voice weirdly high-pitched. I put my arms around her, peeling her hot back from the wrinkled drapes.

"It's all right, honey," I say. "Where are you?"

"In the cage, in the cage, and the master's coming, oh he's coming, Mommy, get me *out*."

"There's no cage, Christel." I hold her just a little away, so she can see my face. Hers is still heart-shaped, the cheeks pudgy around the bone, the forehead just a little bit aggressive, the sort of thing you notice in a girl child. The lips are too dry for a pout, the teeth between them starting to strain. "I'm Phoebe," I say, almost sternly, "your aunt. This is a friend's—well, apartment. Somebody screwed up your misconception, and you've got a fever. You've got a fever, that's all."

She stares; her breath comes fast. She forms the word once, then screams it out, "*Mommy!*" and twists in my arms.

"I'm *here,* Christel," I say. "We're going to take you somewhere to bring the fever down."

"*Mommy!*"

"I'm here, Christel. Where are you?"

"I'm . . . I'm . . ." She looks past me, over my shoulder. I can hear the pitch of her voice lowering, like a kettle taken from the fire, but her body's still stiff, raging. "I see things. Things you don't see," she says.

The woman, who's managed to fill a bucket with cool water and a cloth, reappears at one point with white pills that she says are for pain. I feed Christel four of them, until she waves the pills and the water glass away. For a while she doesn't talk or cry out, only clutches at me from time to time. Her hands have gone cold now, the fingers rubbery. When she comes more to her senses, the talk spills over. She keeps apologizing. "I'm sorry," she says, "we never played tennis."

"When you're better, Christel," I say, "and I'm—more available."

"I'm putting you in danger."

"No, no."

"I don't want my mom to know. She found out—before—did I tell you she found out?"

"Tell me when it hurts," I say, pressing gently on her abdomen. The muscles there are tight, under puffy skin, but I can feel the heated swelling of her uterus, the distended bladder to the right. The skin itself is crusty; she hasn't bathed, though the main smell overpowers any unwashed odor.

"God found out too. Only—no—He didn't find out. He *knew*. He always *knows*, that's the trouble. And now He'll have to forgive me, He'll have a big job of it this time, don't you think? And my mom'll never know—"

"Your mom's been looking for you. Lloyd'll get hold of her." I tuck a drape around Christel's body, at once clay-cold and pulsing with heat.

"Only it's not so much the sin He'll have to forgive me for, it's for being so stupid. So stupid," she repeats, and her eyes look as if they would cry, but the fever's dried up her tears.

Ten minutes after they come, the ambulance people are wheeling Christel away, an IV pumping antibiotics into her poisoned veins. "Peritonitis, right?" I ask the head paramedic—maybe he's a doctor— that Lloyd's managed to send.

"Worse," he says, keying something into his Minilap. "Septic shock, and we're damn late."

"What can you do for her?"

"Keep her hydrated. Use the biggest guns we have. She'll need a hysterectomy right away, if we can stabilize her temp."

"Is she going to be—will she live?" I say.

He frowns at his screen, not liking the scenario it blinks at him. "You next of kin?" he asks.

"No, not quite."

"Better notify them. This'll go one way or the other in the next twenty-four hours."

Before they wheel her into the ambulance, I pepper Christel's face with kisses. "Sorry," she murmurs for each one.

"I'm the one who should be sorry," I say, holding her chin in my hands, trying to get her overbright eyes to focus for a moment. "You thought I could fix this."

"No," she whispers, shutting her eyes, ready to drift into another fever dream. "I thought God could, at first. Isn't that funny? That I thought God could?"

Her thin nose twitches, and she smiles off-kilter. I don't answer. I won't code my name or number onto the doctor's screen, and he nods as if he was warned I'd refuse. "Her mother will be there," I tell him.

"You sure? Sometimes, these kids—they've drifted so far, you can't even track the family."

"Not this one. Guarantee," I say. But I don't climb into the ambulance with him. I wave and say a swift prayer to who knows what. I sink down on the cold, shaded curb when they've pulled away, my failure a blanket around me. Christel, I say over and over, under my breath, Christel. Like the thing you don't want to shatter. Come with us, says the woman, and the man lays his thin fingers on my shoulder, but I don't move. For hours I sit there, until they've gone and night fog has fallen, and then I rise and find my suitcase, with the food and the book, the bit of money and the hat; and begin my journey out of the city.

CHAPTER 23

Rudi—misunderstanding, as always—is quick to declare Christel better off. "You have no idea," he says, "what kind of life those retros lead. We're talking serious drugs, rampant TB-2, a short miserable life in the underbelly of this myopic culture."

"I don't care. I want her alive."

"You're just thinking about yourself."

"I am not. How can you be so cold?"

He shrugs. "You see it so much, young people fallen off the edge. Some folks I work with think there're galactic rays at work, corrupting the atmosphere in ways we can't detect. Makes hordes of people suicidal."

"Christel's not suicidal."

"*If* she's alive."

"Well, maybe she is. Alive, I mean. Maybe someone performed a miracle."

"Then," says Rudi, "you have nothing to blame yourself for. So stop bashing your head, okay? You look like you've gone a round with a revolving door."

It's the next morning—or later in the morning, I should say, since it was well past midnight when Rudi let me into this apartment where he's staying. Always cannier than he looks, he asked no questions, made no advances, but fed me and led me to a high-ceilinged, lemon-colored bathroom with a deep whirlpool and then a terry robe and a soft couch for what was left of the night. Now it's past ten, pouring rain outside, but coffee and sweet rolls in Rudi's friend's kitchen, everything to make me feel safe.

Once they'd taken Christel away, I thought I knew where I was going. I had failed at everything—at extinguishing Lydia, at saving Christel. There was only love left to try. "Love Is All You Need," sang one of my mom's battered old CDs—sold, no doubt, when they emptied Marie's house. My need for Arthur was like the simple hunger people wake with in the morning that sends them to the kitchen in search of toast or an egg. If Lloyd could be trusted to send help for Christel, surely he could be trusted to get a message to the Coast. To lend me greenbacks for a bus to the Canadian border. How Arthur would manage—quit his job or take a leave, set up a Canadian file, try to keep his card afloat until charges were pressed against him—wasn't my concern. I knew he'd meet me, that was all. Knew he'd be with me as long as he could and wherever he could. And his touch would be honey and fire, iron and silk, and I would stop choking on my own failure.

Dark as it was, I headed uptown to Lloyd's office. Love, I was thinking, love. *Love Is in the Air,* like this night spring, daffodils coming up through the fog around the carefully planted trees on Genesee. Surely Christel had reached the hospital in time; surely they'd be able to do something. She would not die tonight, or tomorrow, or this week, and then she would be out of danger. Everywhere around me, things were conceiving, coming to life. And surely I, too, was running from death to life, revenge to love.

I almost missed the license plate of the car parked in front of Lloyd's building. CITY9, it read. In the driver's seat sat a young man in a dark suit playing games on the dashboard system while he waited. I stopped on the sidewalk and glanced up at Lloyd's ninth-story window, as if it could tell me something. The lights were on, inside—Lloyd has always kept late hours. I stepped in, keeping my sunglasses on, gave Christel's name to the door monitor, and rode the elevator up.

Lloyd's office has a minuscule waiting room with an electronic secretary, then a thick oak door leading to his chamber. No one was in the waiting room as I slipped through the glassed entrance; but the oak door was ajar, and there was no mistaking the voices, with their detectives' sneer. Tonight, one was saying, at eight thirty-five. They brought in a young woman with blood poisoning, a critical case. Lloyd's name was in the file, but the young woman named someone else.

A message was delivered to me, said Lloyd. You can see for yourself, it's got no signature. I was obligated to help my cousin if it was a real emergency. Sounds like an emergency.

May we see your system?

One of them was moving toward the oak door—maybe to check messages on the electronic secretary, I'll never know. I backed out and into the hallway, my bag bumping behind me. Then I ran.

If Lloyd, then the two retros who helped Christel. Then Christel, if she managed to pull through. How many people could I prevent being linked to me? By the time I got to the dark street I was panting, running like a rabbit away from everything and toward nothing but shelter. People glanced at me and my sloppy suitcase as if I were a retro dressed clownishly like a member of society. I didn't stop for five blocks, and then it was just to lean against a chain-link fence and shut my eyes.

Crouching there, I dug my Minilap out of my case. I had a couple of handles for Arthur; maybe he was checking in, maybe I could use the card just once, leave a text message in some kind of code that only he would understand. No, it was too risky, too damn risky. My little screen glowed like moonlight in a puddle. I keyed in *friends,* just as a way of thinking through my options that weren't really options, of naming the people I didn't dare contact.

And there, still on that link, was Rudi Hauser. "Rudi," I said out loud. Miss MacDonald had said he was looking for me. Rudi whom I'd regretted, Rudi whose life I probably couldn't invade even if I tried, he went around with such a natural indemnity. All right, Rudi then, while I tried to find my way to love. I pulled his latest address from the Trash, a number on South Franklin that I seemed to recognize as belonging to a friend of his, a guy he met through the UFO Room. People would be expecting me to go to Arthur; they wouldn't expect me to go to Rudi. I picked my way around bags of recyclables left out for morning and headed past the misty town park, onto the sloping, ill-kept avenue that ran down toward the river and the old brewery. At the intersection I hesitated.

"Help you get somewhere, darlin'?" said a man at my elbow. I turned; he was tall, stooping, unshaven but not unwashed, smelling just faintly of wine. Two prominent moles punctuated his right cheek, just below the watery eye, like great brown tears. In a few years, the gang Christel had been wandering with, possibly the man who'd gotten her with child this time, would turn into something like this. But Christel was in the hospital, Christel was with her mother, she'd be fine.

"I'm okay," I told him.

"Over there"—he pointed, his hand in a fingerless glove, wool just covering the scabbed knuckles—"they're hirin' dancers. No video, just live. Only you better change your gear."

"Thanks," I told him, and with the distinct sense that this was the only way to keep him from tagging along, I headed the way he pointed—across the avenue and down, to a tawdry marquee whose neon raced around a circle, lights splattering the sidewalk. VIRTUAL SEX, promised the billboard, plastered across what must have once been a window. INTERACTIVE MODELING. The image between blurbs was of a startlingly real red-haired woman wrapping her legs around a shadow. High heels dangled from her toes; her head was flung back, exposing her white neck; and somehow, on either side of the hulking shadow, erect nipples peeked, like children playing a game.

A square-shouldered man hurried out while I stood there, buttoning his jacket as he went, checking his watch as if he were late for a meeting. Inside the place would be women who worked, like Roxanne's Marta, for cash. No doubt they harbored misconceivers among them—Pockface, whom I'd last seen a year ago, might well be humping air in a dark room, a night job she could take and quit at will and where patients could be referred and find her as soon as the need arose.

"Looking for someone?" came a voice from above. I looked up; a heavy, sallow man in a dirty white undershirt leaned out from the window.

"Work," I heard myself say.

"Jus' sec." The head disappeared. I glanced back, across the street—the stooping wino was gone. I looked back at the building; I couldn't see where the door was, but in less than a minute the face from upstairs would appear, opening it, beckoning me into the darkness. My head hurt as if it were being pressed between irons. Fever, I thought, and my warm blood throbbed in my neck. And aloud I breathed, "Oh, Christel!" and knew she would not pull through, would not be alive next week. Was dying even as I stood outside a porn house, pretending I could be anybody I chose. Was dying because I'd brought her into a land of death, where her own poisoned blood would kill her because someone like me had botched it. "Christel!" I cried again. My hands clenched. With my left fist I struck myself in the forehead, punishment driving out pain, struck myself twice and then three times as hard as I could.

"What the fuck?" said the man, his face indeed in the doorway—at the end of the building, to my left, a sweatshirt covering his sagging chest now, a cigar in his mouth. I balled up a fist, again, and he ducked back inside. I didn't hit him, or myself, this time. I just clenched my teeth in my mouth, clenched them as if they were the only thing holding my head together, and without looking back I ran on down the street, away from Virtual Sex, the truth racing against me, my throat dry and lumpy, as if Christel's death were lodged there.

But none of this matters to Rudi, who has a plan for me. He spent, he's saying—pouring more coffee—all summer and fall in Prague. "Missing your fireworks," is how he puts it. He didn't make it into the shuttle, but there were new atmospheric tests on the biolaser, an alteration in the ultraviolet rays breaking through the ozone hole over Belarus. Breakthrough stuff, he just knew it, but then his work visa expired and he had to come back. By the time he learned I'd been arrested, I had slipped from Softjail and disappeared. "I kept hanging around that little red house where your sister lived," he says, his thin handsome face broadening with nostalgia. "I was sure I'd cruise by one day and find the new people gone and your little Access parked in the drive and the smell of orange bread drifting out the window."

"You and the detectives from the first precinct."

"Yeah. Yeah, I guess. Sorry." He smiles on one side of his mouth, that cheek dimpling as if at some inward amusement—not a joke exactly, but an odd labeling on the inside of the world's fabric. He let his hair grow in Europe—it's longer than mine but straight, melting onto his neck like a cat's fur. He kept thinking about me, he says, when he was in Prague; and by the way he crinkles his eyes and lifts his head as he says it, I know he means sex with me. That was always Rudi's talent, a way of suggesting with his eyes what he never really put himself into with his body. Ever since he learned what happened, he says, he's been thinking he's the perfect one to get me out of the country. There's another fellowship, this one to study the meteor fall in Argentina, the one where there are signs of fossil evidence. He has that degree in geology—do I remember?—and he knows the guy who built the lab down there. If he can get the money, he can get two visas instead of one. The Argentines don't do credit checks.

"So I can live out my days happily as a gaucho girl," I say.

"Better than living them out in court."

"Or maybe the next craft will choose to land at the meteor site down there, out of nostalgia for the remains of their ancestors, and I can hop aboard."

"All right, I know it's a joke to you," Rudi says. "But it *is* real to two million people around the world, and when you consider that Alexander Bell would have thought the idea of hammering out a contract face-to-face in your own language with someone sitting at a little screen in China was a joke, then you begin to question who the real visionaries are."

His voice has taken on a familiar edge that coincides with an angry, sexy tilt to his jaw. The argument is one we used to have early in our relationship; I would play the part of the cynic while he played the fanatical prophet of other worlds, until there was nothing for it but to tumble into bed together and let our bodies tussle it out, usually according to Rudi's somewhat off formula. The fact is I'd far rather side with the other-life-forms idea. The arrogance of our little species, I'd argue, has ballooned like a cartoon dragon—but arrogance doesn't prove that there aren't other votes getting cast out there. And yes, I used to say to Rudi when I let him inside my armor, you can apply that belief to misconceptions, too. Morality is local—who knows what other forms of life, floating about on their little star-warmed islands, would think of the fatal link between desire and fecundity that's got us programmed? Perhaps it's no great matter at all, this human debugging that I do.

Perhaps, he would say, it enrages them.

And I had to admit, yes, perhaps. Which was why it was easier to scoff at Rudi and why, once it became clear that having sex with him was going to be just as disturbing as talking to him, I had to break it off.

"I'm supposed to leave in a week," Rudi says, buttering a sweet roll for me. "And for once in my life, there's plenty of money in it."

"Whose money?" I look around the kitchen. The place is in a high-rent district—an old warehouse like the one Christel was lying in, but full of newly renovated units with built-in systems and workstations, even a pop-up unit in the kitchen counter. It's not Rudi's style at all.

"The guy who owns this building," he says, "opened up the first rhizome specifically regarding extraterrestrial history. You know, for theoreticians tracking biological evolution in the Alpha Nebulae, that sort of stuff."

I glance sharply at him, but there's no way to tell if he's joking. Argentina with this man, I think. "But how'd he make his *money?*"

"Netbetting, they say." Rudi is leaning nonchalantly against the counter between the kitchen and eating area. I can't stop moving, opening and shutting the empty cupboards, cruising out into the hallway and the bedroom that's got the system built in. I've gotten dressed, my gray clothes wrinkled and heavy, and hung the terry robe up on a gleaming brass peg. "This guy would actually like it," Rudi is going on, raising his voice so I can hear him around the corner, "if I brought someone along with me. He has this theory about libidinal susceptibility."

"Libidinal who?"

"Susceptibility. That single people are either more prone to alien influence, or more apt to fantasize about it. Either way it makes for warped reports. He would prefer it if all researchers were sexually active, balanced, you know."

"Who is this guy, your boss?"

"No, just a big donor. Not one to be ignored."

"Are you sexually balanced?"

"I was scared of you before." His voice is soft, now, but I jump because he's suddenly right behind me, having slipped silently across the smooth floors. "What you did. And your sister, the two of you together. Remember that trip we took to Maine?"

"Sure."

"There was that guy Clark that she brought home. He asked me if you two worked for the FBI."

"Why?"

"That's what I asked *him*. He said you were like a two-woman SWAT team, he didn't see how anyone could get past you. I almost told him you only went after helpless unborn babies, but I—"

Rudi doesn't finish. I've slapped him; did it before I knew my arm was moving. My hand stings. I go to get my coat, then remember I traded it for food.

"It was a joke," he's saying, his left cheek blotched, trying to catch my elbow as I move into the main room.

"Didn't sound like one."

"Look, I *know* what you were up against. Christ, that's why you're running, isn't it?"

"I am not running," I say. My voice sounds surprisingly calm; inside I'm screaming. "I had business to take care of. I couldn't do it from prison."

"Oh, so you're going right back."

"You do not know *anything about it*." There's an old sweater on the back of the entrance door; I take it and shrug it on, retro morals.

"Phoebe, I am trying to offer you something. I am trying to offer you a way out." Suddenly Rudi's between me and the door. The blush on his cheek is fading already, but his whole body seems agitated, not calm the way it was a minute ago. "I don't care what you've done since you got out. Maybe you've killed somebody. Fine. That's really what I was trying to say about you and Marie. You guys had the whole thing licked—and you, you've still got it licked."

"Only I don't scare you anymore."

"No." He runs his tongue over his lips, as if they're dry. "Because I—I really love you, you know? And if I give you this chance—it would be good for both of us. Can't you see how good it would be?"

"What I see," I say slowly, standing in the sterile hallway of the vacant apartment where Rudi is squatting before the next stage of his crabbed journey toward outer space, "is that you'll get your fellowship to Argentina contingent on your bringing a mate along. I see that you think I'm desperate. I'm not sure whether I see blackmail—no," I go on when I see the shock widen his hazel eyes, "you wouldn't go that far—but certainly a determination to try more than once. Are you going to let me get by?"

He stands irresolutely to one side, not sure if it will advance his cause to confess. "It's not like I have to bring someone," he tries. "It's just a values thing, you know—"

"Yeah, I know. Nothing like batting a hundred on white-guy researchers with families to give your loony project some credence. At least the Jeezoids'll contribute."

"The who?"

"Expression of Marie's," I say. I'm at the open door now, only dimly aware of the possibility of freedom that I'm flinging aside.

"I misread you," Rudi says, entering the doorway with me. "I *thought* you were different from your sister. From the minute you introduced me to her, I thought, 'Well, that's what Phoebe's *not.*'"

It's the old accusation. I'm supposed to protest—"I *am* different from her!"—as if being something other than Marie is already an identity, as if half my choices fall into a "like-Marie" box and the other half into a "not-like-Marie" box. If Rudi had said, with the same tinge of disappointment, that he had hoped I was *like* Marie, I would be protesting that yes, deep down, my sister has been reborn in me.

I'm sick of the question. "Nobody is like Marie," I say, lifting my chin. "And nobody in my life, thank God, is like you, Rudi."

It's still morning, the rain still pours down. I take the bus to the edge of the city, its new neighborhoods and business plazas flashing by, then I walk the rest of the way to Jonathan's place, my legs like pistons pumping. I inhale the cool air as if it's food. For the first time since I pulled myself from the Softjail airshaft, I'm not worried about being seen. I'm invisible, the way they say laser-beamed objects are invisible in the stage between one incarnation and the next. I arrive up the mountain breathless and excited, five hours before Jonathan is due home, and in what looks like a domestic frenzy except for a certain calm at the center of it, I sweep the place clean. Cobwebs from corners, dustballs from underneath parts; I oil his oak counters, polish his copper pans, brush Norman until his coat shines gold. I get going on the loom Jonathan keeps in the corner of the living room, with a barrel of rag strips waiting to be woven in. At twilight I see Jonathan's car winding up the long drive, and I'm taken by a surge of excitement, as though I've got some great news to tell him. Though there's nothing, really, that you can find words for.

CHAPTER 24

If only I had Arthur's locater code, Jonathan tells me, he could tap into a five-state telecom log and find out at least if he's in the area. That's how the police—who must have Arthur's code—will track him, if they want to. "That's how they track me," Jonathan says, heading back into the system room.

"Who's says you're being tracked?" I call over my shoulder. I'm sitting at his big floor loom, keeping my hands busy.

"Think about it," he says, poking his head back out. "Think about Gerald. Think, Phoebe."

I bite my tongue as I shift the warp. Three days ago Gerald was fired. His lifestyle was said to disrupt company harmony—the line they always use, according to Jonathan. When I asked how Gerald was taking it—this was my first night, drinking wine by the fire—Jonathan shrugged. Gerald's looking for something new, he said, something more positive than wiping out viruses. It can be very positive, I argued, if you cut out the glitch and see the system recovered. And Jonathan protested that there would always be more to chase down, systems breeding viruses.

So, what? You just let things get destroyed?

No, you leave the dirty work to someone else. You abandon the theory of infinite perfectibility.

I told him he was full of fine ideas. It has to be admitted that I'm a little sore on the point—I, who once removed viruses and fetuses, and now do neither. I haven't spoken to him about Christel. If I don't speak about her, I think, if I don't let her name pass my lips, she will be alive.

Tonight Jonathan is testy. He had dinner with Gerald, but didn't bring him home, and I know this is somehow my fault. "One thing I've learned," I say, plucking a new set of colorful rag strips out of the oak bin. "They can't track cash."

"So?"

"So if you can get me—I don't know—a thousand dollars in greenbacks, I'll just go looking for Arthur. They can't track my body, either."

"A thousand won't take you far. You've got fifty-two states, not to mention Canada."

"No. He's nearby, I can feel it. You left that message for me?"

He jerks his head: a nod. "Haven't heard back."

"Well, you may not." I've given Jonathan the safest handle I have for Mau-Mau; if it's traced, he can claim he was asking about homeowner's insurance. But if I'm too hot to handle, they won't help, not even if Arthur's managed to get in touch with them. *It's bigger than any one of us,* Marie always said.

Jonathan's house has been quiet during the day—a few planes droning overhead, the chirps of nest-building birds in the woods. It's colder here than in the city. While he's off at work, I wrap myself in one of his plaid wool blankets and stoke the fire. He's convinced I'm ill, and maybe he's right—no amount of water seems to slake my thirst, and my muscles ache as if I've been hoisting bags of cement. I'm always bending my neck to lean my forehead on the heel of my thumb. The barn where I sleep has a space heater; in the morning I wake with its electric warmth on my face and imagine I'm waking on the beach, with the sun's first glow. I dress fast, stamping my feet to stay warm, and trot over to the main house, where Jonathan's got a strong pot of coffee already made and the fire rekindled. All morning I poke at the burning logs and flip through Jonathan's paper books, with their wood-pulp scent. I've read through the *Phaedo* finally, and I don't care for most of it, all that cloudy argument about life after death; it's only the trial itself that captures my attention. On the flyleaf of the book there's a line drawing of Socrates facing the tribunal, a jowly group with dashes for mouths. When it's grown so warm outside that a fire's absurd, I rouse myself and turn into Snow White—I dust cupboards, I bake bread, I clear last fall's matted leaves away from the holly bushes by the front wall. When I find myself leaving the house, walking down the long drive, shading my eyes from the afternoon sun to look down the hill toward the city, where the hospital is, I purse my lips to keep them from uttering Christel's name, and then I turn back and head straight for the loom in the corner of the house.

I've promised Jonathan I'll be gone in less than a week—as soon as this throat feels better and I can tell where to go. Throwing the shuttle between the flexed lines of warp, I beat the pattern into place. I used to tease Jonathan about the Christmas gifts he brought to the office—intricately woven coasters, placemats; once, a silk scarf for me, the slubs of the raw woven silk alive to my fingers. Couldn't he find a program to do this fancy work for him? I used to ask, and he'd answer simply, Yes.

"Did it ever get back to you, about that Hecate virus from St. Monica?" I ask when he comes out of the system room again.

"The one you used to get out of jail? Only for the three hours they were grilling me."

"They grilled you?" I stop shuttling, the rag strip loose in the V of the warp.

"Who d'you think they called in to *fix* the problem? Doctor Spock?"

"I—never thought. I'm sorry." I put my hands in my lap like a penitent schoolgirl; they're clammy, though the room's warm with the woodstove roaring. "Well, you didn't know I had a version."

"Yes, well, that's my *job,* isn't it? To keep track of versions, to contain the thing?"

"I could've been part of the sabotage in the first place."

"They haven't neglected that possibility. *Somebody's* part of it."

"Oh, Jonathan." My smile's nostalgic. "You don't swallow all that conspiracy crap, do you? I mean, the retros aren't even *organized.* They're worrying about *food.* What happens is just mostly . . . accidental. Random."

Jonathan slouches in the doorway; from behind him come reassuring clicks and tones. "Then they'll lose the war," he says.

"What war?"

"The war in which Lydia Anderson's on the other side."

Tim, I think; but I won't. I haven't told Jonathan the whole story; it may not be finished yet. "Lydia's left Viratect," I remind him, my hand resting in the warp. "She had nothing to do with what happened to Gerald."

Jonathan takes off his glasses and rubs the bridge of his nose—a gesture that reminds me of Arthur; oh, where is Arthur? "Yours," says Jonathan, "is not the only network operating. It's not illegal to be a faggot, but let's face it—you don't get a place at the table. Gerald's a lot more militant than I am. She was on his ass before she left, and the company was on his ass after. It's not just misconceivers getting nailed, Phoebe." There's something very naked about Jonathan's face, backlit with the fluorescent light from his system room outlining the sloping muscles of his neck.

"I thought Gerald didn't care particularly. About the firing, I mean."

Jonathan sighs and looks at the beamed ceiling. He's wearing only a T-shirt, says he gets warm easily. "You know what I wish?" he says. I shake my head. "I wish you'd grabbed that gun and used it."

"It was just a stunner," I say. I turn back to the loom, to its comforting susurrus and clack. "Lydia's fucked up."

"She is evil."

I could push this—*You said you cared about her*—but I won't turn the knife. "You used to tell *me* there were no conspiracies," I said.

"That was before I knew you were in on one."

"That's not fair."

"Tell Gerald what's fair. Tell Gerald who can't get work with a blacklisted file."

"All right, Jonathan."

"Tell Gerald who wants to split off with me because I still work for them."

"All right!"

"Tell him next week when he has to leave his apartment!"

"Why not tell my dead sister?" I burst out.

"Exactly!"

"Look!" I jump up from the stool, knocking over the basket of rag strips. As I step down into the main room, bright with firelight and the glow of old lamps, I catch sight of the *Phaedo* at the end of Jonathan's row of books, huddled together like children hiding in the dark. I step over, lift it off, wave it at him. "I do not," I say to Jonathan, "want to rid the world of all its crazy evil people. I do not want to revenge my sister anymore, or make things better for you or Gerald or anyone. I just want my niece Christel to be alive. I want to find Arthur and go hide away somewhere, and live my life."

"People like Lydia have got to pay the piper sometime, Phoebe," says Jonathan.

I pace, fingering pages. I take the iron poker and stir the fire in the woodstove. I try to erase Christel's name, too late. "Lydia *is* paying," I say.

"Nice of you to think so," says Jonathan.

Behind him, there's a two-tone beep, an urgent message in over the textlink. He turns away, leaving me in the cathedral-ceilinged room. Unaccountably, I shiver. Waking in the barn before dawn this morning, I had the uncomfortably familiar sensation of waking in an enormous tomb, dark and silent, with smells of earth and rotted wood, of mold-lined cement. I'm still trying to escape the inner sensation of cold, stalled blood. "What is it?" I call to Jonathan.

"I think we've got your friend," he says.

As I start across the rug, breath caught like a bird in my lungs, an odd light flicks across the room. On the wood floor, Norman's tail thumps, and he gives a hesitant bark. Jonathan leaves the blinking screen; he comes out of the system room as the light sweeps over the loom and reflects off the oak-framed mirror next to the coat closet. "Gerald?" I say tentatively.

"No." Jonathan moves quickly to the front window. He's right, of course: Gerald's headlights are low, I've seen him pull up the drive after dark. But these were headlights, surely. I race into the system room. *Phoebe darling,* the screen reads, *tell me where you are and I'll be there in a matter of hours.* Oh yes, oh yes at last.

"Where's your stuff?" Jonathan's voice, behind me, in a stage whisper.

"In the barn. This is Arthur, Jonathan, he's here—"

"All of it?"

"What?"

"Your stuff. It's all in the barn?"

I tear my eyes from the screen and turn to look at his face, moving toward me, moving to shut off the screen. The lights outside are pointed at the kitchen. "Yeah," I say. "Except that shampoo you bought me, maybe, and—"

"Go out by the deck. Take the path through the woods as far as the well, then double back to the barn. Don't turn on the light in there, just get your stuff out. If there's a light on already, turn back to the path. Head to that abandoned foundry—you know the one—half-mile over the hill?" I nod; I'm backing away already from the screen, from my love. Outside, the car's shut off its lights. Norman's at the door, sniffing. Jonathan pulls me out of the system room and opens the back door for me, and I run.

Everything I do, breathing especially, feels loud. I can hear the voices behind me as they call to Jonathan from the front door, as he answers them sluggishly, as lights come on in the main house. I'm stumbling over roots, hoping I shut the door behind me—surely I did, surely the latch clicked—keeping my head down, below the hesitant greenery of the spring woods. I reach the barn, still dark. Feeling my way through the rusty back door—loudest creak in the world—and up the open wooden stairs at the back, I fumble my clothes together and into the suitcase. My Minilap goes in too, and the cheap shoes I bought, already wearing thin. Only as I stuff them into the case do I realize I'm barefoot. Even the zipper, sticking then sliding, sounds loud, *zzvvt*. Outside something crunches on the gravel, and there's no time for the stairs, I jump from the loft and land, thank God no sprain, the bag plummeting painfully into my side, and I push up from my heels and tear out the back door.

Now I'm silent. Like a cat or a garter snake, the suitcase notwithstanding, I slide into the forest and slither away up the path. Still I can hear their voices—carrying, the way voices do in the hills at night, with a distinct edge that the trees lack after sundown. Male voices, three of them plus Jonathan. And yes, they're cops. They're saying there was a report of a young woman going in and out of the house, the barn. They're insisting there must be a light switch in the barn; Jonathan claims the wiring's bad, he never goes in there after dark. He sounds disgruntled, an innocent man being harassed. The screen, I think, the screen with its message—but no, he shut that down. A yellow light streams out from the barn as I hit the top of the rise. "Nope!" the deepest man's voice calls out, but I don't stay to discover what he's negating, I'm over the rise and into the thicker growth of the south-facing side.

It takes me an hour to reach the foundry. I must have followed a decoy path around in circles. In the dark, all landmarks look the same. The suitcase, stuffed with small men's clothes Jonathan bought for me, pulls harder and harder; I shift it from hand to hand and twice consider stashing it, but the bushes are thin, still, and I don't want to leave any clues. Finally, when I'm turning left at the same bend as twenty minutes back—the moon's crept out from clouds, whitening a stand of birches—I decide I've got my sense of direction twisted completely around; and so turning against instinct, right rather than left, I finally descend, over a stony path interrupted by a spring stream, to the hollow where the foundry once did business.

My feet are bleeding. There's another stream down here; they used to cool the ingots in it, Jonathan told me once. After I've dropped the rock-heavy case by the crumbling stone wall, I limp around the foundations, feeling with my hands, until the ground slopes downward and moistens and at last I can set my feet in the chilly glowing water. I stand at first; my arms and chest give a convulsive shiver when the shock of the cold water travels through to them. Then the moon slides out again, and I spot a pale flat rock and step over to sit on it, letting my feet go numb while my teeth chatter.

Surely there's something I'm supposed to do next. I listen, as if the quiet sounds of the hollow can translate into instructions. Faint scurryings in the brush provoke owl hoots and the quick silent swoops of bats. The stream gurgles, and I imagine it saying, *Gimme this gimme that gimme this.* For the first time since leaving the city, the old spot on my head aches; I keep reaching a hand around and rubbing. Finally I pull one foot out of the stream and turn it over, propped on my thigh. I can't see much, but my fingers feel a couple of torn spots and one place where a sharp rock's gone right into the callus; I pinch and pull it out, releasing a fat drop of blood. Then I pull both feet out of the water and rest them on the rock to dry, before I try walking back to where I've dropped my things.

Either Jonathan will come find me or he expects me to come back when the coast is clear. Or no, they could have found something—my shampoo, a pair of earrings, anything—and taken Jonathan down for questioning. Depending on the questions, they could keep him overnight. He could decide the whole damned thing isn't worth it, and anyway, if I've got half a brain I won't have stayed at the old forge but will have pushed on and found shelter elsewhere. Oh, what was Arthur telling me, where is he? Stubbing my toe on a rock as I limp back to my things, I set up a shout that seems to fill the hollow. Then I freeze, like everything else. Surely they heard that back at the house—back there, waiting there for just such a moment as this, and now they'll come tromping through the woods with their sweeping flashlights. But time passes like a dream, and no human sounds come from over the rise—only the scurryings, again, and tree limbs creaking in the night wind.

I've flung the suitcase onto a bed of moss that creeps from the stone wall to the edge of the woods. As I sink down on the spongy surface, I realize what nonsense all my questions are. I can't move anywhere—not in this dark, not with these feet, neither back nor forward. If they come for me they'll find their quarry tethered. I dig a pair of socks out of the case, to cover my blood- and mud-spattered toes; just looking at the shoes makes the bruised skin ache, for now. Then I pull out what clothes I can arrange, on the weed-patterned floor of the ruined forge, to make a pillow and to cover myself. Sweat, gathered along my back and belly from running, has begun to chill. The nights have still been dropping to freezing; sometimes in the early morning Jonathan's had to scrape frost from his windshield. I throw Jonathan's dowdy acrylic jacket over my shoulders and drape my new pair of pants across my hips. If I start to freeze, I tell myself,

I can always walk the perimeter of the forge, keeping my blood moving but saving strength.

Shutting my eyes, I beam out signals to Arthur—*Know where I am, you must know. Come find me where I am.* In my shut eyelids, I see again those amber letters on the screen, not even his voice and yet still snatched away. I can't envision him whole, just bits and pieces, like a set of Marie's drawings—his mouth, his chin, his chest, the disinfectant smell of his hands that first time, in St. Barbara. His muscled legs—he used to run on the beach there, he told me once—that could hike up this mountain and carry me down.

I don't sleep, of course. Over my head the ancient trapezoidal chimney of the old ironworks rears against the piney side of the mountain. They chose this place because of the stream and the brief flatness of the terrain and perhaps because the Indians had no interest in it. They lived in hastily built cabins among the trees while they worked the iron; then, when the ingots had been prepared and brought down the hillside by a caravan of mule-driven carts, the lull hit and they could pass the bitter months of winter in the bars and brothels of Fort Schuyler. Come spring, they wended their way up here again. They worked bare-chested with the great rocks from which they smelted the iron; at the smaller forge, downhill from me, they buried their foul wood and smoldered it into coal. At night, they masturbated in their cabins, as I'm doing now, the musty smell of their private parts filling the chill, still, silent air around them. They came with huge, impersonal grieving that the sweetness in this world, like the nitroglycerine they handled, could in its small measure send them rocketing, and that there was no one to handle it but themselves.

CHAPTER 25

I must have slept, in the end, because the morning light and a raucous mockingbird wake me, though not from dreams or any sense of restfulness. Except for a pulsing pain in my feet, my body's numb, the muscles of my neck a stiff cord. At first I think I'll just lie still, a cocoon of almost-warmth; but my mouth's dry, my bladder full, and I finally push myself up, scattering clothes. I force my feet into the thin leather shoes and stand, trying to stretch the wishbone of my spine. My stomach growls. I squat by the wall to pee, then hobble to the stream and cup handfuls of cold water into my greedy mouth. Around me the unfettered world relaxes into its waking; pale blades of grass unstick themselves from the slimy dew, slender-stalked mushrooms tip their caps to the scarce breeze that strokes the muddy ground. Buds the color of caterpillars have opened on most of the trees over my head. By sunset tonight, they'll have spread and flattened, and the ones with flowers will have shot out a spray of pistils. Puckering the tall meadow above the ruined ironworks, red tulips gone wild cry for mulched beds and vases. They pop up earlier every year, my father used to complain. Just like the country—sexual activity way too young.

I wish I knew how to make fire from wood, like my father. He had me make a nest, that time he showed me, of dry grass and moss, and he dumped into it the ember he'd made by spinning hickory into pine. Then he crouched, his weight on his elbows, cupped the nest with his right hand, and blew. One breath; two, and the thing flared up orange. *More grass,* he said, and I poured more on.

But I don't have a prayer of starting a blaze here. I'd select the wrong kind of wood, and I have no shoelaces or ties of any kind. It's find shelter or freeze. I load my body up with clothes—sweater over blouse, jacket over sweater, rain parka over jacket; on my legs, hose and two pairs of pants Jonathan got for me and the old wool skirt I bought myself. Discovering an old trash bin—maybe the ironworks was a tourist spot once, before the road was abandoned—I stuff the suitcase in. After hesitating, I toss the *Phaedo* too—it's too bulky for my shirt pocket, and somehow I don't want to be found with it on me. My Minilap's in my jacket; I have no greenbacks now, and of course no cards. I can travel as lightly as, say, a woman in the Bronze Age. Probably a great time for misconceptions, I think, at least in winter— surely no one condoned giving birth when stocks were depleted. Let the spring babies live. Weaponless but well clad, I stand on the path, hesitating. Up and over the rise back to Jonathan's, or down into the next valley, mist lifting over clustered towns? Finally—coward, be- trayer—I turn away from whatever eagerly awaits me at the barn and house. Computer bouncing against my ribs and hip, I start down through the thin, lime-leaved trees.

The thing about Socrates, I would have told Jonathan if we'd had time, isn't that he was noble or brave. In the end, it's both foolish and immoral, what he did. He considered himself a good man, innocent of whatever crimes the guys in that courtroom were listing. They had a peculiar system then, too, where if you didn't consent to do away with yourself there was nothing the authorities were going to do about it; if Socrates hadn't drunk the hemlock, he'd have walked around preach- ing just as before, only people would have said, "There goes that guy who was supposed to commit suicide." What's more, by getting him- self out of the way, he was allowing a stupid, brutal government to go on without himself to resist it.

All he did was to prove to history—if there was going to be history— that the system was flawed. That when you rate what most people think above reason, you get the wisest man in town drinking hemlock by court order.

Is that what he was proving? Jonathan would have answered, if I'd told him. Then he was one arrogant old coot, to think history would remember him specially.

I haven't got an answer to this. By the time I think it through, I'm miles from that trash bin, and whatever smart reply Plato would've had ready is left behind on the mazy path. The day has warmed as I've descended, budding brambles crowding my way, so that by the time I get within view of a town I'm sweaty as well as absurd in my layers of clothes. I step behind an abandoned gas station and pull most of them off, bundling them in my jacket and tucking that under my arm. What was once a bathroom is locked—I can't see how I'm combing my hair, or relieve myself decently. My feet hurt, especially the right. I sit on the stoop behind the gas station and kick off my shoes, letting the bruised parts pulse a little in the cotton socks I've put on, to remind myself not to punish them much more today.

Tracking, I think. That's what Jonathan and I were arguing about, when the headlights came. I should be figuring how they tracked me—whether Lydia was behind it, or Rudi—and how they're tracking me now. Because they are, surely. They didn't stop at Jonathan's house in the mountains.

They can't track me in Canada, though. No extradition. Way back in the days of the ranch house, there were people who'd slipped down from Canada to report on how they'd pulled a new identity together, to learn if and when it would be safe to come home. No one looked down on them, no one called them cowards or runaways. Five years is five years; for some, the WDU might as well be Socrates' hemlock. Isn't the Coalition in Canada, too? I asked Marie. The Coalition is everywhere, she said. But they can arrest you in Canada only for what you do in Canada.

North and west, then, I'll make my way to Canada; and when I get there, I'll become a woman who commits no crimes. This is my only agenda, my one goal. Forget how they tracked me. Later I can find a way to Arthur. Later I can mend the past. North and west for now.

First, though, I need to rest, to find food. My throat's still sore. A quarter-mile back I passed a sign with this town's name, Little Falls. Rudi said he lived here once, before he moved into the city, but I've never even passed through it. They're benefiting from the boom, these villages; the one near the WDU, on the other side of Utica, has its own Corpstation, with two hundred terminals for monied cybercommuters. Looking down the main road, I can see Little Falls hasn't done quite so well, but still there's fresh asphalt on the street and signs of fresh cable lines running through the ground. And the air, unlike the air in the time when this was (according to the sign) "New York's Oldest Mill Towne," is clear as dew. They don't tolerate retros here, or suspicious-looking wanderers carrying clothes. It's only hunger that impels me to seek out these frame houses, these church steeples that rise—one, two, three—from the town center, by the old barge canal.

Don't get caught, I order myself; and yet I slip my shoes back on and stand, hesitating and obvious, in front of the gas station.

"Lost?" says one kind-looking man, pulling his Chip onto the shoulder and buzzing down a window.

"No, no," I say brightly. "Taking a stroll."

"Nice day for it," he says, and buzzes closed. A little later on, there's a mother pushing two kids in a stroller down the first sidewalk I hit. Everything about her's a little wild—her hair scarcely combed, her jacket misbuttoned, her baby things slung awkwardly across the back of the stroller. One child is fussing, and at each breath it takes she presses her lips together. No doubt she's a good mother; the other child, slightly older, sits happily and wisely, her spring outfit patterned with yellow ducklings and her white shoes kicking the stroller's splashguard. The mother takes one glance and gives me a wide berth—I'll have to stay clear of this street, she's the sort who would report me just for staring at her.

Behind the Nice 'n' Easy, just before the road I'm on turns into Main Street, I pick through the trash. Half a candy bar, a stale bag of popcorn. As I bear my find back up toward the gas station where I started—a private spot to eat—a gang of late-teen boys leans out of a truck and wolf-whistles me. "Eat me too, babe!" one yells, and I'm frightened in a way I've never been before, as if they will pull off and knife me, now, for possessing a face. But they charge on.

North and west. I eat and then crouch in the sun. How far can Canada be? Three hundred kilometers, max. I can skirt the town and start there tomorrow. They're probably already tracking me that direction; better to come on their tail.

Once long ago, when Marie was on a kick of downloading really old movies, we stayed up late and watched one by a man named Buñuel, *The Exterminating Angel,* in which a group of people at a private party can't bring themselves to leave the house. It's as if there's a force field keeping them in, for days and nights, until they start dying of illness and starvation and suicide; but really it's just their own lack of willpower.

That's what it's like for me, outside Little Falls. If I'm not headed to Canada right away, I need to go into town, to steal more food or ferret out a sympathetic face. But I can't bring myself to advance closer than the Nice 'n' Easy. Each time I stash my clothes and start toward the center of the village, I'm distracted by a stain on my skirt, dissuaded by a drive-by glance. I go back behind the gas station and rest, as if I've just made a huge effort. Or I head along a gravel road that fronts the station and dead-ends in the woods by a seasonal stream where I can slake my thirst.

Anyway, I *am* heading toward Canada. I can make that distance on scraps. If I get far enough out of town, I can hitch a ride to Buffalo, and then slip across the bridge. This is what I tell myself, behind the gas station.

A day passes this way, then another.

I know I'm hungry, but my stomach's gone very quiet, like an empty house, owner on vacation. Around me, the weather's shifted: colder, with patches of drizzle. There were pictures of me in our family album, the year I was born, on a sled in April snow. *Hasn't fallen like that since,* my father used to say. I wear more of my clothes. Though I relieve myself in the woods near the stream, I don't stay in there most of the day—there are paths around, a big parking lot down hill, and posses of mushroom-pickers. As if going to visit a neighbor or pick up milk at the Shopway, I follow the streets that form a perimeter around the town. My feet haven't healed, but they don't hurt anymore, and I need to stay in motion.

I'm headed toward Canada. Where is Canada? North and west. Getting farther and farther away, like a bottle drifting out to sea.

I notice things I never would have paid attention to, before. The little gray system box below windowsills, like a hearing aid tucked under the ear of every house. The play equipment in each backyard, yellow and blue and tangerine red, each climbing structure a variation on the other but isolate, as many as eight separate modules in a block. The stamped-out shapes on the vinyl shutters, hearts and pineapples and ivy leaves, borrowings from some Alpine culture a couple of hundred years back when people carved symbols into wood. No wood anywhere, except the trees stretching into spring—the houses are vinyl and foam, pastel colors that clash with the backyard toys. The second day, when I go walking early—determined either to make the village or push on northwest—I see the wives and mothers bidding their stern-looking husbands off to work then turning back to their jam-faced children with a sort of horrified look on their faces. Later, coming back the same way, I catch sight of several through their picture windows, gossiping on their system screens; one's playing with animation. Such smooth hair they all seem to have, tied back against the nape of their necks. I never see any children playing on the colorful outdoor equipment, not even when they come home after school and it's not raining. Their houses swallow them like snakes swallowing mice.

Still it's a pleasant neighborhood; the trees are lovely, daffodils are out, I could live here. The third day dawns drier and warmer, and three couples step onto the tennis courts in the park just inside the perimeter where I hover. I step as far as the chain fence and watch them, imagining one of the women to be Christel, with her neat muscular body darting up to the net and jumping like a spring to go after a lob. Tennis had been the one time when I felt Christel wasn't completely a Christian. She moved without reflection, without time to contemplate a higher course. She liked to win. She was the only friend I had who was younger than me—this matters terribly, as I watch these people run around the court, as if age has entered me like a weed in a garden. Early in the morning, she'd call me and get me out for a set before I left for work at Viratect. When she first moved East, she was eighteen to my twenty-four, and she'd had summer year-round in California, so she won easily. Soon, though, I was beating her—six-four, then six-two—slicing deep to her vulnerable backhand and volleying a weak net shot. She took it in stride; hugging me afterward, she'd laugh in that bell-like tone over the turnabout. Back home from one game, the week after Marie died, I collapsed on the couch in the little red house and fell asleep, still skeined with sweat in my tennis clothes.

Clairvoyant in California, Christel dreamed of losing only half her baby. Tonight, the sound of the tennis balls ponging in my sleep on the hard ground, I dream of losing half of Christel, her body melting away behind her face. Then it's half of Marie, then half of me. When I wake I need to look at my body, and even then I'm not sure it's there. For the first time since Marie's death, I will my period to come back, that identifying pain. I drink more water from the stream. My stomach's a dry knot. I can't remember where I was going. Into town I think. Food.

That day, I stay in the woods, and the twelve-year-old comes to me.

She's not pregnant anymore, but bruised around the eyes and on her collarbone, which peeks out from a loose V-neck sweatshirt. She's got a round face, like Christel's, and thin blond hair that fluffs around her head like dry cotton. When I raise myself up, she's sitting on a rock, across the stream from me. She's been wearing sneakers, but has taken one off, and trails a bare toe in the cold water.

At first I can't get my breath; my chest is filled with stale air that won't release, and my throat blocks any more from coming in. But finally I tamp down my fear and ask, "Does it hurt much?"

"No," she says. Her voice has that way of cutting off peculiar to adolescents. "Not as much as before."

"You should have just waited," I said. "One week, it wouldn't have mattered. You were early still."

"I could feel it moving," she said.

"No. That was gas, or something. It couldn't move, at that stage."

"I could feel it. Like tiny shrimp just inside my skin, wiggling around."

"You imagined it."

She looks at me, and there's something of Marie in her eyes—an unpredictable play of light, as if she's listening to a melody I can't hear. I'm astonished by how almost-grown she is—her legs in tight black jeans, as long as they'll probably get; her hesitant breasts camouflaged in the loose shirt; her hands, balancing her on the rock, still a child's hands, dimpled on the backs of the palms. "It wouldn't've worked," she says, and cracks a mischievous smile, slightly ghoulish under the bruised eyes.

"What do you mean? The operation itself is simple. You'd have been free to live your life. You're only twelve, for Christ's sake!"

"Sure, you can say that. And then what?"

"Then you get help. You file a court order against your father."

"You ever do that?"

"No, but my father—"

"You don't know. You don't know how you're—just not *anybody* anymore. Once he puts that baby in you, I mean. You're not even *there,* you're not real to anyone but him. And then I'm supposed to make someone take him away?"

"Okay," I say. I've stood up now, and come down to the edge of the stream. I crouch, trying for another full look at her face. Her nose is broken, I think. "Your father's another matter. But you were *right,* to come to us about the child. I don't care what anyone told you at school, or what you heard. You were right, and you should've just hung on, a little." She shakes her head, still a ghost of a smile on her pouty lips. "Okay," I say, sitting back on a rock, "I'm selfish. I don't want the blame for your death."

"I didn't give it to you."

"But if we'd done the misconception on time, you wouldn't have."

"I don't know," she says. It's like she's considering whether she wants milk or lemonade. "Once," she says, leaning forward as if to tell a secret, "I promised my brother I'd play MegaMan X with him if he'd help me comb all my Barbies' hair. And he did—he combed them out, every one, until they were all slick and shiny, even though my dad teased him about it, and he helped me stand them all up on the windowsill. And then I wouldn't play MegaMan. I just wouldn't. He screamed at me and went to my mom, but she was too tired to do anything about it. Wasn't that awful of me?"

"Yes," I say.

"That's what I was thinking about, when I did it," she says. "Not the baby. Not anything to do with the baby or how it got there or how it wasn't getting out. Just that I wished I'd played MegaMan the way I said I would. Only if I could go back, it would probably all happen the same way."

She leaves before I can ask her name.

CHAPTER 26

Then I am in the world, and then I am not. Light and dark, dream and real touch. Jonathan had a younger brother who killed himself by immolation. We were talking suicide when he told me about it, the day I confessed the twelve-year-old. "When you are as way down as my brother was," Jonathan said, "you can't stand to be in your body, you can't stand to be in your mind." So you are not there, I guess, when you burn. I could be burning, the fire peeling off my eyebrows. No, freezing. My body doesn't move.

Then there's activity around me. Voices, stirrings, the ground shifting under my back and legs, I'm being lifted. I am light as the wing of a bird, I must not have eaten in years. Mice nest in my hair. It's been raining; I'm wet through, though not cold. As Jonathan's immolated brother was not warm? I can't follow this train of thought, though I try to speak. My tongue works in my mouth—dry, thick.

"Phoebe," comes the voice that lives in my heart. "Phoebe, do you hear me? Phoebe."

"Arthur," I say.

Then his voice goes indistinct, but I'm enough in my body to recognize his touch. He's carrying me, holding my head tucked into his broad shoulder. Underneath his feet the ground's bumpy; we jerk and sway. Why won't my eyes open? Maybe I've gone blind. "Arthur, Arthur," I say again, but he doesn't answer; maybe I just think I'm speaking, making no sound. My right foot's in pain—a great blossoming pain, like the swelling of a symphony. The pain shoots up my calf, behind the bone. Bump, bump down the path. He's saying something to me: soothing words. I stop trying to speak and just tuck my head in tighter. Breathing, I inhale his scent, I fill all my passages with it.

Now we're in a car, in the backseat. I'm prone, feet curled with the throbbing foot on top, head on Arthur's lap. I could swear my eyes are open, but I can't see, really—just blurry images, gray and black. There are women in the front; they speak in high, light tones and explain things to Arthur. He presses his hand to my forehead. "Fever," I hear him say in his wonderful sandy voice. He bends over me, to get something off the floor of the car. We're moving—a rough road, then smooth. "I'm going to give her a shot," he says, and this time his voice is so distinct it might be coming from inside my head. I try to adjust my position, to look up at him, even if he is only gray and blurry. But his strong hand holds my shoulder still, and then he's peeling back my sleeve and dabbing at my upper arm with something icy, and then the needle goes in.

When I wake again, the needle's still there—or no, not the hypodermic, but an IV, stuck in the back of my hand and neatly taped. I've been dreaming, oddly enough, of the last day I met with Mau-Mau, to unpack the delivery of supplies, when we got as far as the IV frames and then ran across that box filled with feces. In the dream, I kept trying to keep the IV frames clean of feces, which kept smearing all over the shiny metal. I must have felt the IV tap in my hand, as I slept. Now I open my eyes—and yes, I can see: light and color, a small blue room with translucent white curtains, a wooden table next to the bed I'm in, sheets tucked over my chest, the one arm extended, with the IV. My hurt foot feels as if it's stuck in a bowling ball.

"Hey," says Arthur. I turn my head; there he sits, big as life, in a chair drawn close to the other side of the bed. "You've been out awhile," he says.

I don't speak at first. I just want to look at him. "You have," I say, a little dopily, "a hooked nose."

"Not hooked." There's his accent again, so slight—the *oo* sounds like *hoo*. "Curved. The better to nuzzle a woman."

I squint my eyes and look closer. He's right—it's a wonderful nose, rather short in fact, but smoothly arched from the bridge, with neat nostrils just barely flaring beneath the tip. "How long?" I ask.

"Two days since we found you. I don't know how long you were unconscious by that stream. Twenty-four hours, at least."

"So you rescued me, after all." As I say this, I try to lift my head, but dizziness undoes me.

"Not me," Arthur's saying, "though I'd have liked to. I'd been looking for you a long while. But it was your colleagues who tracked you down."

"Colleagues?"

"They're in the next room. Ssh—you mustn't talk too much. Let me have a look at that foot."

Peeling back the starched sheet and basketweave blanket covering me, he exposes a foot swaddled past the ankle. I'm astonished not so much by that sight as by the rest of me—I've been washed, dressed in hospital scrubs; the bitter smell of antiseptic soap wafts up from under the sheet. My body's thin, like a girl's. "No more oozing," Arthur says, a professional tone to his voice, turning the foot so he can get a good look at the bottom. "I'll re-dress this as soon as your friends have brought back some new bandages. There are a couple of toes broken— but nothing to be done about it, I'm sorry to say," he adds, tucking the hugely wrapped foot back under the sheet and turning to me with what must pass for bemusement. "You haven't yet called on my specialty."

"Well, I'll try to crack my clavicle or something, next time out."

He laughs at the lame joke—a slightly hysterical laughter, like hiccups almost, that ends with his removing his glasses and clutching the bridge of his nose while tears drop onto the edge of the bed. "Oh," he says, still laughing. "Oh God, oh God." And I see, when he finally lifts his face and takes the tissue I hold out to him—there's a box by the side of this bed, just like the hospital—that he's exhausted, his eyes great hollows as if he hasn't shut the lids for days.

"Come to me," I say. He reaches over, clumsily at first, to embrace me. His rough beard on my cheek, his lips skimming my eyes, my throat, finally coming home to my mouth. He moves his body closer, lifting the loose teal-colored cotton top, touching my diminished

breasts with his hand, then his full mouth. He strokes my hair and finally moves his torso fluidly onto the bed and lets his weight press
against me—and yes, yes, I am being brought back to life, every pore
from the injured foot to the old scar still marking my skull, though
I'm too weak to move beneath him. He buries his face in my hair, his
hands clutching my hips, his need matched to my joy. My bony body
can't imagine the act of love, only this passionate chastity, kissing and
rubbing on one another like sticks working toward flame. And then I
drift, drift, drift.

When I wake again Arthur's gone—the sheets straightened once
more, the IV drip undisturbed. "My throat's dry," I say. Missing his
body against mine, I can't bear to open my eyes yet; I want to hear his
voice, first.

But it's not his voice. "There's some water, right here by the bed,"
says a woman gently. "Let me help you sit up a little."

I turn and snap my lids open. It takes me a minute to place the person I'm seeing, bending over with an extra pillow to prop beneath my
head. "Pockface," I say, when it comes to me. Then I remember that's
not her name, but an insult; I don't know her name. "Oh, I'm sorry," I
say, tears starting inexplicably in my eyes.

"That's all right. My name's Audrey. No harm your knowing it
now, I guess."

"But I-I didn't mean . . ." I haven't got a good explanation, though
the acne scars on her face aren't what I notice now. She's short, not
much older than I am, with thick waves of hair around her damaged
face, and round green eyes. "Thank you," I say as she lifts my head
and hands me the plastic cup. I taste the water the way a plant must
taste rain after a drought. "Where's Arthur?" I ask when I've drunk
and settled my head back against the pillow.

"Sleeping, thank goodness. He'd be in as bad shape as you if he
kept it up much longer. He said, when you woke again, we should see
if you could eat a little."

"Yes," I say, as if this is a novel idea. "Yes, I think I'm very hungry." Only as I say it do I sense my stomach, a great aching cave.

Pockface dutifully tells me I shouldn't ingest too much at once, and whisks off to get some bouillon and crackers. Carefully, while she's gone, I sit up. My head aches toward the back, at the old place; otherwise I feel light, just on the edge of dizziness. Probably because they've been pumping fluids into me with the IV, I need to pee. Across the square blue room, there's another bed—more of an examining table, really, with the standard stirrups at the bottom. I must be in Pockface's place, or another misconceiver's—obviously not a clinic, they wouldn't have risked that unless Arthur had insisted. I try to remember how I got here. A lot of blanks. There was the twelve-year-old girl . . . but of course there wasn't, that was my imagination. A hallucination. Then other hallucinations, Rudi and Marie. At one point I had the dream again, the dream where I'm stalking a stranger in a warehouse until I kill him, then I go out into the world with blood on my hands and no one noticing. The misconceiver's dream, Heather called it. Or maybe I didn't have that dream, maybe I only rehearsed all the dreams I've ever had, until Arthur and Pockface and that other woman found me like a pile of sodden clothing on the cold ground.

Pockface is back with a little tray: beef bouillon—a slightly nauseating smell—and poppyseed crackers arranged in a semicircle. Saliva springs into my mouth. "Slowly," she reminds me, but the bouillon still scalds my tongue, I'm so eager.

"How did you find me?" I ask when I've eaten two of the crackers and can force myself to slow down.

"Someone tried to reach Arthur earlier," she says.

"Yes. Jonathan, my friend Jonathan, I gave him the alert handle for Mau-Mau. I didn't know what else—"

"It's okay. He got the word to us that you'd taken off from the south side of Scrabble Mountain. When the police team beating the bushes up there couldn't locate you, we figured you'd made it down. There's a misconceiver in Little Falls, heard about a vagrant. They don't talk much to official people, over there in the Falls. They're suspicious. This lady's not even a member of Mau-Mau; she's not a joiner, she says. But she knew enough about you to want to help—because . . ."

"Because of my sister," I finish for her.

"Your sister?" Pockface gives a little chuckle. "No, babe," she says, checking the IV bag. "Because of you."

"What've *I* got to do with it?"

"Sweetheart, you're a legend. They offer you serious bennies for a few names, and you give no names. You pull a jail break. Then you've got your enemy at the end of a stun gun, and you let her go out of pure goodness. They'll be writing ballads about you, girl!"

"Let her *go?*" I almost choke on a poppy seed. "You mean *Lydia?*"

"Don't recall her name. She said on the Web she didn't know what you had it in for, except for politics, but we all knew. You told her it was about choice, and then you chose not to harm her. Best piece of P.R. we've seen in ten years."

The joke's muffled, but I'll get it when my head's clear. Oh yes, Tim—that's got to be it, Lydia's story that she mollified Tim with when she couldn't produce me as convert or hostage. I can see the outer-space look on her innocent face, . . . *and then Phoebe just pointed the stun gun away and said she didn't believe in violence, either.* . . . Clever of you to leak it to Newsweb, Lydia. Pockface turns to go; I don't need watching now, I'm awake. I spy a bathroom door on the far side of the stirrups and wonder how I can make it there. "There was another woman," I say suddenly. "When you found me. I heard another voice, in the front seat of the car."

"Did you?" says Pockface noncommittally. But then a shadow crosses the doorway, behind her. I crane my head, nearly spilling the bouillon. But it isn't Arthur. She enters the room tentatively, all her old assurance gone, made smaller and a little stiffer by her losses. The blood rushes to my face.

"Roxanne," I say.

CHAPTER 27

"If only you'd just come to me," she says, picking at the edge of my thin coverlet. "You could have come and said, 'Roxanne, I am going to steal your fiancé and drive your child away, and you cannot stop me.' I would have thanked you for warning me, at least."

"I never meant to do either of those things."

"The point is not what you *meant*."

Roxanne's voice is patient, modulated. I have no way to satisfy her. I cannot give her back Christel, whose name I spoke aloud—she never regained consciousness at the hospital, though her mother got there in time and held her hand and pleaded. I cannot give her back Arthur, whose passion isn't mine to give. Roxanne knows these things, and still she wants satisfaction. She's lost weight; her hair hangs straight, the natural roots showing gray and brown under the frosting; there's something forlorn about her big, strong teeth, over which her lips pull and purse, zipping up griefs. We sit through the afternoon and she pelts me with questions: *When did Christel ask you to do it, did you consider the guilt she'd feel after, did you think I wouldn't help if I'd known the truth, what sort of person did you think I was, did you realize Arthur really cared for me, or did you think, because I was older . . . ?* And I get through them knowing there will always be more and more.

I don't have any of the answers. I know the twelve-year-old came to me in the woods, that's all. I know the word *naked* means more than not having clothes on. Lydia stripped away the first layer, Christel the next, then Lloyd and Rudi—other people, my outer layer. Underneath them, memories, and the woods stripped those away.

I sleep and wake, eat, and sleep again. My body's recovering quickly though I can't reckon time; Arthur tells me it's been a week since they found me in the ravine, but it could as well be a day, or a year. Roxanne's going to New York City. "I've got family there," she says. She's sold the place in St. Barbara already, to an optimist who thinks the ozone hole can shrink. Marta has the Russian wolfhound, the white cockatoo, the big pots of flowering plants. She'll be back, Roxanne says, to get me fixed up. I tell her to pick up her life, surely she's done enough for me—and that starts the litany, never angry, just the cold edge of irony slicing her kindness. *Did you think I'd done enough before, is that why you took over with Christel, did you think Christel was too perfect, did you think I'd had my marriage and family and so didn't need a younger lover, did you . . .*

Then at last she leaves, and I sit very quiet, chastened, watching the shadows of new leaves move across the living room window.

That day I move into the spare room where Arthur's been staying. Pockface says nothing; she's got her hands full. For her day job she makes quilts, and there's a commission to finish in the afternoon with a misconception scheduled for evening. She's even asked me to duck out of the clinic. I see her—the patient, that is—as I ease my crutches through the cheery kitchen. A slight, dark-haired girl, her face averted, twisting her hands in front of her like yarn. Behind her stands an older woman, with both hands pressing on her shoulders. For an instant Lydia's voice battles me again; *I was coerced,* she said. I smile encouragingly at them and hobble on through. As I'm out the other door I hear Pockface explaining: She's not a patient, just a friend, you won't have any trouble afterward, don't worry.

Arthur is in a shedlike space with a skylight, off to the side of the house. When I come in I go straight to the narrow bed and sink down, leaning my crutches against the wall. He's been sitting at a small table, his Lap open, working with patient simulations—treating people three thousand miles away. For ten minutes he says nothing, just presses keys and gives directions to the speaker. When he finally removes his glasses and swivels around, I've lain back on the hard mattress, the thin pillow. "Tired?" he says.

"Yeah. Though I haven't done anything."

"You're still getting your strength." The *r*, like the *l*, he says back in his throat. "Roxanne's gone?"

"I think she's working on some plan."

"She is a clever woman."

I nod. "I wonder what she used to do."

"Before what?"

"Before Frank. She told me once she had a profession."

"Ah." He's tight-lipped, and I glance sharply at him. "I will always," he goes on, "appreciate Roxanne."

"Well, it's not fair to any of you. All this trouble."

"Eat," he says, stepping over to the bed with a box of cookies. "You need calories."

"No nutrition in these," I say, nibbling.

"Then we'll get you fat."

I smile. I seem to purr, just hearing his voice; Roxanne's questions blow away like dust. "I hope so," I say, taking another cookie—vanilla creme, a design like one of Pockface's quilts stamped on the biscuit. "I want you to bite my cellulite."

"Oh, love," he says. And he makes a sound in the back of his throat as we kiss, something between a coo and a groan.

It's still adulterous, our relationship. Roxanne, after all, has left. And now he touches me everywhere, but always delicately, as if I may break. His thumb on my inner thigh, his lips on the backs of my knees. His blunt fingernail traces the muscle that ropes my shoulderblade; his hands lift the green scrubs off me as if they're peeling a grape. As he unbuttons his shirt, I ease his hips onto the bed until he's straddling my waist, and I can hold his cock like a pommel, my knees up against his buttocks; when I reach back with my hand he shivers, and I squeeze my breasts together to embrace him. Finally naked, he slides underneath me, and reaches up to lace his fingers in my cropped hair. When, thrusting upward again and again and again, he brings his hand to touch me at my center, I hold him by that wrist and come like a waterfall, but with such a clear rush that I can make no sound. He, on the other hand, shouts.

"Was that Russian?" I ask when we're calm again, lying like spoons in the drawer of his narrow bed.

"What?"

"That word you shouted."

"Did I shout?" he says, but already I'm not sure, as his arm stretches the length of mine and my swaddled foot, faintly throbbing, rests against his shin—maybe the shout was mine.

Early next morning I get up, brew coffee; Arthur goes out for bread. I can stand for ten minutes or so, then my knees seem to give way, and I find one of Pockface's straight-backed chairs in the kitchen. "That girl," I say when she's come downstairs and poured herself a cup.

"Which?"

"The one you misconceived, last night."

"Uh-huh?"

"She was what, fifteen? Sixteen?"

"Going on twenty-one, believe it or not."

"This was her first?"

"Third," Pockface says, picking up a plastic watering can from a side table. "She's just plain retarded, in fact." She starts to sprinkle the ivy pots that line the window over the sink; their tendrils are trained to the window frame. Elsewhere, her kitchen is full of little hangings that Marie would find cheesy—oak placards with cheerful greetings, cartoons of tyrannical cooks. "She slips out and walks the street, looking for love. Her mom sends her here whenever she gets knocked up. Her mom's trying to find a doctor who'll tie her tubes, but she's afraid to tell about the miscons."

"Does she want the babies? The girl, I mean," I say.

"Who knows?" Pockface's face looks drained, her acne scars brownish, as she turns from her plants. "She says not, and I get her alone, without her mom, and she says not again. But I have a feeling if I put up resistance, or just said no, her mom would take a coat hanger to her—so why should she refuse me? They don't have a lot of money."

"Someone could report the mother," I say. "For trying to sterilize her daughter against her will."

"Yes, and Mom would go right ahead and report us. It's the devil's work, Phoebe."

There falls a long silence. Somewhere in Pockface's backyard the retarded girl's ur-baby lies buried. I'm thinking it's time for me to leave. We don't know one another, really; I don't know why she does misconceptions, or how she lives her life so as to hide what she does. There's no sign of a man around, no pictures of anyone.

Roxanne is back. Her hair's freshly frosted; she's had a manicure—thin pearly polish, neat moons at the cuticle. She's secured an apartment in the city and made plans to ship the wolfhound east. Canada, I tell her when she asks where I'll go. I can't meet her eyes.

"You'll never make it," she says.

"Plenty do. It's a long border."

"It's a different border from before. I talked to people in New York."

"Well"—I look out to where Pockface is on the phone; we're in the blue clinic room, where I've hastily moved back—"I can't stay here."

"That's why I brought you a present," Roxanne says.

Arthur doesn't say anything for a long while. He turns the card over in his hand. "I've heard," he remarks at last, "of companies that set this sort of thing up. It's not enough to have the name and number, you see. It's the card and the locater codes, the credit history. Good for her," he says, meaning Roxanne.

"But I can't just turn myself into Christel Chambers. Christel is dead."

"That's exactly why you *can* do it."

"Just for a few months. That's what Roxanne said. They give the system companies six months to catch on."

"Six months, then. It gives us a chance to decide where we're going."

"We," I repeat.

Pockface hides little; she's relieved, grateful. "You're heading for a border anyway, aren't you?" she says.

"I don't know, now. Arthur's got a plan."

"Well, it's safest. This'll just give you time, and someone to be when you cross."

"But to be Christel . . . I don't know."

"Suspicious?"

"Why should Roxanne *help* me?" I ask. "She never lets *up* on me."

"She was determined to track you down."

"She *could* have tracked me in order to turn me *in.*"

"Then you'd be out of her reach."

"But the state would have me. The state would put justice to work."

"Oh, Phoebe! Her gripe has nothing to do with the *state's.*"

"I performed a misconception on her daughter. That's the same charge as the state's."

"Will you listen to yourself?" Pockface's voice shows a trace of annoyance. I stare at her; I don't get it. She sighs. "You have your back to the wall. You deny, deny."

"I just admitted!"

"But you deny the—the—" Pockface's hand clutches at the air, as if she can catch the right word in it. "The burden of responsibility," she says.

"Are you sure?" I ask Roxanne, holding the reconstructed card out to her as if she might do me a favor by taking it back.

"Sure I'm sure. Weren't you?"

"Wasn't I what?"

"Sure. When you talked Christel into an abortion."

"Roxanne, please. Take it back, forget the idea. I'm not asking for this."

"I'm just saying there are always risks involved. I am trying to help. Weren't you trying to help?"

. . .

If you are guilty, in the case of Christel, then I am guilty too, says Arthur. If you are guilty in the case of our love, then I am guiltier.

Have you told Roxanne that? I ask.

No, because I'm not guilty. But I will, if you ask.

I squeeze his hand. I tell him I am well enough to travel.

You have not, says Pockface, finished with repentance.

There's my picture on Christel Chambers's ID, her number in my head. I have a fifty-thousand-dollar line of credit. As with being born, I seem to have no choice in who I am. My foot is down to a single wide bandage along the sole, and a loose wrap to protect the injured toes.

Pockface's village is one of those tiny outposts heading into the Adirondacks that gear up for tourists in summer and sleep away the wet, once-snowy winters. Shops have just reopened; dressed in borrowed clothes, I walk with Roxanne into town—her idea—to try out my new identity buying things for Pockface. A basket of cheeses, a blown-glass hurricane lamp, a half-dozen romance hypertexts—I noticed a pile of them, in her bedroom—and an overpriced selection of coffees in little glass jars. Only in places like this can the recreation of shopping beat out the Webmart, which has surely got everything these shops carry at half, only you miss smelling the bayberry candles.

I hand each shopkeeper my spanking new card, thinking *Christel Chambers Christel Chambers* as it passes from my hand to theirs. I sign my name on their dark reader just as I've signed it on the back of the card, on the strip that Roxanne magically restored to its original, unsigned state. "Thank you, Miss Chambers," they each say, and we exchange smiles, it's all too good to be true. Outside one shop, a town cop pulls up in his gas car, and I nod right at him. Not the slightest tremble, not even under my ribcage where I always panicked before, sure that they had my profile on their beepers and were hunting. My new name's a shield, miraculous. Roxanne buys a pile of cotton scraps for Pockface's quilting. "And I have to get something for you," I say.

"Don't be silly. You need the money, I don't need anything from you."

"It's a token, Roxanne. A token of thanks."

"I don't want thanks."

We're walking past the last gauntlet of shops, onto the curving road that leads to Pockface's house. I'm nervous, waiting for the questions to start again; my hands carrying the bags of presents seem to tremble. "You can't be completely unselfish here, Roxanne," I say. "It's not fair."

"Why not?"

She's walking just a little ahead of me—the foot slows me down—and suddenly she looks as I predict she'll look when old: tall, too thin, finally beautiful in a brittle-boned way. "Because," I say carefully, "it doesn't complete the circle. It doesn't answer the *why* of what you're doing. Finding me, hiding me. Arranging Christel's card. The account."

"Look," she says, stopping so I can catch up. "I just want you to get wherever you're going. Safely, that's all."

"But I'm the last person you should owe! And it's not as if you believe in what I *do*."

"Did."

"Did, do, whatever."

I'm too weak to stand. There's a large rock at the side of the road—we're outside the village, now—and I sink down on it. Roxanne doesn't start asking questions; she stammers. I can never see, she tells me; it's not up to her to explain. She's dressed all in white again, like the first time I saw her last summer—but her skin was tanned then, her arms toned. It occurs to me that I am punishing her, but I can't figure how, or what for. "Three of the people I've cared most about," she says at last, "want me to help you. Or would want me to."

"You mean Frank," I say, "and—and Christel."

"And Arthur," she says quickly.

"Arthur. Right, of course. That's good of you. You're so good." I've set the packages down. Leaning one hand on my knee, I stretch the other out, as if holding her by an invisible leash. "But what about you, Roxanne? What do you want?" I ask. Inside me there's a nut with a seamless shell, hard and glossy as shellac. I like to think that my sister Marie put the nut there, with instructions—*Don't let them crack this!*—stenciled on the side, but I know in fact that it grew there all by itself. I do not know what's inside the nut, but I fear that it's a version of myself, minute and vulnerable as a moth in its chrysalis.

Roxanne levels her wide-set eyes at me—the pale lashes more startling without makeup, the eyes of a woman in a painting. She takes a step closer, onto the gravel of the roadside. Her voice is hoarse. "I want my daughter back," she demands.

And the nut cracks everywhere, like an egg, and the person who is me crawls out, and the first thing she does is to go down on her knees in the gravel. And when she receives forgiveness, she draws breath. She lives.

CHAPTER 28

Finished with watering plants, Pockface smooths the quilt displayed over the back of her long couch. She's watching me backward, through a mirror on the far wall. Finally she asks, "Will you go back in the business? Once you get really free, I mean. New identity and all that."

"No," I answer—without thinking, though I hear Lloyd's voice in my head, *You never get out of this business.*

"Well," she says. She turns, leans her hip against the couch. Light shafts between the open blinds of the window, stripes on the floor. "We'll miss you."

"Tell me something," I say, that line of Lloyd's sparking an uneasy premonition at the back of my neck. "Does my cousin send them to you?"

Pockface approaches the window seat where I've settled, watching for Arthur to come back with the car he's bought. We leave tomorrow. Roxanne's gone to New York, to her new life. Above Pockface's round cheeks her eyes are so serious—neither hard nor cold—they could be blue coins from an ancient civilization. "They picked Lloyd up," she says.

"What? When was this?"

"Three weeks ago maybe. I heard about it a little after, from a girl who came to me direct. Word of mouth."

"Well, he can get off surely. There can't be a case against him!"

"They found everything. All the records."

"He hid those records in a total labyrinth. You can't tell me—"

"They got them. I am telling you. I don't know how. Some people say he'd gotten sloppy. This girl said she thought he wanted to be picked up."

"Then what about you—? What about the rest, that he—?"

"*That* part he hid well," she says. Taking a seat next to me, she picks up a quilt—a special design with a golden cross in the center, commission for a church. Lloyd had a scrambler on his system, she explains, so he had to have kept all his miscons' names in his head. On the other hand, they're questioning women who are still coming to him. I nod—I know how patients can be intercepted, how they'll trade a name or two for a lighter fine. I try to picture Lloyd in the Men's Detention Unit, fitting his fine gear and his bulky frame into a narrow room, narrow cot.

"He'll get five years," Pockface volunteers, stitching. "Same as you, same as anyone on the first arrest. Next time he'll get eight."

"If there's a next time."

Pockface smiles, close-lipped, and glances out the window. "There's your boyfriend with his new wheels," she says. "Time for your last supper."

Nothing, it seems to me in the end, is simpler than this. This free movement over the road, no one ahead of or behind us, the window open, sun in my eyes wind in my hair. Rudi explained to me once how they film chase scenes for movies—with the camera set up to run ahead of the car, shooting what's coming up next, so viewers feel always as if they're craning their necks around the next curve, anticipating the dodge, the crash. That's what I'm doing as I lean out the side window, feeling the *whoosh* and vertigo. I pull in my head, buzz the window shut, and try to tell Arthur about it. He nods, driving, not really listening to my chatter, happy that I'm safe and with him. He has plenty on his mind—he possesses a job still, the identity he was born with, a real life that can be threatened by anything and everything we do.

Whereas I am a sloth mentally. I haven't even asked where we're going. When he offered to tell me, I put palms over my ears and said,

"Not yet, not yet." My griefs flow behind me like the long hair I once had. *Christel Chambers,* I name myself, Christel Chambers for six months. Six months is an eternity. When I can no longer safely be Christel Chambers, I will have to become someone new, but my only reaction to this problem is to wonder idly *Who?* and to smell the lilac we pass along the road.

But we are not driving north, that is one fact for sure. South, then. South and west, through Binghamton, where the high-security prison is housed in what used to be a state university—you can still make out the chapel tower, on the rise of the hill—and into Pennsylvania, where we stop to recharge and grab a soyburg-and-fries lunch. I tell Arthur I feel as if I'm eloping, and he says, "Why not?" and cranks a ring out of a gum machine to give me. It's the color of dish detergent, with a hologram of a dancing girl in its square plastic bracket. We kiss across the sharp-edged square table; he tastes of fried potatoes Cajun style. I'm tempted to ask where we'll stop for the night, but I don't want to know. I want to be led, to be dictated to. "My mother would be ashamed of me," I tell Arthur.

"*I'm* ashamed of you," he says, sliding his card a second time through the charger to confirm the sale. "I thought an escaped convict would be an independent female. Thought we could quarrel, keep ourselves awake. Here"—and, grinning, he tosses me the car card—"you drive."

Only behind the wheel do I realize how much this happiness of mine is nerves masquerading as joy. I haven't driven a car in nine months. My thumbs fumble on the switches; my right foot feels suddenly inflamed. "Where to?" I ask as we hum away from the charger.

"Where d'you like?"

"I don't know. . . . You've got a plan, don't you? I mean, look, Arthur, I'll be as assertive as you like along the way, but I haven't really thought about this."

"Neither have I."

"But you headed us south. You chose Eighty-one over the Thruway."

He shrugs, mock-slacking. "It was the first entrance."

I glance over at him, his hands folded obediently in his lap. I almost can't bear how handsome he looks to me now, with his broad chin and calm shoulders, his well-formed hands; I can't recall or imagine what I thought plain about him when we first met. "Well," I say slowly, searching his face for a reaction, "there's no point doubling back, or zigzagging. I figure I'll keep on this course."

"South-southwest, then," he says, his eyes enlarged behind his glasses.

"South-southwest."

"Whatever you say."

"I say south-southwest. Toward Mexico," I add, and that gets a slight curl of his lip. So that's it: he's thinking Mexico, not Canada. Well, except for the water and the ozone hole, it makes no difference to me.

Nothing could be simpler—but it's only with the chance to be alone, driving, Arthur nodding off beside me in our humming Electra, that I can pull away from the straight line of the expressway and acknowledge the wrinkles in our landscape. Jonathan, for one. When I told Pockface—after the last supper, while Arthur finished a round on his Lap—what I wanted, she rolled her eyes; she'd known this was coming. "You can call him," she said. "You've got a number now, you can code it in."

"I don't know who's on his system, and neither do you."

"Call him from a kiosk."

"They'll trace the locater code."

She knew I'd make these objections; she was trying to get me to talk myself out of it so she wouldn't have to.

"We just go up there," I said, "in a car. It's too risky for me to go by myself, but they haven't got the right to ask who you are, or Arthur."

"Unless they have warrants for all of us. Remember Lloyd."

"Wouldn't you know if they did?" Behind her quilting-bee demeanor, Pockface is very smart, very careful; she wouldn't have lasted as long as she has otherwise. And I knew Lloyd gave out a double-mirror program to anyone who asked. If someone was watching Pockface, surely she was watching the watcher.

"Look, Phoebe, leave a loose end or two." Her face, so round and scarred, looked for half a second as if she'd been every place I'd been; as if she could, in a moment like this, pinch-hit for my lost sister and give advice.

"What are you hiding, Audrey?" An edge cut my voice; I didn't like it. "Are they holding Jonathan?"

"No."

"Okay, is he helping them? What?"

"No. No! He's a *fag*, goddamnit."

"So fucking what?"

"So it's the one group worse off than miscons."

"Give me a break! I've been in Softjail! They get maybe two months for breaking a specific ordinance. Otherwise it's a suspended sentence, maybe they're harassed back at their job. Period."

"That's only because dykes can't get convicted of raping anyone!"

I colored suddenly, violently. "Jonathan would never—anyhow, this is way off the point, isn't it? Even if they could pick him up sometime and do whatever unimaginable stuff they do, he's either picked up or he isn't, and if he isn't, how's this relevant?"

I spat this last out, fast, stumbling over my words. Pockface didn't answer; she paced around her living room, straightening quilts, their bright colors and intricate swirled patterns shining in the sun that was pouring through the picture window for the first time since I'd been brought to her house. "If there's one thing we learned from the nineties," she said, not looking at me, "it's that you can't fight all the battles. Maybe, at some level, it's true that your friend Jonathan's queerdom is tied in to what we do. That's what they used to believe, that it was all one big ball of freedom."

"That's what Marie believed," I shot back.

"Yes, she did. And that's where she fucked up. Because even if it is true, it's just as true that a ball that big cannot be rolled. We're fighting this thing as a medical issue, we've got lawyers and a network and international suppliers and what have you. *They're* still mourning a so-called right to privacy that never existed, in the Constitution or in life. And Mau-Mau, may your sister rest in peace, has nothing it cares to keep private. The faggots simply drag us down."

"So it's not police you're worried about," I said. "It's other miscons. It's the word getting out that you took me to see Jonathan, against regulations. You're scared of your own."

"*Our* own," she said, but still she didn't look at me.

Though she took me, anyway, very late last night, refusing to tell Arthur where we were going and swearing me to secrecy as well. Already I regretted shaming her into it, but still I gave her directions from the back of the car and then huddled under one of her quilts as she made the last, sickening turns up the narrow mountain road. At last I heard the familiar crunch of gravel under the tires, and then she stopped. In a voice barely above a whisper, she said there was a dark-colored Polar and a whitish gas car parked by the barn.

"That's Jonathan, and Gerald too," I said. "Anything else?"

"Fluorescent on in a room to the right; more lights on in back."

"Kitchen and system room. I think we're okay."

I started to move out from under the quilt, but she pressed a hand on my shoulder and promised to check it out. I heard the driver's door open and shut; a whiff of cool mountain air sifted into the backseat. Seconds passed, then a minute, maybe two, and I panicked. What if she had something to gain by turning in Jonathan? What did I know about pockfaced Audrey, anyway? And Jonathan—what had those detectives put him through at my expense, what might he figure I owed him now?

The back door of the car opened with a sharp click. "We're okay out here," came Jonathan's voice. "Step on out, Phoebe-bird, let's have a look at you."

Awkwardly, I threw off the quilt and untangled myself from the floor of the car. Outside, under a waxing moon, Jonathan's face looked even leaner than I remembered it, his body in white T-shirt and jeans like a birch tree, its upper limbs dark. "Oh, baby," he said, and folded me in his arms, and then I saw Gerald behind him, solid, wax-skinned, stubbornly patient.

"What did they do to you?" I asked, pulling away and glancing from Jonathan to Gerald and back.

"Nothing," Jonathan said. "They saw you weren't here, and they couldn't prove anyone had been here, really. There were little signs I'd had company, but that's not against the law. I'd logged off the system. So they went looking, but you were too smart for them. I'm certain they bugged the house afterward—but they stopped driving by almost two weeks ago. It's no *problem*."

I knew his voice too well. He kept holding onto me, his strong hands on my upper arms, but I found a place in his eyes—the moonlight helped—where he wasn't looking straight on. "How do you know," I said at last, "that they bugged the place?" Not answering, his eyes darted toward Gerald. "They heard the two of you, didn't they?" I pushed on. "Heard you and cited you. And your job—?"

"I've got my job," Jonathan said. His eyes returning to me, now, checking out my face. "I'd started to think you were dead," he said.

"They're using it as leverage, though, aren't they?"

"Sort of."

"As blackmail. If you don't produce something on me, you'll be outed—to Viratect, anyway."

"I haven't got anything to produce," Jonathan said. His faint, ironic smile played over his features like the moonlight that was passing in and out of high, smoky-blue clouds. I could feel Pockface's vigilant presence behind me and had to hold back from turning to her, my protector, and rubbing her nose in this: *You set yourself up against this man?*

"Well," I said to Jonathan, instead, too softly for Pockface to hear, "I'm on my way out. So you won't be tempted, or you can lead them on a chase if you like. Even *you* won't find me, friend."

"Well, c'mon," Jonathan said, steering me toward the house, past Gerald, who bent, as if demonstrating for Audrey's sake, to give me a kiss on the cheek. "I've got something for you."

The something is tucked in the carrying case of my new Minilap, under the front seat, next to my battered copy of the *Phaedo*, now green with mold and still damp. The *Phaedo* was the greater surprise—Jonathan produced it first, when he reemerged on his front stoop after he'd shushed me there. He'd found it along with the wrecked suitcase, he said. Two days after my dash into the hills they'd finally started to leave him alone, and he was able to hike over the ridge to see what had become of me. He'd burned the suitcase and hadn't looked for me further, afraid he would only lead others to wherever I was.

And anyway, by then he had his own consequences to face. Gerald's stony face, the way he folded and unfolded his arms the whole time Jonathan and I were whispering, told me that. When Jonathan started explaining about the other thing he'd brought out, Gerald turned away into the darkness—pacing, I could tell by instinct as much as his footfalls, around the barn and back toward the patio.

The something is three disklets, stacked and banded, their little grooves tucked into one another, that will let me change from Christel Chambers into anyone I please, whenever I'm ready. Jonathan's latest lab prodigy. I haven't told Arthur, his head thrown back against the seat, about the something. I didn't tell Pockface that night. I slid back into her car, the front seat this time, as public as you please, and when she asked what my friend had given me—*friend* said with just the barest trace of a sneer, like an eyelash in a bowl of clear soup—I showed her the book. She shrugged; she didn't like to collect old things, she said, not even quilts. And then Jonathan bent his head down by the driver's window and thanked her for bringing me by, said he understood the risk but had been worried about me, and now he would rest easy. Said he understood she was a quilter; he was a weaver, he said, they should compare notes sometime.

"Christ," she said when we were curling our way back down the mountain, "he is a real queerball, isn't he? Did you smell the cologne? Wow. It's amazing he doesn't try to hide it more."

And I was grateful to Pockface—am still grateful, down in this new set of mountains, safer than I have been for months and with my love beside me—but I felt my stomach turning at her words, and I went under such a wave of homesickness for Jonathan's chilly barn and the smell of his bread oven that it beat anything I'd ever felt for Marie's red house, or my father's apartment, or the home my family and I had once made.

Now, beside me, Arthur sleeps the way my father used to in the car—arms crossed over his chest, chin tucked into neck. I set cruise control to 120km. Cars pass me. Back in Softjail, in poor health, Heather is rooting for me, thinking I'm underground somewhere, carrying on Marie's work, not taking a Mexican vacation. That scar, like a caterpillar on her lip—I never learned where it came from.

Cracking the window, I put my fingers out to feel the cool wind. Just then, I catch sight of a police cruiser in the rearview, tooling along just behind me in the faster lane. I snatch my fingers in, as if he could recognize them. I keep the speed down, but he stays just there, hovering, like a mosquito behind your ear. Panic—the panic I thought owning Christel's name had buried—creeps back into my stomach. He knows me. While Arthur still sleeps, I feel like Alice in Wonderland, growing the way she did in the white rabbit's house, until her neck stuck out the chimney like a giraffe's and her arms crashed through the windows, and everyone could spot her from miles around, the girl poking out of the house. I touch the top of my head, as if it might have gone through the car roof. Of course not—but something, something has tipped this cop off, and he's on line with others, there'll be a cluster waiting at the next entrance. They'll order me out of the car, and the first one—this one—will step forward with his holstered gun and point a finger at me and he will say, *I accuse.*

I'm shaking poor Arthur awake—crying, jouncing his shoulder back and forth. "C'mon, Arthur!" I shout. "Come *on.*"

"Hm?" he says, lifting his chin—but just then the cruiser finally speeds by, the guy's eyes on the road and the lights flashing, intent on bigger game.

CHAPTER 29

Pennsylvania, a wink of Amish country. As we approach an overpass I see a black buggy drive across, and then it turns down a dirt road parallel to the expressway; standing in the open door of the buggy, a little girl in white bonnet and black dress watches the twenty-first century hum by. West Virginia, Virginia. When Arthur wakes for real he sits up, startled.

"We're in the Blue Ridge," I explain. I've been driving for six hours; I'm not the least bit sleepy. Being Christel keeps me awake.

"Why are we on this *road?*"

"You said I should drive. I took the exit for the Parkway. I couldn't stand those methane trucks another second."

He rubs both hands over his face and scratches the back of his head. "You know what I was dreaming?" he says. He takes off his glasses and cleans them with a tissue. His forehead knots, then relaxes. I want to touch his hair—pepper-and-salt, thick at the back, a tight curl at the end of each lock—but keep my hands on the wheel, my eyes on the road. Christel is a responsible driver.

"What?" I ask.

"You won't believe this."

"What?"

"I was pregnant," he says, "and you were going to perform an abortion on me."

"Misconception. We call them misconceptions."

"In the dream, it was an abortion. And I don't know"—glasses back on, he sets his chin in his hand, looking out the window at the tall pines—"if I wanted you to or not."

"Why didn't you know?"

"I think," he says slowly, "it was a very selfish reason. Yes, I'm sure now it was. The baby in me was dead already. So it had to come out, that's why I wanted the abortion."

"Misconception."

"But I didn't trust you to perform the procedure without puncturing something vital inside of *me*. You had sharp instruments in your hands, the kind I use for surgery. I thought it likely you would kill me."

Long pause as I approach a pair of bicyclists, wait for one to pull over, pass. "You didn't have to tell me," I say quietly.

"It was just a dream."

"I'm good at it, you know. I've never hurt anyone."

"Phoebe, I'm a doctor. I can't help fearing incompetence—I'm trained to it."

"I was trained, too."

"Let's not quarrel." He puts his hand on my knee. His *quarrel* sounds like *squirrel,* the *r* in the back of the mouth. "Your profession—your former profession—scares me. I've never even seen an abortion performed."

"We call them misconceptions."

"That's a euphemism."

"It's the word we use."

His hand slips from my knee. He's looking out at the mountains, layered in the distance like rows of lifted knees. I feel the nutshell growing again, a place to curl up safe, not even a door for anyone to open and find me inside. "The woman I told you about, the dancer," Arthur says at last, almost meditatively, "had one once." He pauses; but I'm just being Christel, driving. "I don't know where she went for it, she wouldn't tell me. I paid for it."

"Must have cost you," I manage.

"Cash, I remember. Eight hundred, a thousand? What's the going rate?"

I won't answer this. Instead I say, "But she wasn't in your dream."

"No. It was her child, though." His voice cracks, a little, and now

I'm not angry. It was only a dream he had. "Oh, look there. Let's stop a moment," Arthur says as we draw onto the crest of the ridge, mountains sloping downward on both sides and undulating into the distance. I pull into a deserted turnout. As we get out of the car I feel the vertigo of long-distance travel, as if I could pitch off the mountain at a slight misstep. There's a thunderstorm brooding over the next range, with an occasional yellow flash; here, the sun lingers in a cool haze. "I am glad you took this road," Arthur says. He's looking at the topographical map posted for tourists—showing where battles were fought or rocks quarried—but he isn't focused on the Blue Ridge. He's trying to be nice, to make up. I don't, I'm forced to admit, know much about this man. He's fifteen years older than I am; he heals people's bones; he once loved my sister-in-law and, before her, a dancer. Back at his home in St. Barbara, a cello stood in the corner, but he never played it, and I've never asked if he can. He does not practice his religion. And now we're headed into nowhere from nowhere together, all on my account, because I do a thing that gives him nightmares.

"Rhododendron," he's saying. "Look." I follow with my eyes, and yes, there's an intermittent burst of dark pink, in the thick growth below. "They grew like this," he says, "in the hills outside Kiev, where I was born. We used to scamper up the great bushes, my brother and I."

"Do you still love her?" I ask.

"Who, the dancer?"

"I know," I say—and in that moment, I do. "I know your dancer isn't a long-lost shadow. Your dancer is Roxanne. Or was. And if you still love her, you should go back. You don't owe me anything more."

He's stiffened. Shaking his head, he bends to pick a long twig from the ground, then swishes it over the high grass behind the wooden tourist sign. "I'm sorry," he says.

"Why didn't you tell me?"

"I couldn't figure it out myself, what was happening to me."

"But then you did figure it out. And then—"

"And then I'd have lost you as well as her. Look," Arthur gestured, an empty hand. "When we used to . . . when we—when Roxanne and I—loved one another, I set up certain demands. Tried to—to stop her from *dancing,* put that as the price of my staying. And she *paid* that price, only she paid it to your brother. By the time he—when he died, I was living in the north, I'd cut off all communication. When I got a job offer, in St. Barbara, I thought . . ."

He stops and thrusts one hand in his pocket, his head tilted toward the sky, as if stumped for a quiz answer. "You thought you could start things up again," I try.

"No! I thought it had been long enough. I could call, say hello—"

"Hang Japanese lanterns."

"Yes! It turned out she had been a widow for a decade. And not once in all that time had she gone back to dance."

"Well," I say, sarcasm smudging my words, "she'd learned, hadn't she?"

"I am ashamed," he says. And in those words, without *r*'s or *l*'s, he sounds more old-world than I have ever heard him.

I step around, the breeze up the mountain lifting the hair on my arms, to try to get his face to bend down to mine. "Did—did *her* profession scare you?"

"No." He shakes his head gently. "I think women scared me. Real women. Roxanne thought—if she put that part of herself aside—" He tosses the stick he's been holding. "I think I didn't know my own heart," he says. Then, after a silence, "Before you met me, the woman I'd loved was already gone. Sacrificed, if you want to put it that way. What was left—between Roxanne and me, I mean—was memory and duty. Nothing more. And she knew that."

"Maybe she'd have changed back," I say.

"Doubtful." He pulls a long blade of grass, something new to hold. Touching his shoulder, stepping downhill from him, I see tears in his eyes. "But we'll never know, will we?" he says, his voice steady, like warm sand through my fingers. "Because you came along."

"Saint Roxanne," I say.

"No." His cheek seems to tug. "Only a good woman in an ungrateful world."

"Go back to her."

"She won't have me." But his eyes shift to mine, and his shoulders just barely straighten. "No," he says.

We don't say anything for a long time. We barely touch, just the tips of my fingers grazing his hips. I'm looking at his broad chest, he at the top of my unkempt hair. When I speak, the wind seems to catch and swallow my words. "I want you," I say, "to pretend I'm her sometime. Make love to me as if I am your dancer."

He steps over to a rhododendron bush; picks a blossom; comes and tucks it into my hair, behind my ear. Then he kisses my ear. His eyes are dry. "I will do better," he says, tracing the curve of my neck, "loving you."

Night, Arthur driving, we switch off the Blue Ridge back to the expressway. We take a three-hour recharge outside Knoxville, then push on. We talk about everything. That phrase has always annoyed me— the sure sign of love: "We stayed up late and talked about *everything*." Better perhaps to say we talk about nothing, except that the triviality of nothing leaves an image of small talk. This is big talk. Only what we are saying has little relation to the effect of the talking. Roxanne, my brother, London. Rudi, Marie, Lydia. Hungrily we imbibe one another's words, because eventually—we know this already—our bodies will become familiar and tired, and it is only the words that will knit us together. So we talk, and slake our thirst, and talk more. Start at the beginning, I tell Arthur, and he takes me back to Chechnya, to the war there and how his family removed first to the Ukraine, then to Israel, where they were living by the sea when the Iraqis dropped the bomb at the millennium. "Year I was born," I say.

He was fifteen, the oldest boy. "My father went to Tel Aviv that day, starting at the new hospital, chief of orthopedics. He was so relieved to have a hospital again." An ironic smile plays on his face. It's what everyone knows about the Tel Aviv bomb—they scored a direct hit on the city hospital and vaporized everyone. Then Arthur's mother brought the family to California, and he grew into his father's legacy—medicine, the language of bones.

"That's two things we have in common," I say.

"What?"

"One, we each lost a parent to a bomb attack. Two, we work in the family profession."

He draws a quick breath—to point out that his was a *hydrogen* bomb? to quibble over that word, *profession?*—I'll never know, because he thinks better of disputing. We pass another plaza. They're everything, these plazas—food and recharger and ethanol, system and stock market, health clinic and shopping mall, motel and spa. Like Pockface's town, the plaza is a place to get off-line and shop by touch. It comes, Marie used to say, of putting the country's infrastructure in the hands of private enterprise. She made me feel wicked, I tell Arthur, for liking the plazas so much. He nods, as if he knew Marie, but he doesn't stop at this one, or the next. We finish the soda and spring water we brought with us. By the time we swerve into the great plaza outside Chattanooga, our throats have gone raw and we fall silent, our batteries dead.

That night, against the door of our bland little expresstel room, seven stories above the twenty-four-hour bustle, Arthur and I fuck like a chambermaid and a busboy grabbing their seconds of lust. We don't have time to get our clothes all the way off, and the bed feels miles away. At first, being tall, I can stand on tiptoe and let him inside me. But then when that's not deep enough he lifts my hips and I let my legs go high and my feet against his back, and between the door and his urgent rhythm I stay like that, above the ground, my pants in a heap far below; and he steadies himself with one hand around my hip and the other against my mound of Venus, pressing downward. He doesn't say *Roxanne,* but he doesn't say my name either, just *this,* and *Yes.* When I feel myself start to come I manage to pull my shirt up, and he takes one of my breasts—larger now, almost as full as before—into his mouth. And I do come, but with the quick, sharp release of the fast fuck, and he brings himself to it with a cock-happy frenzy that I think may shake the flimsy door from its hinges. And then he lets me down, semen trickling down my thigh, and we laugh; and then I feel shy for having liked it so much, like that. Hard and impersonal, flesh on flesh.

Christel Chambers—the original Christel—would be horrified. But I am not Christel Chambers. Christel is dead.

Marie is dead.

"C'mon," whispers Arthur, when he gets his breath back. "We ought to be able to find the shower, even if we missed the bed."

As I follow him into the bathroom, a queer pain starts in my lower back—a familiar feeling, just a little sickening, a sort of groan that reaches through and around my whole pelvis, and I wonder if I've hurt myself somehow, with the position and all. But then Arthur flicks the light on in the bathroom. After I've taken him in with my eyes—chest hair springing from the half-buttoned shirt, his bobbing purplish cock below—I look down at the slipperiness coating my thighs.

"Oh my God," I say. The stuff is pink—deep red at the very top. Pulling a tissue from the vanity, I dab between my legs, and it comes away rich with blood. "My period," I say in wonderment.

"I haven't hurt you—?"

"No," I say, and with the pain in my back spreading I manage a low giggle. "It's been a long while, that's all."

"Well, you've been ill."

"No," I say. He's run the shower, and I step in ahead of him and start to rinse myself. "The body," I say. "The body is just the damnedest thing."

And then he is holding me, soaping me from behind. I breathe with the cramps, feel my egg and its nest sloughing away from me. Two weeks ago it must have happened, that brave little egg making her way down the fallopian tube. Did she wonder at how the path had been abandoned for so long? Was it overgrown with weeds and decay? Arthur holds my breasts and I feel their weight in his hand, their readiness for milk.

If you go too long without your period, girls used to say, the hormones back up and make you crazy. But I'm not crazy; I've only been in mourning, and it's over now, over for good. There have probably been dozens of tribes who displayed their mourning by the letting of blood. And all right, this too is a mourning, every month an alchemy of relief and sorrow. But not for Marie. Time, my body said, time to let that go.

Stay here, Arthur says, when we're both clean. I'll get whatever you need downstairs. Everything's always open, these places. I nod, rubbing my belly; I'm the princess. When he comes back with tampons and Midol, I'm sleeping so deeply that he has to bite my shoulder to get me awake.

· · ·

Tennessee, Arkansas, Texas. While I drive Arthur clicks off the audio and flips through my ragged copy of the *Phaedo*. "Don't read that," I say.

"Why not?"

I shrug. "Depressing."

"What are you doing with it, then?"

I'm sucking an ice cube, booting up the map on the dashboard system. "I sort of found it, in Softjail."

"You stole it!"

"Don't be silly, it's a paper book. You can't steal what no one wants."

"You've read it?" I nod, and Arthur lifts the book to quote. *"Whatever you do, know that I shall never alter my ways, not even if I have to die many times."*

"I know," I say.

"Know what?"

Crunching my ice, I glance over at him. I want to snatch the little gray pamphlet from his hands and throw it out the window, but I don't. *"You* know. Majority rule, and the philosopher dies. It sort of tangles you up morally."

"In med school I learned," Arthur says, tucking the book carefully into the door pocket, "they couldn't get a physician to attend Socrates when it was time for the poison. They'd all taken the oath."

"What oath?"

"What do you mean, what oath, silly girl? The great-grandfather of the oath I had to take in this very country in this century!"

"Oh, that oath. What's-his-name's."

"Hippocrates."

We've got three hundred kilometers until Laredo. Around us, it's still hilly, not yet like the Texas of movies. Logging off, I ask the car about its battery, and it tells me it can last that long. I check the rearview mirror—though I'm not afraid of being spotted, not like yesterday. Cramps are worse, a knot of pain around my hips. I wonder if they noticed, at Softjail, how I never got my period. Heather did, I think. Heather, who pictures me underground somewhere, agitating for the greater good. I picture Heather pregnant, getting back in the pickup with her husband, *It's just not meant to be.* Bubble of hilarity in the gloom. As I take my exit, I start hearing Arthur again; he's talking still. "What?" I say.

"I said, that's why the women doctors never took it."

"Took what?"

"Why, the oath!"

"I didn't know there were women doctors."

"I just told you. Thousands."

"I wish there were thousands now."

"They've almost all retired."

"*I'd* take the oath."

"No, you wouldn't!"

"See, that's just like a man. You think that—"

"You haven't heard a word I said!"

"Sorry."

"'Neither will I administer a poison,'" Arthur recites carefully, and now I hear the echo of what he was saying before, when I was back with Heather and her Valium phobia, "'to anybody when asked to do so, nor will I suggest such a course. Similarly I will not give to a woman a pessary to cause abortion.'"

I'm extraordinarily aware, as Arthur's words—no, I correct myself, the words of Hippocrates—sink in, of the dense green landscape around us, of spring sweltering in north Texas. *A pessary to cause abortion.* Common knowledge holds that this area is being badly blighted by the Texarkana ozone hole, an amoeba-shaped rip tearing northeast from Dallas, but the trees and kudzu hugging the expressway on either side don't seem to have heard the news. We could disappear into this greenery, surely, and make our own laws the way people did when they first arrived here, when no strip of asphalt cut through the undulant growth.

And we would make laws, at first, that let people choose in this messy business of babies the same way they would choose to kill a rabbit or live on berries and roots. Until a plague struck, or an earthquake, and we found ourselves at war with this growth all around us, and needing more strength. So that what I could make with my body would gain a value greater than my own—and Arthur, being stronger, would name that value and cleave to it. *I will not give a woman a pessary,* he'd swear. And then when we'd won the fight with the dense undergrowth, I and my kind would claim our own value again, along with the value of the undergrowth itself which nourished us. And we'd strike out that line about the pessary.

But we wouldn't quite be able to erase it, and it would be like a line drawn on the sand between us.

All this comes to me in the time it takes to pull onto the new expressway.

"What's a pessary?" I ask Arthur.

"A suppository, a purgative. Worked no better than the purgatives women try these days, I'm sure."

"Did you swear that?"

"Not those exact words. But the gist is still in the oath."

"Why do you think I do—what I do?"

He glances quickly over at me. I'm making him nervous. I say we've talked about everything, but the truth is we've talked about everything but this. I feel as though what I do is like one of those astral bodies Rudi used to talk about, that either carry no weight at all or carry so much weight that we mistake the gravity they exert for something coming from the bodies all around them, because it seems impossible for an object so small to bear such mass.

"I asked you yesterday if you still did it," Arthur says.

"No, you didn't. You referred to my former profession. That's not asking."

"*Is* it your former profession?"

His words brush against my cheek. I can't answer as Marie, because Marie is dead. I can't answer as Christel Chambers. This is between me and the world, now. "No," I say, with barely a beat skipped. "Not former."

"Then," he clears his throat, raises his voice just slightly—I can hear the scratch in it, from talking and talking all yesterday—"you do not do it to advance the status of women. You do not do it because women might die otherwise. You do not do it to reduce the disaster of overpopulation. You know of all these arguments, and they are good arguments, and you might use them in your defense, but they are not what make you an abortionist."

I start to object to the term, but check myself; let's put the worst face on it. I hold my breath.

"You will destroy the fetus inside any woman who asks you to do so," Arthur continues, carefully, formally, "because it is the thing you do best, the work you do beautifully. And you thus arrive," he looks full at me, less nervous now, "at a state of grace. A shocking grace, maybe, but grace nonetheless."

I let out my breath, like a long rope paying out along the road. "And will you have me this way?" I ask.

Arthur reaches behind the seat for the new mineral water we stocked up on, at the plaza. A rare grin spreads across his features, turning them almost boyish. "My secret," he says as the expressway begins a slow arc, down to more arid land, "is that I have no moral compass in this matter. I would buy you from the devil himself, at whatever price he asked."

But the grin's still on his face as, leaving the car to recharge, we stroll into the cluttered mall of the Dallas plaza—junk food lining one side, kiosks on the other, advertising NOzone sunglasses wholesale, Minilaps and Laservues, disposable Webnews browsers, Texas souvenirs made in Ethiopia. Glancing at Arthur, I think how much a grin is like paint, camouflaging fear for me and hope for him. The hope that he has indeed bought me. The hope that, by the time we're done, he'll have redeemed me. The hope that I shall never again desire the devil's grace.

CHAPTER 30

Odd things, these, that I hold in my heart.

The way Arthur checks in at the motel, awkwardly sliding his card through the slot and clicking on the usual answers (Will you desire a wake-up connect? *No.* Twin bed or double? *Double.*) as if he misses the gold-toothed girl who once stood behind the counter, as if this need for cheap lodgings is new to him. The way he hoists my bag without pausing to look at it or offer.

His physical peculiarities—the large ears; the slight pointiness of his head, just where the hair begins at the top of his crown; the way he tips back in a chair, elbows out, and scratches at the back of his head when he's listening to someone else talk; his small feet; the burn scar on one shoulder, where his mother dropped the iron when he was small. All these I hold closer than his beauty, the perfectly carved eyes and magnificent forehead, the kissable mouth, the muscular legs.

The smell and taste of us, sweat-slicked chest sliding over cheek and shoulder, sharp musk under the arms, enzymic saliva. Scant-haired balls tightening as he comes, like pouches of elephant skin softened and sewn up, cupped in my stretched-out palm. The trape-zoid muscle of his neck in my teeth as I lie on him, salt stinging my chin. The picture that keeps coming to me, as skin harnesses to skin, bucking and rolling, of pleasure like a chasm filled with sweet foam-ing milk, deep and endless as the earth.

The old woman who collapses in the St. Anthony heat, our last af-ternoon of travel before we'll be out of the States, the one bit of tourism we've allowed ourselves, a glimpse at the old fort where they fought off the Spaniards. Only a low groan from her—a heavy Hispanic woman, shuffling behind the group—and Arthur reacts like a cat caught by birdcall, a quick spring from his knees and he's turned around, moving through the crowd, *I'm a doctor, please.* The way the motley group of tourists separates at his authority, *Let the doctor through,* and his agile crouch, the swift surety of his fingers going for pulse, breath, blockage. How he calls for orange juice without looking around; and while we wait for the boy who runs to fetch it as if ordered, how he bends his head like a lion going for drink and puts his lips to the old woman's as if they're an instrument separate from himself, and breathes life into her. Insulin reaction, is how he explains it, later, when the local medics have arrived and thanked him, but I'm not listening. I'm noticing the quickness of his step, the calm energy in his face; I'm remembering the lunch we had in St. Barbara, when he was between patients, how he looked this way then. You need to be healing people, I tell him, and though he turns it around on me— "There are plenty of ways to heal people, my love"—I see the hunger for it in his eyes, hear the catch in his voice.

The blood-red sun that pulls us west, across the border, the night before we go into official exile—our cards given a quick glance at the crossing, network's down but we promise we're only hopping across to Matamoros for dinner. The way it's half a joke, when we stumble across the Mexican chapel and the tubercular priest; we are playacting—why, we can marry each other under any names we choose! Names are kept on paper, huge ledgers, and licenses done on cheap ink-smudged stock; we're back in the Stone Age. Phoebe Chambers, I say, already the name strange in my mouth, and so he gives his own as well, Arthur Eli Levinsky, and there's the plastic hologram ring on my finger and the one Marie gave me, the onyx, fitted snug onto his pinky. Kiss like wax melting. How when we come out the sun's down, the Mexican sky a great purple bruise, and we eat sopaipillas washed down with cheap beer, the dusty sugar and the bitter hops mingling strangely on our tongues.

How his nostrils tighten, how the irises flatten in his eyes, how he passes his hand across my cheek and down my neck, my arm, my hand frozen cold in that hot air, when I tell him I am going back.

I'm holding Jonathan's magic program in my other hand, when I tell him. The program that will let me be whoever I want, that will give birth to entirely new, adult female human beings complete with credit histories and tax IDs. If Viratect ditches him, Jonathan promised me, he'll go straight underground and start selling these and become a rich outlaw. Fuck up the government, subversive activity. "And if I do that, someone at Viratect or whatever will start working on the cure," he said, standing outside his door that night while Audrey waited by the car. "It will take Tim's team at least a year, I can guarantee that much—after that, I don't know. But if I stay on the payroll, I'll be a good boy." A lean dimple dented his left cheek. "In which case only you and I have copies, and this could maybe last you for life, if you change who you are every six months or so. Just be sure to use your imagination in the specs. Don't create a string of young widows living on eighty grand a year. I've given you templates for a dozen identities already—check those out."

"Every six months," I repeated. "I change like the seasons."

"More than the seasons. You never repeat yourself."

"Would you really do that?" I asked him. "Drop out of the mainstream and—? This would count as terrorism, Jonathan."

"No, just sabotage. And yeah, I'd do it." Jonathan held onto my hand for a second, placing the little stack of disklets in it. "If I'm going to live in a closet, it might as well be one that lets in fresh air."

But he hasn't yet. I've checked the one disklet he's programmed to receive such a message, and nothing's come. It's morning in our little hotel room, the sun high in the sky; we've had coffee and rolls delivered. I'm tired—a restless night, holding back from Arthur the decision I must have made—when? When we stepped out of the restaurant? No, before; it had been coming for days, or I had been coming to it, the highway like an equation with the sum at this end. *Chattanooga+Little Rock+Dallas+St. Anthony=time to go back.* But I couldn't tell him last night. He'd have said I was out of my mind—the Mexican beer making me crazy. Go back where? There wasn't anywhere for me to go back to.

Now it's morning and no beer, only crumbs across the white sheets, and my decision percolating with the same satisfaction that you feel when you've planted a garden, seeds snug below ground. This is what I came all the way to Brownsville, Texas, to do.

"The point is not that we'd be marooned in Mexico forever," I tell Arthur, setting a disklet back in its slot. I've explained the program, the aliases. "We could come back as soon as the APBs are cached. We could live six months here, six months there. Or you could go back to St. Barbara—"

"No, I'm staying with you."

"—and I could come and go from the States. But I don't want to."

"I don't have to be a doctor, Phoebe."

"It's important to you."

"*You're* what's important to me."

"That's what you think now."

"Will you let me be the judge of what matters in my life?"

"All right. All right. This isn't about you." I'm rubbing the stack of disklets like a worry stone. I'm still in Arthur's white T-shirt that I slipped on when the night grew chill. Next to Arthur's tanned arms, my skin looks pale as cream. "I don't want," I say carefully, the shadow of Roxanne between us, "to be the thing that's most important to you. I don't want that responsibility."

"You'd rather go to *jail?*"

"No. No, I'd—rather find a way—to come to each other with our whole selves. Not making people up. Not hiding."

"Aren't we our whole selves now?" he says, keeping his voice steady, forcing me to look into his wise-seeming eyes. "And if we stay out of the country, we're not hiding."

"You can't practice medicine in Mexico."

"I already told you—"

"And I can't help anybody. Not the way I used to. I mean, what's Lloyd doing in jail, what's Heather doing there? What's Marie's death worth—or my mother's—if people like me make the slip?"

"You're not going to change the law, darling, or the past."

"I'm going to call Miss MacDonald, all right? For starters."

"You want to be a hero." The word said with the full force of his accent, coming from a place in the world where heroes are cartoons.

"No," I say. We keep touching each other there on the bed with the precarious breakfast tray. I try explaining to him how I just want Miss MacDonald to plead my case, how she swore she could hold the sentence down to time remaining. How I'm not even a good candidate for a big court battle anymore. He's not listening. He's shaking his head, shifting his gaze from me to the drab motel room, our bags packed by the door. "I finally figured out," I say, the words thickening as they get past the lump in my throat, "what that guy Socrates was up to. He wasn't aiming to be a hero. He just didn't want to be ashamed of his life. Punishment—even death—isn't any way your fault. It's the other guy's idea. I want to pay them," I have to swallow as I say this, "the least amount that they demand. Three and a half years, if we're lucky."

"Three and a half years," he repeats, with something that in another man's voice would be called a snarl.

"You don't have to wait for me. You have a life."

"I just bound my life," he says slowly, "with yours."

"Then you know!"

"I don't know a damn thing."

"You know we don't make sense unless I am who I am. You don't love Sally, or Celeste, or Ruth, or any name I'd give myself—"

"Who cares about names!"

"Okay, forget names. You loved Roxanne the dancer, remember? And she became Roxanne something else, and you didn't love that."

"This has nothing to do with Roxanne. No one was going to lock Roxanne up! Three and a half years, Phoebe!"

"All right. All right." I shut my eyes; morning light filters through the lids. "It's taken me a long time to put any meaning to what I do. I kept screwing up, blaming—well, not that, but—finally there's something— I mean, there's going to be fallout, when you figure—well, there's bound to be—"

"It is *not*," Arthur says adamantly, his weight leaving the bed, "worth the price."

"No. No, it isn't," I say, and I've swallowed the lump, only my voice is shaking, tears salting my cheeks. I try a sip of coffee; cold. "I'm not trying to make sense," I say, bending my head to my chest. "I'm just saying, if I hide away with you, our love will die. This way, it will live. And you know it, Arthur. I know you know it."

He doesn't answer, only comes back to stand by the bed. His face is everything I've dreaded. But when I rise, he kisses me, and then keeps kissing me.

Oh, Marie, Marie, is this what you would do? Fly back over the landscape you traveled with your love, this time accompanied by two stocky men in dark suits who talk over your head about how the government's got to crack down on the cash economy? Let Miss MacDonald fit you in a white-collared dress and train you to lower your voice in court? Join the political clique—Heather, of course, and her sort—agitating in Softjail for improved work conditions, healthier food, a home page? Of course you would—that last one, at least. Your eyes would shine as you huddled with these other feisty women, holding fast to principles, elated by each small victory. Deprived of love, you would find new ways to fire your blood, because you are Marie.

But I am not. I look down at the old courtyard from my new cell— my new and noisy cellmates behind me, comparing lawyers—my place freely chosen, and I count the days. When I'm released, I'll be two weeks short of thirty. Is that still young enough, Marie? *For what,* she would ask wryly, and I wouldn't answer, though I might be thinking, oddly enough, of children. After we had torn that fetus, that miniature girl, out of her, Marie couldn't stop thinking of children. This was the one thing I knew about her that she never admitted to me. I saw how she picked up the babies of her married friends, how she breathed in their smell and drank them with her eyes. After every misconception, from that point forward, she would weep—a short, silent interlude, her back to me as I cleaned up the last of the mess, and we both pretended I didn't notice the blotched face, the wadded-up tissue.

Oh, Marie. I love a man, and yes, it weakens my will. Arthur's moved his practice to Utica, and the people whose bones he mends don't ask about the onyx ring or his wife. Only a few, he tells me, have sniffed out his politics, the money he gives to the legal arm of Mau-Mau, the opinions he lets fly when the hospital board meets in closed session. A man, he admits, they don't condemn so quickly. Would you love him, Marie? I think you forgot how to love the way I love, sexually. Or not forgot, but shelved. Poor Marie, I start to think, but I don't pity you anymore—isn't that a relief? No one who chooses wants to be pitied.

Since I came back here, one woman's arrived pregnant and been misconceived—I did the work, with instruments Heather had smuggled in, a simple D&C. Another's given birth, and they've let her keep the baby; she won't say how she managed to conceive, locked up in here, but she's only got two months left on her sentence. We hear the cries at night, thin walls. Two women have died, one a suicide. So we run the gamut.

Jonathan comes by; Gerald too, though not so often. We talk about Jonathan's new job, designing culinary software, KitchenText they call it. We don't talk about Lydia or Tim, who's still at Viratect. *Will he go after others?* Heather asked me when she heard the story, and I said Yes, and she said, *Then the most cunning will be the ones left.* Lloyd's got the highest paid lawyer in the county; I think he's trying to pull some strings for me. But they're sewn fast—and that, Miss MacDonald says, is part of the point. I'm not the solidest case she's had, but I will stand up—so long, I've made it clear, as she won't pin my past on Marie. I own my life; at least, all but this patch of it.

It is high summer now. I spend my hour of free time outside, in the light clothes they let us wear, feeling the hot breeze pass beneath my shirt and along my skin. Sometimes when no one is looking, I step over to the great oak tree that still stands in the center of the courtyard, and I wrap my arms around its trunk, too big for me to encircle. It is alive, however hard. Squeezing the rough bark, I send my longing shooting through the trunk, its branches, out to the green leaves. The time passes quicker, Marie, than you would think.